For Julie

Other books by Jad Adams

Non-fiction

Decadent Women: Yellow Book Lives
Women and the Vote: A World History
Hideous Absinthe: A History of the Devil in A Bottle
Gandhi: Naked Ambition
Kipling
Pankhurst
The Dynasty: The Nehru-Gandhi Story
Tony Benn: A Biography
Madder Music, Stronger Wine: The Life of Ernest Dowson

Fiction

Café Europa
Island of Last Chances (stories)

Jad Adams

CHOICE of DARKNESS

MELES MELES MARKS BOOKS

Published by Independent Publishing Network for Meles Meles Marks

www.jadadams.co.uk

Designed by Ian Lynch, Inkandsocial.co.uk

Printed in England by Mixam UK, Watford

ISBN 978-1-80517-538-4

'The fairyland he creates for you is not beyond the sky or beneath the sea, but nigh you, even at your doors...'
John Ruskin

Chicago 1892

A forest of pillars stretched out into the total darkness of the far reaches of the cellar. Two hurricane lamps picked out objects in the musty light: two zinc lime pits sunk into the floor, a rack, a noose, a pile of clothes, a partially dissected skeleton.

The light picked up a small man in his shirt sleeves, who could have been a dentist or a druggist going about his business. He was bustling between his instruments on a small side stand, and a man in pain, strapped to an operating theatre table.

Some of the instruments had recently been used and lay in an enamel dish in a small splatter of blood. Others were lying on a canvas roll, gleaming in the light of the lamps and showing signs of wear and re-sharpening. From among them the man in his shirt sleeves picked a scalpel.

He turned towards the man on the table who was straining as much as his bonds would permit him. The light was concentrated on the lower part of his body where fabric had been cut away to expose his left leg. The knee had been largely detached from the leg, the blood vessels ligated with clamps to prevent excessive bleeding.

Though muffled by a gag, the squirming man was clearly trying to say something. His eyes were staring, his head moving from side to side.

The standing man leaned in to hear, his ear close to his gagged companion's mouth.

The moaning sound came as if from another room, or a long way away. It was an indistinct, 'Why?'

The man with the scalpel stopped still to consider. 'Why?' he said, as if not understanding, 'Oh...why all this?' he waved his arm to indicate the cellar with its instruments of pain. He adopted a didactic tone, 'It was an idea of mine, a scientific experiment to see if suffering ennobles.' He interpreted the man's agonised incomprehension as curiosity, and added, as he moved in to continue the dissection of his leg: 'It doesn't.'

Chapter 1

Philadelphia 1894

Each new day had its own fresh horror. Today it was through a door half off its hinges in an immigrant district of the city, a reeking shanty of sloping roofs, close built houses and tiny alleys. That summer was a hot one and the two-storied house already had the smell of decay about it, like rotting flowers. I looked in on a uniformed cop in a bare downstairs room, sitting at a table opposite a jittery little man who stared up at me as if I had come to hit him.

'He found the body?' I said to the cop.

'Yessir.'

'Detective Frank P. Geyer,' I said, 'Philadelphia Bureau of Police'. The jittery little man went to speak but I held my hand up.

'I'll talk to you after I've seen what we've got upstairs,' I said.

A heavy, sick aroma inveigled itself, mixed with the sharp scent of the unseasoned wood they had used to build the place. As I climbed the stairs into the darkness my nostrils and throat grew full of the fouler smell until I reached its source.

It was a room cluttered with bottles and wiring, bits and pieces of what looked to me like junk, a cross between a druggist's and a hardware store. A strong chemical smell lingered in the air and sunlight streamed in through the window on to the face of the dead man. I walked over to him and observed his peaceful face with relief, his days of putrefaction in the sun had not yet taken that from him, he didn't look as if he had suffered much. He was a man of maybe forty, the right arm was stretched over his body and he lay back on the floor as if he had just drunk too much cheap whiskey and fallen backwards, where he stood, in a happy stupor. Next to him was a pipe which I picked up with that thrill of shame I always get when handling the possessions of the dead. There was compacted tobacco inside, a cheap variety, which was slightly charred as if he had started to light it. A box of matches was scattered around him as if they had been flung, and on the bench in a direct line to the place where he lay was a smashed glass retort. From its base it looked as if it had been round. I examined the place quickly: there were no papers and almost all the stuff in the room looked like real trash, like there was no way you could ever fit it together to make anything useful. I glanced out of the window. This house on Callowhill Street backed on to the dead house, the city morgue. How convenient, I thought. We were close to the Delaware where the chug and hoot of steam barges never stopped, and in front of me the roaring city stretched out as far as I could see. I sighed, it was a case of only routine awfulness. I searched for a word, as I did in the face of the regular depredations of my life, 'Amurcous, putrilage... ptomaine' I murmured, like a reckoning machine clicking through its motions, passing the precious words through my mind like passing gems from one hand to another.

Downstairs the uniform stood up for me and I sat opposite the sandy little man and lay my notebook on the table.

'So who are you?' I said.

'Eugene Smith, sir,' he said, 'I'm an inventor, at least, that's what I'd like to be...' His freckled hands moved in meaningless spasms, not emphasising what he was saying, just jerking. I slowed him down, looking into the blue eyes staring out of the tiny skull.

'S'pose you tell me how you know the deceased, upstairs, how you came to be here, how you found him, that sort of thing.'

'I'm a carpenter, really,' said Smith, talking too fast, 'and a week or so ago I saw this sign go up here, outside this building. "B.F.Perry" it said, "inventor and dealer in patents." He indicated the window where an inexpertly drawn sign had been stretched across the store-front. 'Well I had made a saw-setter... sets any saw in minutes with no excessive labour,' he recited, 'it will sharpen any dull saw...' I nodded and waved him on. 'Well I'm very good with my hands, but no good on paperwork, and I had this invention but I wanted to get it patented, so other guys couldn't take it off me, see, so I would be the one to make the fortune. So when this sign went up I said: Eugene, "this is what you were waiting for,

3

wait no more" and I got my saw setter and brung it round.'

'So you saw B.F.Perry, inventor and dealer in patents?' I asked.

'Yeah,' he said, 'He was OK, that guy, but he didn't seem like no inventor or nothing, just like an ordinary guy. Still, he said he'd look at the Eugene G. Smith saw setter so I left it here. Then today, this morning, I thought it was about time I came back to see how he had got on. I knocked and I called and in the end, that door being in the shape it is, I just pushed it open and walked in. His hat was downstairs, hanging on that hook where it is now, but when I called out there was no one there, so I went upstairs. That was when I found him, just lying there. And I ran to the police station on Buttonwood Street.'

I looked at his sinewy, skilful hands, and peered into his blue eyes as if I could see through them to the back of his skull. 'OK, you can go,' I said, 'we know where to find you if we need anything else.' He got up to leave, surprised I was dismissing him so quickly, then paused at the door as if uncertain whether to say something. 'Yes?' I said, not moving from the table.

'Would it be possible...' he said 'could I... that is, may I have my saw-setter back?'

It was what I was waiting for. He was telling the truth. 'Sure.' I said, and turned to the cop, 'do you know what a saw-setter looks like?'

'He showed me it when he showed me the body,' said the young officer, looking hot and uncomfortable in his blue tunic.

'Bring it down for him,' I said, 'but don't touch nothing else.' I smiled at Eugene G.Smith to put him at his ease. You could always afford to be kind to the little people.

I sent the officer off to get the wagon from the dead house and spent a while talking to neighbours who come out of their shops and houses to gawp like insects banged out of rotten wood. The little carpenter's story checked out.

Back in City Hall I saw my chief, George O'Brien. He was a bear of a man with greasy hair streaked back from his puffing, pink face. His hair would have been iron grey but for the nicotine from his right hand, that he kept passing from the front to the back of his head, that had stained his hair yellow like his fingers. I had some respect for O'Brien, who was one of the cops who had come up from the beat, one of the first Irish cops to be enlisted when the ban on Irish recruitment ended before the war. The story was still told of how on his first day on the beat he went into a bar, picked a fight with the two toughest thugs in the neighbourhood, clubbed them unconscious and pitched them through the window of the place. They had a lot of friends there, but no one wanted to join them.

O'Brien leaned over and asked me in his bronchial wheeze if there was anything in the Callowhill Street death. 'I don't much like it,' I said, 'a man sets up shop as an inventor. He's got nothing in the building that looks to me like an invention. Within a week he's dead. It looks like he's tried to light his pipe close to a retort – a glass jar of some chemical, chloroform I'd say, and it's blown up in his face. But...' I looked from the used mugs on my desk to O'Brien's sagging eyes, 'but there was glass from the retort inside its broken base, so how could it have blown outwards in an explosion? It's more likely to have been smashed inwards. And his face, it wasn't the face of a man whose died in an explosion, it was too calm. No glass I could see, either.'

Through the end of this O'Brien was drumming two fingers softly on the desk. 'So,' he said, 'the muscles of the face relax after death. So what? And since when have you been an expert on explosions in bottles? Any suspects?' I shrugged. 'It was an accident,' he said, 'don't make work for yourself, Geyer.' He started to waddle off, his fat ass swaying between the desks. Then he looked back, 'And don't think too hard,' and he went off chuckling to himself as if he had made a joke. 'Nescient,' I said quietly to myself, 'ignorant, nescient.'

There wasn't really much to do. I checked out the landlord of 1316 Callowhill Street; he had been paid a month's rent in advance by B.F.Perry using a check from a bank which returned it saying no B.F.Perry had an account there. But the landlord found this out only on the day the body was found. I told the morgue to keep the body on ice for a while and put a notice in the Philadelphia Public Ledger saying, 'Deceased: B.F.Perry, inventor, residing at 1316 Callowhill Street, Philadelphia. Would any person wishing to claim the last mortal remains of Mr Perry make contact with the Philadelphia Bureau of Police, Detective Division.' There was a contact number to identify the case. So there it was: another body, another mystery. Another unsolved case for Detective Frank P. Geyer.

I got on with the task of clearing up the results of the nightly mayhem of the city and making no sense of it. I went off to hunt down a jealous Italian butcher who had chopped up his wife with a meat cleaver. A task of more than routine awfulness.

A few days later - very few - the chief called me in to look at a letter he had just got from the Fidelity Mutual Life Association. Under their circular crest there was a polite request written by a typewriter asking for help in identifying the remains. A Chicago lawyer called Jeptha Howe had written to Fidelity Mutual and they quoted part of his letter: 'B.F.Perry is, in my opinion actually Benjamin F.Pitezel of Chicago, who last September took out a policy in your company naming his wife, Carrie A. Pitezel, also of this city, as beneficiary. Mr Pitezel has for some time been in financial difficulties, and it was for that reason that he went to another city and took an assumed name.'

O'Brien looked at me sideways. 'So what do you make of it?' he said.

'I think, that this is an extraordinarily well informed lawyer,' I said, 'Given that he's got nothing to go on but a false name.'

O'Brien nodded, 'I've already cabled Fidelity Mutual,' he said, 'and they are sending on a couple of people to identify the remains – one of them not connected with the family.'

I looked at the cable. The Fidelity Mutual party were coming on Friday. 'It's their money,' I said, 'you want me to see them?' I took the cable, it may as well rest in my jumble of papers as in O'Brien's. I cabled their man, Edward Cass, to get them to go straight from Penn Central Station to the dead house, I didn't want to lead them around the city like a kindergarten class.

The City Fathers in their wisdom had decided to make the

morgue a gothic monument. Maybe it was under the influence of trashy novels, but spires and spikes pointed to the sky from every angle, and the opaque windows arched upwards. I walked through the offices to the hall. All around, seemingly haphazardly scattered on raised marble slabs, were the fresh cadavers, some with the familiar Y-shaped opening in the chest thrown open to show the gaping abdominal cavity. Most had the waxy features of the newly dead, with rosy red patches on the back or sides where the blood had sunk to the lowest point when it stopped being pumped around by the silent heart. A negro, Joe Stitch, was hosing down the white-tiled walls in a rubber apron, squirting water so the blood and small fragments of gore from the morning's post-mortems ran into the channels in the floor and the slabs and walls dripped with fresh water. Stitch wasn't his name, he was called that because he sewed up the bodies with a huge needle and rough thread after autopsies. I motioned to him and he turned off the hose to hear me.

'Joe. I've got some people coming in for an identification of a party we know as B.F.Perry,' I said.

'He's pretty far gone,' said Joe, 'we got him on ice.' He laughed, showing his, brilliant white teeth.

'It's nice to meet a man who enjoys his job so much,' I said.

'You know me,' said Joe, 'none of my guests complain about the service,' and he went off to the cooler chuckling at his old joke.

The cooler was a cupboard covering one wall which opened with a creaking sound to reveal ranks of feet, all labelled with a tag on the right big toe. Joe looked along the middle row of feet and humped out B.F.Perry or Pitezel or whoever he was, and slung him on a trolley then wheeled him in to the identification room where he pulled the canvas covering off his face and tucked it under his chin, almost as if he was making him comfortable in bed.

The Fidelity Mutual Insurance group would be coming by cab from Penn Central, so I just hung around in the office talking to Muriel, the spinster who worked there, until Joe came through to tell me the party had arrived. 'The man from the insurance company wants to talk to you first,' Joe said in a hiss of conspiracy.

'Show him in,' I said, taking a position opposite the door where Edward Cass entered. He was a personable character, younger then me, twenty-eight or so, clean shaven and wearing a grey suit. He wasn't big, but he was solidly built, and he had the questing air of someone who was alert to his surroundings. He was a man I could get along with. 'Welcome to Philadelphia,' I said, 'what can I do for you Mr Cass?'

'This case,' he said, shaking my hand heartily, 'Anything suspicious about it your end?'

'Suppose you tell me what makes you ask,' I said.

He shrugged, 'This, among other things,' and he produced a document with the Fidelity Mutual crest. 'This is policy number 044145 on Mr Pitezel,' said Cass, 'it was due to expire on August the ninth, but on August the eighth someone wired $157.50 to keep it going. On September the seventh, according to the information you have given us, Pitezel was dead or, at least, this man we are going to see was dead. Now what do you think of that?' he said expectantly.

I waved the policy under my nose. 'I think it stinks,' I said. He waited while I chewed my little finger. 'I've got suspicions,' I said, 'a man rents a house with a false name, dies in an accident a week later. Then up pops the family to claim the insurance. It's just too neat for me.'

Cass stroked his chin, 'But you've got no more than that?'

'That's about it,' I said, unwilling to confide my suspicions about the death when I had been told not to investigate it and I had little to go on anyway. Why let a man from another city think I was inefficient? 'So who have we got to identify him?' I asked.

'Alice Pitezel,' he said, 'she's fifteen, the second eldest child in the family. The eldest is looking after the other kids and the mother, the mother's too upset to travel.'

'Shame,' I said, 'I'd like to have spoken to her. She's the only beneficiary of this insurance?' he nodded, 'So what's it worth?'

'Ten thousand dollars,' Cass said, looking me in the eye though he was shorter than me.

I whistled, 'A neat sum for someone who was living the way he was,' I said, 'just as well they renewed the premium. Who's the other party? I was told there would be three of you.'

'Holmes,' he said, 'Henry H. Holmes. He introduced Pitezel to the Fidelity Mutual, we had that on the file: we paid him a commission. So when we got suspicious about the case, the office decided not to accept the identification of the family alone, we needed another person. Holmes agreed to do the identification if we paid his rail fare. He said he hired Pitezel to work in his drug store in Chicago, that's how he knew him. Holmes is quite a guy,' Cass became animated with mirth, 'we were talking on the train, did you know…' and he went like he was going to tell me some story, but saw my expression and thought better of it, 'well, let's get on with the job,' he said and went to get the witnesses.

He can only have been gone away seconds, a minute at the most. But it was the most important minute I have ever endured. It gave me time, had I but known it, to turn around and leave the room, leave the city, the state, the whole damned continent.

I didn't do that, I stood and waited, and in came Edward Cass with, behind him, a girl of about five foot tall with long black hair, wearing a pinafore dress. I scarcely looked at her because just behind her was a slight man with the easy manner of someone who has not a care in the world. He had a moustache and a shock of black hair pushed back across his brow. My eyes locked on to him and it was as if sound had ceased. There was no more noise from the office, from the morgue or from the street outside. It was as if reality had been suspended, I was transfixed by the sight of this ghastly man. I recognised him immediately as the man who had taken my hopes and burned them to ashes, had ground the ashes to dust and scattered them to the winds. That man was the nearest thing to Satan in human form that ever walked this earth. And he was the best friend I had ever had.

'Well how are ya Frank,' he said, extending his hand, 'it's sure been a long time.'

Chapter 2

New Hampshire 1870

Henry Holmes wasn't his name of course. One thing you learn in my job is that nothing is as it seems. When I knew him he was called Henry Mudgett, and I am as sure as I can be in the shifting sands of this life that Mudgett was his name, but it is simpler in this account to call him Henry Holmes which was his favoured appellation. He went through other changes of name anyway. Everyone in this case did, it seems, except for me.

Henry Holmes had one of those open, honest faces that made you want to walk up to him, even across a room, even if you didn't know him before, and say, 'How you doing? What's going on with you?'

It was like that when I first saw him in the schoolyard in New Hampshire when we were both maybe ten years old. We had just moved to Gilmanton where my pa had got a job as sheriff, and I was alone in the schoolyard and feeling a bit sorry for myself as a new boy does, and up comes Henry. He just fell in beside me and introduced himself with an easy self-confidence. He was small for his age, though not diminutive, and was decently dressed, like me. He came from good, respectable folk, he wasn't the kid of one of the tenants or dirt farmers who went to the school along with us. None of us kids was rich, of course, but we were far from being the poorest.

He had very dark hair and twinkling, mischievous blue eyes. His slightly buck teeth pushed his upper lip out a little. He was still a good looking boy, however, and despite the teeth, he had the sweetest speaking voice I ever heard. He always had that, as a child and a man.

'Now don't tell me who you are,' he said, holding his head as if to shut out the information, 'don't tell me your name. Let me guess. Is the first letter of your Christian name in the first five letters of the alphabet?'

'No,' I said, after a little thought, entranced by this Pan-like creature who danced around me.

'Is it in the second five?'

'Yes,' I said.

He scrunched up his freckled face, 'Is the second letter of your name in the first five letters of the alphabet?' he said, and after going through this incantation a few times he held his white hands to his head in deep thought and then said with some solemnity, 'Your name is Frank.'

'That's great,' I said, 'just how did you do that?'

He laughed merrily, then looked serious, as if he was going to tell me, then said, 'It wasn't magic,' and the bell rang so we went off into the schoolroom. For the next six or seven years we were inseparable, our folks called us the twins.

He never did tell me how he did that trick with the name. Years later of course I realised it was because his father was the postmaster and Henry was looking at the mail, that's how he knew everything that was going on in the town. He certainly would know the name of a new sheriff who was coming to take up a post and needed somewhere to live and a school for his son, all the sort of things that get handled by mail. The stuff about the alphabet was just a blind. When I confronted Henry with it years later, when I knew his ways, he just laughed and said, 'Have you only just worked that out?'

Old man Holmes was the postmaster when I knew him, but earlier than that he had started to train as a doctor. Something had gone wrong, probably lack of money, and he went into the post. He wasn't a very prominent character in my life so I can't really remember him except in shades of grey. Compared to my big pa with his strength, his loud voice, his guns and his colourful vests, old man Holmes fades into non-existence in my memory. Plus he died early, but I don't remember Henry making much of a fuss about it. His ma was our schoolmistress for a time, a sweet woman who adored Henry. She was a regular mom, she did the cleaning and the baking and washing and making sure the kids' clothes were clean and neat. There was no suggestion in this

11

family life of what was to come later. There were another three kids but Henry was always the star of the family.

It was pretty obvious Henry was going to grow up to do a job where he kept his hands clean: a schoolmaster, a lawyer or even a preacher. His parents were Christian enough in the unpretentious way of country people–going to church on Sundays and saying grace before the evening meal. Holmes later made a point of it, that he was 'well trained by loving and religious parents', but that was later. No one would have thought of saying such a thing in Gilmanton in the 1870s, no one would have needed to. Good folks were religious and hard-working, the folks that weren't one of these things generally weren't the other one either, but even then you wouldn't say they were bad, they were just wasters, or they were referred to in lowered tones as 'not good folks,' and we didn't mix with them.

It was a white picket fence sort of town, looking much like any other town in the north-east. There were hitching posts and horse blocks down the single main street and the locks on the doors of houses were rusted from lack of use. Most of our neighbours were plain types, farming people mainly, and everyone else's business was the inevitable topic of conversation in the general store.

Not far from town you were in dense, dark forest land, in the shadow of the Moose Mountains; just outside town was Crystal Lake: the whole country was our playground. As young children Henry Holmes and I played around the grey granite boulders and went tracking animal prints in the snow. We would climb up the birch trees until the trunk got narrow and we could swing down to the ground on them, just under our own weight.

Henry encouraged me to take fruit that we had no right to; taught me to creep round the back of the neighbouring farm in the dark to watch Hanna, who was a particularly well developed girl, taking a bath; to trick Mrs Gotcham into thinking we had already paid for our sodas at the drug store. His ability to dissimulate with a smile always fascinated me.

Only once in the early years did Henry do something which disturbed me, though I would not have given it another thought but for later events. We heard a squealing in the forest, of something in pain, and followed it to find a rabbit, caught in a trap which had failed to kill it, but in the hours since being trapped it had struggled to free itself then started to gnaw the trapped leg off. We both stood, transfixed by the scene of the whining, bloody creature in the low grass, 'Poor beast' I said, 'I'll kill it,' and I looked around for a stone to use.

'No,' Henry said, gesturing with his hand, and I waited a moment for him to speak again, above the whimpering, 'Let's watch,' he said hoarsely.

'Watch what?' I said, but saw his face, curiously glowing in the light which filtered through the trees. I watched him in bewilderment for a few seconds and was then distracted by struggling from the rabbit which had overcome its initial petrifying terror of us and had started a last, desperate struggle to escape.

I was impatient of getting any further information out of Henry. He normally led, but in these outdoor matters there was a tacit agreement that I knew what I was doing better than he did, and it was one area where I did not defer to him. I spied a stone which I quickly picked up and, in one movement, went down by the rabbit to grip its head in my left hand, bringing the stone down sharply on its neck and it flopped, limp and bloody by the trap.

'You killed it,' said Henry, as if in disappointment.

I wiped my bloodied hand on the grass and looked at him. I don't remember what happened after that, the experience probably just drifted off into another commonplace day among the buzzing insects and the green shapes of the foliage, and by evening it had been overlaid by other experiences.

As we got older we could go hunting, questing through the forest where we stalked the whitetail deer - I can still smell the scent of pine needles in the fresh air of morning. Sometimes we went night fishing, rising long before dawn on balmy summer nights, too hot for sleep anyhow, and we would sneak along to where old man Moses tied up his rowing boat and would slip it out on the glassy black water. We'd return it towards dawn before the morning star had gone out, famished and eager to drink milk fresh from the cow, milk that clung to the side of the pitcher.

It wasn't just the adventurousness which distinguished Henry, but the methodical nature of his reactions - he really thought about things. I remember once we were asked by some farmer if we would clear a field of weeds for a price which I have now forgotten. Well, when we had finished and the weeds lay in a pile by the side of the field, the farmer turned mean and said he didn't have the money right then but he would pay us next week. Henry said, 'We'll just take the weeds away, then,' and went off with the wheelbarrow.

'What are you doing?' I said when we got out of earshot, 'He's not going to pay us, why don't we leave the darned things there?'

Henry just said, 'Wait and see,' and back home he carefully lay the weeds out in his yard so they dried in the sun. We returned to the farmer the next week and asked again about our money but it was still not there and Henry said, 'Are you sure about that?'

The man said, 'Of course I'm sure, get away from here,' and made to hit us with a hoe. I walked along beside Henry grumbling but he took me back to his yard where we opened the now dried seed pods of all the weeds and shook out the seeds onto paper. That night we went back to the field and sowed it to a three-inch density with weeds. It took almost as long as the original weeding but when it was done it was so much more deeply pleasurable than a simple act of revenge would have been. It was Henry's pleasure, something I was to come to understand only years later.

Whenever he saw that farmer again Henry would say, 'How's that field coming along?' and the farmer would grin good-humouredly, until late that summer he realised he had the richest crop of weeds in the neighbourhood. We laughed until we cried. This was the difference between Henry and the other kids: he planned, looked ahead. Anyone else would have cursed and bad-mouthed that farmer, Henry never did, he just went for revenge, even if it took time. It was a paradox that he acted much older than us other kids, but was far more mischievous. He was always

14

the most daring, despite his unathletic build which did not alter as he got older, he was always slight.

So Henry was smart. Well, we both were, but Henry had such a quick mind it dazzled me. I'd come to the same results through my plodding, deductive methods that Henry would reach instantly, in a kind of intuitive flash. Henry read a lot, and read quickly. There were books in his house, as there weren't in the houses of most of us, and when I looked at them I found most were medical books, darned hard going. Still, Henry devoured them and developed an intellect that was knowledgeable without being booky, but which always suggested he knew more than he was telling, but there was no point in divulging information that we kids just wouldn't understand.

Henry's quick wits more than once saved him from trouble. They also attracted attention from mean kids who resented him. I once remember him being bullied by Bill Bellow, a big loudmouthed kid who would never be anything in life but a bully. I tried to intervene with some time-honoured phrase like pick on someone your own size.

'I can look after myself,' Henry snarled, one of the few times I ever saw him angry, and it hurt me because the anger was so clearly aimed at me for interfering.

The next time we saw Bill Bellow together there were just the three of us. Bellow wasn't with us, but he was hanging around, when Henry pulled a poke out of his pocket and said, 'Hey, I've got some candies, want one?' I looked in the bag, they were large marzipan balls in different colours, green and yellow, they weren't too fancy by later standards, but candies were a big deal to us. They were present for Christmas and birthdays in families who had a little money to spare, and were absent from families that didn't.

'That's great Henry, is this something special or something?' I asked and selected the top one.

'Oh, my aunt gave me some money to... ah, indulge myself,' Henry said.

I was taller than Henry and could see there looked to be three there. I was surprised that Henry had produced the candies when Bill was around because etiquette demanded that he offer them around, even if it weren't the case that Bill Bellow would obtain what he wanted, because it was his way.

'Give me some of those Hen-ry,' Bellow said, mimicking Henry's voice.

'Well, Bill, it's such a nice day, I don't think the time is right for quarrelling,' said Henry, 'look, I've got three left, I'll have this one,' and he popped it into his mouth and handed the poke to Bill Bellow.

'Nice day,' Bill sneered, and reached for the bag, greedily stuffing both small candies into his mouth and going off home with a laugh and a 'Thanks.'

'You're welcome,' said Henry placidly, picking up the empty poke which Bill had dropped on the ground, out of a concern over littering, I thought.

The following day while serving dinner my mother mentioned, along with other gossip, that she had met Mrs Bellow in the drug store and Bill was awful sick. The following morning Henry trotted round as I was chopping logs in the yard.

'Big Bill Bellow is sick,' I said, in the course of exchanging other information.

Henry was unsurprised, 'I put a curse on him,' he said, examining his fingernails. I grinned and went on with my chopping logs, but a few days later Henry's ma, our teacher, came into the schoolroom and announced she had some bad news: Bill Bellow had died from some stomach complaint, we ought to pray for his folks, and everyone ought to be careful about what they ate, and to be particularly careful not to eat unidentified things from the forest.

I don't know if I realised at the time that Henry had laced the candies with arsenic. Probably not, or I treated it as just one strange event among many. After all, children used to die, we were accustomed to it: they died from whooping cough or measles or untreated problems like a burst appendix that it was hoped would be better in the morning, so's you didn't have to pay for the doctor.

Bill Bellow died of the gripe, what more could you say, except you were sorry to hear about that, and get on with your life?

The knowledge to analyse a crime came much later: there was the use of an agent which would conceal the taste of the poison - the candies would be entirely devoured by the greedy victim, thus removing any external evidence; it was at the end of the school day so Bill Bellow would soon be eating at home which would delay the effect of what was probably white arsenic derived from rat poison; arsenic mimics the effects of food poisoning and kills within about thirty-six hours. Only the bottom two of the candies were poisoned, so if anyone indicated the candies as a possible source of food poisoning, then Henry and myself, the sheriff's son, could testify that we had eaten them and were uninjured. Of course, no one would suspect the truth, not seriously. Poisonings didn't happen in Gilmanton. Grown-ups didn't kill each other, and certainly children didn't.

It is all pretty obvious for a middle-aged detective, but at the time, awful though it may seem, I was so innocent, so absorbed in all the other wonders that exploded like springtime around me as I was growing up, that I didn't give it close attention. I might even have thought, 'Henry poisoned Bill Bellow,' and let it drift in and out of my mind with the other panoply of wonders: Gallup's cow has produced a calf with two heads; war has broken out between the Sioux and the prospectors in the Black Hills; there is a mile-wide swarm of grasshoppers eating the crops in the midwest, so many that their crushed bodies grease the rails so the trains can't run. A world of wonders.

I talked to Henry about this world all the time, we had an insatiable appetite for novelty. Folks knew things and could do things now that our grandfathers never dreamt of: almost every day there was a new marvel that my pa would be talking about. 'Soon there will be nowhere to hide,' pa had said to me one day, 'today bad men ride out west and we never see them again, but soon we'll be able to contact every other lawman in the country just by flicking a switch.'

This excited me and I repeated it to Henry, sitting on our porch one afternoon. I quickly warmed to my subject, 'Trains cross the entire country, from New York to San Francisco, isn't that something? There are telephones where you can talk from one place to another,' I held my open palm to my face as if talking over a telephone though I had, of course, never seen one, '"Hey, look out, there's a bad guy coming your way, you make sure you catch him, he looks like this..."' I went on excitedly: 'There's a telegraph cable under the Atlantic Ocean, under the ocean! People could be tracked down even if they are in Europe or some place like that. Where can a criminal hide?'

Henry looked at me in his lightly amused way, 'I just think the criminals are gonna make use of the same things the lawmen are gonna use,' he drawled, 'maybe sometimes they'll use them better than the lawmen. I don't think there's any knife that cuts only one way. I mean, if you got a gun, and the other fella ain't got a gun, then you have the upper hand. But only until he gets a gun himself, and then he may have the advantage over you, because he's mean enough to use it and maybe you ain't.'

I couldn't see it, for me the world was a good place and was getting better, and the best place in the world was the U. S. of A. I was proud of living in a country where the war had been fought and won so men could be free, proud of the New Hampshire men who had fought for the Union and sad for the ones in the graveyard with iron flags marking their resting place. These ideals never seemed to interest Henry, he listened politely, but then went on to something else. He was much more interested in things: in designing a perpetual motion machine which could be sold for thousands of dollars; or a windmill which also acted as a bird-scarer as its sails turned round, to scare the crows from the cornfields.

Two things happened in our youth which were strange and unusual and now I think about it, frightening, and which didn't appear to be connected: I fell in love, and Henry began to tell stories. I had seen Georgiana Yoke almost every day of my life, at least every school day. She was the minister's daughter, a little fair-haired girl, virtually indistinguishable from many of the other girls, with two plaits and polished lace-up boots with tassels. Not all the kids had footwear, so you paid attention to the boots of those that did.

So I had seen her all the time, but not seen her, not really seen her until one day when I was coming back from inspecting my traps, whistling as I went, with my jacket over my arm because the sun had warmed the earth since I went out that morning and I was hot.

As I was approaching the hump-backed bridge, I could see the figure of a girl approaching from the other side. The sun was behind her so I saw her figure in relief up against the sky, in darkness until she came close. The sun was out of my eyes when we both trod on the narrow bridge from opposite sides and I blinked as I saw her clearly for the first time. It was an effect of the sunlight, but also of our proximity in such a restricted space, that I saw with a shock of recognition as she approached, through her thin dress the suggestion of her hips. I had no intention of staring, but the observation led me to look up to see almost with horror that on her lithe torso, though the cotton fabric, there was the swelling of two budding breasts.

My whole being gave a jolt, and I was covered in confusion. I looked at her face, and saw anew the familiar: the fringe of golden hair over her high forehead, the pure skin, the extraordinarily large blue eyes.

'Well good morning Frank Geyer,' she said.

'Excuse me Georgiana,' I said, somehow wanting to detain her but feeling awkward and embarrassed at not knowing what to say. She looked as if she expected me to say something and we had both halted, 'I mean excuse me for being in your way,' I said, and immediately felt foolish and blushed hotly. She smiled a radiant smile and fluttered a hand to indicate it was nothing, and squeezed past with less than six inches of space between our bodies, as I looked down at the raging water tumbling the pebbles beneath me.

I walked home bewildered, pondering the banal words we had spoken as if they contained the secret of life itself. Could I have said something different? Could she interpret what I had said the wrong way and think badly of me? Did she even like me? All the things that had been dear to me receded behind a confused glowing of need and expectation, she was in my heart forever.

After that I took every effort to see her, which was not too laborious in a town the size of Gilmanton, though it was testing my wit to think of a new thing to say if I encountered her three times in one day.

It became so I couldn't go a day without seeing her, it was as if my life depended on it, and then that I couldn't go an hour without a glimpse of her face, the arch of her long neck, her graceful body. I saw her so often, waited to see her with such expectation in those early days, that the vision of her is permanently branded on my mind... those remarkable blue eyes, her perfect ears with tiny wisps of golden hair in front. Soon she stopped wearing her lovely fair hair in pigtails, and wore it in a band. Sometimes, on Sundays or when she went shopping with her ma, she had it tucked into a bonnet.

Over months, or even weeks, it seemed to me, she became a willowy delight, every day more lovely. I started going to church with enthusiasm, even to the evening service which was not, in my family, obligatory. The object of my devotions was sitting in the front pew wearing a pair of white gloves, looking up at her father in the pulpit, and she seemed to me a heavenly angel. How good I could be, I thought, with the love of a girl like that.

I began to look at myself: what did I have to offer? I was tall for my age and strong, people have said I was a good-looking boy though I guess I'm not the best judge of that. I tried hard to do well, and where I didn't succeed I put in a decent effort. My family was good, I had enough pride to think I was a boy well worth having, and if anyone should love Georgiana, the best girl in town, it should be me. Sure, I was nervous I might do something wrong and embarrass myself or, still worse, embarrass her, but I had always been praised for the things I could do, and I was not tormented by self-doubt. On the whole it would have been better for me if I had've been, but I wasn't.

I took the opportunity to walk from school with Georgiana, and carried her strapped-up school books in time-honoured fashion. We didn't actually have so much to say to each other, though she welcomed my attention and smiled sweetly so I felt I had been blessed. One day after I had started walking with her, I asked Georgiana if she would accompany me on the Sunday school outing to Lake Winnipesaukee: which meant sitting with me rather than with a girlfriend, as everyone went on the outing, it would have seemed downright irreligious not to. In the limited confines of courtship in Gilmanton, walking together was a private friendship, but going to a communal event together was a public declaration.

I thought she'd blush and lower her head and look up at me through her eyelashes and kind of consent in a whispering tone. Actually she looked directly at me with her huge blue eyes, for she was almost my height, and said, 'Yes, I'd like that,' as if she had been just waiting for me to ask.

She used to teach the little children Bible stories, and they gathered around her on the outing, which was welcome as we were limited for conversation, and the infants provided us both with a current subject. I went down on my hands and knees and made a horse for them to ride one or sometimes two at a time, and that made everyone laugh. Georgiana was not passive in these times requiring civic organisation, these outings and picnics: one of the things I admired about her was her ability to plan, to gather up and send people older than her running off to tasks she set them. She was a skillful strategist, something that often gave me pause to think in later years: she could bring organisational ability to the fore when it was needed, and perhaps she had more to do with the events that transpired than was ever revealed.

Georgiana always reciprocated my attentions, but no more than that. We didn't make a vow or anything, but it was understood between us that we were together. We would sometimes hold hands and look out over the fields and forests, go berry-picking together. When we talked it was of inconsequential things. She had a natural reticence, which I regretted, because I wanted her

21

to talk more about herself, I wanted to know what she thought about everything, what she felt inside, what it was like to be her. But she didn't disclose much, a lot of the conversation we had would be me talking about things, and hoping she was interested. She was a maddeningly private and contained self, but she was always thoughtful and affectionate towards me, always looked at me as if she loved me, and that she bathed in my adoration of her. I suppose we did what we had been brought up to do: I was the more active one; she was beautiful and quiet. I can say we were happy and I know I am not talking only for myself. Whatever anxieties and challenges stirred in that soft breast, whatever compulsions drove her to her destiny, I am a witness that Georgiana Yoke laughed and teased and played like a girl without a care in the world and that her time in Gilmanton was innocent and idyllic. It was a fresh, if uncertain love, and the air was purer and the meadows greener than they ever were before, or would be again.

Once I said, on a summer evening with the low buzzing of the insects in our ears, 'Do you love me?'

'Why, yes,' she said, as if she were talking to one of her kindergarten class.

Then she saw my crestfallen expression and said, 'You may kiss me, Frank,' and I brushed my dry lips against hers as the droning of the whirring animals grew and mixed with the sound of the blood pounding in my head.

Sometimes there were dances in the church hall, at Thanksgiving, Christmas, Mayday and times like that, and we would go and dance to the tunes of a fiddler. Henry would go too, of course, and he always had a partner to dance with, even if he didn't arrive with one, he was never at a loss for a word or a compliment to charm the farmers' daughters, but his eyes always seemed to be on the horizon, somewhere ahead, plotting the next move, never here with us.

Henry had lain low in all this business of my developing affection for Georgiana. Either he didn't understand or didn't care, his route to grown-up life was different from mine. He had taken an interest in girls at an earlier time than I had, but had taken a pretty languid, indiscriminate interest in any girl and every one. He seemed to find this, like so much else in life, easier than I did. Anyway, when Georgiana and me were confidently a couple, Henry used to hang around with us, or we did with him.

One reason why we came to spend a lot of time together, Henry, Georgiana and me, was that we were among the few clever kids who stayed on at school–or the kids whose parents could afford to let them. It magnified the distance between ourselves and the other kids in town, and increased our feeling of closeness. We got lessons in American history, algebra, geometry and bookkeeping, as well as carrying on with the standard subjects. I know Henry's ma taught him Latin and maybe some Greek, he certainly knew about Greece, and maybe it was the language that stimulated his interest in Greek stories.

Henry started to tell us stories, sitting on the grass or on a wooden porch, or in the barn when it was cold. I don't know how it started, probably he just said, 'I've been reading a book, do you want to hear a story?' Nothing much surprised us about Henry, if he wanted to tell us a story, we'd listen.

'These things, they happened in Fairyland, which was a land of golden roads and perennial flowers and wine,' Henry said. Everything he told us was alive and sparkling as if it had just happened in the valley over yonder and Henry was telling us fresh news. The stories were often strange and terrible, but they were always shimmering with light, as if they were the entrance to another world. Henry told us about the lady in a tower who the god came to in a shower of gold; the man who was pulled into the stream by the nymphs; the father who so feared the revolt of his sons that he ate them soon after they were born, until one son was helped to escape and who he returned to rend the flesh of his father himself.

I remember how Henry told that last story, looking round at us with his flashing eyes, and whispering, 'He tore off a part of his father's body, tore it off, and what part do you think he tore off?'

We were wide eyed.

'The part that made him a man!' he croaked, with an emphatic nod.

I was undecided about the right response to this kind of talk but Georgiana laughed, put her hand to her mouth and touched Henry's sleeve, as if to push him away, 'I declare you're a demon, Henry Holmes,' she said, and noticing my uncertain expression, said, 'It's just a story, Frank.' That was Henry, he always knew just how far to go to tease and fascinate without repelling.

There was one story I remember, that Henry told us sitting in the shade of a willow tree alongside the river: 'Once in Fairyland there were no men, or women either,' he said gallantly, with a bow of his head to Georgiana. 'One part of Fairyland was inhabited by the Titans, made by the god Zeus who ruled over the heavens. They were great, dark, hairy giants who roamed the plains and the valleys looking mean, and they hunted their food with clubs and didn't do much else. Now Zeus didn't think the Titans had much fun and he wanted them to enjoy themselves, and as his son Dionysus was the god of wine, he was exactly the right person to send down to teach them a few things. Well, Dionysus came down, in his wine-coloured robes and his head crowned with vine leaves, and he set about civilising those Titans. He taught them how to gather grapes and instead of eating them, to tread the juice out, and leave it, and mix it so it was fermented. And they did this and then they drank the wine and they had a gay old time, singing and dancing and making merry. But none of the Titans knew when to stop drinking the wine, and they just went on and on, and after they got merry, they got loud, and after they got loud, they got mean, and they started picking fights with each other. This wasn't what Dionysus had wanted to happen at all and he told them so, but they were in no mood to listen and they started saying, "Who is this guy to tell us what to do, we're the Titans, we're in charge around here!" And they tore him apart with their bare hands. They tore him limb from limb and ripped the flesh from his bones. Then they tore open the rib cage and ripped out his liver and his lungs and even his divine heart, and they fought with one another in the blood to each get a piece of it.' Henry paused and shook his head, as if condemning such very bad behaviour. 'Soon the wine was finished, and the meat,' he added with a grin, 'and they fell down in a drunken stupor. Now Zeus came down looking to see what good works his son had done and he came into the clearing by the river, just like this place here,' Henry swung his arm round and we shuddered as if we could see the sleeping bodies of the murderous Titans with the evidence of their bloody feast all around their twitching mouths.

'And the great god he roared a terrible roar, and called down thunderbolts from the sky, like he was used to doing, and struck the Titans with them and struck them again, until what had been a race of giants became just a few piles of smoking dust.' Henry paused for effect, then delivered his epilogue. 'And from that black dust, Zeus made men and women, thinking he might make a better job of it this time. And that is why people feel guilt, because people were made of stuff that shared the shame of having killed a god; but it is also why, base creatures though we may be, we have something divine in us, because we were made of the dust that still contained part of the divine Dionysus.'

Georgiana had nestled close to me as the horror of it began to unfold, which made me as grateful for the story as I was of the warm air around us and the mossy earth we lay on. 'That's a Temperance Union story about Fairyland,' I said, laughing, because Henry and his folks didn't drink–it wasn't at all unusual to be an abstainer in those parts.

I envied Henry that he could always make Georgiana laugh. Sometimes I could make her laugh too, but he was a master with the choice word or glance. Henry graduated at the top of the class and got a scholarship to go to college. Applying for scholarships was something the Holmeses would know about, it wouldn't have occurred to my ma and pa. I was going to get a job as a deputy in a neighbouring town, and when I had enough experience I'd become deputy, then sheriff in Gilmanton. Some time along the line I'd marry Georgiana and we'd have beautiful children and live happily ever after.

I said something of this to Georgiana and was surprised when she said, 'I think I'd like to see something of the world before I settle down.'

'What world?' I said, stupidly, I was sixteen or seventeen. Thinking it was a manly thing to say, I said, 'I'd want my wife to stay home and look after the children, isn't there world enough in that?'

She pursed her lips, she wanted to go to a teaching college. We talked a little about it, I wasn't against her being a teacher till the kids came along. I mention this trifling difference because it was the only one we had, and the only hint I had of what was to come.

I was away a lot after I'd passed seventeen, helping out at Pittsfield which had more deputies and a bigger jail. I was really just hanging around getting experience until a post came up, but I put a lot into it, arriving early and leaving late, looking eager. So I saw less of Georgiana, and hardly anything of Henry who was studying to go to college. Once I called at her house unexpected, I'd ridden over early from Pittsfield and Henry was there, sitting at the table in the kitchen which always smelled of baking, talking with the very efficient Mrs Yoke. He was a little surprised to see me, but not excessively. He had some school books on the table which he was slowly clearing up. 'I was just going through some mathematics with Georgiana,' he said.

Hearing my voice, Georgiana came through from the parlour. 'Oh, hi Frank, what a surprise, Henry was showing me some geometry,' she said. Only later did I think, when suspicion had become second nature to me, that for both of them to need to explain his presence was dubious behaviour.

So what happened? Nothing, really, or almost nothing. No event intervened between me and my happiness, not that I knew of anyway. It would all have been easier if there had been a sign, a blazing portent of what was to come, but there was only a lesson as hard and blank as a granite block. She whose movements were poetry to me, whose lips were all I desired; for all the hours of sitting, of talking with Georgiana Yoke, of being blissfully together, I didn't know her at all.

One rainy autumn night after I had ridden home, I settled the horse and walked through the fallen leaves over to Reverend and Mrs Yoke's house by the church, just to say hello, to stand on the porch maybe, just to look at Georgiana a little. I knocked and Mrs Yoke came to the door. She was a tall and rather austere woman with hair which might once have been fair but was now silver, pulled back into a harsh bun,

'Well hello Frank. I didn't expect to see you,' she said.

'Oh, I just decided to come home early to see ma and pa,' I said, 'and I thought I'd see Georgiana, is she around?'

'Why she's gone Frank, didn't you see her?' said Mrs Yoke, her lined face leaning out of the warm house into the darkness, genuinely perplexed.

'Gone?' I said.

'Gone to college, I thought you knew,' she said, 'I thought all her friends knew.' I almost reeled back at the shock but I knew even then the value of keeping calm to gain all possible information.

'Must have slipped my mind,' I said, regaining composure.

'Yes, she went to college in Burlington this morning with Henry.'

'With Henry.' I repeated stupidly.

'Yes, he called for her, surely they told you.'

'I didn't know it was going to happen so soon,' I said, trying vainly to extend the interview to obtain more information.

'It was, for many weeks,' Mrs Yoke smiled sweetly, wanting to terminate the conversation.

I backed away into the night, 'Thanks Mrs Yoke, sorry to bother you.' My footsteps felt heavy as the blood roared in my ears and I walked impervious to the cold and the rain which had started to fall faster. There would be a simple explanation, I told myself, there was a misunderstanding. My life was breaking away and scattering. The life I had lived, seeing Georgiana, thinking of Georgiana, loving Georgiana, flowed off broken like gossamer thread smashed by heavy rain, like leaves in the wind.

My doubts came flooding in on me. What had I said or done to upset her? Georgiana's mother had never liked me as a suitor for her daughter anyway. It wasn't anything obvious, a tilt of the head, a look of forbearance when I called for her once too often. She may well have thought Henry came from better stock, or had better prospects, or just the old thing about his family being total abstainers while we weren't. It wasn't that we were drunkards or anything, just that my pa enjoyed a drink and gave no one any problems with it, and we'd never stop doing something because some stiff-necked fuss-budget said we should. But Mrs Yoke wanted her grandchildren to be brought up in a teetotalling household, as her children had been, and she said as much in one unguarded moment to my mother in the general store.

I was heading for Henry's house, some way out of town, as the thoughts rushed through my head like water through sluice gates. Maybe Mrs Yoke had misunderstood: Henry had helped Georgiana with a carriage or something, he had gone with her part of the way and put her on a train, there had been a mix-up with the date and she only just found she had to go. By the time I got to Henry's house I had explained it all and was making light of it, all I needed was confirmation of the innocence of the events.

I went to the kitchen door. Mrs Holmes was there immediately, a plump, fussy woman, who had dressed mainly in dark colours since her husband's death. 'I didn't expect to see you Frank, well what can I do for you? You'll be missing Henry now he's gone.'

'Oh... where has he gone?' I said with as much nonchalance as I could muster.

'Why, don't you know, when you and Henry were so close?' she peered into the dark. I was less guarded at looking hurt before Mrs Holmes. I just shook my head.

'They went this morning,' she said.

'They?' I said blankly.

'Didn't Georgiana tell you?' she asked.

'She didn't mention much, she was a quiet girl,' I said, choking on the words.

'They applied to the same college,' she said, 'they said they did want to keep it quiet in case they didn't get in, you know, but I would have expected them to tell you, Frank. Henry's doing medicine of course, and she's studying to be a teacher. A long way away, too far for my liking, but they'll make a fine couple.'

'What do you mean?' I said, dry mouthed, inwardly cursing the silly woman.

'Well, there had been talk of marriage,' she said winsomely, her head on one side, 'and I can't help feeling it's romantic, even though a wedding is a long way off yet, they will want to finish their education...' I stood on the porch looking at her soft, fat white face babbling on, until she noticed my shocked expression, 'It must be hard for you, Frank,' she said, now realising how little I knew and feeling uncomfortable, 'you were sweet on Georgiana, weren't you?'

'We were friends,' I said, 'excuse me,' and I went stumbling out into the rain with the world slowing down around me. I was engulfed in shock, as if I had been in an explosion or a railroad accident–that such a thing could happen was too terrible to countenance. My mind would not encompass it.

I just stayed out in the dark, letting the cold rain lash me, listening to the wind whip the branches and tear the leaves from the trees. Summer was over.

I was ill after that. It shocked my folks, who had never known me to have a day's illness. I couldn't go in to work and lost my reputation for health and reliability, and so lost the chance of a job in Pittsfield, but that was just more suffering of a different sort thrown in as a kind of relish. My mind was obsessed with Georgiana, her sweet gentle face and her terrible betrayal, and Henry's cursed friendship. Ma thought it was a chill and blamed me for being out in the rain. She knew about Georgiana, of course, everyone did. It was a small town, and a town which looked to its children to provide continuity–people were supposed to marry and bring up families in Gilmanton, we were the future. None of us three did that, we all went away.

Even now it is hard to measure what was taken from me on that night of betrayal. Friendship, love, the possibility of new life were all of them blighted. I had believed that your best buddy was always your best buddy, you'd be sitting on the porch with him smoking tobacco and watching the sunset when you were both old. I had believed that two people meet and are right for each other, and they marry and have kids, and the process begins again. I didn't think that things changed, not for the worse, anyway. This is dumb of me, I know, but this was New Hampshire, this was the Granite State, for God's sake: the rocks stayed under the ground and on top of it the trees grew, there was always new lumber to send through the scything steam mills, pumping the sounds of power through the forest, there was always new growth, new trees. To think there might be an end to friendship, to finding your sweetheart and having a family, that just wasn't natural, it wasn't conceivable, it was like there being no more forest. What Henry had taken away from me was a whole way of seeing and believing in the world.

My nights were void of sleep but filled with pain and anger. I was so tired I just wanted to sleep all day. I was less angry than empty, but also sore and tender to the touch. Now I am older and have experienced such things, I know what that gritty tiredness was: it was the tiredness of bereavement.

My face was lined with unhappiness, sorrow must have aged me ten years, my soul wrung out with futile passions. It was perhaps, also, not just that I had had and lost, but that I had never really had her. That she could do this - I never knew her at all, in any sense. We were, I should say, chaste. It was just the way we were then, at least in the country. In the city I don't know. I can't imagine Holmes showed such restraint, and the image of that tormented me. I went through stages of feeling: first I was angry, so angry I could have torn the head off his neck with my bare hands. Then I was consumed with bitterness and self-loathing. If this had happened to me, why didn't I see it coming? Because I was dumb, that's why. Because I was unworthy. Because I deserved it. Why didn't I go ahead and do the act with her? I had ample opportunity, but because I thought we had all the time in the world I didn't, or because I was timid, or respectful of convention. Because, because, because. Because I was me.

Then I got to the stage where I didn't care, where the hatred had burned up any feeling from me. And I thought he may as well have her, the trash, because if she would have him and do that with him, she was trash and beneath me. But a glow of desire still pulsed in me somewhere: for I loved her still. My dearest darling, why did you do what you did?

Georgiana Yoke destroyed me for good women. That is, I couldn't believe there were any anymore. I knew there must be, perhaps I have even met some, but they were not for me. My feelings for Georgiana were more difficult to deal with than those for him. Him I wanted to kill, wanted to kill in their bed, beside her, so she could see what she had done. I wanted her to plead with me for his life. I wanted to take a gun and find him and blow his brains out. No, I wanted to shoot him somewhere fatally, in the gut, and go over and watch him bleed and hear him plead with me looking down the barrel of a gun at him letting him know for every last minute it was me, me, me who had killed him.

I understand that people later regret such thoughts, or find them childish or not worth remembering. Me, I was so often in the months that followed my reassociation with Henry Holmes in 1894 to lament that I hadn't played out just those fantasies and tracked him down, even to the last place on earth, and killed him dead.

Chapter 3

Philadelphia 1894

Henry Holmes walked into the morgue office, extending his hand in friendship, blithe and bold. The same flop of hair fell over his forehead, the familiar smile spread over his whole face. A lot of things in my job required self-restraint under challenging circumstances. I had gotten good at it. I recovered my composure sufficiently to say, 'Good afternoon,' and swiftly grasped and released the proffered hand.

'You two know each other?' said Edward Cass in amazement.

'We went to school together,' I said, trying to regain some control of the situation. 'Good afternoon young lady,' I said to the girl, 'what's your name.'

'Alice. Alice Pitezel,' she said and brought her sleeve up to rub her nose then thought better of it, in this company. She was an ordinary little girl with dark hair hanging loose and cut in bangs. She was poorly though not shabbily dressed and her brown eyes were more frightened than questioning. I guessed she wasn't very clever.

'I'm sorry this isn't such a nice, place to be,' I said, feeling awkward as I've never had children and have no particular skills with them. 'Miss Robertson will look after you,' I said, and called on Muriel who was employed for her kindly manner with the bereaved and the timid.

Muriel led the girl away and I turned back to Holmes and Cass. Henry Holmes' blue eyes were as bright and smiling as ever they were, and the years had not greyed his hair nor coarsened his features as they had mine. The most noticeable change was a moustache which virtually concealed his buck teeth. He wore a smartly tailored, dark business suit with a waistcoat with a heavy watch chain running into the fob pocket. He looked as if he had done well for himself.

'I do hope, Frank,' Holmes said, with a manner as easy as if he had last seen me yesterday, 'that we won't have to put that poor girl though the torment of seeing a cadaver, perhaps of her own father, for I fear it is he.' His voice was still smooth and melodic, his turns of phrase a little florid for everyday use.

Cass pursed his lips and looked at me. 'We'll see,' I said, 'let's go through.' I was letting the situation convey me along like an automaton, or like a carriage where the driver has stopped thinking and the horse has taken the lead. We went into the autopsy room where the pathologist William Scott was waiting for us and Joe was taking away the remains of the last fellow who had been opened up.

The rank, discoloured body was exposed, still in his clothes, like a grotesque carnival dummy. 'There's been no autopsy,' said Scott, a ruddy faced old man with mutton chop whiskers and an apron that looked like it came from a butcher's shop.

'I see,' I said, not wanting to give an opinion. There should have been an autopsy. An autopsy should have been ordered, but to comment on it would be to draw attention to my impotence in being unable to give the order myself. I had to deal with that someplace else.

'Just an identification then?' asked Scott, clearly hoping he wouldn't be needed so he could go off for his coffee and cookies.

'Yes,' I said, 'but stick around, it may not be straightforward.' I turned to Cass, 'Didn't you say something about distinguishing features?'

Cass nodded and said, 'Can you help us here Mr Holmes?'

'Why yes,' said Holmes, his arms on his hips, pushing his jacket back so I could see he had not lost his figure with the passing years. He began as if doing a high school recitation in front of the class, 'His front teeth were most distinctive, he had a wart on the back of the neck, just here,' he indicated on his own neck, 'there was a scar on his left leg where he dropped a crate on it back in 1889, and one of his fingernails was badly blackened,' Holmes looked at his own immaculate manicure as if in demonstration.

'That's quite a list,' said Cass slowly, 'a pretty thorough identification. I bet my own mother couldn't identify me that well.' Cass was new to this work, still at the stage when he thought it was clever to reveal his insights immediately to show how clever he was, the sort of thing that tipped off the bad guys that they ought to be careful.

'I have known the deceased for a long time,' responded Holmes, 'He was my friend,' he said looking down, with that quiver in the voice which commands sympathy.

I exchanged a sidelong glance with Cass, 'Let's get on,' I said, 'Doctor Scott...'

The doctor started to lift the head with its bulging eyes, looking for a wart on the neck.

Holmes said, 'There it is,' and put his finger on the protuberance. Scott, Cass and I looked at it and nodded. Holmes then started to roll up the left trouser leg with Scott's help. Even through the discoloured tissue it was possible to see there was indeed a scar stretching three or four inches from the shin back to the calf.

'Which finger was it you were interested in?' Scott asked.

'I'm afraid I can't remember,' said Holmes, and we all looked at the puffy, blackened hands .

'The only way to recover a bruise like that,' said Scott, wiping his hands on his already soiled apron, 'is to cut off the finger and place it in alcohol.' I nodded and he grasped a silver lancet and started to cut off a finger. 'The index finger of the right hand is the most likely candidate for this kind of injury,' he said, and with some difficulty he cut it off and dropped it in a glass beaker of spirit that Joe had poured. We watched as if it were a miracle taking place in the glass jar, scenting the sharp fumes as the discoloration seeped away and left us staring at a pure, white man's finger.

'Let's try again,' I said.

'I'll help,' said Holmes, and he extracted a linen bundle from his pocket, unrolled it on an instrument table and selected from a range of surgical implements a gleaming stainless steel scalpel which he held a little before him with an experienced gesture.

'Well God damn' said Joe Stitch emphatically, his lower jaw hanging open. Holmes shot him a cold look of admonishment for his profanity, and Joe cast his eyes to the ground in deference.

'I am medically trained,' said Holmes to Dr Scott, as he approached the cadaver from the other side and held the body's left hand as if in a gesture of courtship.

With some expertise Holmes severed the tissues of a lower finger joint, digging the point of the scalpel into the cartilage with an audible squelch. Dr Scott took off the main fingers of the other hand. As they worked longer on the body its temperature rose slightly, and a range of foul scents billowed from it. There was putrefaction; the chemical odour I had noticed in the building where I found him; and more familiar smells as his bladder and bowels had emptied in his clothes. *Carious, putrilage, dissolution*, I thought. During the removal of the fingers Edward Cass visibly paled, then found something interesting to focus on over the other side of the room.

I now had my first time to think. Of course, Holmes had known from the insurance company that he was going to see me–once he had the name he knew it had to be me. There can't be that many Frank P. Geyers in law enforcement. That was part of the secret of his perfect equanimity. But as the name he now used was not the name by which I knew him in childhood, I had no idea I was going to see him. He was prepared and I wasn't, just one more time Henry Holmes was a step ahead of me. *'I have to get him alone,'* I said to myself.

Finally a finger with an ugly bruise across the nail revealed itself in the beaker. Holmes looked round with a beam of satisfaction. 'I don't have any doubt that this is B.F.Pitezel,' he said.

'Show me the teeth, doctor,' I said, and Scott pulled back the blackened lips to show a poor set of uneven, yellowing teeth. They were so uneven, so ill-fitting, that one front incisor was slightly crossed over the other. 'Joe, get the sheet to display the teeth,' I said, 'and move this guy into the public viewing room.'

I explained to Cass, who looked as if he needed reassurance, 'It's a technique for identifying people when the body is too far gone, or where we don't want to upset the witness unduly. Very often people can be identified by their teeth, and if anyone can be, I guess this fellow can.' Holmes went to object, knowing I was going to ask the girl to identify her father, but thought better of it and looked resignedly at me, as if in regret.

We went back to the office while Joe prepared the body and Dr Scott washed up. Muriel had got the girl drawing on sheets of coroner's office paper. 'I'm sorry to ask you to do this, Alice,' I said, 'but do you know why you are here?' She nodded her head meekly. I said, 'We've found someone dead and we think it may be your daddy, but the only way to be sure is if someone who knows him really well has a look. We've made it easy for you, we've covered him all up except for his mouth. I'm going to have to get you to take a look and see if you can identify him just from that.' The dark haired girl made an almost imperceptible movement of her head and looked down again, as if she were going to continue her drawing. Muriel went to give comfort but Holmes already had his arm around her.

'Come on champ,' he said softly into her ear, 'you can do it.' She looked round at him and smiled weakly. I felt jealous of his easy relationship with the girl, and was momentarily angry for having felt such a thing: I was confused about my own feelings as I had not been for years, and discomfited that I was being plunged back into doubt. I led the way into the viewing room where Joe had wheeled out the body with a green canvas sheet covering it entirely except for a small space over the mouth.

'This needn't take long,' I said to Alice, 'come here and a have a look.'

The room was illuminated by shafts of watery sunlight shining down from the high gothic windows on the plain plaster walls. There was no furniture in the room but the trolley with its green drapery over the man-shaped lump. I pointed to the teeth, visible through a hole in the fabric, and Alice nervously leaned over, stared for a long two seconds, then turned and sought Henry Holmes' arms, sobbing into his shoulder, 'Yes... yes.'

'OK,' I said and we all shuffled out, 'that's it as far as the identification is concerned.' I said to Cass, 'can you wait here for me, I'd like to spend some time with Mr Holmes on his own.'

Cass was boyishly eager to please, 'I'll stay here,' he said, as if it was an honour. He probably needed some time to recover.

'Let's talk a little, Mr Holmes, Henry,' I said leaning over Holmes and noticing the scent of lavender water. I immediately regretted using his name, by using a name we both knew to be false, it was as if I was being drawn into his conspiracy, but any other form of address would have seemed discourteous.

'Of course, Frank,' he said, but pulled his fat little gold watch out from his fob pocket and opened the front, 'but mind we've got a train to catch to get back to Chicago.'

He seemed pretty confident he was going back and, indeed, I had no reason to detain him. 'I'll get you a beer at a place a few doors down the road.'

'You can get me a soda,' said Holmes. So he was still teetotal. We walked outside, through the big pointed arch of the morgue entrance into the dying sunshine of fall. 'I'd pay thirty dollars to have the poor boy cremated,' he declared extravagantly.

'That would require the permission of the widow,' I said.

'Yeah,' he said dismissively, 'all too much trouble. So this is it, the city of brotherly love!'

'It's your first time in Philadelphia?' I said,

'Sure is.' he said cheerfully, 'and impressive, from what I've seen.' Was he actually trying to win me over by playing on my civic pride?

'How did you know the deceased?' I asked as we entered a simple, decent-looking bar. Holmes and myself were reflected in the gilt-edged mirrors covering all the walls: he shorter than me and slighter, standing there in his alertness and his dark business suit; me brooding over him, big and powerful but somehow lumbering next to his jauntiness.

'Ben was his name,' Holmes mused, 'he worked in my drug store in Chicago, did some of the heavy work for me—unloading supplies, that sort of thing. I got to like him and his family. They're great kids.'

One thing I did not want was a disquisition on family life. 'So how did you hear about his death?'

Holmes shrugged, 'The attorney, whatever his name was...

37

Howe, he contacted the insurance company and they contacted me.'

'So how did the attorney know?' I asked, realising I was running out of questions.

Holmes shook his head, 'A newspaper report I guess. Maybe they circulate information about this sort of thing among attorneys. I'll have a kola soda,' he said in response to the barman's inquiry. I had a beer and we sat down.

'Let me ask you something,' said Holmes brightly, 'You know I've heard about that Lexow committee investigating the police, saying detectives wouldn't work on cases unless they were promised money beforehand, is that true?' He was referring to the scandals in New York City where the captain of one precinct had a fifty-foot long steam yacht, not something he had acquired on police pay.

I kept cool, 'How should I know,' I said, 'the Lexow committee is investigating New York cops.'

'Oh,' he said, 'and it's not the same everywhere?'

I shook my head and got out a ten cent cigar. 'Didn't I hear you had gone to Vermont to study medicine?' I said. Police corruption wasn't my favourite topic of conversation.

'In Michigan,' he said, 'Ann Arbor.'

'So why did you get out, I would have thought being a doctor was a good position to hold.'

'Sure,' said Holmes, 'it was good when I could be some use to people. But you know...' he looked into the middle distance as if wondering whether to tell me something. 'Do you know what diabetes is?'

'I think so, but tell me,' I said, curious to know where he was leading.

'It's an inability to metabolise food,' he was recounting a story just as he had all those years ago, he still had a superb skill. 'The body won't use it, and the blood gets filled with sugar. Diabetics have a craving for water and for food but when you give them food it makes them worse. As a young doctor I was on a ward that dealt with these cases. I'll never forget the smell on the ward, like rotten apples, the by-product of some internal process when the bodies were trying to digest food they couldn't handle.' He looked into the yeasty air of the bar, as if reliving the smell of the hospital.

'They lived quite a while, maybe a year from first diagnosis. There was time, you see, to try to make them better. A lot of things were tried: mainly they were treated with opium which at least relieved the pain but it did nothing for the diabetes. But there was always something new, there were the special diets: the rice diet, the potato diet, the high fat diet, the sugar diet. We tried them all, or other doctors did and we read about it. Nothing worked. there were lots of hopes, then failure. Then came a new method, the starvation diet: you had to put only as many calories in as a resting body needed. You reduced food intake to the mere maintenance level. That was so hard for everyone, but hardest for the children. They were always hungry, and of course there was food a-plenty in the hospital, we just couldn't give it to them. I remember one little girl who came in, she was called Dorothy. She was about twelve, and the cutest little thing but real sick, pale and wasted. And while I was having her weighed and checking her pulse and things, like you have do, when she was admitted, while I was holding her wrist to take her pulse she said, "Are you gonna make me better doctor?" Well, I was new in the job and full of self-confidence and pretty blasé about the whole thing and I said, "Sure I will honey,"

'As the months passed she got worse and worse. We were starving her to death day by day. We were doing it to try to treat her, but it wasn't the disease, it was us doctors. When people are starving, their eyes seem to get larger as the flesh of their face wastes away until you get these huge eyes staring at you, imploring you to do something when you know, and they know in the end, there is nothing you can do.

'Dorothy couldn't have any of the fancy things, any of the nice things that children like. Her birthday cake was a cardboard hatbox with coloured paper around it and candles on top. She weighed about forty pounds at the end.

'I used to go home and cry my eyes out. How could this be happening? What was the good of being a doctor if I couldn't help someone like her? She was a living skeleton, it was all she could do to talk. She never reminded me of my promise to her, but I was reminded of it every time I saw her.

'Well, on the day she died I packed up my things and walked. I just didn't have the heart for it anymore.'

Somehow I was again under his spell. After all the pain, I was feeling admiration, even respect for Henry Holmes. I had to get out of it.

'Was that when you changed your name?' I said.

'Yeah,' he said unhesitatingly, taking a sip of his kola, and looking up at me in joy across the smeared table, 'new name, new life, that's the way I look at it. You can be what you want. This here is the land of opportunity. You make your own chances.'

I looked down at the table, the suspicious nature of the name change overshadowed by Henry's spirited love of life and all its possibilities. For me, I couldn't be what I wanted, I could only be what I was. I drank some beer without pleasure.

He caught my mood and, bold as ever, took the initiative again. 'Look, Frank, don't get mad, but you're still sore at me for going off with Georgie, aren't you?'

My mouth twitched involuntarily at the familiar mention of her name. I had a natural reluctance not to show if I was hurt, it gave the other man the edge. I took my time, 'That was all a long time ago,' I said with more ease than I felt. Inside I was crippled, incapacitated, enervated. 'But one thing I do wonder: why didn't you tell me, why did you let me go on thinking till the end that she,' I couldn't even say Georgiana's name, 'that she was going to marry me, why was it so sudden?'

He literally slapped his thigh with amazement and his blue eyes lit up. 'I begged Georgie to let me tell you,' he said earnestly, 'but she kept telling me it was her duty to do it, she was your girl after all.'

'Where is she now?' I said trying not to introduce an emotional tone into my voice.

Holmes shook his head. 'It wouldn't be good for you, Frank,' he said, 'she is happy, has little ones,' I nodded miserably. This was the worst: thinking that their life had gone on, *continuance.*

'Do you still...' he said, and then retracted, 'no, it's nothing,' and finished his drink.

'No, go on,' I said, fascinated by the way he had retained his charm.

He looked at me boldly, 'Do you still believe in progress? That things are going to be better in future because of locomotives and telephones and the Gatling gun?'

'I think the century that is to come,' I said, glad I was on familiar territory, 'will hold many wonders, and not all of them will be good. But the slums will be cleared and decent houses built; sick people will be made better by new medicines we don't even imagine now; and people will be able to talk to each other more easily through the telephone and other machines not yet invented; and travel will become much easier – yeah, I think progress is going to make things better. How could it not do?'

'You sound less sure than you used to,' said Holmes with a merry laugh.

'Just older,' I said

Cass was waiting for us in the office with Alice. We went to one side out of deference for her feelings. Holmes said, 'I am sorry to say, gentlemen, that I think there is no doubt the deceased is my friend Mr Pitezel.'

'I've seen nothing to suggest he isn't,' I said.

Holmes addressed Cass, 'I should therefore like to claim my expenses for this journey,' and he brought out of his waistcoat pocket a thin sheet of paper on which were written some calculations, 'and I will leave this fair city with young Alice.'

Cass looked at the note and murmured, 'It all seems to be in order,' and wrote out a Fidelity Mutual cheque.

'I was hoping for cash...' said Holmes.

'Sorry, just don't have it,' said Cass, getting a signature on a receipt, 'but you can cash that at the bank at the station.'

Holmes shook my hand. It felt wrong but I could hardly

withhold the gesture and remain polite. He touched Alice's cheek and said, as much to me as to her, 'It's a sad day in fairyland.' The words brought back a torrent of memories from my childhood and youth, all the times we had been together, and the times we had been with Georgiana. I pressed my lips together and nodded as they walked off, the jaunty man with his hand solicitously on Alice's shoulder as they went out into the clattering tangle of horses and carriages in Second Street.

I watched them dwindle in the distance, a deep well of sadness within me. I was trying to understand what I felt about the case, about Holmes, about Georgiana. Everything converged into a heaving mass: the things I ought to think about for my job; the things I shouldn't think about because they gave me pain; the memories of far-off summers befouled. Seeing Henry again made me realise what I had lost. It was too much to handle all at once, I needed space to breathe.

After a period of silence Cass said, 'So what happens with this case now?'

I sighed audibly, 'Let's go to City Hall and talk about it in my office,' I said. There wasn't a very good reason for doing this but I was feeling I'd taken a beating and I wanted to be in familiar surroundings.

We sat in silence in a cab down Broad Street to Penn Square, with Cass peering out of the window as we approached the new City Hall. As we walked up to it he looked up in pleasure at the elegant French-style building and lingered a little in the courtyard to hear a guide telling a group of visitors from out of town, '...it covers four and a half acres, has over 750 rooms, is 547 feet high which is twice the height of the Masonic Temple...'

I nodded at him to hurry up. 'Sorry,' Cass said, as we walked to an ornate elevator door, 'I just like to take everything in when I'm in a new city.'

He looked at all the doors as we walked down the corridor: the brass plates announced the Orphans' Court Record Rooms; Board of Health Milk Inspector; Turnkey and Surgeon of Police... Finally we were at the detective's room where I led him through past my desk to see O'Brien. The closer we got to the chief's office the more the muscles in my neck tightened. This case was going to be quietly dropped, it had all the makings of a case that wouldn't go the distance: no obvious crime; no obvious suspect; out-of-state witnesses. But I liked Edward Cass, and he looked up to me with his round, fresh face, and I didn't want him to think that dropping the case was my doing.

I could see O'Brien's greasy, yellowish head of hair bent over his desk through the window glass that surrounded his office. I knocked and we entered. O'Brien stood as I introduced Cass, 'The insurance investigator in the B.F.Pitezel case,' I said, 'the identification seems OK, it's him. The stiff is still in the dead house, but the coroner hasn't ordered an autopsy.'

O'Brien looked down as if he was going to spit. He raised his arm and struck the heavy board of his desk softly with the flat of his hand, in a moment of frustrated resignation. 'Well,' he said, 'that's out of my hands. But what would it prove? Death by explosion, chemical poisoning? It doesn't affect the insurance payout.'

'It would if it was murder,' said Cass quietly.

O'Brien gave a look of forbearance, 'What have you got?' he challenged, 'to say it was murder?'

'Man rents a property,' said Cass, 'a few days later is found dead. Very soon afterwards insurance money is claimed for the death on a policy that has only just been renewed.'

'How did his relatives know this guy was dead, when he was using a false name?' asked O'Brien.

'The only way we could be sure is to go to Chicago to interview the widow, or the lawyer in St Louis,' I said

O'Brien wiped his nicotine-stained fingers through his hair, 'Hell,' he said, 'Mr Cass, this is suspicious as I don't know what, but I've just gotta have more to go on. I got pressure on me to get results. I just can't keep men working on a difficult case that only might show results, if I can have them working on a case we can be pretty sure will get results, you follow?'

Cass nodded, 'Thank, you for your time, sir, I'll wish you good day,' he said. 'I have to tell you Fidelity Mutual wants to pay the claim and get it over with. I was here to oversee the identification and if that was positive, they'll pay up, unless you guys had any further investigations to make.'

O'Brien nodded and sat down again on his fat ass behind his desk, 'No, we haven't Mr Cass,' he said, 'thanks for dropping in, good day.'

We went over to my desk where I looked miserably at the pile of useless paperwork, Cass didn't want coffee, 'I ought to get back if there's nothing else I can do here,' he said.

'I know you're mad about this,' I said, 'so what do you think this case is about?'

Cass looked pensive, 'Holmes set up some fraud,' he said, 'they fought, or something went wrong.'

'There's no evidence Holmes was ever here before today,' I said.

'Maybe not, but look at him,' Cass said, 'I mean, you can tell what he's like. He's sharp, he's on the make somehow. He's fun, but he's on the make. But you guys knew each other, you were at school together, weren't you?'

'We lived in the same town in New Hampshire when we were kids,' I paused, 'We weren't friends,' I lied.

'What about the coroner?' Cass said, 'in some states an autopsy would be routine. If there's a sudden death, there needs to be an autopsy.' His earnestness was almost tangible as he seemed to be pleading with me to squeeze wholesome justice out of this garbage.

Suddenly the uselessness of it all crowded in on me and I shook my head angrily. 'The coroner,' I said, with some vehemence, 'used to be a coal merchant. He's been serving since 1883 and his dearest wish is to use the post to become Mayor. To become Mayor he's got to please the maximum number of people. His real function here, as he sees it, is to make this city look like a better place than it really is by reclassifying hard cases as easy ones. He sees his job as being to label the homicides that are easy to label and to mislabel the tough ones. Hopeless cases are thrown away. They are filtered out, misdirected, disposed of.' Cass swallowed hard but made no response. I continued to talk to his blank face, the words feeling like gravel in my mouth, 'Do you know the crime of infanticide virtually doesn't exist in Philadelphia? Babies are overlaid. That is, if they have been suffocated, it is said that their mothers have rolled onto them while asleep, and that's what killed them, not wilful murder by their parents. Or they die of inanition. Do you know what that means? It means emptiness. They die of emptiness.' Here was a long silence. 'Let's go. This case is over.'

'But...'

'This interview is concluded,' I said coldly, 'Let's go.'

'I'm sorry boss,' he said, the first time he had called me that, 'I didn't realise you cared so much about it.'

'I don't,' I lied, 'it was just another case.'

I took him to the elevator feeling awkward because I had offended a good man without reason. And I had shown more friendship than was necessary to Henry Holmes without a reason for that, either.

'I'm sorry, Cass,' I said. 'It is me, I don't like to leave a case, but there's nothing more I can do. If anything else comes of this, you tell me, alright?'

'Call me Ed,' he said, and extended his hand, 'I'd better get back to Chicago and hand over some more money to the bad guys.'

I patted him on the back as the elevator doors opened, 'Look after yourself,' I said.

That night I went to McQueen's Suicide Hall and talked with the girls and got drunk. I sat near Molly, dejectedly watching her working with the grimy banknotes, feeling aware of the chasm within me between what I was and what I might have been. I left before she was through, so I didn't have to go back with her and didn't have to explain why. I knew it would make her unhappy but in a world of misery my tiny spoonful didn't count for much.

I slowly walked off alone. This case hurt me like a chronic ache. I had nothing to go on, and so nowhere to go with it: it was suspicious, but that was all. But it wasn't just that. Worse than another case full of loose ends was that I had to face the possibility that I was interested in it beyond all reasonable suspicion anyway, because I wanted to get Holmes, because he had stolen my girl, he had stolen my life, my certainty. The police service instruction for such cases was stay off, keep out, do not enter. It was prohibited, disallowed.

Maybe it was me that was sick, and everything else really was going right. Everyone was busy forgetting their past, earning their living, being happy, getting married and raising a family. Everyone except me. This is a decent town. No one kills babies, and there are no unsolved murders. Inanition.

Chapter 4

Philadelphia 1880

I had taken a long journey from Gilmanton and the intervening events had served to suppress the betrayal of my youth. I had leaned out of the window and watched the grey granite rocks and green pines of New Hampshire flash past, catching a fine spray of cinders and ash from the engine on my lips. It was the taste of what I had become.

Even as I was, benumbed with pain, I felt the thrill of travel, the rhythmic song of the pistons propelling me into the unknown. From Laconia to Boston then a change of locomotive in the busy station, and another train down along the coast, giving me my first sight of the bleak, grey Atlantic Ocean. We speeded through Providence, New Haven, the bewildering cacophony of New York, and on to Philadelphia.

I was going to be a city cop, going out of the fresh air and into the smoke. It didn't have to be Philadelphia, there were other cities, but Boston was too close for me; New York would have been my choice, but my mother had had some bad experience there when she was a girl and begged me to choose someplace else, so I did.

Police work was sought after in those days. It was steady work, there were no layoffs, and there was a pension at the end of it. Once it was said that only locals could get a job, or men who had been in the city at least five years. This had to be changed, the city wasn't kind to its boys: men who grew up in the tenements were small, five foot three or thereabouts. They might be strong, but height was needed as well as muscle. So the cities started recruiting from us country boys, thereby increasing the resentment from the street toughs for the cops who were seen as outsiders coming to tell them what to do. Still, we weren't there to please the plug uglies.

So I had height and physical strength in my favour, a good

school record and a recommendation from the Pittsfield Sheriff. It didn't even occur to me that the City of Philadelphia Bureau of Police might turn me down.

I left the crowd surging inside Penn Station and entered the body of the city. The streets seemed so full – the women in big dresses; messengers carrying mysterious packages tied with string and curiously shaped objects piled high; hacks and carriages continuously rolling past with a clatter of hooves; the insistent display of advertising in bright letters and pictures on every available surface; elevated chairs on every street, as if for a visiting personage, but in fact the province of shoe-shine boys who plied their custom with imploring cordiality; street trades with their floating aroma of hot cakes or coffee or sticky candies; stores at every step, with vast expanses of glass window and their doors opening and closing while more people entered and departed the street than I had ever seen before I started my travels. It was never-ending: I could stand and watch for a minute, then two minutes, then an hour and the picture of the streets would still be unfolding. Something else: everything was so covered, so paved and cobbled over, so curbed and gullied in stone, the earth so encased in hardness. I was always thinking in those first days, walk a little while and the street will end, and there will be grass... fields, but the end never came. I was possessed with the feeling there was something behind the buildings–the trees and the mountains if I could only see round the grey and brown hulks of the streets. I was continually trying to shrug off the closeness of the city like it was a jacket I had on that was too tight.

I got some lodgings at a boarding house near the station, at a price I later realised was too high, and I went out walking. I saw Penn Square, Independence Square, the Treaty Stone, the immense Masonic Temple, the Greek columns of the Girard National Bank, the Western Union building, and Moyamensing prison that looked like a medieval castle. I wondered at how real people lived in the big houses on Rittenhouse Square and walked back down Chestnut Street, lined with elegant dress and fancy goods shops that made me think of Georgiana and turn away. I wish she had been there to enjoy it all with me.

You could get a good dinner for fifteen cents then: vegetable soup, hamburger, potatoes and gravy, apple pie, bread and butter. I had such a generous meal at the end of my first day, feeling very like a man as I paid the bill. For the first time since Georgiana left I felt I was doing something, I was going someplace. I wasn't happy, but I was regaining my pride. I left the eating house and walked the long streets, illuminated by gaslight that hissed and fizzled but never went out. What a wondrous place. A ragged woman edged out of an alley off Market Street, she was crouched down and in her arms she held a baby close to her breast. The sight touched me and I put a dime in her dirty, outstretched hand to her effusive thanks. Everything was going to be better.

The next morning I turned up at City Hall, the old building, and asked to see the Superintendent of Police. I had wired I was coming from my pa's office, and the Superintendent's office had wired back that he'd see me. I had my letter of recommendation and I had my youth, and vigour, and honesty. There was never such a picture of idealism in country boots as I presented that day.

I waited in a wood-panelled room adjoining the office of the Superintendent's assistants. Every time someone walked past I started as if to get up and meet the top man but it was never for me. He surely was a very busy person, and after four hours I wondered if I would ever see him today, or if I would have to come back to wait tomorrow.

Eventually, there being no one else available to put in front of me, the assistant beckoned me and ushered me into the Superintendent's office. He was a silver-haired, proud-looking man sitting behind a huge desk and showing me the crown of his head as he finished what he was doing with his papers. The office had the smell of power about it, all leather and polished wood. I stood up straight and answered questions about my education and the Superintendent looked at me as if he was listening. He hardly glanced at the letter from the sheriff.

'And you want to be a Philadelphia police officer,' he said, clearly a man with a talent for stating the obvious.

'Yes, sir,' I said, rather more loudly than the occasion merited.

'You're a fine-looking specimen,' he said, like he was talking about a horse, and he nodded as if to wave me away, 'you keep in touch, tell us where you're staying. If we have a vacancy for a rookie, we'll let you know.'

'Sir, you mean...' I said.

'Yes, you'll be considered when there's a vacancy, Geyer,' and he nodded towards the door, more definitely this time.

I said, 'Thank you, sir' and walked out. What more could I do? I felt my new-found confidence drain out of me like milk from a leaky bucket. I left City Hall in a daze, the bottom had opened out of my world, where was the safety net?

I sat in my bare lodging room with nothing but a water-pitcher on a table, a bed and a chair, and tried to hold off the panic. It wasn't so bad, I told myself, I could find a job somewhere else. I could wait till they needed a rookie and I would be there. I would let them know regularly that I was available. Maybe I would just come upon a crime and apprehend some real badman and I would be welcomed into the police bureau, and experienced officers would smile to themselves and nod to me and wonder how they had ever got along without me.

In the meantime, I must find work. For days I traipsed around to the places which I thought were promising: hollow ware foundries, bottle mould manufacturers, wire works, ice dealers, only to traipse out again. Sometimes there were even 'No hands wanted' notices up. Days drifted into weeks. Everywhere there were other men also calling on the same errand, most of them a bit older, a bit shabbier than me, but I knew they looked how I would look. I saw the beggar woman with the baby whenever I passed that place in Market Street and always looked on her with sympathy, until one night the baby rolled off her knee and into the gutter, and I saw it was a rag doll, and the woman was drunk and leering stupidly.

I wrote cheerful letters to my folks back home about the things I had seen in the city, when I could afford the stamps. One day my ma wrote, without further comment, that she thought I would like to know that Georgiana and Henry had married and they were both working as schoolteachers.

I picked up some days casual work as a labourer for a few cents an hour, digging holes in the road with the Irishmen. The work was dirty and backbreaking, I was almost glad it didn't last long. The fifteen cent meal before going to the City Hall was my last good dinner. Then I lived on dry bread, knowing I must keep what little money I had to pay for my lodgings. I had seen the homeless people huddled in doorways, had heard the wagon trundling round in the morning to pick up the stiff and frozen bodies. I had to have somewhere to stay, I could not return. I'd sooner jump off the Schuylkill Bridge than return abjectly to Gilmanton, the boy who had such dreams, whose girl had run off and who had failed to make his way in the big city, who had come back with his tail between his legs. If that was what I was, why survive?

It was in one of these dark moods, when I had called at John Bower's Packing House and Abattoir to see if they wanted hands and had met two men leaving, having been there on the same fruitless errand. There wasn't even any point going in, so I turned around and walked off. A few streets away I almost fell over an advertisement for a job. It was chalked on a board standing outside a bar, where normally they would list the day's specialities: 'Bouncer wanted. Apply within'. The main sign on the bar said 'McQUEEN'S' in bold squared-off gilt letters under glass, surrounded by sprouting wooden mouldings of foliage, and the premises belched a warm, yeasty smell out onto the street. I had never been into a drinking hall before and my first experience of McQueen's was not welcoming. A man was being propelled out of the swinging doors by a waiter in a grubby apron who was holding his collar in one hand and the seat of his pants in the other. As the shabbily dressed man exited, a look of surprise and indignation on his face, the waiter delivered a kick to his backside, and then stood slapping his hands theatrically. I had witnessed my first bum's rush.

Inside it was warm and smoky with the scent of old beer in the air and the noise of a bar in the early evening. A girl in pink tights danced on a stage to music provided by the 'professor' at the piano. I looked at the waiter who had thrown out the bum as he tucked his tray under his arm and straightened up for more business. He had a cauliflower ear and a broken nose.

'You looking for a bouncer?' I asked him, standing up square so he could see my broad shoulders.

'Yeah,' the waiter said, 'see him over there.'

He pointed to the bar where a man in a jazzy waistcoat was chatting to a couple of well-dressed drinkers before a wall of glittering glasses stacked in front of a mirror. I walked up and offered him my services. Now Patrick McQueen must have been the ugliest man who ever stuck his hand up a woman's dress. He was a squat guy, with a pasty white face, knobbled and pitted with scars where acne pustules had been; and carroty red hair that stood up from his head like an electric shock. He looked me up and down like a farmer at a cattle show and said, 'Can you fight?'

'I can,' I said, and paused, 'if I have to, but I prefer to get things over with before the fighting starts.' He liked that, I suppose because the speed of my answer showed him I wasn't dumb rather than because of what I had said.

'Then you're ma man,' McQueen declared, I could see the saliva in his pink mouth as he spoke, 'Only two rules: you're always here when we're open, and you don't drink.' I nodded, 'Five dollars a week and you get your food free,' he said. 'We'll give you an outfit, if you haven't got one, and you'll pay for it out of your first two months' wages. OK?' extended my hand and he put his clammy white paw into it.

I hesitated a moment, 'Any questions?' he asked.

'Why's there a vacancy,' I said, 'What happened to the last guy who did this job?'

McQueen paused, then said, 'Hospital case,' and let a well aimed gob fly into the spittoon by the end of the bar, he turned back to his friends.

The cauliflower-eared waiter, Sam, showed me the ropes, but I could see for myself what sort of a place it was. The clientele were sailors, toughs, students, prize-fighters, or well-dressed young men looking for entertainment on the seamy side of town. There were also the usual scattering of bums and derelicts who had managed to scrape together enough for a drink, and there were girls sitting at most tables, to keep the men drinking. Even with my innocence of the ways of the world, I could tell they were girls gone wrong.

Though the sign outside simply said McQueen's, I soon found it was generally called McQueen's Suicide Hall. The picturesque name came from the number of girls working there who had just had enough of sadness and had drunk carbolic acid in the back room. The girls were there to entertain, I was there to keep order in the entertainment, to duck the clubs, bottles and brass knuckles and hit back hard–but not too hard. A violent drunk ideally should be dragged out unconscious and propped up in a sitting position around the corner. The drunk should not fall down so hard he would hit his head on the tiled floor of the bar, because that might make him not a hospital case but a dead house case, and if that happened I was in trouble.

My helper in this work was a long rubber hose filled with sand, kept behind the bar for troublesome customers and for starving boys who rushed in to grab fistfuls of the crackers, cheese and cold meats that were the 'free lunch' at the opposite end of the counter from the door. It was free to those who drank there, of course. I normally missed those boys when I whacked them, getting just close enough to give them a warning and to keep me on the payroll. I knew what it was like to be hungry in Philadelphia.

I soon got to know the regulars, the clerks with their forced hilarity, who were only a few dollars a week better off than the bums that they despised; there was a lonely old German who had once taught at a college but now scraped a living teaching poor immigrants English, who used to quote Goethe when he got drunk; there was a seedy hardware salesman who came for the women, but the women told me when he got them alone he didn't do anything, not to them, anyway. And there were any number of folks from out of town come to see sin at close hand so they could moralise about it back home.

The girls used to mock me for my slow speech and countryboy

manners, but they came to like me in the end, particularly because they knew they could rely on me to deal with any man who was giving them trouble. I received something of an education in the ways of the world from them, and more than once I was able to prove the value of gallantry when I moved some masher out of his seat and through the door with a speed he previously wouldn't have thought possible.

Normally there wasn't trouble, particularly once a few of the toughs had tested me out and found I wasn't taking any. There were always ones to watch out for, though, men who didn't feel they had had a good time unless they had picked a fight and given someone a beating. Sometimes prize fighters would come in with their entourage, wanting to prove they were cock of the walk.

The meanest of the fighters around those parts was Schwartz. I knew him by reputation: he did not just like to fight, he liked to see blood. The way he could get the most blood in the shortest time was by cutting his opponent before the other man even knew he was in a fight. He would do this by smashing a pint mug glass on the marble counter of the bar, leaving him with the handle in his fist to jab in the face of his opponent who was still trying to work out his tactics.

Someone had tipped me off when Schwartz walked in and I watched him, a mountainous red-faced shape, bigger than me, even as he slouched on the bar. He knocked off a few beers with whiskey chasers and began to look around, like a bull hoofing the ground before a charge. His eyeline fixed on a man standing next to him at the bar, a regular drinker who had never been any trouble, a man a head shorter than Schwartz in a faded business suit. I was behind Schwartz but I could see he held the smaller man in his gaze, Schwartz's right hand was gripped around the handle of a glass. I couldn't move too soon, or I would be acting without justification, or too late, as the injury would have already taken place. The little man, clearly uncomfortable, was making an inquiry of him, 'Excuse me, have we met,' that sort of thing, I couldn't hear.

I held my hand behind me in a gesture Sam knew to mean he

had to slip me the cosh, and without taking my eyes off Schwartz, I gripped the thing comfortably in my right hand. Now I saw Schwartz raise his glass mug deliberately, taking it not to his face but above the marble bar-top, still fixing the smaller man in his gaze. I whipped the cosh up and brought it down like a thunderbolt with every ounce of strength I had right on the top of Schwartz' head. He spun round and for a moment terror gripped me, for I feared I hadn't hit him hard enough and the next blow would be his. But he was moving unsteadily, like he was a performing bear. I had moved round to face him and now saw him reel around very slowly, as if enticing me into a dance, with a silly expression on his face, then his knees went and he began to fall in a heap on the floor. I gripped him by the lapels as he went down, and dragged him face downwards out of the door and round the corner where I propped him up like a dummy. When I walked back into McQueen's they cheered, they literally cheered, and I smiled as I hadn't done for months. It turned out that it was Schwartz who had done for my predecessor, and everyone was waiting to see if I would go the same way. Schwartz was a quieter man after that, and he mumbled a lot. He didn't remember who had hit him, even if he remembered being hit.

I enjoyed renewed respect subsequently, and I came to accept the job I did without too much resentment, though there wasn't enough to do, and I certainly didn't tell my folks I was working as a human guard-dog in a drinking hall watching half-drunk men crying at the words of Home Sweet Home. It made me sad, too, even without the benefit of drink. I was the son and grandson of lawmen, and here I was working in the next-to-lowest dive in town. The lowest was full of syphilitics and was called the Paresis Hall. I even held my breath when I went past that place. Still, the work at McQueen's gave me food, companionship of a sort, and the experience of handling tough guys. I didn't fear anything in the city after that.

That is, I didn't fear anything outside of me. I still feared my own ignorance, my lack of understanding of the world. I felt dumb in the city, which set me to wondering what the difference was between smart people and dumb people, how you could tell, even when they were drunk, that a man had an education. When a dictionary fell into my hands like a blessing it gave me the clue to that conundrum: it was the words, the understanding of words that gave the secret knowledge of what things really were.

It was a good dictionary with bold definitions first, then etymology and grammar in tiny writing trailing off into invisibility and a mass of tiny symbols, as incomprehensible to me as a nest of bugs, about semantemes and phonemes. I had obtained the dictionary from a poor man, who used to be something, who had died in our lodgings and we had divided his paltry belongings as we did when someone died who had no relatives to claim them. It was better that way than have the landlord take them and sell them. No one wanted that fat, battered, brown book except for me. I took it to my room to muse over, finding in its stacks of type a rich melody of meanings, an echo of all knowledge.

I read story books - Hawthorne, Twain, Dickens - but it was to the dictionary that I turned for comfort, to the book which gave me the internal language to interpret the world. They were words which you could roll around in your mouth, words you could taste, words for things no one ever considered they needed words for like decephalisation–a diminution of the organs of the head; phthartalatrae–a worshipper of the corruptible; calyx – the whorl of leaves around a bud. I set myself a task of learning one a day, but often just sit and hold the pages, marvelling at the revealed world.

After a very few early assays into public use, where my words were greeted with incomprehension and even mirth, it became clear I had better keep them to myself. So that's where they stayed, in my mind, jewel bright, talismanic, a language of my own, one I would use to converse with myself

The only person I get very close to in the Suicide Hall was Molly, a respectable woman a few years older than me who reckoned the cash for McQueen. She was a rosy cheeked, ripe breasted, good, uncomplicated sort of woman with generous, smiling eyes. Her story was no great secret, I think I learned it the first day I met her: she had been the lover of a store owner who had suddenly upped and died on her but he had left her a little house. There was no money, so she would always have to work, but at least she had the security of her home. But it was hard for a woman to find her own way in the world, and being a book-keeper in a bar of dubious reputation was the best employment she could obtain once the store keeper's will was read and his wife made a judicious assumption as to why the nubile assistant had been left a house from her husband's fortune.

We fell into an easy kind of companionship, I made her laugh and she made me feel more at home. Molly knew about the words, 'Oh Frank will have a word for it,' she would say, in reference to maybe some iridescent gewgaw one of the girls was showing and I would say, 'nacreous' somewhat bashfully and she would clap her hands as if I was a performing pet.

I kept in contact with the police bureau, just telling them my lodgings and letting them know I was still keen to be on the force. I slowly came to realise that if you had no pull it was harder than hell to get into the police force, and pull in Philadelphia meant influence with the Republican party, and that I just didn't have.

McQueen, for all his ugliness and unpleasantness, was good to me, he started talking to me occasionally after I had downed Schwartz. He soon found out my ambition to become a cop and he said, 'Why didn't ya tell me? I'm ya friend, what help did you have when you went to the Superintendent?'

'Help?' I said.

'Yeah, who was batting for ya, who was on your side?', he stood with his legs apart, his thumbs in the side pockets of his jazzy waistcoat, the chewed end of a cigar in his mouth.

'Oh,' I said, 'I had a letter of recommendation from the sheriff in Pittsfield.'

McQueen looked horrified, as if he had unaccountably been struck a blow with one of his own pickled gerkins, 'Look,' he said in either mock or real exasperation, I could not tell which, 'a letter from a sheriff in a hick town out of this state doesn't mean a cent in this city, not a damn cent.'

'I gathered that,' I said.

He nodded and raised his hand, revealing the sweat stains on his shirt under his armpit, and put his pudgy arm around my shoulder, as if in forgiveness for my ignorance. 'I'll see what I can do,' he said.

'What do you mean?'

'I'll talk to a friend,' he said, and he turned back towards the bar. McQueen was smart. *Why lose a good man from your own bar?* a buddy might have asked him. McQueen reckoned that if the man's that good, he won't stay long as a bouncer. But if McQueen helped me to become a policeman, he would have a friend in a position to help him when he needed it.

Later I found out the Director of Public Safety had been a candy manufacturer. Quite how this suited him to oversee police work no one really knew, but his generosity to the Republican cause was well known. He was in charge of the police, and of the fire service; and also oversaw the inspection of buildings; inspection of boilers; and inspection of electrical services, so his time for concentrated effort on police work was limited, which was just as well, because nobody had any confidence in his ability to do it. Anyway, McQueen was a frequent if not large contributor to the party and he went to the right meetings where he saw the right people. It was said that if you shouted *'Your saloon's on fire!'* in a political meeting in Philadelphia, the whole room would turn out, the liquor trade had that much influence.

So Patrick McQueen put in a word for me, which I believe consisted of him writing my name on a piece of paper and giving just that word to The Candyman at some fundraiser. The Director of Public Safety passed the word to the Superintendent of Police and I was summoned back into City Hall, where I took a written examination, which was easy, and was told to report to the police college the following Monday. That was it, I had found out how things are done in Philadelphia.

So I went out to patrol the streets, to the rats and the roach infestations, the abortions wrapped in rags and thrust into a trash can, the offal that dogs fought over outside the slaughter houses, the piles of steaming horse shit lying where it had dropped to be trampled by hooves and wheels and swept by the hems of dresses.

Sometimes in the years that followed I would wonder wryly why I had ever exchanged my nice warm drinking hall for the life of a serving police officer, out in howling gales and rain-sodden nights. We would be nine hours on patrol and then seven hours a day on reserve in the bedbug-ridden station house. There was one day off in fifteen. The station house had beds eighteen inches apart, where forty men slept within earshot of the drunks in the cells. Wet clothes were hung on hooks on the wall and the heat in the place made a permanent moist fug of the atmosphere in winter. There was no talk of religion or politics by order, or we'd be fighting like monkeys in a barrel.

On top of all this you virtually felt in the early years that you were paying the police bureau for the privilege of working there, what with $5 a month to pay back for uniforms and equipment, a dollar for the dormitory and the endless round of charity drives to which you had to contribute to show you were a good guy.

The advantage was the comradeship of the other officers. Some of the guys I worked with were there since before the civil service examination and could not read or write but they sure were handy to have beside you if there was trouble. They remembered the great anti-negro and anti-immigrant riots of the forties, before there were even uniforms, and they had all fought in the Draft Riots between the Irish and the negroes. At least things had calmed down some when I was a beat cop. The worst riots we faced were at strikes, and some trouble at the Italian parades, that sort of event, but pitched battles were a thing of the past.

It was the heroic age of dispensing the law with a night stick, seldom bothering to make arrests. If you were called to deal with a Saturday night wife beater you dealt with him. If you had to make an arrest, and you got someone back to the station unbeaten, the roundsman would be outraged, 'What do you mean, bringing in a prisoner in that condition, take him downstairs.' And I would have to take the prisoner downstairs and knock him about with as much enthusiasm as I could muster. It was made very clear to me that we were responsible for law and order, and that meant summary punishment. As the roundsman told me, with extended finger and stern countenance, 'The witnesses can refuse to testify, your prisoner can have political friends who pull strings to have the case dropped, they might jump bail, your case might fall in court. But a man who's done wrong and been beaten for it, he knows he's been whupped. He'll think twice about stepping out of line again. You have maintained law and order.' I didn't like it, but I got on with doing what I was told.

I kept away from the postings where I knew there was a lot of graft–which wasn't difficult, because they were so sought after there was a waiting list for transfer to them. That's serious graft, shaking down gambling houses and brothels, but there wasn't any section of the force where there was no graft at all. But what I did, and the other beat cops, was honest graft without greed. Bars and diners would stand you a meal, and with no break in a nine hour shift you had to take it, and of course you were more favourable to the place after that. It happened, it wasn't good or bad, it just happened.

Something I found out early was that in many ways the bad men were easier to deal with than the respectable folk who would trouble the police station with impossible requests. They wanted sabbath observance and the liquor laws to be policed; and for gambling joints to be closed and streetwalkers to be chased somewhere else, though they never said where. When I worked on the desk, after a few years on patrol, it was from the respectable folk that I learned more dishonesty than I would have believed possible. Shamefaced men who would come with tales of being 'trimmed' by Spanish girls. Now, I knew they were negro prostitutes, the men knew they were negro prostitutes, and the girls sure as hell knew they were negro prostitutes; but in the description of the girls that went in the book for each of these respectable married men, 'Spanish dancer' was what they were. Give me a crook who's done wrong and admits it any day.

I often used to go back to the Suicide Hall, because it was the nearest thing I had to a home in Philadelphia and because Molly was always glad to see me. We became lovers in a congenial and unchallenging way: we both needed the comfort and enjoyed a genuine affection. When we parted it was never with an understanding that we would meet again, though we always did, as I walked into the Suicide Hall to be met with her radiant smile.

She was good, too... after exertion sometimes, with her hand on my chest as the sunlight streamed through the window, I felt a kind of peace.

'Why are you so sad?' she would ask. I had thought it was not so obvious, as I feigned a shallow cheeriness with others, a cocoon of badinage and smiles, but Molly saw through it.

'I'm not sad, just thoughtful' I would say. Soon she need not even ask, but would look at me in an admonitory way with her head to one side and I would acknowledge her with a smile, knowing what she was thinking, half resentful that she had penetrated my secret parts this far, and resolved to be more protective of myself in future.

I worked on secondment to the detective bureau after a while, and pleased the bosses with tracking down a man who married old maids and ran off with their money. With less zeal but equal efficiency, I had located a father who had tracked down and killed the man who sent his daughter into prostitution. I got a taste for detective work, and eventually schemed and toiled my way into room 529, the detective bureau, in the great new City Hall.

Philadelphia changed in my early years there. Mainly the change was to do with the numbers: there were more than a million people in the city, so many people it injured the brain to think about it, double the number of people who were in the city when I was born, and hundreds of thousands of them since I arrived, teeming in to fill the shanties, shacks, airless cellars, backyard houses and alley tenements. Still they were coming, humanity scurrying into every hole and corner in the city. The other great change I saw was widespread electrification with such modern dangers: stock clerks slipped down elevator shafts, old men fell into manholes, everyone tangled with live electric cables. When they electrified the streetcars, that was the real menace. It wasn't just the speed they got up to – going round the city at ten miles an hour – but they had no instinct to avoid people like the horses did who used to pull the streetcars. Well, that was progress.

As for me, I had moved from unemployed youth to bar-room bouncer to cop to detective. I hadn't forgotten my pain, I just let it rest undisturbed. I had nothing to add to or to detract from the sum of my unhappiness, it was there within me like a cyst. In the beginning I thought of Georgiana all the time, then less, maybe several times a day, more often at night. Sometimes, even with Molly, I would catch myself wondering what Georgiana was doing at that time, was she too dressing in a city bedroom that bright morning, her breasts dropping forward as she bent to pull on hose?

'Why are you so sad?'

'Guess it's just the way I'm made,' I would say, thinking internally: 'it is the way I have *been* made. It is what has been made of me.' In the beginning I used to dream of finding Georgiana in the gutter where she had ended up once Henry Holmes had abandoned her. I would help her, feed her, she would be pathetically grateful, looking at me imploringly with her huge blue eyes, and she would realise what a terrible mistake she had made, and I would pity her, and she would beg my forgiveness. Later I just thought it would be good to see her again, to talk to her, tell her how I'd been, ask about the turns her life had taken, just talk.

The first time I returned to Gilmanton, at Christmas to see my folks, I was sick with dread that I would see her, yet I knew because ma had written to me, that Reverend Yoke had retired and moved away. I heard nothing of her then, and of Henry only that he was studying to be a doctor at some college in Vermont. Still, I saw her around every corner, in every place we used to be; and walking through that snow-muffled landscape, my wounds were as searing fresh as when they were first cut.

Chapter 5

Philadelphia 1894

There was no inquest. B.F.Pitezel, Ben to his friends, was laid to rest in Potter's Field burial ground with minimum ceremony. I got on with my life, tried to pretend nothing had happened, until one day a week later the chief called me in.

'Is this a branch office of the Chicago police?' chief O'Brien said in that way of his which would have been called sarcasm in a wittier man, but it was just his way of talking. He had the gift of being able to strain my patience in a number of ways on any given day.

'What do you mean?' I asked.

'Your friend Edward Cass, in-sur-ance investigator' he said the words slowly as if they left a nasty taste in his mouth and he was trying to figure out what it was, 'his company has cabled that they want you to look again at that Callowhill Street death.' The chief waited for a response, stroking his hand from the front to the back of his hair. I just nodded.

'He wants you to meet him in St Louis and go interview an informant there. There's more evidence on a suspect called Henry Holmes.' My flesh gave a jolt at the mention of his name.

'Just as well I enjoy travel,' I said, suddenly very pleased the case hadn't died, 'when is this going to happen?'

'I haven't said it is, yet,' said O'Brien.

'It was our case, chief, and we all knew it was suspicious but we didn't have the evidence,' I said, almost pleading. I knew the old man could be stubborn and once he had set his mind against something, nothing could change his course.

'Weeell,' he said, rubbing his chin, how often can we go out of state to get a collar? We've got our hands full here.'

I decided on the perilous course of a full-frontal attack. 'Can't we just once do some detective work that doesn't involve greasing some bad guy's palm or shaking down deadbeats to get them to talk?' I said in exasperation.

O'Brien coloured, 'That's the job, Geyer, you knew that when you signed up for it,' he shouted at me.

'Well the world is changing,' I said quietly and insistently, 'the crooks are getting smarter, and they don't keep within city boundaries for our convenience. They've got business suits and accounts books now.'

O'Brien looked at the floor away from me, trying to compose a formula that would save his face. He didn't have many ideas, he found he could get along well enough without them. But he knew an idea when he saw it, and he knew when an idea offered the promise of expansion. My way of thinking meant more money from the city coffers, more men, more equipment, more glory for the man at the head of the bureau. It wouldn't be right away, but it would happen with or without him so it had better happen with him. He let the wheels of this thought clunk through the slow machinery of his mind and allowed himself to come round to my way of thinking. 'Oh, hell,' he said, 'go. You got a week, no more. Get out of my sight.'

'Thanks Chief,' I said, turning quickly to get out before he changed his mind.

'Wait,' he said, as I was almost out of the door. 'Look, Geyer, don't run up any big expenses on this. I've got six detectives for the whole city, I don't need to be lending them to Chicago and St Louis unless there's a return here. Got me?'

That night I was boarding the express train on the St Louis, Alton and Terre Haute Railroad, 'The shortest and quickest route between the Atlantic and the Mississippi' it said on the posters where a smart traveller stood poised to board a huge, shiny new locomotive.

I looked out from the warm railway car over the countryside as we ploughed on through the night. Clear moonlight from a perfect silver disc over the cornfields shone on the glistening train that I could see curving behind me as we took a bend; out over the great plains where in my boyhood the outlaws, fur trappers, buffalo hunters and cowboys ranged the land. I felt lulled, comforted by the relentless motion of a train running on rails that went all the way to Los Angeles, a solid band of iron across the nation.

The following evening we pulled in to Alton where Cass met me at the station, greeting me more like a long lost brother than a colleague, with smiles and a hand on my shoulder. I liked Cass for his enthusiasm, but resented the way he was constantly having to be reigned in, like a colt, he was always running off on flights of fancy, and looking back to me to me for approbation.

'So why'd you call me, what was wrong with the Louisville detectives?' I said as we walked to get a cab over to St Louis side, across the river.

'Since you knew Mr Holmes and all,' Cass said, 'I thought you might be interested in trying to find him. Plus it's your case, your murder.'

'Not,' I said, 'my suspicious death?'

'I don't think so,' he winked conspiratorially, 'Trust me on it.'

He led me to an expensive diner, brightly lit with electric light, with curtains on the windows and rugs on the floor. There Fidelity Mutual stood me a fine meal of crab and catfish from the Mississippi, with rich sauces, and a choice of imported wines, but I stuck with beer.

'Your friend Holmes,' he said, 'was on the run when we met him. Had been for six months.'

I breathed a long sigh. 'That's great,' I said miserably, 'so if we'd known we could have picked him up then. Where was he running from?'

'St Louis. He had bought a drug store and mortgaged the stock and then arranged for someone to steal if from him so he could claim the insurance on it.'

'So he gets to keep the stock,' I said, 'to re-sell or re-use, and the insurance money. Very clever.'

'Yeah, and the only reason Holmes got caught, the on-ly reason,' said Cass, 'was bad driving.' He smiled his mischievous smile. 'A four horse wagon was being driven down a street in St Louis late at night, and it was being driven so badly, a cop stopped it and questioned the driver who had been drinking as the cop guessed. Holmes was sitting next to the driver, and in the back of the wagon was the stock from the drug store.' I listened with rapt attention. 'Now by a stroke of very good luck – or bad luck for Holmes – the policeman who stopped the wagon was the same one who had been called to investigate the burglary at the store.' He savoured the moment of fortuitous coincidence like a choice delicacy, revelling in the delight of placing these details before an appreciative connoisseur, 'and who do you think was the drunk driving the four horse wagon?'

'He was B.F.Perry, inventor and dealer in patents, alias Ben Pitezel,' I replied unhesitatingly. I was enjoying Cass' company more than I thought I would.

'Right on the nose,' Cass cried merrily, so loudly that some other diners looked at us, and we lowered our tones. 'I called in at police headquarters to make sure I could identify Holmes,' he said, 'cuz he had a false name, H.H.Howard to be exact,' I nodded wearily, 'and I had to make sure he was our man. Here he is.' He passed a medium sized photograph to me. Unmistakably it was a mug shot of Henry, with his head slightly to one side, looking a little indignant, as if this was all a terrible misunderstanding which the authorities would soon come to realise, and deliver him a fulsome apology.

'But Holmes slipped out of their hands?' I said.

Cass nodded, 'His wife stood bail for him,' I gulped. Georgiana? As soon as this case became enjoyable it started to hurt again. 'And he vanished, of course. Pitezel went the same way.'

'OK,' I said, 'I've checked Holmes' record with all the states in the East and Mid-West.'

'And?' Cass said

'Nothing, at least, not under the names I know for him. In Chicago where he had a drug store he was investigated by the police when they found oil-soaked rags in a warehouse he owned. It was suspected he was going to burn it down and, you know,' we said in cheery unison, 'claim on the insurance.'

'But,' I continued, 'police in Chicago say he vamoosed out of there months ago, I guess St Louis was his next port of call. There's a lot on Benjamin Pitezel – larceny, mainly, and drunkenness, going back many years.'

'Just the sort of friend a businessman like Holmes needs,' said Cass brightly.

'OK,' I said, 'So the twelve days Holmes spent in St Louis jail were the sum total of his experience of the criminal justice system.' We mulled over this for a while and ordered some desserts. 'So who's our informant?' I said over the cherry pie.

'Marion Hedgepeth,' said Cass between mouthfuls, 'currently residing in the Missouri County Jail. Known in Wyoming, Colorado and Montana as a cattle rustler, horse thief, gambler, and latterly a bank robber.'

'So he keeps himself busy,' I said,

Cass continued speedily, 'He had the reputation of being the fastest man on the draw in the south west, once killed a man who had him covered, shooting from the hip,' Cass playfully made a gun with his hand.

'He's been reading too many dime novels,' I said, 'get on with it.'

Cass drew out a police record sheet, a carbon copy on flimsy paper, and quickly intoned the major points like verse: 'In 1890 he held up the Missouri Pacific at Omaha and robbed the Pacific Express safe of $1000; then he held up the Chicago, Milwaukee and St Paul Express using dynamite and got away with $5000; then he held up the St Louis and San Francisco Express at Glendale, killed one of the guards, cracked open the safe with dynamite, and got away with $50,000.' He looked up.

'Well, I always like to say something nice about new people I meet,' I said, getting out a cigar, 'so let me say it sounds like he is good at his job. How did he end up in the county jail?'

'He was on the run,' said Cass, putting the flimsy paper aside, 'and was being tracked by Pinkerton detectives on behalf of the railroad companies. They suspected his lawyer was keeping in contact with him, and so followed the lawyer into a billiard hall and picked his pocket after he had hung his coat up. Unethical behaviour, eh?' Cass closed one eye as if trying to get an exact reading on my face.

'Nothing much by way of ethical behaviour is expected of detectives,' I laughed.

'There was a note in that pocket,' continued Cass, 'it was from his client, Marion Hedgepeth. It gave Hedgepeth's address in hiding, so the detectives took the address down and went off to arrest him.' Cass paused, then addressed me directly, as if this was the final question in a life or death examination, 'And who was that lawyer?' he asked.

'Not Jeptha D.Howe, attorney at law?' I said.

'Almost,' he said, 'Caleb Howe. Based in St Louis, not Chicago, and a cousin or maybe a brother of the man who claimed the money on Ben Pitezel.' Hedgepeth, he explained, now wanted to inform on Holmes, tell us what Holmes confided to him in the jailhouse. We walked through the soft night back to the hotel Fidelity Mutual had booked for us, with its ornate gilt entrance hall and red velvet curtains. We didn't say much, comfortably digesting the meal. I kept my reserve: Cass may have been callow and inexperienced but he was smart enough to guess that I had a guilty secret, and I had more at stake than a simple arrest in my quest for Holmes.

That night I sat in my room chewing on the end of a cigar and looking out of the window on the twin smokestacks and rococo galleries of the steamers berthed on the cumbrous, dark Mississippi. So the law had caught Henry Holmes twice, and failed both times to hang on to him. Once it was in the shape of the St Louis police; and once in the restless hands of Frank P Geyer. At least the cops in St Louis put him away. I had had my man, and I had lost him. Not for the first time in this case, or the last, regret and anger corroded my soul.

The next morning Cass and I went out to the poorly paved streets of St Louis, picked up a cab and lurched along to Missouri County Jail. Crossing the forecourt in front of the squat stone building a respectably dressed woman approached us. She was small, with the fresh plumpness of youth, black hair curling out of a bonnet which was worn back on her head so it gave a good view of her face to anyone who cared to look.

'Are you gentlemen going in to see Marion Hedgepeth?' she asked, in a slightly girlish voice.

I stopped short with a jolt, shocked that our mission should be public knowledge before we had even laid eyes on the man. 'Why do you need to know that?' I said.

'If you are,' she said, 'please give him this,' and she attempted to push a lilac envelope into my unwilling hand.

I held the hand flat, 'Just post that through the regular mail, lady,' I said, 'The man you are talking about hasn't been found guilty, he's just being held here awaiting trial so he can get letters, clothes, food, anything you care to deliver to the prison authorities.' A flowery scent rose from the letter still being held before me.

'Oh, I know that,' she said, trying to meld her impatience with the imploring tone she needed to adopt, 'But you see, some of the things I've got to say are of a personal nature' she let her eyes glance down as if she was bashful, 'and I don't want those guards seeing them.'

'I'm sorry, lady,' I said, walking on, 'I can't give anything to a prisoner, it has to go through the regular authorities.'

'So how did she know we were seeing Hedgepeth?' Cass asked as we walked up to the studded wooden doors in the stone wall of the prison.

'She approaches everyone going in,' I said dryly, 'and one of them is either going in to see him or will take her love letter in anyway and drop it in his cell.'

'You know what I wonder?' Cass mused, taking a last look at the free sky before we entered the prison, 'Is why it is that these guys get all the girls. I mean, what is it about bad guys that makes them so irresistible to women?'

'Shut up,' I said, without malice.

After a few words a guard led us through and we were assailed with the stench of formaldehyde used as a disinfectant, and rodent powder that seemed to be spread everywhere, rising dust clouds as we walked.

We did the formalities in an office and were led through to the central hall, a huge, barred cage of several stories, all of them balconied, that were covered at the side and above with bars. The whole of the roof was glass, making the enclosed space into a great light well. Prisoners in grey canvas clothes scurried around the walkways on their duties carrying trays, buckets, mops, bedlinen. Trolleys were being wheeled round some of the balconies, all to the sound of a ringing and clanking of the interconnecting barred gates being opened and slammed shut. It was the very image of a modern prison. 'Panopticon,' I breathed, and ignored Cass's questioning glance.

On the first floor, down one of the corridors which radiated from the central aisle, we found cells containing those awaiting trial. They were pretty good cells, as cells go, with a lot of comforts the prisoners had been able to bring from home, just floor to ceiling bars across the whole of one wall to remind the prisoners of where they were.

Hedgepeth rose and welcomed us into his cell like a madam in a brothel receiving new trade. He was what gushing women writers would describe as 'dashing,': a tall man with black hair, a thick moustache, high cheekbones that suggested maybe some Indian blood somewhere along the ancestral line, flashing black eyes and a wide, sensual mouth.

'Won't you sit down gentlemen,' the bank robber said, 'I'm sorry it's so cramped.'

I looked around: there was the bed, a small cupboard and a few books, and they had given him two extra chairs for us. What was remarkable about the room, though, was the blaze of colour in that grey place provided by baskets and bouquets, and the sweet scent of many flowers. In my line of vision all the time I was talking to Hedgepeth was a note tied with a blue ribbon to a bouquet in a vase, it read, 'To Marion, I see you in my dreams, Edith' with several crosses.

I opened my black-backed leatherette notebook and took a freshly sharpened pencil from my pocket, 'Tell us what you can about Henry Holmes,' I said.

Hedgepeth's eyes opened wide in his eagerness to be helpful, 'I knew him as H.M.Howard,' he said, 'but I'll call him Holmes if you like.'

'Well I was here in this, er,' he waved his hand to indicate his surroundings, 'temporary accommodation, and Holmes asked if he could see me. We have this time here, in this remand wing, of free association, so we can talk to each other, you see. Holmes came in to see me, sat right there where you're sitting. He was a little man, very friendly. He said he wanted to shake my hand, had heard all about my career, said how famous I was and all. He introduced himself as a druggist and speculator. Well, I was right pleased to see him, he was an educated man and you don't get many educated types in here, so I was glad of his company.

'He told me he had a peach of a scheme that would make him $10,000, and he needed some lawyer who could be trusted and said if I could help him, I would get $500 for it. I told him J.D.Howe could be trusted, and how to reach him. So he told me the scheme, and here it is: that his friend Ben's life was insured for $10,000 and they were going to work the insurance company for it. He said how he was an expert at it, had done it before. Being a druggist he could deceive the insurance company by having Ben hire a place and fix it up to look like there had been an explosion. Ben lies low, see, after they have put a corpse in his place to have it identified as him. It was real smart, a real slick operation. I was impressed.'

Hedgepeth smiled warmly with professional admiration at the remembered pleasure of a truly well-crafted criminal plan. I nodded indulgently and motioned for him to continue.

'I didn't think much of what he told me,' Hedgepeth said, 'until after he went out on a bail bond, and J.D.Howe got word to me via his brother, to thank me for putting the work his way. He said he had had the whole plot laid out to him and that he had never heard of a finer or smoother piece of work, that it was sure to go right, and that Howard, or Holmes or whatever, was one of the smoothest men Howe had ever met, and he's met plenty, I can tell you.'

'OK,' I said, 'so why do you now want to tell us all about this smooth operator who made such a big impression on you.'

'Well,' Hedgepeth stretched himself out with his head behind his hands, 'there has to be honour, you know? I mean you have to be able to trust people.' Sitting there in a room full of flowers, with his glossy black hair and his easy manner, it was easy to see him as just a regular guy talking about honesty. 'Holmes had promised me some money when the deal went through. Now I know from Jeptha Howe that the deal did go through, the body was found and identified and the insurance company paid out. I also think this man Ben was killed, and not substituted for a cadaver after all. Now that is wrong, and I didn't see any of that money and that is wrong too.'

'Mr Hedgepeth,' I said, 'Why should we believe you? Let's not mince words, you're a crook.'

'But I'm an honest crook,' he said drawing himself up in a flush of affronted dignity, 'He ain't'.

I let that go. 'OK,' I said, 'will you be prepared to swear to this story in court?'

He looked pensive, in a studied way as if he had practised it in his cell as a response for just this question which he had anticipated would be coming his way. 'Everyone gets something for what they do,' he said, 'and I want you to put in a word for me with the St Louis authorities, just say I helped you to put away a really bad man.'

'You're frightened you'll hang for the murder of the security guard,' I said.

'So I'm asking for a deal,' he said.

'Look,' I said, 'I'll level with you. You got two problems here. One is that we don't have a lot of pull with the St Louis justice department. We have some, particularly because they want Holmes back too to stand trial in St Louis. Also they're not indifferent to us picking up a felon for murder, so we got some goodwill there. I promise I'll put in a good word for you. However, there is another problem that's a bigger one: you killed a man and they don't like that around here. Pleas for clemency tend to fall on deaf ears when there's a death involved.'

Hedgepeth looked exasperated, 'You mean that guard that got in the way? He was a fool he was trying to be a hero for someone else's money.'

'And for that he deserved to die?' I asked.

'Look, I'm not saying I dropped him,' Hedgepeth said, with the air of a man finalising a business proposition, 'or that anyone I know did, but it's just common sense to say if you see a robbery going on you stand aside and let the men do their work, it's only reasonable.'

'I'm not the judge here,' I said, 'and they might not see it like that. But OK, I'll put in a word for you.'

Realising this was the best he was going to get, Hedgepeth agreed to give us a statement, so we spent the best part of the day with him in that cell with the buckets of flowers, and he waved us goodbye cheerily as we left, just as if we had been paying a Sunday afternoon visit to our folks.

'I don't understand,' said Cass, as we made our way through the ringing metal of slammed doors. He had been silent through much of the interview, just taking notes and asking Hedgepeth to pause so he could get it all down.

'What?' I said, 'about Hedgepeth?'

'Yeah,' he said, 'why did Holmes tell him anything. It was a risk, right? Why take it?'

'Yeah,' I said, 'they don't have much to talk about in these places except crime, so they do a lot of talking about that. My experience tells me they swap information about such matters as where to find a crooked lawyer all the time. They don't need inducements, like some $500.'

'And Holmes offered the money,' said Cass with an offertory gesture, 'he didn't need to do that.'

'On one level no,' I said slowly, for I was only realising the truth of it myself, 'but maybe he has deeper needs, he's a confidence trickster of the purest kind. He likes to gain someone's confidence, the more confidence the better, and betray them. Marion Hedgepeth was a class act, a famous criminal. Holmes just felt like taking his confidence and abusing it. I think that's it, I think he just enjoyed it.'

We called in at the office to sign out and look at the records. The turnkey had a shelf of big new books with marbled endpapers and shiny leather corners. All the admissions, releases, visits, court dates and successful bail applications were written down on the thick lined paper in measured strokes. The turnkey was a man who liked to keep a neat ledger. We found the date of Holmes' release with the address to which he had been bailed. The local police had checked it when he skipped bail, it was a hired house, and he had of course left it the day of his release. So who stood bail? I looked along the clean white paper, as stiff as a starched sheet, to see Mrs G.Howard, a woman using Holmes' assumed name. G. Georgiana? Maybe.

I asked the turnkey, my pencil poised on my notebook though I didn't take any notes, it was just for show, 'Did you take the bail details?'

'Yessir'

'This Mrs Howard,' the words stuck in my throat, 'What was she like?'

The turnkey, a barrel-chested short man in shirtsleeves with protectors at his wrists, thought briefly and said, 'Respectable woman, tall, fair hair, handsome figure, very agreeable, not one to be mixed up in crime. I bet she made a good impression on the judge, that's why she was allowed to stand bail.'

'May I,' I said, 'see the signature?'

There it was, Mrs G.Howard and the fake address, in a perfect copperplate straight from the copy books of our old school in Gilmanton. Yes, that was Georgiana. My heart beat like a cart going over a cattle grating. She had been here and she had signed this. It was physical evidence of her presence, a manifestation.

'I'm done here.' I said to Cass.

We trudged on in silence through the administration corridors of the new jail, our senses assailed by the smell of formaldehyde and the rodent powder that rose in tiny dusty eddies around our feet as we walked. In that long corridor with light flooding past the bars, shining through the swirling dust, the significance of the rodenticide came home to me. It was being used to destroy vermin, but if they thought they needed that much, it meant the first dose hadn't been effective, and they had thrown some more down. Again the vermin had increased, and again the authorities stepped up the dose, but they hadn't understood what was happening, what it really meant: the rats had grown resistant, and then had even developed a taste for the poison. They were thriving on it.

Chicago 1893

Nannie Williams, a tall, russet-haired girl, was tied to an upright contraption with a ball-gag in her mouth, her dress torn and her eyes wild with fear. She listened with uncomprehending terror to the voices from the front office room.

Holmes was there behind the desk, talking with Minnie Williams who responded in a lively Texan accent. The lobby was run-down and the hotel clearly not in full operation, but both were laughing and high-spirited.

Holmes took both her hands in his, 'I'll have this place back up and running in no time and it will be like the old days. And you will be queen of the establishment, behind this desk.'

'And we can do more?' said Minnie, 'I love you so much Henry.'

'In Texas, we will do more, much more. All you need to do is to sign. He presented her with title deeds with a Texas state seal. Minnie took the pen and saw that above the space he indicated, Nannie Williams had already signed.

'Why, that's my sister's signature,' she said, 'how did that get there? I thought we were going to go to Texas to get her to sign.'

Holmes laughed cheerily, 'That's the surprise I was telling you about, Minnie is already here, she's in that room.'

The room next door was a room-sized safe. In there, listening to them laugh, Minnie Williams was weeping with pain and frustration as she struggled to be free of her bonds.

Holmes was explaining, 'She was so excited about the development of your real estate in Fort Worth that she signed right off.'

'I gotta go and see her,' said Minnie.

'Business first, then we'll celebrate,' said Holmes. Minnie hesitated, but signed.

Nannie? Holmes called into the next room, 'Oh she's shy, go in and get her.'

Nannie was making the only gesture she could, vigorously shaking her head.

Minnie walked towards the door and into the dark.

'Nannie?'

'Let's put the light on so you can see her better.' said Holmes, Minnie suddenly suspected something in his tone or his phrasing and went to turn around, but then saw Nannie strung up and ran towards her with a shriek.

Behind her Holmes closed the door of the safe. Minnie wildly slammed at the door then rushed back to attempt to untie her sister and embrace her.

Outside, Holmes, with a certain fastidiousness, turned a gas key on the side of the safe.

Minnie heard the sound of the escaping gas and turned round to see a pipe near the floor. She left Nannie still tied, and ran to try to close it off, showing some relief when she put a finger in the pipe to stop the gas entering.

Outside, Holmes turned a second gas tap on, and hummed a little song to himself.

Minnie, sealing the lower pipe with her finger, heard the escaping gas from the upper pipe, beyond her reach. She and the still trussed Minnie stared at each other in hopeless terror.

Chapter 6

Philadelphia 1894

I sat in a bar opposite the smooth, shiny face of Edward Cass, watching the daylight fade outside. The dying sun penetrated through the smoke and lit the golden beer in our glasses.

'What we've got on Holmes is good enough for a warrant,' I said, slowly as if I was explaining it to him, though he knew that part well enough, 'but not for murder. I'll get a warrant for insurance fraud, that much we can prove, or at least I think so.' I was piling up the morsels we had. They didn't amount to much, and my precious few days were slipping away.

'How do we do that?' he asked intently. There was a certain earnestness about Cass that must have endeared him to school teachers and ministers of religion.

'We've got the evidence to have an autopsy,' I said, so let's exhume old Benjamin F.Pitezel, dealer in patents.'

'An exhumation?' he said, it may have been the first time he had ever used the word and he was relishing it. I composed a cable to the chief, putting the best face on the story, asking him to request an autopsy, that I was pursuing Holmes, and to issue a holding warrant.

Cass had already checked out the address Fidelity Mutual had used to contact Holmes, it was a post office box, so a dead end, he wouldn't be going back there to collect his mail. 'We'll get Jeptha Howe for the insurance fraud in the end,' I said, 'He isn't going to give up his practice as a shyster lawyer, we know where he is. But Holmes went to him, he always did, so Howe doesn't know where Holmes is, I'm pretty sure of that.'

'He'd say he had to protect his client anyway,' said Cass. 'Professional ethics and all. And Mrs Pitezel? What d'you think?'

'Yeah,' I replied, 'we can pull them in, but at the risk of alerting Holmes that we are on his tail. You locate them, let's know what Mrs Pitezel is doing, but don't contact her, we'll bring her in when the two of us meet up, and see her together.'

I said quickly that it made sense for Cass to deal with Chicago where I'd meet him later, as he was going back there anyway, and I'd check out Holmes' background to see if I could track him. I didn't give any clear reason for what I was going to do because I didn't have one that could be rationally expressed. I was possessed with the need to get out there on my own to know what this crazy man had been doing after he ran off, though had I known, had I really known of Holmes' activities since I last saw him in Gilmanton, I would have looked up at the vesperine sky over Missouri and howled like a wolf.

Of course, recent leads were more likely to get to Holmes than an expedition into history. But I didn't only want Holmes, I wanted, with a longing that permeated my whole body, to gaze once again on Georgiana Yoke and ask her in the name of God why? I wanted to know what had been done to me, to redeem the past, to recover what I had lost, perhaps just once to understand.

Cass went on to Chicago the following morning. I felt queasy about sending that trusting young man off while I pursued my own course of action but, hell, as my daddy used to say, why be a lawman if you can't kick over the traces once in a while?

A cable had confirmed Holmes graduated from Ann Arbor Medical School in 1884 so that's where I went, changing trains at Chicago. This was going to be my life from now on, the platforms crowded with porters' trolleys and families waiting for reunions, young lovers maybe holding hands in a gesture of humanity against the iron and cement of the world where locomotive beasts roared and whistled and the air was ever full of their smoke and dust and the smell of burning grease.

I arrived late so I bedded down for the night and walked on to the campus next morning with the sunlight piercing through full-leafed trees onto the fresh new buildings. There were big columns and stone stairways where students, men and women, were hurrying to their classes, carrying their books and talking, even boys and girls in groups together. Whether it was the fatigue, or the bright newness after a long journey, or the surreptitiously personal nature of my mission, I can't say, but looking at those students in their starched collars or plain, businesslike dresses, jostling under the twin towers of the library, I was filled with the sadness of regret. Atrabilious, lachrymatory melancholy. This had never been offered to me, the easy friendliness of it, laughing and joking with nothing to think of but their next set of class notes. These students would never know how tough life could be, the pain, the grinding hardness, the unrelenting dangers which had made my life a mirror of the unforgiving city where I lived. And Henry Holmes had taken my youth and hope to join them.

Still, like I had a thousand times before, I swallowed my sorrows and got on with the job, striding up the vast steps of the medical school administration building. I asked for the dean, Professor Charles Beylard Nancrede, and found him in an oak-panelled office that smelled slightly of antiseptic soap and old cigars. He looked more like an old sawbones than a surgeon, with black mutton chop whiskers and big, red, hairy hands, one of which he extended and gave me a firm grip.

He gazed at me as if he was analysing an interesting medical condition while I told him I was looking for a former student, I wonder if the professor remembered him, well... yes he did. I spun out the story about police being interested in him, not willing to say why, I was sure the professor understood.

He sighed, glanced across to the window briefly, as if longing to get out to the cool green quadrangle, and said, 'Things are somewhat better today Mr Geyer, but you have to know student behaviour was a national disgrace ten or more years ago. Not just here, please don't think I'm denigrating my own establishment, but everywhere. I remember one night when the circus came to town and a few hundred students tried to rush the gate, they were fighting for hours with the roustabouts and canvasmen. Policemen were called out, firemen were called out... the president himself had to go down to restore order.' He looked exasperated, tired out with the constant effort of holding back the tide of rowdyism. 'Yet the petty mischief of some reckless students – hazing, fighting, vandalism – will be paraded through the newspapers with more noise than the results of twelve months' manly and undemonstrative study,' I smiled reassuringly, as if I understood his problems and he had all my sympathy. 'In that context, Mr Geyer, Henry Holmes was not a bad student,' he shook his head, 'He was not a rowdy, he was not a drinker, he did his work and he sat his exams. He got good pass marks.'

'This sentence is leading to a "but.."' I said, after a silence had lasted a couple of seconds.

Nancrede nodded, 'Yes, but he was a bit of a scamp.'

'In what way, professor?'

He paused again as if wondering whether to tell me, 'Well, there was a breach of promise episode with some widow, a hairdresser, who came to Ann Arbor from St Louis.'

'Breach of promise? He had promised to marry this woman?' I said.

'And had received some favours in return, as I understand it,' said Nancrede with mild amusement, looking at his fingernails.

'Wasn't he already married?' I asked.

Nancrede snorted and shook his head, 'Not to my knowledge, but it wouldn't amaze me.'

'Is there anything else I should know about Henry Holmes's time here?' I said

'I don't think so, is he still in practice?'

'He isn't', I said, 'so far as I know. He told me he'd quit medicine in sorrow at his inability to cure a young diabetic girl.'

Nancrede raised his eyebrows as if eager to hear more, so I told him, briefly, the story Holmes had told me about his youthful promise to the diabetic girl who he then had to see slowly fade away and die. Nancrede listened with the tips of his fingers together, his elbows on his desktop blotter, a wry smile on his face.

'That,' he said finally, 'was me. It is a story I tell to students near graduation to let them know that they just can't help everybody. It is a true story, that happened to me when I was a callow young doctor. I was going to quit medicine in despair at the hopelessness of it all but my professor persuaded me to turn around and come back again. Dr Holmes simply appropriated the story to himself.'

'Very smart,' I said, with an inward sigh that I had once again been hoodwinked by Holmes, 'and very convincing. Is there anything else you can tell me about Holmes: where he lived, where he might be now, any other misdemeanours?'

Nancrede smiled indulgently. 'We just don't keep the addresses of former students; And nothing else springs immediately to mind about his time here. I'm afraid you're going to be disappointed.'

'That's OK, I'm immune to disappointment, inured by long exposure' I said dryly, angered by this man's manner of taking me as a pedestrian fool and wishing to show him I was smart. I might not have been to college, but I had some tricks myself. He looked down, not catching my eyes. He was a liar, of course, the professor was lying through his over-educated teeth. He was a good liar, though, as liars go, he gave me a little information, enough to suggest he had no more to say.

'And now,' he said, 'if you will excuse me, I have an anatomy class to take.'

'Thank you for your time, professor,' I said, 'I'd appreciate having a look around the campus.' He looked uncertain, 'I'm sure you're very proud of it,' I said lamely but it did the trick.

'Please do, be my guest,' he said, leading me to the door.

We parted on the steps. As soon as he had gone I stopped admiring the buildings and went down a stairway at the back of the entrance hall, descending to the janitors' rooms.

In a corridor made hot and muggy by the proximity of the roaring boiler room I flashed my badge, talked to a couple of men. There was an old negro who either didn't know or wasn't saying; a young negro who would say anything if he thought there was something in it for him, but had only been at the place five years. Finally I was advised to speak to the deputy chief janitor, a fat, warty man. He'd been there fifteen years knew everything, and everything was for sale. Yeah, he knew about Holmes, there was a big hullabaloo about it, but it never got to the cops. It was to do with the morgue. That gave me a jolt of recognition. So who would know more, so who would know everything? The warty janitor sucked his teeth, couldn't rightly be sure. A second dollar did the trick: there was a man still in the area, practising medicine, a Canadian, he was a student with Holmes, he would know. And Holmes, he added for good measure, he was funny, a real gentleman, would always be prepared to give a working man the price of a drink. Yes, I would bet on that.

Ed Grant, doctor E. W. Grant, I confirmed from the university records for 1884, had graduated at the same time as Holmes. The professor's secretary who had showed me the list was also so kind as to show me the state record of those licensed to practise medicine and, glory be, Dr Ed Grant was still there. That was good. If I hadn't found him there I'd have checked on all forty-four states of the union and Canada too, but I would have found him.

He was working in Battle Creek, only a few stops down the Michigan Central Railroad from Depot Street Station. The Battle Creek post office gave me his address and I found a neat, timber-built house with a waiting room, office and dispensary on the bottom floor. It looked like Dr Grant was doing very well for himself. That was good, you could only threaten someone with scandal who had a name worth dirtying.

The waiting room was empty so I walked through to what had to be his office, knocking on the door and saying 'Dr Grant?' as I entered. Grant was a well-built man standing in his shirtsleeves and waistcoat washing his hands in a white basin behind a good solid doctor's desk and a black leather chair. 'Surgery's over my friend', he said in an accent that had something of British Canadian in it.

'That's not it Dr Grant, I'm a police officer,' I said deliberately. He self-consciously slowed down washing his hands, turned to me and took a brief look at my proffered badge.

'So how can I help you officer?' he said, looking as guilty as a boy caught stealing apples from his neighbour's orchard. Maybe he had more to conceal than the events of the 1880s, maybe he was a part time abortionist or used other of his physician's arts to help people out of tricky situations: poisoning unwanted relatives or patching up the gunshot wounds of bad men.

'I'm looking for Henry Holmes, also called Henry Mudgett, H.M.Howard and a host of other names,' I said.

'Yep,' he said, throwing the towel aside, with what may have been relief that it was only past crimes I was interested in, 'I knew Henry, we were students together, and we were pals for a time. I can't tell you where he is now though.'

'That's bad news,' I said, 'because I'm investigating a number of disappearances and insurance frauds,' I eyed him as a predator. He pursed his lips and bowed his head slightly, 'and I have evidence that you are part of them Doctor Grant,' I said sharply, so that he jumped, 'so you give me your help now and I swear I will do my best to keep you out of it.'

'Weell alright,' he said, as if he had considered his decision, breathing out heavily and leaning back as if he expected me to strike a blow. He realised he had to act the man, and recovered his composure, 'but here's the deal, detective,' he said with vigour, 'I'm going to tell you what may have happened, but I'm not admitting any part of it. I can tell you the blueprint. OK?'

I assented, 'Yeah, sure, tell me what the scheme was, we'll take it from there.'

'Well, Henry and me were medical students together, as you know. We did a lot of dissection classes, we were very familiar with cadavers, bodies held no horror for us, you see. One day Henry talked to me about a scheme he had to make some money. he told it to me like he'd been thinking about it for a long time. This was it: someone would be insured, a student let's say, under a false name. We'd bribe a morgue attendant at the dead house to let us know when a body came in of the right age and sex and we'd take one of the carts from the medical school morgue and we would carry the body to where we could stage an accident. The student is declared dead in the form of the cadaver and we collect and split the money. Of course, the city morgue get their body back – they hadn't lost a cadaver or gained one, the same attendant we bribed to get him out puts him back, we've just borrowed a body. It's just a matter of losing some of the paperwork. If any roundsman stopped us while we were wheeling the cart, we were bone fide medical students taking a cadaver from the city morgue to the hospital morgue for use in dissection.'

'Very clever,' I said, 'very slick.'

A winning smile spread over Grant's face, 'It was perfection. There was another variant of it that Holmes told me about,' he said, clearly eager to point the finger away from himself. 'This was one he did on his own: Henry had an order in for weeks with the crooked attendant at the city morgue. Finally one came in, a young man who had fallen from a freight car. Henry bought a trunk with a zinc box that went inside. They put the body in the box, rigor mortis would have worn off by now, so they could double it up, put some ice in there to keep if fresh, and sealed it down. He had an expressman deliver it to Illinois Central station and got the trunk on a train to Grand Rapids. He left it in baggage but when he got to reclaim it, the thing was stinking like a skunk, he'd got to deal with it. Once he'd got to a hotel he had to get the body out so he could line the trunk better.' Grant was grinning, wide-eyed at the horror of it. 'Well he went out and bought a waterproof hunting bag, had it filled with ice and took it back to the hotel. He put the ice in the bath and took the stinking body out of the trunk and laid it on the ice. Well, the body was disgusting, it was pretty plain the man had been dead longer than the morgue attendant said, so Henry had been tricked for once.

'Well, he was working with the body in the bathtub when there's a noise behind him and standing in his room is the hotel manager, he has come in with a pass key, you see. "This is a nice sort of business," says the manager, "I knew it was death, I know what death smells like, I smelled it in the war. Now you show me what you've got there." The manager looked in the bath and pulled back, gagging, it looked like the game was up for Henry Holmes but did he lose his cool? Not Henry.' When Grant became excited a ball of spittle would collect in the corner of his mouth until he licked it away.

'So he's caught red-handed with a putrid body in a bathtub and the hotel manager with all his staff at his disposal. So what does he do, you tell me.'

I motioned for Grant to continue, 'Henry turned to the man, cool as an icehouse, and he said, "My dear sir, you will let me explain, I hope, this man was my brother. He has just died of a malignant and very contagious disease. He had been sent to a medical college for dissection and when I learned of it, I determined to save the body from the demonstrator's knife. Come, look again, and see if you cannot discern a family resemblance."

'And the manager looked forward into the bathtub and he looked at Henry and back at the decomposing body, and his face turned ashen, his hands trembled and he almost dropped his keys. "Now leave me to place my poor brother's body in this trunk and you will no more be disturbed by the odour," said Henry, and the manager just backed away, but he stammered out that Henry had better be gone in the morning. So Henry got a train to about forty miles outside of Grand Rapids and put the next part of the plan into operation. He hired a gig and drove fifteen miles on through roads hub deep in mud, until he came to a small lumber town. He set himself up in a hut there and word soon spread that he was a lumber operator of considerable means. One day he went out in the evergreen forest and just didn't return. A week or so later, what purported to be his dead body was found pinioned to the earth by a fallen tree. It was wearing his clothes, had his papers in his wallet in the pocket, there was even money. There was no question of the identity. When his death was reported his insurance company paid up a cool $20,000.' Grant shook his head and mopped his brow, 'I mean,' he said, 'Henry did some bad things, but you just had to admire the nerve of the man, you just had to love him.'

'Yes, OK,' I said, 'So you say you weren't involved in that one.'

'Nope, he did it on his own, it was the vacation or something.'

'So how did he get the payment?'

'It went to his wife.' My stomach gave a sickening lurch – it wasn't just him, he had involved Georgiana in it. Willingly?

'It strikes me,' I said, reining in my emotion, 'it might be difficult to find a young male body to match your insured.'

Grant pursed his lips, 'yeah, s'pose so, it was a long time ago.'

'Dr Grant, I am conducting a murder inquiry,' he visibly blanched. 'Sometime in 1883 a student was insured and it wasn't another corpse which was substituted that time, was it? It was the student who was insured who was killed.' It was a bluff on my part, but it was worth a try.

Grant was no fool, he judged it was a trap. I just didn't have the detail to back it up. We were still standing facing each other with the waiting-room behind me, the wooden shelves filled with glass jars and the tablet stamp of the dispensary behind him. He shifted his weight so he was standing more clearly opposite me. 'We were caught,' he said, 'that's all you need to know. We were reprimanded, almost lost our places at the university and all those years of study. It was enough, I split with Holmes.'

My bitterness spilled over, 'So the university authorities tied it up for you, judge and jury in their own court?' I said, 'I'll tell the bad men I see if they really want to get away with it they'd better get a college education.'

'When we were caught, that was when I really saw the beauty of the scheme,' said Grant urgently, anxious to divert me from my pursuit. 'You see, the medical school authorities had a lot of trouble with getting cadavers for dissection. They had people who had willed their bodies to medical science, but you don't get so many of those, and John Does who died on the street, and people who'd been hanged in the prison yard. But it was always hard to get them, and any scare like this would reduce the supply still more, like the claim that we dug up freshly buried bodies from graveyards. Now, to my knowledge no one ever did that to obtain teaching specimens for dissection, but you ask anyone in Michigan and they'll say that medical schools do it all the time. Well, everything unsavoury like that makes it more tricky to get cadavers and I think the authorities just couldn't afford the bad publicity. Plus we were near the end of our final year then so they'd be losing a couple of graduates when everyone had put a lot of work into their education, it looks bad on the balance books to lose students like that. They get a lot of money from the State of

Michigan to produce students, graduation lists ought to look fat and healthy. So we were bawled out and let go. It never happened, right?'

My patience was running out. 'Let me give you a way out of this,' I said, 'because I don't want you that much. I want Holmes.'

'You can't have me,' he said aggressively, 'because I never did the bad stuff.'

I chanced my arm, 'You broke with him,' I said, 'after he suggested taking out an insurance on you. That's what happened.'

'Jeez', Grant said, holding the back of his neck and looking down as if ashamed, 'he tell you that?'

'He didn't have to,' I said, 'you just did.'

Grant swung his head disconsolately from side to side, like a horse that couldn't reach its fodder. 'The truth is, I'd broke with Holmes before that man died, and I really didn't know anything about it. I'm just not going to help you with anything about no murder.' His speech had become less grammatical since he had been rattled by my threats.

'So tell me where Holmes lives,' I said, tiring of all this.

'No,' he said, 'I just don't know'

I leapt at him and pinned him to the wall with my right hand under his throat and my left pulled back as if to strike him. 'It's over, where is Holmes?' I said.

Grant was about the same height as me and could probably give as good as he got if it came to a fair fight, but the shock of the unexpected, being attacked in his own home, and whatever respect he had for the authority of the police disarmed him.

'How dare you... you have no right...' he choked, the spittle at the side of his mouth becoming a dribble.

'I need to find Holmes and his wife, the Holmes lair, understand?' I said.

'Yeah,' he said, 'get off,' I relaxed my grip, 'I'd have told you without all that. I don't know where he is, I really don't, but sure, I can tell you where Holmes and his wife used to live.'

'That's good,' I said, releasing him.

'Then will you leave me alone, keep me out of it?'

'Yep,' I said, as far as I can, 'I want Holmes for later stuff, anyway. Things he's done more recently.'

He told me it was Maple Rapids and gave me some idea of where the house was. I thanked Grant politely and left as if there had been no unpleasantness between us.

I sat at the railroad station, I only had to wait a couple of hours. So Georgiana was in on it. I let my mind wander, trying to keep away from the sick implications of her role. As evening drew in I watched the fantastic moths, gnats and beetles buzzing around the gas light. There was a lot lit with the electricity now, that was cleaner and newer, but if anything even more dangerous than gas. Most places, outside the biggest towns, still had public places lit with the singing, incandescent gas mantle.

I suppose, I mused, that if I traced through the record of Michigan deaths during Holmes' period at the university, and I found all the ones who were students, I could ask the local insurance companies and find there was a substantial payout on one particular death. I toyed with doing it, I made a few notes, but what could I prove? That Holmes was the beneficiary of the policy? Almost certainly not, he would use an intermediary, a lawyer maybe, like he had in Philadelphia. That he had killed somebody? No way. No witnesses, the physical evidence long since decomposed. It was going to be a paperchase, and a paperchase through history at that. Well, I knew I could get those details if I had the time to do it, if I wanted them. For now, I wanted Holmes. I wanted to see Georgiana, to redeem my life. Taking hold of Henry Holmes and putting him behind bars was part of it, though I was haunted by one of the last things Grant said, 'You might catch him, Mr Geyer, but you won't keep him.' We'll see.

The next day I went on up to Maple Rapids, on through the wilderness tracts of the dark vegetation of Michigan where the wolves lurked. I don't know what I thought I was going to find. Perhaps nothing, perhaps Grant had sent me some place where he knew Holmes wasn't. But I didn't think so, and anyway, any lead was better than none.

Maple Rapids was as much like Gilmanton as it was like any

other town. There was the row of stores: dry goods, druggist, cigar store, a saloon or two, a post and cable office. Past that were some neat houses set back behind white picket fences. There was a church in the near distance, if I looked around a little I might just find a sheriff's office with a boy like I was in the stables tending the horses.

I spoke to a child in a pinafore dress rolling a hoop, asked for Holmes by his description, 'Does my friend Henry live around here, short guy with a moustache, very nicely spoken.'

'Mr Holmes?' she said, I nodded. She indicated a house, 'Mr Holmes lives there.' Now that was curious, because the name he had been using in St Louis was H. Howard. But at least I knew I was in the right place, and I just went right on up the street. The full realisation could no longer be suppressed that I'd be seeing Georgiana again. I'd been able to displace the thought with activity before this, but now I had to face it. The muscles in my stomach tightened into a ball that an iron fist was squeezing.

It had been all of sixteen years – what was I going to say, that I'd come visiting bringing a basket of fruit? My forehead, my upper lip felt cold and clammy and I faltered in my step as I felt a weakness in the back of my knees. But at that point I saw in a light blue dress a figure cross the street and go through the gate I was headed for. The waist still slim, the long neck, even from behind I knew it was her.

I trod quickly, my heart pounding, I was back chasing the apparition, now one which had gone down the short path and was turning the latch on the door. The pit of my stomach was a ball of pain, my legs unwilling to go on. I lumbered forward, crippled by my need to see her, as if she would go away again and be in my sight no longer.

My mouth was dry, could I even speak? 'Excuse me... G...' I couldn't get the word out, I couldn't even say her name.

She turned, framed against the white door of the little house. The apparition at bay at last. 'Good afternoon, can I help you?' said a sweet, fresh face fringed with chestnut hair. It wasn't Georgiana.

Chapter 7

I struggled to contain my shock at the suddenly unfamiliar face. 'I was looking... for your husband, m'am,' I said, masking my confusion with formality and pulling out my badge, 'Detective Frank P.Geyer.'

She was perhaps thirty, but age had not weighed down her features. She was tall, for a woman, slim and graceful, so like Georgiana it continued to startle me as we spoke. She showed no great surprise at my presence, but pushed the door open behind her as she looked at me with a sort of amused curiosity, as if I was an interesting specimen that kids were gawking at in the reptile house. She wore a two-piece house dress of pink and white striped gingham with a wrap that she took off when she laid down her basket. It was a fresh house that smelled of apples and cut flowers, there were a few good pieces of furniture, a round dark wood table with an embroidered tablecloth; some comfortable chairs with doilies, a neat kitchen leading off and a stairway going up. I bet there were carpets in every room, even on the stairs. It was the sort of house you could be happy in.

'I'm sorry I don't have the pleasure,' I said.

'I'm Myrta Holmes,' she said.

'I was hoping to see Henry Holmes, will he be back today?' I asked innocently.

'I can never say when my husband will be back. He's a traveller in patents, you know, and he could be in any state in the union.' She registered my disbelief, and said as if to placate me, 'He does write me, but he is between hotels all the time, so he doesn't give me his address.' She wasn't at all surprised at being asked about her husband's whereabouts, I guess this had happened before.

'Did you sign your husband out on bail in St Louis six months ago as H.Howard?' I said directly.

'No,' she said, 'No, I didn't,' she seemed genuinely surprised.

'Was your husband previously called Henry Mudgett, sometimes going under the name Henry Howard?'

Her pretty face looked perplexed, 'Is this a case of mistaken identity, Mr Geyer?'

'Well that's certainly possible,' I said, though I had no real doubts, 'Have you got a photograph of your husband?'

'Why, of course,' she said and she went to the piano to pick up something I had already noticed and wanted a closer look at: a wedding photograph with Henry in a neat suit with a formal, high collar, holding a bowler hat in one hand, with on his arm the fetching woman I saw before me. She stood a little taller than Henry in a fine but not too fancy dress with discreet lace trimmings. She wore her bonnet high which showed off her well-sculpted face. She wasn't wearing a wedding dress, though it looked like a marriage photograph. 'That's the Henry I know,' I said, 'where was it taken?'

'My folks' home at Mooers Forks, after our wedding in summer 1883.'

'That would be when Henry was a student at Ann Arbor?'

'Why yes, that's right. I'm sorry to rush you Mr Geyer but I need to get things ready for the children, they'll be back from school soon. You leave a forwarding address, I'll make sure Henry gets it.'

'You have little ones?' I said. Would my shame never end, I who had no family while he had one in every town?

'Laura and Sam,' she said, 'aged five and seven,' she said.

I imagined the tiny forms playing at Henry's feet as he sat in the easy chair in that neat little house. 'And Henry talks to them about fairyland?' I said, not really thinking about it.

'He does,' she smiled indulgently at the remembered pleasure.

'I have heard him tell those stories,' I said, almost wistfully.

'In his home life I do think there has never been a better man than my husband,' said Myrta, with no other prompting, 'He has never spoken an unkind word to me or our children or my mother. He is never vexed or irritable, but is always happy and seemingly free from care. In times of financial trouble or when we are worried over anything, as soon as he comes into the house everything seems so different.'

I remembered Henry in the morgue, chopping off his former friend's finger, 'And when did you last see this paragon of virtue?' I said.

'I'm not sure I like your tone Mr Geyer,' she retorted, 'I'm talking to you freely because I have absolutely nothing to hide, there is no cause for rudeness.'

'Then I apologise, ma'am, but I am very eager to see your husband.'

'Then I will certainly give him that message the next time I see him.' I gave her my police calling card which she looked at briefly and put down.

'Just one more thing,' I said as I was leaving, 'Was Henry married before he met you?'

She shook her head, 'My goodness no, no, I'm sure of it.' Again, she seemed a little surprised at my question, though hardly alarmed by it. I walked down the short garden path and through the white gate in the picket fence. In town I checked with the sheriff only to find what I expected: Henry wasn't known around there except as a model citizen. Like the smart guy he was he had taken the old saying to heart: don't poop on your own doorstep.

In the fly-blown lobby of the only hotel in town I got out my pencil and my black leatherette notebook and examined the possibilities. That Georgiana was dead, died in childbirth, died of a fever, died alone in agony, died in some hovel or back alley, perhaps killed, perhaps she deserved it. Perhaps she had been insured. Maybe Holmes had someone else using her name. But she signed his bail application. I could have been mistaken about her handwriting, it was a standard script, but the turnkey described her to me. Someone looking like her? Bigamy? I wouldn't put it past him. So where would I find her now? Probably, I thought miserably, where I'd find him.

I was let down, deflated... I had been stoking myself up to meet Georgiana and had only come up with another mystery. But in a way I was also relieved: I maybe never would see her again. Maybe that would be better than the torment of seeing her and having to speak, to give voice to the years of suffering, of wanting and not knowing why when I could have died of love. Perhaps I didn't have to know and I could avoid the pain.

The next day I leaned out the window as the train steamed into Union Station giving me that shock of the city that I always got: so vast, so complex, so ineffable. When you looked up the cable and electric lines cut the sky into jagged, unnatural shapes; smoke and steam streamed from the trains thundering overhead on elevated railways which threw bizarre shadows on the horses drawing wagons below. At ground level every street was a melee of dresses, business suits, working clothes, the poor and the rich all jostling together in the crush. Underneath the constant feet of these harried pedestrians were the never-ending coils of pipes carrying gas, water, sewage into the bowels of the leviathan.

I got a cab to the Fidelity Mutual building, a big skyscratcher of a place, eight stories or more, with an echoing lobby decorated with tiles depicting industry, trustworthiness, thrift and so on. Cass came bounding down to meet me and we went up in an elevator with gold-coloured wrought iron work on the gates. Cass's office impressed me, he had a door of his own and another door opening to a clerks' room where three young men wearing cuff shields hunched over their copying on tall, slanted desks. Cass had a map of Chicago on the wall, with reproduction portraits of Abraham Lincoln and of Grover Cleveland behind his desk, so when you sat talking to him you faced both presidents. On his desk looking towards him was a silver framed picture of a smiling plump woman, Mrs Cass I guessed, with other framed picture I couldn't see. More family.

'It's a real modern city,' I said, because it is always welcomed if you say something good about someone's home town.

'All this business district was built since the fire of '71,' Cass said, settling behind his desk and motioning for me to sit opposite, 'It's pretty new. We built it, the insurance companies, we made this city,' He sat looking pleased with himself, as if he had just lain a line of bricks and mortar and was standing back to look at his handiwork with his thumbs in the pockets of his vest, 'How've you been doing on the hunt for our Mr Holmes?'

'Doctor Holmes,' I said, 'he graduated as a physician ten years ago,' and I gave him the story of the trail from Ann Arbor to Grant to Myrta Holmes.

Cass listened, taking notes, his soft pink hand scuttling across the pages of a bound ledger. Finally he said, 'Did you believe in Myrta, that she was telling the truth?'

'No,' I replied, 'she didn't invite me to sit down, and that kind of woman always wants to make you feel at home. And the fact that it wasn't irregular for her to have someone calling asking for her husband. Most people would be shocked, want to know why I was interested in him, what I had on him. She didn't, she'd had callers on that errand before. Creditors maybe, or criminal acquaintances.'

'OK,' said Cass, with restrained excitement, 'now me. I had no luck checking round all the regular routes, I thought he might be going under a different name, which is why we've had trouble getting him in Chicago.

'When all that came up blank I started looking at the places around Chicago, because the city's grown so fast recently you can't keep up with it. And I've found it – not Chicago: Englewood – it's a suburb South of here,' and he threw across a small book titled 'Guide to Englewood' which I flicked through, 'Located twelve feet above the level of the lake, with a perfect water, sewerage and gas system, and an excellent police and fire department, Englewood combines all of the convenience of the city with the fresh, healthful air of the country.'

'Now look at the ads,' said Cass. I flicked to a place he had marked and there it was, 'H.H.Holmes… Drugs Paints and Oils… Linden Grove Mineral Spring Water.'

'Holmes arrived around 1886,' Cass said, 'he'd been working in drug stores and a hospital pharmacy. He got a position as a clerk in a drug store on 63rd Street. This drug store was owned by a Mrs E.S.Holton and the relationship seemed to go just fine, because a few years later he was made a partner in the store. Things went a little sour after that, they quarrelled over the books – Mrs Holton accused Holmes of doctoring them, wangling the accounts –

and then she vanished, she and her daughter, leaving Holmes in control of the whole of the business.' Cass looked up from his notebook and met my eyes.

'A lot of people vanish in this story,' I said, 'Didn't have insurance did she?'

He shrugged, 'There's more–he's built a castle there.'

'A castle?' I said, more in exasperation than curiosity.

'That's what they call it, Holmes' castle, but really it's just a big building that takes up the block opposite the drug store. There are storefronts downstairs, with a hotel upstairs that Holmes built in time for the '92 World Columbian Exposition, the great Ferris Wheel and all, you remember? We had a million visitors in this city, and we needed every foot of hotel space, Holmes did good trade.'

We hired a hack and went straight over there, through the morning snarl-ups of horses, wheels and reins and the crush of pedestrians in the business district, out to the cleaner air of Englewood. The suburb was busy enough to be rich, but far enough from the city centre to feel fresh. We passed a huge new opera house in red brick with iron balconies. It looked a good place to live, the sort of neighbourhood where I'd never lived.

Where 63rd Street met Wallace there it was, a storefront with the painted sign 'H.H. Holmes, licensed dispensary'. Opposite was what we were looking for: a block wide, a block deep, with four stories, the bottom one taken up with storefronts. At intervals along the building were bay window sections which rose to become turrets above the roof, connected on top with a balcony with the sort of gap-toothed sections cut out that you see in pictures of old buildings in Europe, as if it was for archers to fire on an approaching enemy. Great. We hadn't just missed the man, we'd missed his damned castle.

As we gazed, a white-faced, sad-eyed woman, like a decently dressed ghost, plucked at the air as if summoning the courage to speak to us but we breezed past, we were city dwellers, used to the crazies on street corners. I was to have time to regret not speaking to her, but then, my life has been a long pageant of remorse.

Anyway, we were mesmerised by how dilapidated Holmes' lair was... some of the ground floor stores were closed and boarded up, the door and window frames needed a lick of paint, the upper floors looked empty with dirt collecting on the windows rendering them translucent against the bright sunlight. The Holmes store was open, though the display window on one side was empty except for a layer of yellowing paper. On the other was a showing of cheap jewellery and ornaments, gifts of glass or china. We went in and rang the bell in front of a counter full of small pieces of gaudy finery, brooches, earrings rings, and a rainbow assortment of hair ribbons.

Out from some dark room at the back came a cheery bumbling man in late middle age with his sleeves rolled up and a green eyeshade worn high on his bald head.

'What can I do for you gentlemen.'

'We're looking for Mr Holmes,' Cass said, it was taken as read that as this was his city, Cass took the lead. The man paused in his appreciation of the situation, looked from one of us to the other, then slapped his thigh and laughed like a drain. Cass and I exchanged gloomily glances.

'I'm sorry,' he said through his mirth, 'wish I had a dollar for everyone who came through that door saying the same thing. I haven't seen Henry Holmes for maybe a year. But he always made me laugh.'

'How was that?' I said

'He was just so smooth,' the jewellery store manager said, 'he was like an English crook come over the water, just too smooth to be an American.'

'And you're sure he was a crook?' I said.

'No shadow of a doubt, not one, not one itty bitty little one. Let me just tell you this: when creditors came to the door all angry and wanting their money – 'cos I don't think Henry Holmes ever paid a single bill in all his life – he would greet them with such shock, such a surprise that they had any doubts in him. "Let's talk about this and see how I can reassure you." Out would come the beers and cigars and he would sit them at that table there,' he motioned towards a single table and chairs piled up in the darkened side of the shop, 'and he would sit there with a soda and tell them such stories I would have to go out back to laugh to myself. And the creditors, they would go off empty handed but smiling, convinced that Holmes was not just an excellent fellow who had just fallen on hard times but was just so brilliant they never need fear but that their money was in safe hands, glad they had lent it to him.'

'Why was it all so funny?' Cass said, still trying to get the measure of Henry.

'It was just all so...creative,' said the jeweller, struggling for the word, 'let me tell you just one scheme. There was this Canadian...' he put his hand over his mouth to stifle a laugh, 'Henry put it out he was some kind of inventor, and he put a big galvanised tank down in the basement under the store. He put a load of old junk and chemicals in there that made murky colours and stank to high heaven. Then he tapped the gas main that runs below, ran a pipe through the tank and up into the store and burned the gas. He put it out that he made his own gas and it was as good as any in the city; he didn't advertise it, just let it be known by people who came in and soon enough a guy came sniffing round the bait. Little fellow, Canadian, white hair, well he was really taken with this singular device and he gave Henry two thousand dollars for the patent, had to beg Henry to sell it to him, virtually went down on bended knees. Henry gave him the machine and he went off as happy as a sandboy. He came back a few times, unable to get it to work, and Henry was patient and explained it all again. Then I heard the Canadian had died of a broken heart over the failure of the wonderful machine, never suspecting it was a scheme... Then there was Linden Grove Mineral Spring Water, where Henry sold water he got from tapping a water main downstairs for five cents a cup.'

'He got people to pay for water from the faucet?' said Cass incredulously.

'Do you know where we can find the original owner here,' I said, 'Mrs Holton, is she still in Englewood?'

He shook his head, 'Before my time. When I started here it was 1889, Henry leased this part of the drug store to me because he needed all the money he could get, he was building the castle then.

'Even with all his schemes and deals, how the hell did he get the money to build a hotel?' asked Cass.

'If I could tell you that, I'd do it myself,' the jeweller scratched his head, moving the eyeshade vigorously as he did so, 'but one way was by not paying anyone. He'd employ a team of builders, then when they had the work half finished, he'd quarrel with them and dismiss them without pay, telling them they could go to court to get their money because their work wasn't good enough. The company that built it never paid a cent to the builders.'

'The company?'

'Campbell Yates Manufacturing Company. Henry always said he was just an agent for the company, but I never saw anyone giving any orders but Henry and his pal Ben.'

'What would the full name be there?' I said hoarsely.

'Ben Pitezel, he did all the running around for Henry.' I couldn't resist a sidelong glance at Cass, 'He was supposed to be the Campbell in Campbell Yates Manufacturing, but it was a scheme. And there was no Mr. Yates. Now I'd better get back to my work gentlemen if you don't mind.'

'Anyone else live with Henry Holmes, anyone we might talk to?' I said.

'Yeah,' said the jolly man, 'he had a number of women friends, quite close women friends too, if you get my meaning. Pearl Conner and her daughter Julia were here when I came. Henry and her lived together as, you know, man and wife, but she went when Minnie came on the scene, he had a secretary called Amelia, she stayed a while and then I didn't see her again; one day Julia was here, the next she wasn't, that was the way things were around here. Julia left after he had built the castle, didn't say goodbye or nothing, I was surprised 'cuz I knew them quite well.'

'So you don't know what happened to her?' I asked, 'What about this Minnie, was she local? Could we speak to her?'

'No she was a Texan girl, from Fort Worth, Texas. Fine accent she had, that girl, her and her sister with a name that was similar - Nannie, that was it. Minnie and Nannie Williams. They went, probably back to Texas.'

The man was tending to ramble, his store of nervous energy had been expended and he was running down like a kid's clockwork toy. I made one last effort at squeezing a lead out of him, 'Anyone else around here who we could talk to, anyone who worked for Henry perhaps?'

'Joe Quinlan the janitor,' he said, with the air of a man having a truly great idea, 'lives out where the negroes and Irish are around Constitution Street.'

We went down to the wharf where kids played in the narrow streets and mazy lanes ran off to who knows what den of iniquity. We found Quinlan by giving a few cents to the stale bread vendor on a street corner. He was a negro, probably in his late fifties but looking older, he was well built but his face was deeply lined, with dull, rheumy eyes, and a stubble on his chin as white as snow.

For a small consideration he told me how he'd worked for Henry virtually since the castle was built until one day, when he was owed a few weeks' wages, he turned up to find Henry gone and the place crawling with creditors.

'What was it like there,' I said, 'how did he live, was there a woman with him? Julia... Georgiana?'

'There was always women around,' he said, as if surprised I might think it would have been different, 'women all over the house, it was like a damned harem.' My stomach turned, horror piled on horror, 'But they never seemed to stay long. I remember Miss Amelia who was right good to me. Tall, she was, much taller than Dr Holmes, lots of red hair like an angel. I remember once though,' Quinlan's big eyes looked down, as if ashamed and amused at the same time. I nodded for him to continue, 'I remember once going into that office to do a little cleaning and there he was with Miss Amelia,' He looked around furtively as if seeking eavesdroppers, though we were alone, and lowered his voice., 'fornicatin' like a hog,' he hissed, then repeated it for emphasis. 'Fornicatin' like a damned hog... with her stretched over that big old desk of his, and him coming in from behind.' He jerked his hips to mimic the sexual act and let out a leering laugh.

I thanked Quinlan with some money that felt dirty in my hand, and we repaired to questioning the neighbours who weren't quite so accommodating as the jeweller. Real estate agents, brokers, architects and other folk who might have been expected to know what was going on with a man in business on their own street had all suffered a memory loss. No sir, they didn't know a thing, could only just recollect seeing Holmes around and about, no, not in this neighbourhood, nothing like that, nothing bad. These people were worse than criminals for keeping their mouths shut when there was trouble. Holmes' negro washerwoman was more use, her rolls of fat and voluminous breasts seeming to merge with the basket she carried. 'He wanted to get me insooorance,' she said, her eyes wide, 'Well I never had no insoorance and I don't want no insoorance and I told him that straight.' No negro was taken in by him, it seemed: whatever sorcery Holmes had did not cross the race barrier. Perhaps negroes were just less trusting of the things white folks said.

We passed the ghostly spectre several times on our rounds but ignored the timid woman in our routine. We had put an ad in the Englewood Gazette asking for information, and cabled Fort Worth police so that when we dragged wearily back to Cass' office there was a reply: yes, they knew our man, wanted him for 'larceny of one horse'. Edward Cass and I looked from the cable to each other. Holmes was not a horse thief, this was not his modus operandi, as the lawyers put it. Maybe it was the wrong man, or something had happened there, something different. It was the only lead we had, so it had to be followed. I'd done enough travelling and my time was running out, so Cass said he'd go while I stayed in Englewood.

Cass took me to his home that night to have dinner with his family. I resisted but politeness decreed I had to go. The truth is, I didn't like to see it, I didn't like to see family life because it made me sad for what I had lost: the two little children that I brought candies for who were playing on the rug, the homely but pretty wife, given to embonpoint. The children had been kept up so they could meet me, so I could feel the glacial hand of frozen time on my heart as I looked at the family I would not have.

Ed was in his element, running about the neat house putting things in their place, referring all the while to Mrs Cass, as he called her, 'Mrs Cass doesn't think so do you dear?' 'I'll take this through to Mrs Cass in the kitchen...'

She was an open, ebullient soul, full of simple family jocularities about Cass's general incompetence around the house, hoping he was a better insurance man than a handyman and such like. They had a kind of vaudeville routine of challenge and recrimination over household tasks which was put on for the entertainment of guests. I carried myself off pretty well, told some stories, kept in with the high spirits of the occasion while inside I was haemorrhaging with isolation and waiting to be alone with the vacuity of my heart.

The next day I covered every house in the vicinity of Holmes' castle without result while the ghastly sentinel followed me with her eyes. She was respectably dressed with a bonnet and shawl but with the careworn expression of impenetrable grief. By twilight I felt I had nothing to lose and I approached her. I wouldn't normally have taken a lot of notice – many on the streets bear the haggard expression of the haunted, nameless fears and obsessions that possess them, and if you take them seriously you become part of their delusion. But I reckoned if she had been hanging around so much there was a chance she had seen things that might give me a lead.

I took a chance, 'Excuse me ma'am, I'm looking for someone,' I said. Her eyes were a dull grey-blue, her face waxen and deeply lined, wispy grey hair, once fair, trembled in the wind.

'You looking for my Emily?' she said sharply. She spoke in the accented English of a first generation immigrant.

'No, I wasn't ma'am, but tell me about Emily,'

'Emily, she is my daughter, she was missing from three years ago, one day she go out alone, she don't come back.'

I established she was Mrs Van Tassell, a widow, and there had been a thorough police search for Emily who had gone missing at sixteen.

'Did you know Henry Holmes, used to run the drug store on 63rd and Wallace, I motioned to the place.

'Yes, I knew him,' she said, 'I used to go there to drink the spring water, for my health, Emily would haf an ice cream... when my Emily went missing he put up a poster in his store.'

'What was she like?'

'Oh, pretty as a picture,' she said, touching me on the arm, full of the pride of motherhood, 'tall for her age, blue eyes, two pigtails.' She lapsed back into melancholy, it was obvious I couldn't help her. 'Now I go the places where we went together, you know, in case I see her,' she said. 'You tell me if you see her?'

'Yes, sure I will,' I said, but I knew that a runaway teenage girl was no great story. A mystery man friend was more likely than the white slave trade to have taken her off. Moms were as like to be the last people who knew what their daughters were doing. Still, it was another disappearance. Nothing connected it to Holmes, but that corner of 63rd and Wallace was coming to look like a natural spot where people disappeared, one moment they were there, the next they were gone, like a weird freak of nature.

I returned to the hotel weary, as the light was failing, and the evening rush of horses, reins, carriages and people started to clog the Chicago streets. I looked through the shambles of advertising signs, down at the hats of the men and the bonnets of the women, any of them could have known Henry Holmes. Where were all the people who knew him, where were Mrs Holton, Julia and her daughter Pearl, Minnie and Nannie Williams, Amelia? Even young Emily. Were they all discarded lovers? Were they all involved in his schemes and had taken off to other cities to try their luck elsewhere, or had he done away with them? It was too big and too crazy a thought for my mind to work its way around, but through that long lonely day of the cobbled streets and the neatly painted woodwork it sat in the centre of my mind like a boulder in a field you have to plough. All the people, all the people who left without saying goodbye.

Chapter 8

Clots of hair and dust lurked in unswept corners of my hotel lobby. I checked for messages and the deskboy indicated a lanky man on one of the decrepit armchairs, who looked like he could do with a libation of carbolic along with the lobby. I took his hand without enthusiasm, 'What can I do for you?'

'Charles Chapman, sir, at your service. I've come about this,' he held out a crumpled newspaper, it was the ad we put in the Englewood Gazette asking about Holmes.

'How did you know Henry Holmes?' I asked. You got a lot of cranks when you advertise, people who said they knew things and didn't, or confessed to heinous crimes for the attention, a talk with a policeman and a night in the cells being the best they could hope for by way of human contact.

'I'm a skeleton articulator,' Chapman said. I eyed him inquisitively until he explained, 'you know, when cadavers need to be stripped so you've just got the skeleton there, and when you've got to put the skeleton back in the right order,' he could see I was still mystified, 'for medical schools you see, museums and other things like that, well I'm your man. I'm a mechanic really, by trade, but I worked with meat in the stockyards and when there was a strike I did some work with cadavers.'

'And how did you meet Holmes?' I said.

'Just the way I met you,' Chapman said with vigour, 'he put an ad in the Gazette looking for a skeleton articulator and I applied. Once he knew I could do the job, he set me to work on two real striking cadavers. It was all above board, he said he'd got orders for from the Hahnmann Medical School.' My stomach jolted. It was surely a way of making people disappear.

'He gave me thirty-six dollars for stripping each cadaver, not a bad rate at all, not so bad. I've had worse.'

'Where did all this happen?'

'Downstairs from his hotel, in the cellar. But what happened when I started the job was really interesting, just really interesting.'

He stared at me as if his bright blue eyes would pop out of his grimy face, I was wondering if he was a hop-head, an addict, and in that case not the most believable witness. 'What happened then was that Mr Holmes went to get a dissection kit, rolled up his sleeves, put on an apron and got to work with a scalpel. He was good too, real efficient, stripping that meat from the bone like an expert, yessir.'

'What were these bodies like?' I asked.

'Women, both white, and both young – that struck me as odd you know because you'd see ten old cadavers or dead-beats for one fresh, young one. Both of these were right presentable women, the sort of women you'd touch your hat to in the street, very fresh cadavers too, it was a pleasure to work on them... there was a tall woman, fine looking...'

'How young,' I interrupted him, 'what sort of age?' Was this Georgiana's fate, to be cut up by this crazy man with his brilliant blue eyes and his dancing limbs?

He looked at the ceiling, 'The older one in her late twenties, the younger one maybe ten years younger,' he said.

'Could you give me a better description, distinguishing features, colour of hair?

'The tall one was a redhead,' I breathed a secret sigh of relief – not Georgiana. Was this Amelia, Holmes' secretary, who had been laid over the desk, *fornicatin' like a hog*?

'The younger one,' I said, 'Did she have pigtails?'

He shook his head, 'The hair was cut, maybe even shaved, it often is, you know, and the hair, you sell the hair to wigmakers. But I'd say she was blonde because of the hair you know, in other places.'

'Yes' I said sharply, this had already been as disgusting as I wanted it to get. I asked a few more questions, took his address and gave him five dollars, which he probably went off to spend on a few pipes in a Chinaman's den.

I'd had a long day but I was too anxious to eat, I lay on the hard, musty bed in my hotel room, staring up at the fan rotating against the peeling paintwork of the roof with the thoughts closing in on me. What if all the people who didn't stop to say goodbye became meat stripped from the bone and thrown in a bucket, Chapman and Holmes slicing away to reveal the gleaming skeleton sticky with blood? Slice and snip with the sharp silver tools until a presentable young woman, the sort you'd lift your hat to, is a grinning grotesque of white bone still flecked with red... My natural caution hauled me in, this was all supposition. Henry Holmes could have been doing legitimate business, even though it was business that made me sick to my stomach. I had no leads but this one, and my time was running out. Irresistibly I was driven to the conclusion: I needed evidence, and the only place to get it was back at the castle. I had to go in now. I leapt from the bed in a fever of resolve.

I borrowed a hurricane lamp from the hotel manager who passed it over without suspicion, as if he had had stranger requests. I went out into the streets, looking like the guy in the story who toured the streets with a lamp looking for an honest man. I got a cab across to Englewood through dark thoroughfares now cleared of people, the armies of clerks had all left their little coops of offices and were at home eating dinners of warmed-over fish left from the night before when they had had it fresh. The shutters were down on the shops and signs offered Wright's Indian Vegetable Pills or Alaska Down Bustles to no one in particular. My jaw was clenched and my limbs stiff with tension but I was not afraid. I was accounted very brave in my early years in the force, because of the dangers I was prepared to go into. Men with knives, bottles, shotguns, suicide risks from bridges, all that sort of thing Geyer would do when others would not. Actually I was neither brave nor foolhardy, I assessed risk without regard to my personal safety because I just didn't care if I was alive or dead.

Now I faced danger in the same way, calm and uncomplaining, though my hands shook as I used my pocket knife to open a weak back door at the back of Holmes' castle in Wallace Street. The dry wood around the latch splintered as I pulled it out and dived straight into the darkness, pulling the door behind me. I squatted in the dark and listened for noise. Nothing, just the distant clattering of horses' hooves. From the carpeted floor it seemed I was in a hallway, from the smell of old grease, I must be by the kitchens.

I lifted the hood on the lamp, struck a lucifer and lit a guttering yellow flame which pumped up to a bright luminescence. It revealed stained wallpaper and a red carpet stamped into blackness by the feet of waiters and kitchen hands, in front of me a corridor stretching into the dark. I walked along it, looking for a way down.

I quickly got the layout of the place from the inside. Shops on this floor had their doors opening on to the street; behind them the hotel kitchen and dining room, and upstairs the hotel rooms. After a few minutes of fumbling around the corridors I found what I wanted: a cellar door. I opened it and felt a fetid odour of damp and decay billowing up at me as I descended the creaking wooden stairway, the lamp throwing crazy angles of light into the dark, my heart beating hard with exertion and the excitement of daring. I leaned on a clammy brick wall and peered into the gloom where I could see the pillars that supported the building leading off until they became invisible. Above were rafters like the ribs of a dinosaur that had lain here millions of years ago and been encrusted with dirt and forgotten; under my feet was a beaten earth floor. I listened to the sounds: there was a dripping in the darkness where the light didn't penetrate, somewhere past the sentinels of pillars. The dank air filled my throat and nose with the smell of mildew and dissolution. '*Crepuscular... occultation*', I said quietly, as if naming the darkness could drive it back, '*nefandous night.*'

I began to walk, watching my feet for hidden dangers. I almost crashed into a wooden chute with a slide which descended from the ceiling. There were piles of clothes and other rubbish that I nervously stirred with my foot, in case anything had a human shape. I looked at the clothes for a while but they were too dirty and torn to make much out.

Pools of greater darkness in the dark showed something else at my feet - I gingerly approached and knelt down to see two pits perhaps six foot deep each, probably made by sinking galvanised tanks into the floor. By the smell they had contained quicklime, but now there was just sludge on the bottom, I saw a stick lying nearby and picked it up to poke the mess but something made me hesitate – the stick felt strangely light as if hollow. I looked again at it and dropped it in shock: it was a bone. Sickness rose within me at the thought of what I had touched and I looked up at the wooden rafters, gasping in misery at the awfulness of this lonely job. But this was evidence, here was something I must assess calmly. I was breathing shallowly, so as not to gulp into my lungs the putrefactive air. By my feet the earth was not beaten hard, it was soft as if recently disturbed. A little scratching on the ground, like the scratching of an animal, disclosed small fragments, white or brown, that I shook free of earth and dropped in my pocket, slowly and methodically, trying not to think about what I was doing. *'Fuliginous, penumbrant...'* I said.

I rose again to explore further, but now I was disorientated, trying to maintain equilibrium in this putrid hell. I stumbled on and found something white and angular. It was a table but a cold table, a marble-topped table. I didn't get it, what was a table doing here in the cellar? Who was sitting down to dinner here? I stroked across the smooth surface then found the runnels at the sides. My hand whipped back in an involuntary spasm and I let out a cry as I realised what it was: not a table for eating, but a slab. A mortuary slab. This was where Holmes and that crazy hop-head had cut up two fine women, the sort you'd lift your hat to. That smell, that grease underfoot showed he had told the truth, ghastly as it was.

I started to approach huge dark shapes which finally gave way to form the outlines of something familiar: a coal heap, a heating furnace. But next to the heating furnace, a door with a lock, another furnace, a lockable furnace what's the point of having a lock on a furnace? My fingers curled round the edge of the steel door and my throat tightened as if there wasn't enough air in the place. I held my breath, I had the sense that I wasn't alone, that somewhere in the darkness there was someone else. The light started to falter and I stared round wildly into the unknown as far as my fading vision would take me. I squatted to pump up the lamp, sweat running down my face despite the cold. I fumbled with the mechanism, my fingers refusing to obey. Darkness closed in on me as the lamp offered again a weak yellow flame and I struggled to work the lever, pulling with one hand and pushing with the flat of the other. Finally I had it, I relaxed, my eyes were dazzled with staring at the luminous core. I breathed a heavy sigh. A metallic click sounded out like a shot, I spun round as it echoed off the walls. It was a revolver, it was the sound of a revolver being cocked. I froze. Dive to the floor? Where could I go? I was the point of light which would attract the shot. I went to leap into the unknown, leaving the lamp, but I was too late. 'Good evening Frank' said a familiar voice. My heart stopped as I saw the small, elegant figure of Henry Holmes as if rising out of the dark.

He had approached me silently in the darkness and now stood in his business suit illuminated by my lamp with the light glinting off his watch chain. In his right hand he held a revolver outstretched towards me, the thumb of his left was implanted in his vest pocket.

'Well Frank, I am sorry our previous association did not teach you to have more respect for an old friend's property,' he said, as calmly and easily as if we met every day like this.

The sweat on my body froze. 'You can't get away with this Holmes,' I said, though my voice was faltering, 'the Chicago police know I'm here'

'They certainly do, Frank,' he said, still holding the revolver at arm's length, 'I have just telephoned them.' I believed him, telephones were good over short distances at this time, and a hotel would have had one. Great, now I would have to explain away the break-in.

'I want you back in Philadelphia,' I said, 'I have a warrant.'

'No immediate plans to revisit your lovely city, Frank,' he said.

'Where are the women who used to work with you and then disappeared - Amelia, Julia, Minnie?' I said.

'You have been busy looking into my affairs,' he said, still standing stock still with weapon outstretched, 'But it's you who need to be answering questions, not me Frank. We'll just wait for the police to come.'

I shivered in the icy cold, feeling impotent at my lack of ruses to use to trick him into incriminating himself.

'Zeus's father ate his children you know,' he said, absently, as if passing on some neighbourhood gossip in a grocery store.

I felt the words *'You're stark crazy'* come bubbling up but I didn't say them, Henry Holmes showed every evidence of being the sanest man I knew.

'Zeus's mother was unimpressed by this behaviour,' he continued, 'and she sought to protect her children. She wrapped a stone in the swaddling clothes the baby Zeus had lain in, and when father Cronos – that means time, you know – when old Cronos came to eat his newest son, he was tricked and ate the stone. Why didn't he know the difference? Must've had pretty queer digestion those ancient folks. Well Zeus was hidden in a cave, you see, a cave just like this one, and that's why I tell you this story,' and he looked around his subterranean domain, 'because this cave is just so like the cave where Zeus hid before he could grow big enough to return to earth to kill his father and set free all the other gods.'

'You're very clever, Henry,' I said, 'you're clever enough to know it will all be easier if you co-operate, you can't keep running.'

He didn't respond to this, except to say, 'Shall I sing you a song, let me do so.'

He started to sing in a voice not strong, but melodious enough, 'The road to the forest is plain to see
The river runs freely out to sea
Come all those who would be free
Who choose darkness come with me
Pleasure and plain are all the same
Streams that run through the dreams of man
Winter sunsets and leaves that fall
The glamour stays when the reason goes
Into the night go one and all
The silver girl and the golden girl...'

110

I stood gloomily through this queer exhibition, silently lamenting my plight. Henry had decided to keep talking in order to give away nothing, and in his position it was the right thing to do, I couldn't fault him on that. There was a commotion behind me and out of the gloom came two cops carrying night lights, a tall one and a short, stocky one who did all the talking. 'Bejesus what a stench, what's going on down here?' he said when he was in earshot.

'I am a cop and this is a wanted man,' I shouted excitedly as he was still yards away.

'This man broke into my property,' said Henry, at once in command of the situation, lowering his revolver and putting the catch on.

I went for my badge, but too quickly, 'Keep your hands where I can see them,' the cop shouted, and I obeyed, I didn't want to be hit over the head with a night-stick.

'I was just...' I said.

'Just don't you say anything, you can explain all that down at the station,' he brayed. I chafed at the humiliation, but at least Henry would be under control there.

Henry led us out, thanking the police for coming so quickly. 'I'll follow on in another cab after I've locked up,' he said.

'Alright Mr Holmes, we'll see you there,' the cop said, to my mounting horror. Was I to lose him again?

'He's got to come with us,' I shouted, my voice high with desperation now I realised what was happening.

'That's enough from you,' the cop said.

I had to make them understand, 'If you don't make him come with us we'll lose him, we'll never see him again,' I shouted over my shoulder as I was bundled into the wagon

'Hey, you're the one who's under arrest brother,' the fat cop snarled.

In the enclosed police wagon I smelled the odour of the horse, the wet tobacco smoke from the driver's pipe as we clattered through the streets, and said nothing to the cop opposite, fidgeting in his uncomfortable uniform. It was the first time I was in the position of prisoner, I didn't have a lot to say.

The roundsman raised his eyebrows when he saw my badge as he checked me in and ordered I should be taken to see Sergeant Norton. I was left in an office, sitting in front of a Bertillon cabinet for storing the vital measurements of criminals. I gloomily reflected on how I always used to say that would be very useful in detective work if the bad guys left such measurements as the distance between their nose and outstretched index finger handily at the crime scenes. But my set-piece of analysis on how fingerprinting was the crime detection system of the future was not called for here. Here I was playing the bad guy.

Norton was a man with a face like a bloodhound and no physiognomic evidence of high intelligence. He greeted me without ceremony, and sat impassively as I told him about the investigation; about Fidelity Mutual and what I had found in Holmes' castle: the chute which could take a body, the lime pits, the mortuary slab, the clothes, 'They were complete sets of clothes, not just dresses, as you might think, but dress, chemise, petticoat, stockings, as if they had been taken off people who were wearing them all, not just rags.'

Norton looked at me warily, as if in criticism for taking such an interest in women's clothing. 'Mr Holmes is a respectable businessman,' he said finally.

'Yeah, I get it,' I said understanding the drift of his remarks, 'a friend to the police, a little packet of dollars every year for the Christmas party; the back door left on the latch so the beat cop can come in at night and have a warm; hotel kitchen always willing to make up a sandwich for a hungry cop...'

'Don't tell me what police work is like in Philadelphia, Geyer, it's here you're in trouble,' he barked.

'I've got a warrant for Holmes' arrest,' I said.

'So you said,' he snapped, 'for insurance fraud. Well you should have come with that warrant to us and we would have helped you execute it.'

'I was looking for Holmes,' I said, 'Anyway, that's a holding warrant, the fraud in Philadelphia involved a murder, and like I said, I suspect him of many more murders which have taken place right here in Chicago.'

'But what evidence do you have for that? You've already said there's a reasonable explanation for the presence of cadavers, Mr Holmes is a medical man, why would he advertise for help with dissecting bodies if what he was doing was illegal? In my experience people committing murders like to conceal the bodies.'

'That's what he wants you to think,' I said, almost pleading, and Norton looked away in exasperation. *Evidence*, I said to myself, *he wants evidence*. I looked at my hands and remembered digging in the soft earth. The bones, how could I have forgotten the bones?

'I've got evidence I found in Holmes' cellar,' I said, thrusting my hand into my pocket and pulling out a handful of white bones. I scattered them on the desk between us. 'I picked these up not two hours ago in Holmes' basement.'

Norton pushed the bones around with the end of his pencil, then went to the door and called a colleague to come over. Norton and the other man each looked at some of the bones. To my slowly dawning dismay, even to my eye they didn't seem right.

'I don't claim to be an expert,' said Norton's colleague, 'but I've had some experience and they don't look like human bones to me. Maybe a dog.'

It was the first time I had seen them in the light. 'But this...' I said, suddenly lost for words, 'this looks like a human knuckle bone, and here's another... Norton, you've been taken in: Holmes has mixed animal and human bones together for concealment. Explain away one bone and it looks like you can explain away them all.' I was like a man slithering over a cliff and clutching at tree roots. They looked at me with something between pity and contempt, that a policeman could sink so low.

The other man left and Norton settled down in his leather chair as if resolving to perform a distasteful task, 'Look, Geyer,' he said, 'we've cabled Philadelphia to check up your story and we've put in a call to Fidelity Mutual. Neither of them have responded, probably because it's too late for office work. Mr Holmes hasn't yet come in to press charges, so I'm going to keep you here overnight, to give Mr Holmes a chance.'

'He won't,' I said, 'he's got away again.'

Norton didn't respond to this and I was led off. For the first time I saw the inside of a holding cell with the door closed. I sat down and looked at my hands. I, who pride myself on my restraint, had lost control. What was worse, I had once more lost Henry Holmes. I lay down on a hard bench and tried to rest but my mind was raging through the night. What was Holmes doing now? In another state already, I would guess, perhaps at home. At home with who? With Myrta? With Georgiana? In a house with carpets in every room bathed in the smell of apples and fresh cut flowers. How welcome he would be, and how tenderly he would look in at the little children, sleeping in their beds. I seethed at the deceit of it. I'd find Georgiana and tell her about Myrta, tell her she loved a bigamist, that would wipe the innocent smile from her face. But in the end it was my problems I had to groan over. What would happen to me now? I stayed contained within my own shell of sorrow as the derelicts and casual robbers were brought in, filling the cell with the smell of poverty and old drunk.

By about nine in the morning I was getting restive, as my bleary-eyed comrades in misery were being packed off to appear in court, the drunks to ritually receive the sentence of a night in the cells, which justice had already been accorded them, the robbers to be charged. Eventually Norton called me in. He looked not much better than my cell-mates.

'Mr Holmes hasn't come in, he clearly doesn't want to press charges,' he said wearily, 'We cabled Philadelphia and your story checks out, so you can go. But if you want to do any police work in this city, just come to us first.'

I nodded a grudging acceptance that he had let me go, 'There's something else,' he said, 'Your Chief O'Brien says you've got to go back to Philadelphia. Here it is,' he read it out, "Tell Geyer return city hall immediately O'Brien" would you like this cable?'

'I think I can remember it,' I said. Would I even have a job to return to? I was given back my lamp and carried it ridiculously into the daylight of the street. I was unshaven and looking like, well looking like I'd spent a night in the cells. As I was leaving the police station Ed Cass, the last person I wanted to see, leapt out of a cab and raced towards me. It was just what I didn't need, his questions and his puppy-dog enthusiasm, peering from his clean and simple life into the nest of thorns which surrounded my heart.

'So you're out then?' he panted.

'Looks like it,' I said.

'They checked with my office. The police checked with my office,' he said indignantly, 'How could you? I mean, we have to work with these guys.'

I tried to make light of it, looking over his head at the crush of advertising signs, Cass was irritating me, 'Well, I'm sorry, these things happen.'

'No they don't just happen,' he said, his eyes crackling with fire, 'I brought you here and you are giving us a bad name.'

'Yeah, well I've said I'm sorry,' I said, then using the conspiratorial voice of experience which had worked so well before with Cass I said, 'I've been in worse scrapes.'

'Great,' he said, refusing the bait, 'but you haven't taken Fidelity Mutual along with you. I can't believe this is happening I can't believe I am seeing you like this. How did you get arrested?' His face was a mask of outrage.

I gritted my teeth and told him briefly about seeing Mrs Van Tassel, and the skeleton articulator, and meeting Holmes in his cellar.

'And that couldn't wait?' He was right, I should have waited, I didn't reply. 'I've come over to bail you out,' he said, 'I trusted you, and I respected you, and now I've got to come and get you out of the goddam cells.'

'I am sorry,' I said, 'I mean it. That wasn't right, I mean it didn't happen like it was supposed to... I'll do what I can to clear it with your boss, anything that went wrong was all my fault.'

Cass listened impassively, 'There is more to this' he said menacingly, 'How well do you know this guy Holmes?'

My blood froze. I said, 'I knew him way back, in Gilmanton,' but my tone could hardly have been less convincing.

'How well did you know Holmes?' he shouted, his face red, 'What have you got against him? This isn't all police work, is it? Who is this Georgiana Yoke woman? Is she the cause of all this? Just how stupid do you think I am Geyer?' I looked big, unshaven, a lumbering bear on the sidewalk while this sleek-coated fox flashed around me.

'Yeah,' I said resignedly, beaten to the ground, 'I should've told you earlier. Georgiana was my girl, Holmes was my best friend, they went off together.'

'Jeez,' said Cass, taking his hat off and mopping his brow, 'Jee-sus.'

There was a long silence between us while the sounds of the carters and the cabbies harrying their beasts continued in the street, 'How did you find out?' I said.

'When I was away you used Fidelity Mutual cables to get the Pinkerton Agency to find out about Holmes' marriage to this woman, and to try to trace her.'

'I can cover the cost,' I said meekly

'It's not the cost of the damned cables,' he exploded, 'it's using Fidelity Mutual facilities to pursue some private quest, it's taking me for a fool.'

I didn't have much of a choice. I could get angry and storm off or I could get humble and apologise. I stuck with that. 'I should have told you Ed, I should have told you it all,' I said, 'but I thought I could keep these things separate. Holmes was a real bad guy, there was no reason why he should get away just because I had a grudge against him. Then you asked for me personally when you got the tip off about Hegepeth and the insurance scheme.'

Cass observed my imploring tone dispassionately, 'Anything else I should know?' he asked.

'No,' I said, 'no more secrets. I've been called back to Philadelphia anyhow, so we won't be working together. Maybe I won't even get to keep my job.'

Cass nodded regretfully, 'I'll get you breakfast,' he said, and we went over to a shack where they served fresh rolls and steaming coffee in full view of the bustle of people going about their business. The food was welcome, I had forgotten how long it had been since I last ate.

'So what did you find out?' I asked with a mouthful of roll and butter.

'They were real helpful in Texas,' said Cass, 'the picture is roughly what it had been here, Holmes arrived in Fort Worth to secure a loan of $16,000 on property owned by one Minnie Williams, which he had the deeds for, signed by her. No one ever saw Minnie Williams, or her sister Nannie, just Holmes who said he was her agent. He started building another castle, another three-storey building with a hotel and storefronts.'

'I guess he was going to build them all over the USA,' I said resentfully, 'a real business empire. In a year or two he'd be as rich as Vanderbilt or Morgan and then we'd never be able to touch him.'

'He got material and work on credit,' Cass continued, 'but met some pretty tough cookies in Texas, and they started pressing real hard for payment. He had a meeting of his creditors that he had to make a quick getaway from, hence the "larceny of one horse".' I smiled grimly, relishing the scene of Holmes at last on the run. 'I've got a Texas warrant for that offence anyway, just in case we have trouble holding our man when we get him again.'

I held my head in my hands, 'If we get him again,' I said.

I looked at Cass nervously, 'No one needs to know about my previous connection with Holmes do they?' I said.

'It doesn't look so good for me if they do,' Cass replied, 'so it hasn't happened. It wasn't there. OK?' I thanked him and left him to return to my hotel and clean up before I trudged sorrowfully to Union Station where I had arrived with such hope barely a week before.

I suppose it was on the train that the reality of my situation presented itself in stark clarity: Holmes had finally beaten me. The best I could hope for when I got back would be a demotion to uniform, pounding the beat again. This was the future then, which had given me such hope: trains, steam carriages, gasoline-driven carriages, maybe even flying carriages, electric telephones, all the things I'd dreamed of we now had, things I'd talked excitedly to Georgiana and Henry about. But my future wasn't all that, it was an endless descent. Every time I thought I'd reached the bottom, there was another place to go down. He had stripped me of love, self-respect and now my job, mechanically taking it all away like the flesh from a skeleton.

I went to the end car and stood there in the open as the darkened shapes of the countryside flashed past me. I gripped my knuckles to my mouth to stop myself shouting out. Why could I still not understand it? What was Georgiana doing with this homicidal maniac? How could she dare to spend one minute in his company? Had I died inside for the love of a woman I didn't even know?

Chicago 1892

Holmes was leading a man with a walrus moustache into the cellar, taking him down the creaking stairs, holding a lamp.

'Of course we are going to have electricity down here,' he said, 'this hotel will have every modern convenience, but the guests must come first.'

His companion, a mature man wearing a suit, looked uncomfortably out of place on the stairs of the dark cavern.

Holmes watched the somewhat portly man waddle down the wooden stairway as he extended an arm as if to help him down the last few steps.

He kept up a continuous crackle of talk, 'Your inspection is very welcome, sir, I always had the utmost respect for the insurance industry...'

The man followed Holmes through the forest of pillars to a large brick and iron structure, like an outhouse with an iron door large enough for a man to walk through. 'It's the most modern range,' said Holmes, 'an up-to date-appliance in keeping with every scientific development of the present age.'

'It looks,' said the inspector, 'like a furnace.'

'Yessir, an oil burning furnace, made to the highest specifications.'

The man snorted, 'Looks like a cremation furnace to me,' he said.

Holmes put his head to one side and assumed a serious expression, 'it was the people in that line of business,' he said, 'who developed the finest contrivances for conveying heat,' he said, 'that I improved with some adaptations of my own, to make it a heating furnace, let me show you these improvements.'

He opened the iron door, 'If you will just step inside and let me show you...'

The walrus-moustached man walked towards the door but stopped to gauge the height of the furnace.

'Just step inside...' repeated Holmes, 'inside is where all the real work is taking place.'

Holmes held open the door and the portly inspector made to go in, but thought better of it. 'I can see pretty well out here,' he said

'Oh, you don't need to go all the way in, there's just something I would like you to see,' said Holmes, 'just put your head around here.' Holmes stood in the door beckoning his companion eagerly.

The man advanced a step, looked at Holmes, then pulled a gold watch on the end of a chain from his side pocket, 'Think I'd better be heading back...'

Holmes picked up a wrench and looked down on it as if he were inspecting it for blemishes. 'Of course,' he said, 'Would you like to return to the stairs?' Holmes gestured for the inspector to go ahead. The man turned towards the darkness, Holmes tightened his grip on the wrench.

The fat man turned, 'I'd rather you go first, Mr Holmes, I can see better that way.'

Holmes shrugged, put down the wrench, and held the lamp in front of him as he ascended the creaking stairs with the insurance man behind him.

Chapter 9

Philadelphia 1894

I was bruised from a night of agitation when the locomotive pulled into the station. I didn't want a rest, didn't want to see Molly, I had nothing for her. I didn't go to her place or to McQueen's to tell her I'd got back. I went direct to City Hall, unable to fix on anything, moving like an automaton, having no words now to express my feelings. I just had to go through the procedures now, nothing I did could any longer affect what would happen to me. I wasn't deciding any more, it was just things happening, it was just being. I washed and shaved in the soap-encrusted mirror of the locker room and gave a moody greeting to my colleagues who were talking about the election. I was away for the election, but taking a bet on the outcome was, anyhow, a standing joke: the Republicans always got in. The assessors' list of voters was packed with the names of dogs, children, non-existent and dead people. The signers of the declaration of independence, the fathers of American liberty, first voted in Philadelphia and every election they voted again, or at least their names did, swelling the rolls of the electorate with further fiction in the Republican cause. That was politics in this city, so I gave it all the attention it deserved.

I walked briskly up to O'Brien's office and knocked. He looked up, 'Oh it's you,' he said, 'Let's go.' He threw on his jacket as we went down the corridor. O'Brien was a man of few words, unusual for an Irishman, but I was being treated to almost no words at all today, which deepened my gloom. I guess they thought there was nothing to do but get rid of me with the shortest ceremony possible.

We stamped down the panelled corridor to the elevator. I didn't even acknowledge people we passed, I was headed for execution and in no mood for pleasantries. I guessed we were going to the superintendent's office but we went on and up, and eventually O'Brien knocked on the door of the Director of Public Safety and announced us to two female secretaries. Even in my numbed state I was shocked – was what I had done so bad I had to face the highest police authority in the city? Were they going to make some kind of an example of me?

We both walked over the thick carpet into a room of rich, dark wood with wide windows showing a panorama of the city, and a desk the size of a bed. Behind it sat an energetic looking man in his vest and shirtsleeves, with a black moustache and hair just beginning to grey at the temples. This was not the Candyman, the election must have replaced him. 'Good morning gentlemen,' he said to us as we stood to attention on the other side of his desk. This was a surprise, he was almost genial, was this a refined kind of torment? 'Please sit down.'

He finished what he was writing and turned it over onto his blotter, lifting it up to make sure it was dry before placing it in a wire tray to his right. Clearly a methodical man, who liked to take his time and see things done right. 'I'm very glad to see you, Mr O'Brien, Mr Geyer. Now,' he said, placing both hands palm downwards on his desk, 'you'll find me showing more interest in some aspects of police work than my predecessor did.' He was as alert as a hare, constantly glancing round the room to check if anything had changed since he last looked, gauging our faces and movements for our response to his words, his bony hands first touching fingertips then clenching knuckles one after the other, never at rest.

'I am, as Mr O'Brien will know, but you perhaps won't, Mr Geyer, James T. Honeycutt. I have spent the days since the election assessing some of the work currently being undertaken in the Bureau of Police and I am very happy to see how seriously Chief O'Brien and yourself have taken the matter of insurance fraud. I worked in insurance for twenty five years, starting as a boy, and there is very little you can tell me about it, but seeing your reports Mr Geyer has shown me a new level of depravity in criminal undertakings calculated to defraud the insurance business on a large scale.'

The room was very silent. It was hard for me to stop my

twitching mouth from cracking into a wide grin, or even bursting into hysterical laughter. For once when the wheel had turned I had come out on top. This was why O'Brien didn't want to speak to me, he didn't want to acknowledge that I was right.

Honeycutt continued, 'In the past these crimes have been a matter for the companies themselves, often aided by privately hired detectives. Sometimes they would do deals with the criminals to recover stolen goods. This must stop. These are not private matters but ones which affect the security of our society as a whole. The full resources of the Bureau of Police must be made available for these investigations.'

He invited me to tell my story from the beginning. I did, all the way from the body in the Callowhill Street house. I even said I'd known Holmes in my youth. I mentioned his two marriages, but not my relationship to Georgiana. I told him what I knew, and what I believed to be true, and what I suspected about the dungeon of horrors under the castle. Honeycutt listened intently to my tale, like it was straight from the Arabian Nights, making periodic ejaculations of 'shame!' and 'I never did hear such a thing!' He was the most appreciative audience I had ever had. When I reached the story about my apprehension by the Chicago police, where I feared I would lose his sympathy, he burst out, 'If a city could be built out of corruption it would be named Chicago!'

When I walked out of there it was to order the autopsy on Pitezel which had been held up by the coroner; to order that Mrs Pitezel be brought to Philadelphia for questioning and to wire Cass to let him know I was back. I never breathed sweeter air than I did that night, when I whistled out on to Broad Street on my way to Molly at the Suicide Hall after that long day of writing reports and sending cables.

The next day I stood in a square tent on Potter's Field while labourers dug into the moist earth, sod by sod down to the coffin, their breath making clouds in the cool morning. Soon Benjamin Pitezel, B.F. Perry dealer in patents, one half of the Yates Campbell Manufacturing Corporation, husband and father, now very dead, rose again. Con-man redivivus. The box creaked heavily as it was hauled up with a winch before being carried, in a bizarre reversal of the funeral process, to the square, green tent where we would jemmy open the lid to reveal Ben's bloated form.

The putrefaction was masked by the oppressively fresh smell of carbolic acid and turpentine sprayed in the air to keep the flies down, but there was no mistaking the smell of death. Pitezel was lifted up by the gravediggers and placed on a table. He lay blackly with one eye closed as if winking at us in acknowledgement of a conspiracy, his swollen lips giving a clownish, pouting expression.

'Can you be sure, Mr Geyer, that this was the body you found in the Callowhill Street building and which was given up for burial after identification?' Dr Scott said out of the corner of his mouth, watching the corpse as if frightened it might get away,

'Yes,' I said. 'I'm sure.'

Dr Scott's assistant cut off the damp clothes with steel scissors, sharpened to surgical perfection, and the morbidly discoloured body of a man was revealed, well built but running to fat, a fact discernible even given the decay.

The assistant sat on a bench next to the wide-mouthed bottles he had brought and made notes as the doctor intoned, 'This is the body of a well nourished individual, around six foot and 180 pounds, with no external signs of bleeding or physical damage indicating a struggle or the cause of death. There is moderately advanced putrefaction consistent with burial for a length of time.' He had the body turned over and conducted a close examination, his face inches from the bloated flesh, as he passed from head to foot, stopping to open the buttock cheeks to examine the anus. *'Putrilage,'* I thought.

He had the body turned on its back again, the gravediggers making light of the cumbersome weight, and again made a minute study, staying close to the surface of the body. 'There are marks of a corrosive substance on the lips and in the mouth,' he said, as if addressing the remarks to Ben himself, 'by its smell I'd say chloroform. I'm conducting an internal examination.'

He opened up the body from chin to pubis with such deft knife-work it seemed the dull red slit he created down the front of the corpse could so simply be reversed, the edges of the gash joined up like a Judson zipper and the body would be whole again.

The doctor intoned, 'I'm placing a ligature round the lower end of the oesophagus – that's so the stomach will not lose its contents, Mr Geyer. I am also ligating the stomach at its lower extremity, and removing it complete.' He placed the grey bag, curling round on itself, in an enamel dish. Into jars with glass stoppers went the spleen, the liver, and both kidneys. 'Considerable cirrhotic hardening of the liver,' he said as he passed the organ over, 'consistent with a history of hard drinking.' He gave the organs to the assistant, who pasted the carefully prepared labels and stuck them on the bottles. The procedure was so slow and methodical it took on an air of ritual, as if I was witnessing a scene from ancient Egypt, the slow placing into jars of the organs from the body cavity.

'I am going into the chest,' Dr Scott said, 'and removing the thoracic organs.' He pulled open the mouth and the flashing silver knife worked inside to cut the tongue from its moorings. I am not squeamish by nature, but I was glad I had skipped breakfast that morning. Scott struggled to free the trachea and oesophagus and presently out came the whole bundle, a slimy grey mass of tubes and flesh like a stranded octopus.

'Corrosion' Scott intoned, 'destruction of tissue around the oesophageal region consistent with the ingestion of a corrosive substance. Severe inflammation around the mouth, but corrosion further down. Let's see what's in the stomach. He sliced open the bag of the stomach to let the murky contents spill out into a square bowl and stood back to look at it as if he had done something great, 'As I thought,' he said, 'chloroform - it doesn't mix well with water, see, I'd say we have chloroform and alcohol here.'

'What happened?' I asked, 'can you say what happened?' The assistant looked at me as if shocked that I should interrupt the great practitioner in the process of making his art, but Dr Scott answered coolly enough, holding his hands up with the fingers outstretched towards his neck as if considering strangling himself, 'I'd say this man was rendered unconscious with alcohol, and perhaps then anaesthetised with chloroform – which would accounts for the barely visible burns around the mouth. Then chloroform is introduced into the throat, perhaps poured in, perhaps someone used a tube pushed into the throat and a funnel held above him. But you can see with a transverse section of the oesophagus' and he picked up the cut morsel to show me the slimy, half tunnel, 'this corrosion doesn't start till some way in. Ergo it was introduced at that point, presumably with a tube,' and he smiled a pat little smile. 'Now I must get on.'

At length I walked away from the tent through the green of the graveyard, rubbing my hands as if to shake off dirt though I had touched nothing foul, and my clothing was covered with droplets from the carbolic spray, like dew. So my early suspicions about chloroform were vindicated, and I had at least one proof that Holmes was a killer.

Back at City Hall I enjoyed a reunion with Edward Cass, he was almost as bright and full of ideas as ever, though he had a wariness about him now, as if I wouldn't recover trust so easily once lost, and I sometimes caught him watching me out of the corner of his eye, as if afraid I would do something stupid.

Our first task was the interrogation of Mrs Ben Pitezel, Carrie Pitezel, brought from Chicago for the purpose. She was a nervous, sniffly little woman who spent the interview twisting a rag of a handkerchief this way and that, such a state of a woman you wondered why nature didn't just give up on her and start again with someone else.

Cass sat next to me as I questioned her. I went in boldly, 'You are in trouble Mrs Pitezel, you are accused of being a party to a conspiracy to cheat and defraud an insurance company.' She gave a whimpering squeal and tore at her handkerchief more fiercely. 'But it doesn't have to be so bad,' I said, 'because we don't think you are really wicked, we want to get to Henry Holmes, if that is the name by which you know him.'

'Yes,' she whined, 'I know him.' She wore a dark blue dress which showed the stains of feeding a small child.

'How well do you know Mr Holmes?' I asked.

'Oh very well, he was always at our house, coming to see my

husband'

'Did you hear what they talked about?'

'No he would ask my Ben out into the courtyard, they wouldn't talk business in front of me. I always pleaded with my Ben not to join Mr Holmes but he was led away. Mr Holmes was good to us but...' she mused, but trailed off.

'You are saying you didn't know anything? But you had to be in on this scheme, to get money from the insurance company, didn't you?' She denied this for fifteen minutes in her dim-witted way, but later saw sense and admitted a limited role in the scheme.

'I was just told,' she said, 'that when we was contacted regarding a body, we should say it was my husband. This is what Alice had to do, whatever body they showed her, she had to say it was her daddy.'

'And who told you this?'

'Mr Holmes told me, told me over and over again.'

'Did you ever see any of the money from the scheme?' I asked.

'Why yes,' she said, her eyes black points of light in the swollen red, 'I saw it. I saw a bank draft. He got a wire, he said, saying he could pick it up, after Mr Holmes and Alice had gone to Philadelphia. The lawyer came to give it to me.'

'Mr Howe?'

'Yes,' she said miserably, sorry she had given away so much but perhaps resigned to letting it all out now. 'He had about seven thousand dollars – such a lot of money,'

'The insurance was for ten thousand,' I said.

'He took some,' she said, 'because he was owed some of it, Ben owed him some of it, Ben always owed everyone money, always people coming round our door asking for money... and there was expenses.'

'So is that what you received, seven thousand dollars?' I said, interested that this stupid woman could still do reckoning, even though she was incapable of keeping the money in her own hands.

'Well no,' she said, looking at me as if it was I who was foolish, 'Mr Holmes told me my Ben had a half-interest in a property in Texas,' I glanced at Cass.

'...and he said, Mr Holmes said, unless we made another payment on the mortgage we would lose it altogether, but if we paid it I would get the rents on the property, lots of money for the rest of my life and for the children's future, so I signed to have $5000 paid into a bank.'

'Did you receive any money from the rents?' I asked for the record, I knew very well what the answer would be.

'Noooo,' she squealed and pressed her sodden handkerchief to her face.

'OK. Mrs Pitezel,' I said, 'so Howe took his cut immediately, then five thousand went to Holmes, where did the rest of the money go, just short of $2,500?'

'Well, Mr Holmes needed his share as agreed with Ben, it should have been more but he only took $1,700, so he wouldn't leave me and the children short, he was good like that, you see. Then there was expenses to pay, so many expenses, and I was left with just over $500.'

So that's all you got for your husband, I thought scornfully, but then corrected myself. Holmes had defrauded me of more for less return.

'Travelling round to meet Mr Holmes, trying to get to see Ben. There was a lot of expenses...' she trailed off as she had a tendency to do. It seems that she had seen Holmes once to give him the money, and then at least twice after, in Indianapolis and Detroit.

'I wish to ask you one question direct,' I said, 'do you believe now that your husband is alive?'

'Well, there must be something in it,' she muttered, 'I am sure I could not swear to it for I don't know for a fact that he is alive. All I know is what you have been telling me, and what Mr Holmes has been telling me, that is all I know.'

'Have you had confidence in Mr Holmes all along, that he would finally take you to your husband?'

'Why, I thought so.' It may have been, curiously enough, that this was the first time she had been obliged to think about exactly that question.

'Has your confidence ever been shaken?'

'Well, sometimes I thought maybe he was fooling me... I have just been heartbroken, that is all there is about it...' and she started crying in full flood.

This was wearing our patience and not getting us very far in the investigation. I tried a gentler tone, 'We are not doing anything to undertake to make you feel bad,' I said, 'we are trying to get to the matter and sift it. Holmes has kept you moving about the country from point to point and you look as though you have been through a good deal. We want to get all the light on this we can.' She looked downcast, as if too much light would make her wither up, 'We don't believe in Holmes very much. That is why we are asking you these questions.'

She held her hands together around her handkerchief, looked at the floor and then was silent a minute to make sure I had finished with my lecture, then said, 'Can I see my children now?'

'What?' Cass and I said together.

'Don't you have my children here?'

We both shook our heads and she said, 'Mr Holmes went off with Alice and Nellie and Howard. I thought you would have them here. Don't you know where they are? I want to see them.' She looked from one face to another.

It is not practice in a police interrogation to look as if you don't know what is happening, but that is how me and Cass looked then. Mrs Pitezel caught our uncertainty and fully realised, for the first of many, many times, the hopelessness of her situation. The whining subsided and gave way as we watched a chasm, an abyss of despair, a face of mute agony I hope I never see again.

Before we had coaxed the story out of her, now it came all in a flood. It turned out she'd been talking about the children all the time to the cop who accompanied her from Chicago. She had just assumed that we had got Holmes and had got the children with him and the game was up and we were just building up a case against Holmes. The officer who'd brought her knew nothing about our investigation and didn't contradict her.

The story we deciphered from what she now told us gave a little more of what Holmes did when he left us in Philadelphia after identifying Ben Pitezel. He didn't go straight back to Chicago as he said he would, he went somewhere else, because when he arrived at Chicago Union station to meet with Mrs Pitezel, he didn't have Alice with him. *All those people*, I thought involuntarily, *who didn't stop to say goodbye*.

Carrie Pitezel had already been brought the money by Jeptha Howe who deposited it in a bank for her. In Chicago, in the station diner, she and Holmes divided up the money as she had described it before–or to put it more accurately it was there that she'd been smartly cheated of it. Holmes had cabled her to tell her she must bring two children so he could take them to their father. She had with her Nellie, who was eleven, and Howard, who was seven, 'they went with him when he left.' Howard was a favourite of Holmes, he had even been named after Holmes – or had been named after one of his fake names. The mother thought she was going to see Alice, but Holmes said Alice was already in Indianapolis with her father. She had a few letters from them but nothing after that. Holmes had seen her a couple of times, and given her letters from the children and taken hers to them, but she never knew where they were, and her last contact was more than a month ago.

'He said Dessie should come with him too, she's my oldest daughter, she's sixteen, but I told him I needed her to stay to help me take care of the baby, and he said that was alright, we could all come together later.'

Once she had reached this point I listened in silence. Her voice in the small interview room bounced thinly off the green painted walls and cheap official furniture. I motioned Cass outside and ordered an attendant to get refreshments for Carrie Pitezel. Suddenly I felt old again while Cass looked young and fresh and full of excitement.

'Why'd he take Alice away?' Cass said, arguing his way through the case like a detective in a storybook, 'he had to, she was the only one who knew her father was really dead and it wasn't a substitute corpse.'

I almost grasped his lapels in frustration, 'So why take the others?' I said sharply.

'Maybe... maybe an insurance policy... a ransom,' Cass suggested, 'against the probability that he'll be caught he can give the children back if we do a deal.'

'Maybe,' I said, knowing in my heart it was wrong. Holmes didn't plan to get caught, he wasn't like us: he didn't know the meaning of failure.

I shook my head and turned away from Cass as I pressed my closed fist so hard on the wall it hurt. Once more, just one more time, Henry Holmes had completely dumbfounded me, had wrong-footed me, had left me sprawling on the canvas to get up again and punch at a shadow. I was clumsy, gauche, ursine. Now he had those children too, all I knew was that we had to find them.

Chapter 10

We let Mrs Pitezel stay in a remand cell, not the general cell where she would have had to mix with midwife abortionists and girls gone wrong. She had suffered enough and was in danger of losing her reason over the fate of her children. Her stupidity made the interviews an exercise in frustration, not helped by her reluctance to talk about the schemes her husband and Holmes had been in. I can't say we weren't moved to pity by the sight of the wretched woman still trying to shield him, as if she might betray the trust of a man I had seen lifeless and decomposing only the day before.

We were weary with it but at the end of the day we went for a coffee in the City Hall canteen. 'So what's happened to them?' Cass asked, 'Who takes children? Even a double-dyed criminal like Holmes, why go off with a bunch of children. Is there,' he strained at the unthinkable, 'is there a *market* in children?'

'Nah,' I said, though I could see he was sceptical, 'Look, all that stuff about the white slave trade, it's a story dreamed up by newspaper editors to sell their papers. You get girls sometimes lured to the city with a promise that they're going to get to be in a vaudeville show, they sign a contract, and they end up in a bordello working to pay off their travel and living expenses to the pimp who ruined them. That happens, but those are grown up girls. You get kids working in sweatshops who should be in school, but I never heard of a case like this, kids just taken away and their mother doesn't know where they are. Where kids are sold to do work they shouldn't, it's usually the mother who does the selling. There are kidnappings but this isn't one, no ransom note, and there's no money in this case that Holmes hasn't got by other means.

Cass looked pensive, like a man wondering which horse to bet on when he knew nothing about them but their names. I had no further guidance either, I couldn't tell him why Holmes had done it. All I knew was, with an insistent urgency like hunger, we'd got to find those kids.

'So what's our best chance of finding him?' asked Cass finally, 'Following this trail that's two months old?'

I nodded, 'It's sure easier to look for a man with three kids than a man on his own. Plus, I'm worried about them. I want to find them... before they come to harm.' My words fell out tonelessly, I didn't have a lot of doubt that they had come to harm already.

We fell to looking at the facts. Ed Cass busied himself with the calculations, his pink hand gripping a pencil that filled the pages of a blank book with dates and figures. 'We saw Homes on September 5,' he said, 'with Alice Pitezel. He saw Mrs Pitezel on the eighth in Chicago, and he didn't have Alice with him, but he took the other two children. So where did he go?'

'How far could he have gone?' I said, 'in time to lose Alice, whatever way he did that, and appear in Chicago three days later? Where were there trains running that afternoon after he left us? My guess is he could have only gone back a short distance, say to New York, before he turned around to get to Chicago in time. But more likely is he went to a place between Philadelphia and Chicago, left Alice there – with someone, I hope – and then went on to Chicago to fleece Mrs Pitezel of the rest of her money. Then he saw her again in Indianapolis, to get her signature on the Fort Worth papers, so he was still moving round the mid-West a month later...'

'So what have we got,' said Cass, 'the train timetables, and that letter, the one Holmes delivered to Mrs Pitezel from Alice. He told Carrie Pitezel that Alice was in St Louis with her dad, but I guess if there's one place we know she wouldn't have been that's it.'

We went back to the office to look at the letter. It was a single page of blotted white paper, written on both sides in a child's hand, with slow deliberation but not without a certain expressiveness in the use of language. The excitement of travel showed through, so that commonplace events took on the air of adventure, 'Yesterday we got on the C & O Pullman car and it was crowded so I had to sit with someone. Mr Holmes sit with some man, we sit there quite awhile. Mr Holmes is alright but I don't like him to call me babe and child and dear and all such trash.' She seemed to have stopped writing here, only to recommence sometime later, in a hotel of some kind, 'I wish I had a silk dress. I have seen more since I have been away than I ever saw before in my life. There is so many buggies go by that you cant hear yourself think. I first wrote you a letter with a crystal pen but I made some mistakes and then I am in a hustle because Mr H has to go out at 3 o'clock I don't know where. It is all glass so I hafto be careful or else it will break, it was only five cents. There is more bicycles go by here in one day than goes by in a month at home.'

I could see the shape of evil hovering above the child's cacography. 'So it's a city,' I said.

Cass wrote our suppositions down as he spoke, 'A city served by Pullmans, and I guess a hotel not a boarding house. A hotel in a busy street, near the centre of the city.'

'Good for trains,' I said, 'like they say in the ads, a convenient staging post for anywhere in the United States. They could be anywhere.'

My pessimism was irritating Cass, 'I know what you think of this man, Frank,' he says, 'but why d'you think we'll never find them? Alice was alive to write this letter and it doesn't look like it was written under duress.'

I strained at this. 'Maybe to calm any fears Mrs Pitezel might have, or she wouldn't hand over the money... but you're right, we'll find them... we'll find them wherever they are.'

'They couldn't be just anywhere either,' he said, the first time he had directly contradicted me, 'The last part's a real clue, "Mr H says we can go to the zoological gardens and see all the different kind of animals, theres a fountain here be the height of a big tall building that you have to look into the sky to see it. I will have to close for this time now so good bye and kisses and love to all, Your daughter." So what cities between Philadelphia and Chicago have got a zoo and a fountain?'

He was right, I acknowledged, it could get us somewhere. We asked around the office to find who knew what about other cities and soon we had our own departmental gazetteer. All the cities had a zoo, or at least a menagerie that a child might call a zoo.

Most had a fountain of some kind, but only Cincinnati had both, a big sized fountain and a big sized zoo, and there was a train on the Dayton and Columbus line going out an hour after Holmes and Alice had identified Ben Pitezel in the dead house. There were other trains, other destinations we considered, but in the end we set off to Cincinnati, ploughing through the countryside, uncertain searchers after a moving target.

Cass and I looked pensively out of the window throughout the journey, rehearsing in spurts of conversation the mysteries of time and travel on the eastern rail network and the practical difficulties of moving children around. We leaned forward in anticipation as we approached the city. The Pullman chugged through the stockyards where the open doorways of warehouses showed row upon row of racked pink bodies. Signs offered 'Extra Sugar Cured Hams' or announced a company's prowess as 'Slaughterers, packers and dealers in live and dressed hogs.' From some of the yards came a whine, a sound of a thousand squeals merged into one, arising from the writhing pink mass of backs and tails and ears as hoards of pigs were herded into the halls. Men in bloodied white aprons carried huge stiff carcasses on their shoulders or loaded scores of legs or backs onto barrows. Once, more alarmingly, I saw a barrow loaded with heads, glassy-eyed ranks of limp-featured pigs stacked bloodily row upon row on top of each other. Closer to the city it was quieter and just the thump thump of steam machines could be heard above the rhythms of the locomotive as the conveyor belts rolled out products from the rendered down pigs, 'Robeson's Glue,' 'Neat's Foot Oil', 'Chatterton's Bone Dust', everything pounded down through a city of factories, a labyrinth of processes, until all that remained was the dust of ground bones to be packed into sacks and cast on fields far, far away. Bone dust.

In Cincinnati we bought a state gazetteer, marked out the hotels radiating from Union Station, and started on the quest. About the second hotel I called at, Atlantic House ('rooms with hot and cold water daily 50c and upward') I entered a lobby where the fresh paint on the walls contrasted with the threadbare uniform of the bell-boy who slouched against the counter picking his nose. I got him to summon the desk clerk, a man so diminutive he was about the size of Alice herself. He had to stand on a box to have full command of his desk and he answered questions with a clipped delivery which indicated that he was quite aware about how small he was and could get along pretty well without you mentioning it to him, thank you.

He remembered a man and three children around the right time. He couldn't remember even if the kids were boys or girls but just recalled a very polite man with three children. He showed me the ledger, the black ink line above his tiny finger showed they were entered for the right day, for September seventh, 'Alexander E.Cook and three children.' It was a new alias for him but the dates and description fitted. 'Have you got an account with a cab company? Have you got a record of journeys and payments?' I asked. He pulled a battered ledger from under the counter and opened it up to read along the lines for they day Holmes left.

'Nope, he said, nothing that fits, but... ' he paused, 'I remember it now, he was standing there where you are with the three kids and two big trunks. I offered the express service and he refused, it's all coming back to me, he didn't want to use expressmen, said he'd had some kind of problem. He said he'd look after his own trunks, went outside and got a man and his helper to shift the trunk and take him where he needed to go.'

'Do you remember the cabman?' I asked without hope.

'Nah,' he said, 'not a chance.'

'OK,' I said, 'I'd better talk to them all.' Very clever, I thought, so very clever of Holmes not to use the express service which would have meant there was a record of the transaction: how much it cost, where the luggage was taken from, where it was taken to. Just what honest folks want, a record of what was done with their baggage, just what Holmes didn't want.

I went out through the turmoil and tumble of the street, the rows of cars pulled by slipping horses and the jangling street car bells, to question the cab drivers enshrouded in their waterproofs. While it was no light task questioning cab drivers about a passenger they had two months before, it wasn't a case of asking every driver in the city. Only a limited number waited for custom on the hack-stand near the Atlantic House and in a day I could expect to see them all. There was another thing; cabbies were always helpful about missing children, even talked about them with a catch in the throat and hoped they were safe, wished me well with unaccustomed gentleness. It was as if my questions provided a mental sanctuary for them in the roar and crash of the streets, as if they needed an occasional wash of sentimentality to redeem their usual brutish behaviour.

But today, standing in the tussle of reins by the heads of the snorting horses, none could help me, and my spirits dwindled as the rain began to settle on my clothes and slowly penetrate through. Late in the day Cass came running up excitedly, 'I've found where he was, he booked in as "A..Cook and three children" at the Hotel Bristol.'

'But he was here,' I said, 'he was booked in here.'

'I've just come from the Bristol,' Cass said indignantly, as if I was calling him a liar, 'he was there for weeks, left on September 30, they remember them all well enough for a good description.'

Suddenly I realised what he had done to put us off the scent. My day spent asking questions of cabmen in the rain would have left me, at the apex of its success, just at another hotel in the same city. He had just changed hotels. I could almost hear Henry Holmes laughing at me.

'Great, so now we know where he went from here,' I said, looking from the stately entrance of the hotel to the cobbled stones of the cab rank, 'just to another hotel, very clever.'

Cass shook his head, 'He's going to an awful lot of trouble to conceal his movements,' he said, 'why's he doing that?'

'Because he knows we'll be after him,' I said, 'he knows. And maybe, maybe just because he enjoys it.' Cass pondered, with a slightly open mouth, this insight into a man's soul. And back we went to see what more we could glean from the staff of the Hotel Bristol, 'A strictly first-class European hotel, recently refitted and refurbished.' Mrs Pitezel had furnished us with photographs from the Pitezel family of Alice, Nellie and Howard, and the mug shot of Holmes we had picked up from the police in St Louis, and even catalogue pictures of the trunks Holmes had with him. We showed them to Miss Klausman, the German maid who had seen the children more than the other staff, a thick-legged, full-breasted young woman who looked at me intently with beady blue eyes as if I was going to have her deported if she made a mistake. She spoke almost no English so I communicated with her in the street German I'd picked up as a beat cop – Ed Cass was greatly impressed. But all she could tell us was the children were crying when she went up once with their meal, homesick to see their mother, she thought. She had been very sympathetic but her English was not good enough to understand more of their plight. The children were always drawing or writing but nothing that they had written had been saved.

We checked the cabs, and made a lightning check of the other hotels, but there was no more here. The only other sighting of Holmes that we knew was in Indianapolis the day after they'd left the Hotel Bristol. Holmes had met Carrie Pitezel there to get her to sign some papers over the Fort Worth business and to ask her to send the other two children to him – sixteen year old Dessie and baby Wharton. He'd given her another letter from Alice and one from Ella but neither of these said much to help, 'I have just finished Uncle Tom's Cabin and it is a nice book. We hafto get up early if we get breakfast. We have awful good dinners pie fruit and sometimes cake at supper and this aint half. They are all men that eat at the tables we do not eat with them we have a room to ourselves. I wish I could see you all. This is another cold day' and so on.

Sometimes he left the children for days at a time, 'on business' he said, with the hotel staff bringing the children their meals. It was on one of these days, I reflected with pain and bitterness, that I saw Holmes in the basement of his cellar and he had me taken in by the Chicago police. The children were alive then, the knowledge of it corroded my soul – they were alive then, but where were they now?

So we were on our own again, with nothing but intuition and

luck to guide us. At the roaring station on Broadway and Vine we tried to imagine what he would have done. Cass said his instincts told him Holmes had stayed in the east, he'd had a bad experience in Fort Worth, chased out of town, had to steal a horse and all, he wasn't going west of the Mississippi again. We ticked off the number of destinations which were possible but we knew he had to have been in Indianapolis, even if he didn't stay there, and eventually we boarded the Indianapolis and Cincinnati Short Line Rail Road.

I struggled with despair as we passed each painted sign which heralded the arrival of the train in each pretty little town: Shelby, St. Paul, Greensburg, New Point, Spades, Harmans, Lawrenceburg...they could have got out anywhere. But I had to go with my hunch, that Holmes was a country boy like me and he knew it was harder to hide in a small town than a big city, everyone knew your business in the stations on route, but when you got to Indianapolis, no one knew nor cared who you were or why you had those children with you.

Indianapolis was harder to cover than Cincinnati, we had less to go on – we weren't even sure he had stayed for long – he had met Carrie Pitezel in a station diner. But we checked out the hotels, hotels where there was 'rooms open for the reception of transient guests'; hotels with 'Turkish baths for ladies and gentlemen (elevator runs all night)'; refurbished and First Class European Hotels, 'breakfast for early trains, polite and attentive servants ready at all times; day board $1 per day, pleasant rooms'; Birch House in Water Street conveniently placed next door to the Excelsior Bedbug Exterminator; and McEwans Temperance European Hotel between two saloons. And there seemed to be no end of those so, so convenient hotels like Globe House 'the most favourably located house in the city for travellers, being near the Union Depot where trains leave for all directions.' That's progress, I thought, bad men escape in all directions, taking little children with them. What would the pioneers of the railroad have thought of that?

I watched the honest Edward Cass day after day with his

dogged pursuit of the most ephemeral of clues, his brow creased over his notebook, his voluminous reports to his head office. I sat through many dinners with Ed, mainly steaming tureens of chicken or ham stew, with fresh bread and butter and a welcome beer after a long day questing, watched him methodically eat his way through his dinners: first meat, then peas, then potatoes, his bowed head showing the first developing tonsure of premature baldness. Sitting through so many such meals, I more than once caught myself disloyally thinking quite what an interesting companion Henry Holmes was, how if it was him travelling with me, instead of being sought by me, what a time we would have of it, how we wouldn't have long pauses while we tried to rekindle the conversation, how Henry would have known everyone in the place and everyone's business on the first night we got to the hotel, how he would have kept me laughing. If only I didn't have to hate him.

It was over one such dinner that we heard the grating sound of our hopes scraping the riverbed. It was after a bad week. We had gone through the guest list of every hotel in Indianapolis: Indiana House, Palmer House, Spencer House, Oriental House, California House, Phoenix Hotel and so many more damned hotels and boarding houses my head swam with it. We had reached the end of the list of hotels in town and in the surrounding areas, and we were running out of ideas. There wasn't much left to do. 'It's months since he passed through here with the kids,' I had said wearily, 'what if there were hotels open then that've closed by now? You know what a business the hotel trade is.' So we checked our list of hotels with an old city directory, one from last year, not the up-to-date one we had been using. One hotel was on the old but not the new list: Circle House, 'located in the quiet part of the city and particular attention is paid to the comfort of guests.' We asked at an artificial florist next door to the closed hotel, and discovered it had been run by one Herman Ackelow who now ran a beer saloon. We found him standing polishing his counter in front of a large pyramid of glasses under a mirrored sign advertising fine ales and London porter. He was no great friend of the police, but by threats, bribery and appeals to whatever better nature he had, we obtained his co-operation and he looked though a box of ledgers.

The books of the Circle House were kept without much system but at the beginning of October we found the entry we hardly dared hope for: 'Mr Howard and three Canning children.' Canning was Mrs Pitezel's maiden name. It was them. But our elation dispersed like the bubbles in Herman Ackelow's beer when we realised that it all led us precisely nowhere. He knew nothing more about them, could only just remember them even when we showed him photographs. Normally we'd have a lead to looking for other locations, but not today, we'd already covered all the hotels in Indianapolis. We tried a last desperate measure: looking for the trunk we knew the children had with them, asking at freight depots, omnibus companies, hackmen, express offices. This last was an errand of despair, we had already established that Holmes didn't use expressmen.

That evening was our lowest point as we sat over a tiny table in our hotel, the pretty calico tablecloth mocking the grim nature of our assignment: to track down a murderer and three kidnapped children. We examined our dwindling number of options. Giving up was unthinkable, starting the search again in another city where we had no clue at all as to Holmes' whereabouts was almost as inconceivable. 'Let's go back to the biography,' said Cass. We had been producing a record of Holmes' life between 1878 when I last saw him in Gilmanton and 1894 when I remet him in the dead house in Philadelphia. I didn't have the heart for more of this as I indicated wearily to Cass. 'But something must tell us where he is,' he insisted, 'with all we know about him, he must have let some clue slip. He's talked to both of us, can everything that came out of his mouth have been a lie?'

'I guess so,' I said, wondering what I could tell Director Honeycutt after he had placed all his faith in me. But I went through the exercise, starting with Cass's recollections of everything Holmes had said to him from the time the insurance claims clerk had passed the case over to Cass's investigations department and when Cass and I had met in Henry Holmes' presence what seemed like half a lifetime ago. Holmes had just kept Cass entertained on the train journey, telling amusing stories about city characters, anything to keep Cass from doing his job and asking about Holmes and the dead Ben Pitezel. Then Holmes walked back into my life, and I took him for a beer, or a cola. I went through what little we had said together: it was his first time in Philadelphia... used to run a drug store that Ben Pitezel helped with... the lawyer Jeptha Howe contacted him... he told me a fake story about the diabetic girl that he'd met when he studied medicine... that was in Michigan, not Vermont. I stopped recollecting for a moment. This wasn't right somehow. This wasn't right at all. My ma had told me he had gone off to Vermont to study medicine. Well of course she could be wrong, she was just repeating Gilmanton gossip. But Holmes said he had gone to Michigan and that really checked out, he had gone there.

Cass looked up from his note-taking. 'Henry Holmes has told me the truth about something.' I said, 'Now why would that be? Why why why?'

'What do you mean? said Cass

'Well, Holmes is quite unable to tell the truth, it's a foreign language to him. The only reason to tell the truth would be to divert me from something I already knew. I had Vermont, so why give me Michigan except to keep me away from there?

'You mean we should look for him in Vermont?'

'I mean we pack our bags and get the first train east,' I said. It was a day and a night of travel, back through the clanging din of the stations, the spurting steam and belching smoke and the giant's scream of the brakes on great locomotives.

We clattered and rocked onward, up to the green mountains, another granite state like New Hampshire, the grey boulders flecked with black attesting to the sea of rock below. In the distance I could see the steeples of white wooden churches rising above small, mountain-bound towns, close by the pulling train were herds of dairy cattle on sloping pasture. I almost felt like I was going home. We stretched and gulped in the cool air as we passed White River Junction then Montpelier until we reached Essex Junction, all alight here for Burlington.

The University of Vermont was less protective of its reputation than Ann Arbor, they gave us permission to look at the records, what they had of them. So between us Cass and I flattered and cajoled the spinster who filed the administration papers and we sat for a day in her tiny office overlooking a trimmed green quadrangle, going through boxes of thick brown files of former students. We looked for him under his old name, that he had at Gilmanton, as I guessed the chameleon ability to change identities had not been developed at this time.

I thought 1878 was too early for him, but we checked that year and every one between then and 1882 when we knew he was at Ann Arbor. Finally Cass found him in 1881, he had spent one year at the University of Vermont and had then left, no reason was given, but there was an address in Burlington. We thanked the spinster and went out into the light.

Maybe he wouldn't still be living there, but there would at least be a trail, we could talk to the neighbours. We got a trade directory with its pages bursting with fancy writing, offers and drawings of things to buy. I traced through the tiny printed lists of private individuals, you could miss a single entry, specially if it was in a false name. It wasn't, though. With a shock of recognition like a slap with a wet cloth I saw it was even his own old Gilmanton name. But it wasn't him, it was G.: *Georgiana*.

My first thought was to go straight there, to John Street between Central and Lake, but Cass's caution and my own good sense told me to wait and think. We called in at a bar where we sat in a quiet corner and ate bread and cheese. To be on a hot trail at last made me dizzy with excitement, the food dry and mealy in my mouth. Cass could hardly sit still for throwing out different trains of possibilities: what if he's there, how do we apprehend him? What if there's no one in? What if the children are there?

We knew we had one chance at this. As soon as Holmes was alerted he would move. We eventually evolved a plan. One of us would go in, one would stay outside to grab Holmes if he ran out the back way. Then one would follow Georgiana or whoever left the house.

'I'll see her,' I said, and caught Cass's gaze judging me, 'I mean I'll go into the house.'

'Are you sure you want to?' asked Cass, in a tone which suggested he wasn't sure he wanted me to.

'Yeah,' I said, 'I have the power of arrest, if Holmes is there, I can take him in.'

He nodded, 'Anything else?'

'Yes,' I said, working it through, 'I want maximum shock value, if his wife is there – or one of them – I don't want her to have time to collect her thoughts. Now we know she got him out of jail, so she's got to know he's doing things against the law, I'm guessing she's in contact with him, I'd make a bet on it. I want to shock her into contacting him.'

'So you're trying to panic her, and you think the sight of an old friend might do that very well?'

'Yeah,' I said, 'I suppose so. And there's the shock of confronting her with evidence of Holmes' bigamy. Let's see how she responds to that.' I looked fiercely ahead in the gloomy bar, as if my eyes could burn holes through the door and see right down the street.

'Frank...' he said, with an expression of tentativeness, as if he wasn't sure how I would react. I looked up, 'Now don't get mad at me for asking, but... why does it matter? Why does following this woman matter? Why after all these years?'

The question showed the vast, untraversable landscape of difference between us. 'I don't know, really,' I said, 'I mean it's been a part of me for so long I don't know when I didn't want to see her. I'd like to see her again, and I'd like to ask her why.'

'Tell me what happened,' he said. I told him a little about Georgiana and me in Gilmanton, just that we'd been friends, and Georgiana had been with me, and one night they had both gone, and I was still there. I spoke quietly with my hands placed together on the table.

'How does it still matter so much?' he said, his normally smooth brow furrowed in questioning, 'why does it still hurt? I mean,' his

143

eyes took on a wistful look, 'I had a girlfriend that I liked a lot, when I was seventeen or thereabouts, and she walked out with me a couple of times then she went off with another guy, at least I saw her with another guy once or twice.'

I thought of the lovelorn Ed Cass, leaning out of his bedroom window in a white painted house in suburban Chicago, smelling the fruit blossoms and dreaming his dreams. 'What happened?' I said, 'what did you do? Did you try to contact her?'

'She didn't say anything,' he said, 'she just wasn't in when I called and didn't reply when I wrote her. It hurt, it sure did, but in time I got over it. Now it's finished, it's in the past.'

I marvelled at how easy Cass had lived, that even such devastating rejection was brushed off, how he would flick his suspenders across his chest and toss his cheerful round head and it was gone, another bad experience to be written into the long catalogue of events before death drew a line under them and that was that, the ledger closed, another life lived.

'I dunno,' I said after a pause where we were both waiting for me to speak. 'I have thought a lot of this as the years have passed. It was very sudden and that didn't help. And it was the first time I had, you know, cared for someone else, except my folks, and that's not the same. Maybe it was just something that fitted in with my life, with the way I was, the way I am.' The churning excitement of being on the brink of discovery bubbled within me. Epiphany, I thought, revelation... but this wasn't the time.

Cass smiled resignedly, embarrassed at having made me reveal so much and too unsure of himself to press the matter, though he wanted to. 'I just don't want to see you wasting yourself on this,' he said.

I nodded and said, 'Let's do it.' We grabbed our coats and strode out, welcoming the cool air on our faces.

Burlington wasn't so big, and Georgiana's house wasn't so far away, but we got a cab so we could drive past it unobserved. The house was in a pretty suburb, it was a comfortable two storey frame house next to a Congregational church. There was a porch shading the front door and making a platform for sitting out on summer evenings. It was a fine, plain house, where the only concession to ostentation was two bay turrets, one on either side of the upper storey. It easily matched what would have been the smartest houses in Gilmanton as we were growing up. 'A girl doesn't need to worry about where she's going to live if she sets up with Holmes,' said Cass dryly. He and I parted round the corner and I walked purposefully back to the house and up the path. Cass followed tentatively some moments later across the road where he remained, concealed by an ornamental bush.

The tendons at the back of my knees felt weak, familiar to me from every state of danger I have ever been in. Trepidaton, apprehension... well, this was it. I pulled the hanging cord and heard the bell ring in the dark interior of the house. A shadow fell on the frosted glass of the door as a figure approached, stepping closer to me down the dark hallway, emerging from the past.

'Hello Georgiana,' I said. She was dressed in a long pinafore, her hair was up and she was holding her hands before her like she had just come away from some kitchen task that she wanted to get back to. She stopped sharply, as if so surprised she was just going to slam the door and run back into the house.

'Hi,' I said encouragingly. She looked round, her head tilted, as if she was peering to see if there was anyone behind me or trying to look through me to see if I was real. Her eyes were still gloriously large and cornflower blue, her sculpted cheeks accentuated by her hair being pulled back so only small wisps appeared; a figure still slender was highlighted by the pinafore tied tightly round her waist.

Finally, hands on hips, she said, 'Frank Geyer, well strike me' (the strongest expletive I ever heard her use). It was her voice, a voice I had not heard for almost a generation. 'Frank Geyer! After all these years!' For some reason, both then and in musing afterwards, the clichés appalled me, repelled me far more than the words or our situation merited. They affronted my sense of of... of propriety, of decency, to have come so far for this, to have taken an epic journey through the soul, a trek across America with heart outstretched for her and this was it: a suburban housewife greeting an old school friend.

My attitude had to harden, 'I was looking for Henry,' I said, 'and it's an official visit.' I showed her my badge.

'Oh,' she stopped, only slightly perplexed, 'well you'd better come in.' Once again, I had encountered a lady who showed no great surprise that a policeman was looking for her husband. When I entered, following her slim back, it was like walking back into Myrta Belknap's home. There was the lambrequin on the mantle, patterned antimacassars on the chair backs, an upright piano with a vase of fresh flowers, a bowl of fruit on the centre table, a profusion of trinkets. I bet if I looked I would be able to find, in a scrolled silver frame among the knick-knacks, the smiling face of the bigamist's wedding picture nestling amid the fancy ornaments.

Georgiana turned to me in the sunlit room, 'I'll make myself more presentable,' she said. The task I had called her from was baking, she had been baking, like her mother, always baking. There was flour on her arms and she had transferred a patch of it to her forehead when she pushed back a stray lock of golden hair with the back of her hand.

She left me and I looked around, momentarily entertaining the absurd notion that Myrta and Georgiana were the same person, just with different clothes and a wig, the similarity was so remarkable. I listened intently to hear her alert Holmes somewhere in the upper reaches of the house but she must have just removed the pinafore in the kitchen and taken a look in a glass, for she was back almost immediately, minus the smudge of flour.

She saw me observing her, 'Well I'd have been dressed for receiving company,' she said, 'if I'd known you were coming, Frank, or should I call you Mr Geyer now?'

'Call me Frank, please,' I almost snapped, still mesmerised by the undiminished beauty of her face. 'As I said, I'm here looking for Henry, he is wanted in connection with some matters in Philadelphia.'

'My,' she said, 'he does get about. Well I don't know where he is right now, he travels a good deal for business, you see.'

'What business would that be, Georgiana?' I said

'He is involved in a number of business ventures, property and so on, right now he has the rights to a patent copier which he is making available to people who can use it.' Her eyes were still so wide, the lashes so long.

'And would he have a shop somewhere, with 'Dealer in Patents' above the door?' I said.

'No, he's just travelling,' she said in her tinkling, light voice, 'he stays in hotels, I never know where.'

'So how do you keep in touch with him?' I asked, irritated both at my continued fondness for this woman and her current deception of me.

She detected the note of impatience in my voice and explained defensively, 'I hear from my husband two and three times a week and he continually sends me money for my needs and wants. I don't know when I'll see him again. Of course I'll let him know you were looking for him and he can contact you... where... Philadelphia?'

'Sure,' I said. I softened in my approach, I was going to have to ease information out of her. 'What name would he be living under now?'

'Henry Holmes,' she said, as if surprised that I should ask.

'Doesn't it seem suspicious, that Henry works under a different name from the one he grew up with?'

'Why bless me no,' she addressed me as if she was talking to a class of children taken with an absurd notion about the natural world, 'he had an uncle, Henry Mansfield Holmes of Denver Colorado, who had devised property on him provided he would assume his name, as he had no children and didn't want the name to die out. So Henry took on the name.' Clearly for Georgiana there was a benign explanation for everything.

'Are you sure,' I said quietly, as if worried about shocking her, 'that he's not with his other wife, the one he married after you?'

She put one slender wrist up to her cheek and half turned away, 'So you know about that,' she said flatly.

'You know?' I asked, it was my turn to be surprised.

'It's not what you think,' she said, still turned from me as if to shield her blushes, 'Well, I can tell you what I know. It's a sad story, and a happy one, and no one's to blame really. It was after we had been married about five years, Henry was on one of his business trips out West. There was a railroad collision and Henry was severely injured.' She told it with slow enunciation just like it was him telling the story – the train crash in fairyland. 'When he awakened he found he was in hospital and all memory of his former self had been blotted out, it was as if a curtain had dropped between him and his former self – memory of his name, occupation, home, parents, friends.' She looked to me as if for understanding and I nodded for her to continue, 'There was a woman who came to the hospital and brought flowers to the wards and read to the sick from good books with her gentle voice. Henry and she fell in love and on his convalescence they were married. Through her agency they secured the assistance of a great surgeon who performed a wonderful operation on his head. When he came out of the ether, his memory came back like a flood and he realised he had committed a terrible wrong. He pondered his situation for months. He suffered deep distress and grief for a condition for which he was not responsible. He could not tell this lovely woman she was not legally his wife. He came back to me, but I know he must still see this lady. I am sure there was an offence committed, but I consider it a technical one, no offence committed in the heart, in his heart Henry was always faithful.'

Did she actually believe this ridiculous story? She told it softly with her big blue eyes open wide as if she did. My guess was some scheme had gone wrong and Holmes had to high-tail it to a safe house no one knew about. So he went back to a wife he had abandoned without a word years before, but to grease his return he made up a story so incredible, so incredible... that only someone who loved him very much would believe it.

'OK Georgiana, I said, I think I get the picture.' I had to let it go, it was not as if she had committed a crime. The bigamy was his. It was just another to add to his already extensive list. 'Well we are getting to know one another,' I said. I had tried as hard as I could to get information about Holmes and I deserved something myself, 'Tell me something, Georgiana,' I said, 'back in Gilmanton, that day you left,' she looked up sharply, as if anticipating a blow, 'I won't ask why you went,' I said, to mollify her, 'but why did you go without even telling me?'

She looked at me with genuine bewilderment in her pale blue eyes. 'Why...' she shook her head, 'Henry told me he'd tell you. I begged him to let me but he said it was his duty as a man and as your best friend...' She seemed genuinely aghast, then burst out, 'So he didn't tell you? He didn't? I will have a serious talking to that man when I see him!'

'OK,' I said feebly, 'I thought so.' Of course, how stupid of me not to have realised: he had tricked her into not revealing their plans, to make it easier for them to get away. It was obvious, Georgiana didn't know. That's why her behaviour in leaving without a word never fitted with anything she'd done before. I mused on this, my eyes lying on the polished surface of the parlour dresser.

'What exactly are you seeking my husband for?' she said, presumably eager to change the subject.

'Murder,' I said and watched a flicker in her self control. I pushed home the point, 'You left me for a murderer,' and immediately regretted it, for instead of showing shock, her face broke into a nervous smile, I had lost my advantage.

'Well now you're being jealous, Frank Geyer, and it just doesn't suit you,' it was just the tone and the sort of expression she would have used in Gilmanton and momentarily it stopped me in my tracks.

'I'm here to warn you about Henry...' I said.

'You don't need to warn me about Henry,' she said with mock exasperation, 'he's the sweetest man.'

'But he's got three small children with him.' I said, almost raising my voice to her.

'Then I'm sure those dear little children will be well looked after,' she said.

'Do you know them,' I said, 'Ben Pitezel's children? Alice, Nellie, Howard?'

'I do not,' she said with exaggerated exactitude, 'I have never met them, and before you ask, I have not met Mr Pitezel either, but I know his name because he is a business associate of my husband's.'

'You won't meet him now, he's dead,' I said.

'Well I'm sorry to hear that,' she said with no indication of sorrow.

'You said you hadn't met him.'

'I haven't. I know Henry prized him as a business associate, but he never wanted him to visit this town. He had, you see, a weakness, and he didn't want someone in our home who might be in an inebriated condition.'

'Very wise,' I said, referring inwardly to the ploy of Holmes not letting even his partner in crime know the whereabouts of his safest safe house.

'Maybe I'm not making this very clear,' I said, 'Your husband is under suspicion of murder, and abducting children. These are very serious charges.'

'Then I simply pray that the cloud of unjust suspicion be lifted from him,' she said with her hands folded before her.

She looked over at a standing clock, like a grandfather clock but smaller, 'It's been so good to see you Frank,' she said, 'but if you don't mind, I've got to meet Lucy from school.'

'How old is Lucy' I said?

'Oh, she is fourteen, I don't have to meet her because she's little, she goes to school on her own of course, I'm just seeing her to go shopping. Would you... would you join me?'

Yes, of course I would. I mused bitterly while she got her coat, I knew why she wanted me with her, too. She didn't want her neighbours seeing her receive a gentleman caller unless she was happy to walk down the street with him. A person must not only be respectable, she must be seen to be respectable, and if she was married to a murderer it didn't matter if the murder was in another state. Her husband might be a kidnapping bigamist, but as long as he didn't bring any friends home who were drinkers, that was OK by her. I swallowed my disgust like a mouthful of bile.

We walked together. She talked to me about Gilmanton people, how was Mrs So-and-so who had always been good to us as children. Did I know anything about the Holberts who had just sold up and moved out, I wonder what happened to them, was that crabby old school teacher still scratching on? stuff like that. It was a strange experience, like living life in a storybook, to be walking beside her grown up in an almost familiar town with all the reminders of Gilmanton: the white wooden church spire, the fences and lawns, the polite and sedate people who nodded as we passed.

'Tell me about yourself, Frank, what have you been doing since we last saw each other all those years ago?' she said sweetly.

'Pretty much what you see, Georgiana,' I said, 'I became a policeman in Philadelphia, got promoted, became a detective.'

'And is there a Mrs Geyer?'

Of all the questions, all the options I had gone through in my head, this is one I had never considered, 'No,' I said quietly, suddenly finding my throat tighten, 'no there isn't.'

I was saved from further embarrassment, 'There's Lucy' said Georgiana, raising a small handkerchief in a gloved hand. A fair haired girl detached herself from a group of other girls down the road and came towards us. She was long-boned, tall but not full of figure, her arms folded across breasts hardly developed, wearing a pinafore dress, with hair tied with navy and sky-blue ribbons. There was nothing remarkable about her appearance as such, what made me stop in my tracks was just that Lucy was a miniature version of her, looking much like Georgiana did when I first loved her.

'Meet Mr Geyer, Lucy, Frank Geyer used to know Daddy and me back when we were around your age.'

'That's correct,' I said, a little more formally than the occasion demanded, for though I knew Henry had a child, I had not been prepared for the appearance of Georgiana and Henry's daughter.

Lucy made a little curtsey and smiled bashfully, looking up at me through lowered lashes. She was so like Georgiana, but with elements of Henry: his lively eyes, his slight pout. I felt sickness rise within me as if I had been socked in the stomach. Again, the very teeth in my mouth had been rattled by a blow from Holmes.

'I'll just say goodbye to Mr Geyer and we'll go,' Georgiana said, which Lucy took as a hint that this was grownup business. 'You wouldn't do anything, Frank, to harm us,' she said, too low for Lucy to hear, as she was already looking in a draper's window.

'Any harm,' I said, 'has already been done. I have to get to Henry to stop any more happening.'

'Goodbye, Frank' she said, holding out a gloved hand for me to touch the dry cotton fingers, unwilling to re-enter a dispute about the merits of her absent husband. 'I'll be sure to tell Henry you were looking for him.' I touched my hat and mouthed a thank-you and turned, with a slight wave of acknowledgement to Lucy, to walk to the other end of town, into the loneliness of heart where I was to meet Cass.

I walked into the grey, smoky atmosphere of the saloon, ordered a beer and stood at the counter where a few miserable pickles swam in one saucer of vinegar and in another saucer fragments of cheese hardening at the edges failed to tempt patrons to drink more. Finally Cass came in breathless, 'She went to Western Union,' he gasped, 'went to Western Union and sent a wire.'

I suppose I expected no better of her, but it was still with a pang that I realised the extent of her duplicity. She went immediately from denying knowledge of Holmes' whereabouts to me to send a wire to him. 'What happened?' I asked.

'The kid and her, after you'd left them, went into a hat-shop, a haberdashers and then the Western Union office. She filled in a form like you do, gave it to the wire guy to send. As soon as she left I identified myself and said I wanted to see the form, or at least delay it, but he wouldn't do either.'

I swore softly, like it was a prayer. 'What did he say?' I asked urgently.

'He said I needed a warrant valid in the state of Vermont.'

'OK I'll deal with it,' I said. 'Is she still in town?'

'No,' he said, 'she went back towards home with the little girl.'

I left my drink half-finished and went along with the perspiring insurance man to the Western Union office. The cable office boss was a stocky old guy with white whiskers. I showed him my badge, told him we were looking for someone in connection with a murder inquiry, with a mean sense of inner pleasure that in a small town like this a policeman asking questions about Georgiana would not be a secret for long.

'I have the protection of confidences in my care,' he said, with an antebellum locution, fixing me with a glassy eye.

I had a quiet but determined word, that this was about murder and the abduction of children. That I could easily go over to city hall and get a warrant but it would all take time, which was what we couldn't afford to lose.

The cable man scratched his head, put his thumbs in the pockets of his vest, drew out a gold watch and looked at it and half turned away, leaving his leatherette folder of cable forms on the counter between us. 'I'd better just check with a colleague,' he said, and went though a door to an inner office. I immediately drew the folder towards me and looked at the flimsy scrap of paper on top.

It was addressed to one Henry Mansfield – so much for taking the name of the dying uncle, I thought. It was to a cable office in Detroit, but it was recipient collect, there was no address. The message was in pencil, in Georgiana's school copperplate. It read PHILADELPHIA POLICE SEEK YOU HERE LOVE G

I replaced it and put the folder back as the Western Union manager returned, 'I'm sorry gentlemen I can't oblige,' he said, 'you'll just have to get that warrant from City Hall.'

'I see,' I said, 'well thank you very much for your time.' There was a man who succeeded in treading the chalk line between ethical behaviour and common morality.

'That puts her in the picture doesn't it?' Cass said as we walked out.

'Aiding and abetting an absconding felon,' I said miserably.

'You want to pick her up, see if it flushes him out?'

'No,' I said, 'it wouldn't, and the paperwork and court appearances would divert us from chasing him. We got to get to Detroit. But first... but first...' I went back to the wire office and scribbled a cable to the Pinkerton Agency in Detroit to have them keep watch for the man who collected the cable from Western Union, and to follow him unobserved.

'Now clearly Holmes goes to pick up his cables sometime,' I said, 'I hope it's not till tomorrow or the next day, and then the Pinkertons will follow him and tell us where he is.'

Cass didn't say it, but we both knew that if he had spoken to Georgiana, and I had watched and gone to the cable office, I could have made the manager delay sending the wire for a day, until we could have gotten to Detroit. It wasn't said, but Cass's indictment was that again I had put my own interest before the good of the investigation. Well, that's how it was, I was sick of excusing myself.

We scrambled to the station and I chewed my knuckles as we rolled out of Burlington along the shores of the placid Lake Champlain. The lack of a connecting line to Detroit meant we had to go down and change for the Albany line, so we were going south-east instead of west for 150 miles, which didn't relieve my anxiety. I had no appetite and took no pleasure in the crystal lamps and leather upholstery of the lounge car. I was already thinking ahead and trying to plan. We couldn't afford the time to stop off, so travelled all night but the changes of train meant no sleeping compartment either, so we slept in relays sitting up. I dozed fitfully with the sound of the tracks buffeting my ears, in a desperately close compartment, with my tie loosened and sweat trickling through the hairs on my chest.

The fatigue, the shock of seeing Georgiana and the exertion merged with the rhythms of the locomotive in my mind. I couldn't get away from the image of Lucy – so like Georgiana when she was that age: the fair hair, the white, almost translucent skin, the blue eyes big with wonder; but then there was the brow, the curling mouth and teeth of Henry. I dreamed desperately of Henry and the children.

I see them in a hotel room, the wallpaper faded, an easy chair and a sofa by a bed. Henry is alone with Alice, the other children asleep next door. She is in her linen night-dress, leaning against him as he talks in his low, melodic voice. He says he will tell her one of the great mysteries of fairyland: the exquisite ravishment of the nymphs.

'Once,' he says in his misty, magical way, 'there were two islands. On the south one lived good people who were blonde and smooth and white limbed, and soft to the touch. Theirs was called the island of shepherds, and the way they used to have little ones was to throw stones over their shoulders,' he looked down at the girl in his arms, wide eyed and listening intently, 'and the great mother earth received the stones and fashioned them into little people. The damp earthy parts, containing some moisture, were adapted to make the body, and the solid and inflexible parts became the bone. In a little time, when the moisture in the earth was warmed by the rays of the sun, the bones that were thrown by men became boys, and those thrown by women became girls. And so it went on for a long time. Do you want me to go on?'

'Yes,' she said, snuggling into his arm.

'Now, situated to the north was another island, and there lived the hairy people and their feet were horny and hard, they had long pointed ears, ruddy complexions and glinting eyes, and vigorous temperaments, they were the sort of people you always remembered, even if you didn't like them much when you first met them. And that island was called the Island of Satyrs. On both of these islands there was an abundance of all the necessaries for the comfortable support of life: fruit trees in stately woods and plenty-spreading rivers.

'For many years these islands had no contact with one another. Now the goddess Aphrodite lived on an island nearby. She visited both the Island of Shepherds and the Island of Satyrs and she felt that the Satyrs were having a lot of fun that the Shepherds were just missing out on and she thought this was a real shame. So she called on the god Hermes to help her and she had him spirit two of the Satyrs to the southern island, to teach the Shepherds how to have a good time.

'Well, the Satyrs began to indulge in acts of wantonness, such as touching the bosoms of the nymphs, attempting to raise their petticoats and snatching a kiss from them. It was a little naughty, but at first the Shepherd boys were pleased with the teachings of the Satyrs, but later perceived that the nymphs were enjoying the pleasures of the Satyrs more than from themselves, and became unhappy. You see, the Satyrs taught the nymphs how to love as grown-ups do. They made a choice, you see, the nymphs liked the attentions of the little hairy men, even if it was naughty.'

His hand had crept around her waist and he kissed Alice on the neck and spoke while still close to her ear, 'only a lady could do it, of course, you had to be grown up. Do you want to be a lady, are you grownup enough?' He kissed her again and this time she leaned back and arched her neck to give him greater access; he stroked her thin backside through the night-shirt.

I was shocked out of this when we had to change trains at Springfield and I walked groggily along the platform thinking about Holmes's modus operandi that I had pondered so long that now I saw it in my sleep. In the next train, for Detroit via Albany, in the fragments of sleep I could grasp I entered the nightmare myself and ran down the dark hotel corridors, banging on doors to try to stop the obscenity, calling out 'don't do that, don't do that to my daughter.'

By the end of the journey, when we stumbled bleary-eyed into the corridor, waiting for the train to stop, pieces of it remained with me, like dried leaves stuck to your coat if you have fallen in the forest, and I remembered fragments of the dream as if I was picking off the leaves each after another. One thing I knew: I was sure as hell Holmes had ruined Alice.

Chapter 11

When we stumbled through the smoke and steam into Michigan Central, Detroit, we hadn't slept in a bed for forty-eight hours. We called at the Pinkerton agency to meet the detective assigned to us, a tall young guy like a string bean, a pointed white face peeking out from under a brown hat, the least inconspicuous representative of the profession I had ever seen, he could have had 'detective' tattooed on his forehead.

'I followed him,' he said, his Adam's apple gulping up and down at roughly my eye height. 'I just waited in the Western Union office, I'd given the clerk something so he would tip me off when your man came in, so I just stood and waited, as if I was trying to compose a cable.' Clearly the cable clerks in Detroit felt less ethically constrained than those in Burlington. 'When he came in I got the tip-off and I followed him to 270 Woodward Avenue, it's not far. He went in but I couldn't go up, he'd have seen me.'

The three of us went along to the address, a good tall brick building. I got the Pinkerton's man to stand outside, Cass to go round to the fire exit, and I went in the main entrance. There was a hall with cheap wooden panelling and a series of plates, some brass, some cardboard. There was a range of medical people listed there, like Clairvoyant Physicians and Cancer Doctors. There were two I guessed might give a home to Holmes: Washburn and Fairweather's Dispensary for Private Diseases ('Medicines sent by mail') or Dr Oemisch, who never failed in expelling all traces of disease from the system by galvanism and electro-galvanic puncture. Something about the conjunction of modern apparatus and fake promise made me think the last one had to be him. Some of the businesses had fliers offering their services, so the timid who would venture only so far as this lobby might be tempted to go further. The one for Oemisch read, 'This is the only office in the city where permanent cures of diseases caused by indiscretion can be obtained without the use of mercury. Persons suffering from the use of mercury who have become living thermometers or quicksilver mines from its use may have this dangerous poison removed from the system by this method. Married men and those contemplating marriage should restore vigour to their bodies and minds, ere they entail misery and disease upon those of their posterity.'

Really tugs at the heart-strings, I thought. I took the stairs not the elevator, because of the noise, so I arrived breathless and had to stand outside to recover myself, softly inhaling the light antiseptic smell from the surgery. I opened the door as quietly as I could to encounter an empty waiting room and quickly crossed to the surgery, looking round with sharp movements. There was a rubber and chrome device connected to an instrument box with a dial, a black sleeve connected to a mercury gauge for measuring blood pressure and a small Galvani machine with two silver balls where a current would crackle across, like you would see in demonstrations of electricity in a museum. I guess the trick was to terrify the libertines about their disease, impress them with science, then charm their money from them by sweet talk. Holmes wasn't here, anyway, not in the waiting room, nor the surgery, nor the small wash-room nor the dispensary. This was little more than a cupboard at the back with shelves of bottles filled with dubious liquids and a small stack of books with blank covers and titles like 'Sports with Venus or the Way to Do It' in the Cupid's Own Library series, yours for 25c.

There was a noise in the waiting room that had me spinning around but Cass's voice called out, 'It's me Frank, he's gone.'

I swore softly and looked at him in pained frustration. 'I had to tell the janitor what we were here for,' Cass said, 'he tells me there used to be a Dr Oemisch, then Holmes joined him and he hasn't seen Oemisch for a while, but Holmes kept the business on. Holmes rushed out in a hurry this morning.' I thumped the solid, doctor's desk with my fist. 'He owes rent, the janitor would like us to remind him.' Cass added.

'First thing on my mind,' I said.

The Pinkerton's man joined us. 'From the clutter in here,' I said, 'I think he left as soon as he was tipped off by the cable.

Came back to get essentials then vamoosed. Maybe he knew he was being watched.' The Pinkerton's man started to protest but I waved my hand, 'OK, maybe he guessed that's what we would do, he didn't spot you, he just knew.'

'So where can he go?' asked Cass insistently, 'He knows we know about his safe houses, about Burlington, and Maple Rapids... the castle in Chicago.'

'Castle...' breathed the Pinkerton's man softly.

'Plus he's under suspicion in Chicago and in St Louis. We've asked questions all over Indianapolis and Cincinnati about him, he's going to attract suspicion there. He knows there are warrants from Philadelphia and Fort Worth out for him. What in the name of God is he going to do?' I clasped my head and turned, as if the cod gadgetry of the surgery could give me an answer. 'Let's get going,' I said and I led the way, clattering down the stairs, divided between anger at Georgiana for tipping him off, shame that I had let him escape, and raging anxiety about where to look.

I strained every fibre. Where was he going to be? In the street, gasping for air, I said, 'There are three stations in Detroit, right? Central, Union and Trunk, each of us can get to one, analyse what trains have gone since he left this building, which couldn't have been more than half an hour since he left the Western Union wire office. Check every train that's waiting to leave, check the bathrooms on the trains. Maybe he's still at the station. Meet back at the Pinkerton office, at least we all know where that is.'

I dashed off, buzzing with furious determination, coat flapping open. This would show Henry Holmes, he wouldn't expect us to be raging in hot pursuit. Suddenly a spasm of realisation seized me and I stopped and turned on my heel, my coat swinging around like a madman. 'Ed,' I shouted at his disappearing form, making him wheel round, 'No. Stop. I understand now. That's what he wants us to think.' Other people in the street stared at us as if we were gripped with a collective dementia that might be catching. As we regrouped I gasped, 'No, anywhere but the stations now. He's going to change his modus operandi. He's got to, he knows we know.'

As I pleaded the truth dawned on Cass. 'Yeah,' he said, 'What don't we expect him to do?' We both looked at him, the Pinkerton's man with a kind of bug-eyed amazement that people should say such peculiar things at a time of excitement.

'Water,' Cass shouted in excitement, 'we're on the edge of the biggest inland waterway in the world. He won't go by train, he'll hop the country, he'll go to Canada.'

'How d'you get from here to Canada?' I demanded.

'Why, just across the Detroit River,' the Pinkerton's man said, 'ferries all the time.'

'Damn that,' I said, 'further into Canada? Lake Superior? Lake Ontario?'

'The big steamers,' he said, getting into the swing of it, 'you pick them up at the foot of Grisewold and Woodward.'

'Frequent?'

'Frequent enough.' he nodded, 'most lines run one a day.'

We hailed a cab to race us down to the port, the horses breaking into a bone-shaking canter as the driver flicked the whip for us. The river was scarcely a mile away, we could smell it as we approached: a rich putrefaction of wood, leather and offal, floating round in the murky water in a stew specially brewed for the city. The triangular sails of small boats came first into view, and then trade steamers pulling barges stacked with lumber and finally, so big I was surprised to have missed them at first, a couple of great white steamboats each with two huge funnels, their names in bold characters to defy the elements: 'Traveller' and 'Dubuque.'

I called in to the harbour master who listened to the tale of our mission with weary resignation and told me the order of sailing. This was evidently not the first time a policeman had rushed up breathless in hot pursuit of a criminal. The last ship had gone at eleven that morning which was about the time the Pinkerton's man had followed Holmes.

'What if he's just gone across the river, to Windsor?' Cass asked.

'Then we go to Windsor,' I said, 'keep on the trail. But I think he's headed further afield. We'll search the long-distance steamers.'

We marched down the cobbled slipway to where the huge boats

were berthed, past the booking offices where Cass and I checked each line of passengers while the Pinkerton's man stood outside in case Holmes slipped out the back. No luck, so we tensely clattered on to the first embarkation hall, a wide building at the height of the ship's gangway with windows across most of one wall where you could see the ship.

There was a long line of passengers with packages and luggage of all sizes in the line to go to Toronto. They were talking in German, Russian, Yiddish or in Scottish or Irish accents so strong you couldn't tell they were speaking English. There were ribbons on the rich people and rags on the poor people and a fug of smoke in the damp waiting hall. Standing apart from them, near the end, looking out of the window at the great whale of a ship was our man, Henry Holmes, in his little black frock coat, a carpetbag in his hand. I was filled with wonder that we should come so far, and be so close, attempting to breath lightly lest I disturb the vision. 'Quietly,' I said to the others, scarcely audibly amid the hubbub of the hall. I wasn't so worried about danger. Of course he had held me with a revolver at the castle, but Henry wasn't really a gun man, it was too clumsy a tool for him, I didn't think he would pull that trick. So I wasn't frightened of what he would do, but somehow I was frightened. I suppose it was of what he would say. I walked easily so as not to attract attention by too purposeful a stride when I was still far enough away from Holmes for him to make a run for it.

I needn't have feared flight, given his amazing propensity for doing the opposite of what was expected. He turned at our approach, and I noticed the flicker of recognition that there were three of us. He gave every impression of being utterly unperturbed by the arrival of a posse to bring him in. 'Well Frank Geyer,' he said, greeting me again like an old friend, with no hint of surprise or rancour. He gave no mark of recognition to Cass or the Pinkerton's man, as if they were merely my servants and of no account.

I ignored his outstretched hand, 'I'm arresting you on a charge of fraudulent conduct in relation to the Fidelity Mutual Insurance

Company,' I said. Henry listened to me as if I was a tiresome lad he only just tolerated for the sake of politeness.

He reached out, 'You'd better let me see that warrant.' I handed it to him and he examined it with his quick, blue eyes.

'So, you're trying to arrest me on a Philadelphia coroner's warrant, Frank,' he said, 'are you quite so sure you have a right to do that? Are you sure you have the authority to arrest me, Frank?'

Cass's body froze. Previously he had been standing easy, enjoying being at the centre of the small crowd of travellers who had gathered at a discreet distance and were watching this little side-show of the criminal law in action. Now Ed Cass stood stock still, as if witnessing the last of his life savings wagered on a roulette wheel.

'I'd better see a lawyer about this,' said Holmes, 'of course, you are welcome to accompany me, gentlemen.'

'Slow down,' I said, 'we can take you in on this Philadelphia warrant if you wish, or this one' and I pulled out a second folded sheet of paper and handed it to Holmes. 'The State of Texas also requests your company on the matter of "larceny of one horse"'.

Holmes licked his lips under his luxuriant moustache, as if his mouth had suddenly gone dry. The steamer he was going to board hooted behind us, a line of passengers edged forward, 'Since you put it that way, Frank,' he said, with only the slightest note of regret, 'I will accompany you to Philadelphia to clear up this matter.'

'Hands out,' I said, holding my handcuffs.

'Now is this really necessary, Frank?' he asked.

'I like to do things properly,' I said, and snapped on the cuffs as I got Cass and the Pinkerton's man to frisk Holmes, to his absolute disdain, and do a quick search of his bag to check for his revolver but he didn't have it. In the cab where the four of us squeezed in I could not draw Holmes to conversation, he had suddenly developed an unaccustomed reticence. The only thing he said of his own volition, looking out of the window as we jerked and clattered away from the port was, 'They do treat the theft of horses very seriously in Texas... I'd rather be five years in a prison in Philadelphia than one in Texas.'

I tried to draw him, 'I thought we were going to lose you altogether, Henry,' I said, 'We thought you might be going off to England or somewhere.'

'Not me,' said Henry wanly, 'Nosir, I'm American through and through.'

'Where are the children, Henry?' I asked gently.

'What children?' he asked

'Ben Pitezel's children.'

'Why, they're with their father, safe with their father.'

I could see this was going to be an interview where I would want every word noted, so I saved it for later. We put him in the custody of Detroit police for the afternoon, in a cell and uncuffed, while I arranged travel warrants, settled up with the Pinkerton's man and made a search of Dr Oemisch's surgery. There was no sign of Dr Oemisch, 'He's gone the same way as Mrs Hulton' said Cass thinking about the Chicago drug-store owner who disappeared before Holmes put his own name over the door.

There wasn't much there, the only thing that proved useful was a little packet of letters in a childish hand. My heart leapt when I saw them – other letters from the children, it was another lead, but now I was too busy looking after Holmes himself, terrified at the thought that he might somehow trick the Detroit police department into releasing him. When we returned he was there, sitting in a general cell, having regained some of his good humour. I almost thought he was looking forward to seeing me.

He held out his hand for the cuffs and I put one round his wrist and one round my own. He smiled mildly as he tested the fit, as if pleased to note that we were going to be together. He said little, but when we got to the train to take us on the train to Philadelphia he looked at the open palm of his left hand, the one that wasn't handcuffed to me, as if he was checking his small change. I suppose he was running through the catalogue of lies he could stick in me.

'You know I could hypnotise anyone,' he said.

'Not me,' I said gruffly, then realised I had taken the bait.

'Yeah, really Frank, even you. I'll bet you $500 I can hypnotise you, Frank.'

'I haven't got $500 to bet with.'

'Well if you're so sure you can't be hypnotised, then there's no risk,' he came back, but I wouldn't play the game further. He tried the same trick out on Cass when I went to the bathroom and left Holmes cuffed to a seat, but Ed Cass was now wise to these tricks and showed no interest.

Henry then talked about the science of mesmerism and the great boon it could be in pain relief and overcoming bad habits and unnatural fears such as people who were scared of spiders and such like. We talked amiably, but obviously he was looking for weakness that would give him a way in: for one of us to ask him to cure us of nailbiting or something by hypnotism and he could start to tip the balance of control.

'Did you learn that at Ann Arbor?' I asked.

'Oh I learned many techniques of advanced medicine at Ann Arbor. That's where I learned my surgery. Do you know gentlemen,' he paused as if pondering whether to speak, 'there were women students there also, training to be doctors. Now I am very advanced in my thinking, and I can believe that women should be able to learn to be physicians to deal with women's complaints and those of children. But do you know that in their training the young women students were in the same dissecting room as us, dissecting bodies. Even dissecting male cadavers. Male bodies,' he emphasised, 'and even some of the young women of a more modest aspect were ashamed and petitioned the authorities to allow them to have a separate dissection room. But some of them, some of them were shameless, shameless I say.' He looked out of the window as if appalled at the things he was obliged to contemplate.

'I visited Ann Arbor,' I said, 'then I went to Wilmette, I met Myrta.'

'Yes,' he nodded, 'you were looking for me but I wasn't there.'

'Do you realise that bigamy is an offence in every state of the union? We're not Mormons you know.'

'Bigamy?' he queried, as if genuinely confused, 'Oh, you mean because I have more than one sweetheart, that's a crime?'

'You have been married at least twice,' I said.

'Well, if you want to try to prove that charge you must go ahead, I can't stop you,' he said, in a friendly manner, 'but I do categorically deny it.'

He showed no sign of triumph but he knew he had me cornered on that. The city of Philadelphia was not going to pay for an investigation of a crime that didn't even happen in our state. You needed marriage certificates to prove bigamy, and where false names were used you needed reliable witnesses to identify the perpetrator, to establish that they weren't the person named on the certificate. I could send the accusation to police in Vermont and Michigan to process, but I bet they had enough of their own crime to look into.

Only once Henry seemed to be speaking of the strange predicament existing between us. As we rolled across the night, looking straight ahead, his small head resting on the red leather padding of the seat in the lounge car, his face close to mine as we were still cuffed together, he said in his poetic voice, 'Crisis in Fairyland: After Troy fell and the city was burned, many of the women survived, among them was Helen. And Helen was still so beautiful that the Greeks were still awed by her lovely face and beautiful body. She was so beautiful it hurt, and they wanted to hurt her back because of the pain she had caused them in ten years of war. But she was in part divine, being the daughter of Zeus by a mortal woman, so they could not kill her, for that would bring the curses of the gods on to them. So to relieve their suffering they made her less beautiful... first they cut her lovely hair and then they cut her arms and legs off one by one so she was wheeled round in a trolley and they would call out at her as she was left in the market, "How beautiful are you now, Helen, for whose lovely face a thousand ships were launched?" And Helen cried as she had made countless others cry out of longing for her beauty.'

Cass looked quizzically at me but I was in no mood to interpret Henry's stories. 'Time to turn in, I think,' I said. We went to the compartment where the porter had put down the bunks in the cabin where the three of us were sleeping as we crossed Ohio and Pennsylvania. I uncuffed Henry from my wrist and attached the cuff to the bar holding the upper bunk – I slept on the lower one so I would be disturbed if he managed to slip out of it and tried to escape.

When we were lying down with the lights out I looked into the dark where Henry lay a foot above me.

'You had everything Henry, brains, charm… why'd you do it?' I said, as if speaking to myself.

'Why'd I do what?' he asked.

'Why'd you go bad?'

'Because I could.'

We rode into Philadelphia City Hall to a hero's welcome from Director Honeycutt and a grudging commendation from Chief O'Brien. Now we had to make the charges against him stick.

On the train he had been at his most subdued, as if crossing those empty spaces of America made him wistful and yearn to be at peace. In the lock-up in City Hall he rediscovered his combative spirit. The interviews were lengthy and often without profit. Holmes was greatly given to lying with florid ornamentation, all of his stories were decorated with flamboyant draperies, intended to add depth and colour to the plausibility of his statements. He always had the appearance of candour, and more than one police officer who listened to the flow of his words was taken in and believed him, if not innocent, then not so very guilty either. He became pathetic at times, when pathos would serve him best, uttering his words with a quaver in his voice, often accompanied by a moistened eye, then turning quickly with a determined and forceful method of speech, as if indignation or resolution had sprung out of tender memories that had touched his heart.

The breakthrough, if such it was, came on the second day of questioning. 'I will put it to you,' I said, 'that you killed Benjamin Pitezel.'

'Why Detective Geyer,' he said, using the form of address he employed for more formal exchanges, 'I could no more hurt my old friend Ben Pitezel than I could... cut off this good right hand. Oh, if you knew what pals we were! The times we had together, the scrapes we got out of! Do you know, I'll tell you this though it could count against me for it was not rightly legal, but Ben had been imprisoned in Indianapolis for passing a fraudulent cheque. Well he hardly had fifty cents to send a cable but he did so, calling on me to help him, and I dropped everything and went to him, I impersonated an Indiana congressman to get into the jail house, and bailed Ben out with another dud cheque! Oh, how we laughed at the times we had!'

'But now he is dead, is he not?' I insisted.

'Well,' he said, I suppose I'd better come clean, given the spot I am in.' I held my breath and kept perfectly still, as if even a twitch would destroy the moment.

'I did take money from that insurance company to which I was not entitled. The Philadelphia body switch was Ben and my last caper. I had procured a body in New York which bore some resemblance to my friend. I had it moved in a trunk to Philadelphia where Ben had set up some kind of an establishment where it would attract no attention to have a trunk carried in. I had previously instructed Ben Pitezel on what to do with the body so it was no surprise at all to hear, in fact from an advertisement placed by the Philadelphia Police Department,' he nodded towards me as if in acknowledgement of a virtuoso performance, 'that a body had been found and I contacted Fidelity Mutual Insurance with a family member of Ben's, who had also been instructed in deception...'

'That was Alice,' I said for the record.

'Yes,' he said, as if irritated at the interruption. 'We identified the body of the poor unknown as Ben and claimed the insurance money.'

'But Ben Pitezel did die, didn't he?' I said.

'Oh no, no one died in this caper,' insisted Holmes, 'the unfortunate whose body we used was dead before he entered Philadelphia.'

'So where is Ben now?' I asked

'I can't say, but I've seen him in Cincinnati and Detroit since his demise, as alive as I see you standing there.' Since Holmes was constitutionally unable to tell the truth, I imagined he was visualising me dead.

'When did you see Ben Pitezel in these two cities?'

'I cannot give the day, leave a blank in the statement and I will fill it in later.' Cass and I looked at each other in exasperation, as we so often did. He was just giving himself time to construct more plausible lies.

'So where did you get the body in New York?'

'I refused to state. I would rather not tell, I was concerned years ago with this man and because of the position he is in, it would hurt him very much. Of course I will if it comes right down to saving myself.'

'So how can we contact Ben Pitezel to corroborate your story?' I asked.

Holmes looked thoughtful, and said, 'he may be travelling under the name L.T.Benton, but I don't know.'

'Are you expecting us to believe you don't know the name of your accomplice?' I exploded.

'It was policy,' he said simply, 'if I don't know, I can't tell you, can I?'

'So how would you contact him?' Holmes was pensive, then with an apparent reluctance born of necessity he made a great show of yielding up some information: a simple code in which he would write a message for Ben which would be placed in the personal columns of the Chicago Tribune or New York Herald. Of course we had to go through with the exercise and place such an ad, but no one believed in it. We tried another line of questioning. Where are the children? we would ask in many ways. Why, they are with their father, he would say, maybe gone to Mexico. Ben Pitezel will show up by and by, when the noise has died down, to see his wife again.

At length we had him led along to his holding cell and we went wearily along to meet the Director of Public Safety and the District Attorney. The euphoria of capture had worn off, now we trudged the long corridors of City Hall with just the gnawing need to secure a conviction in our hearts, and pitifully little by way of evidence to cover our nakedness. Henry Holmes would never confess, and without a confession we would be sorely pressed to keep him in jail.

We met in the conference room around a mahogany table polished to a brilliant shine, Honeycutt, O'Brien, the DA, Cass and myself. O'Brien was only there because it would have been bad procedure to talk to me without my boss. Honeycutt was there because it was his show. The real talking was done by the DA, George S. Graham, a bull-necked man, very clean shaven, as if he sliced off the top layer of skin every morning with his razor in outrage at his beard's determination to grow against his wishes, a man with the air of suppressed urgency, as if everything he did was important, but he was consumed with anxiety that the important matter currently engaging him was keeping him from even more momentous business elsewhere.

'So what have we got?' he asked.

We briefly outlined our search for Holmes and the children. 'The children have still not been found.' I said, 'and I fear for their safety. Henry Holmes has confessed to the insurance fraud, but not to the murder of Pitezel.'

'Why do you think these three children have come to harm?'

I shook my head, 'Only that they were last seen with Holmes who now claims not to know their whereabouts. And that their mother does not know where they are. And people involved with Holmes have a tendency to disappear without trace.'

'With no bodies,' said DA Graham, 'we haven't got the shadow of a case.' I assented silently. 'And how much proof do we have that Pitezel is even dead?' he asked.

I shook my head, 'At present just Holmes' identification and that of Alice Pitezel.'

'A fourteen year old girl who was probably in on the plot but was anyway under Holmes's control, and is now missing?'

'That's about it sir,' I said

'I have no doubt at all,' said DA Graham, 'that we have here a very smart crook, who is almost certainly a murderer. My problem is that I cannot hold Holmes much longer. Legally, I've got to indict him or let him go. He has confessed to the insurance fraud so I've got to go with that. In the absence of any other evidence, or a confession to anything more serious, I've got to put that charge to a Grand Jury.'

There was an audible silence as this grim news sunk in, though any of us could have guessed this is what it was coming to. 'Hell,' I said finally, 'I want to get this man for murder, I want to keep investigating this thing.'

'The legal process has its own timetable Mr Geyer,' said Graham, 'of which you are fully aware.' It was a way of reminding me, and none too gently, that providing the evidence to convict Holmes was my responsibility, and I had failed.

'I am prepared to make an appeal over sentencing,' said Graham with resignation, 'we'll have to let Holmes plead guilty, but ask the judge not to sentence until we have completed our investigations.'

Holmes went to a Grand Jury who sent the case for trial. The trial wasn't long in coming, a guilty plea doesn't take a lot of work. Holmes was convicted of insurance fraud but sentence was reserved. Afterwards I walked to the station with Cass. We had hardly spoken since we brought Holmes in. I had been so busy with the DA's office, and he had been occupied with his work in Chicago.

'I'm sorry Fidelity Mutual can't help more with looking for the children,' said Cass, 'putting Holmes behind bars was as far as they'll go. It's just a shame about the kids...'

'Not being insured, you mean? Yeah.' I said, and he grinned sheepishly.

I handed him a cardboard box, just bigger than the palm of my hand. 'Here, I said, a small token of my esteem.'

'Oh you shouldn't have...' he began to say, 'what is it?'

'It's a mould made from a plaster cast of Ben Pitezel's front teeth,' I said, 'I just thought in those long moments between cases, when time hangs heavy on your hands, you might like to check out the dentists near where he lived to see if any can identify him.

He had pretty unusual teeth, with the two incisors crossing over and all. Carrie Pitezel is too disturbed to identify anyone. She'd identify a dead skunk as her husband.'

'With good reason,' Cass said, popping the brown box in his leather travel bag. 'Well, now I know how much you care, I'll think of you whenever I look at it.'

As we got to the booking hall he said, 'If you can't get evidence that he killed Ben, what will Holmes' sentence be?'

'Two years is the maximum in the State of Pennsylvania for conspiracy to defraud.' I replied, and let this sink in. 'So he'd be out in eighteen months. He'd get remission for good conduct, his conduct always is good.'

Cass wiped his brow,' So anything you can do? he asked.

'We can try and ship him out to Texas or St Louis,' I said, 'but they'll have lost the paperwork, or the investigating officers will have moved on. Or the authorities will decide it isn't worth the cost of transferring him across the country.'

'That's justice for you,' he said.

'Yeah,' I murmured, and we shook hands as I said goodbye to Edward Cass for the last time.

Chapter 12

The missing Pitezel children did not stop troubling my sleeping and waking moments alike, but I had to steer a steady course on the only crime where I had a chance of getting all the evidence quickly enough to satisfy the DA.: Henry had to hang for murder. There was no doubt that he was a murderer in my mind, or the DA's, or the Coroner's, or any of the pressmen who now buzzed around the case. Only the law, in its weighty, ponderous manner, sat like a toad croaking 'doubt' on the case of Henry Holmes.

I reacquainted myself with Eugene G.Smith, the sandy little carpenter with the freckled hands who had invented the saw setter that sets any dull saw in minutes with no excessive labour. I called for him along a tenement corridor where cooking smells belched out from a hundred overcrowded kitchens. He was still looking for someone to take out a patent on his saw setter for him. He was pleased to go over the events of September 1894 when he met Ben Pitezel, first alive, then present only in the flesh. It had been a memorable encounter: not every day you see a man dead that you saw just days before as fresh as a daisy. What I needed to know was, had he seen anyone else when he saw Ben Pitezel. Yes, he said with no further prompting, there was another guy there, a little guy, didn't say much but he was very polite, a moustache and a frock-coat. He could identify the accused from a photograph. So that knocked a hole in Henry's assertion that he had never been in Philadelphia and had only read about Pitezel's demise in the newspaper. At least I'd got him at the crime scene.

While I was writing up this encounter I got a message to go to the telephone room to speak to Ed Cass. It was a matter of prestige to be called to answer the call myself, as if only I would do, it was so important. I had used the telephone before, of course, but more often had received telephone messages taken down by the clerks. Now I personally descended to the bowels of City Hall where the telephone rooms were, down the corridor being passed by scurrying messenger boys in City Hall uniform, some rushing away from the telephone hall with paper to pass on while others, their messages delivered, dawdled back laughing among themselves. I entered a small room like a cell next door to an identical room where I could just see through the glass a telephone operator sitting with a steel band around his head which pressed the receivers to his ears, his right hand jerking with a pencil. Each message he had finished was handed to a waiting boy who ran off with it down the grey-green corridor.

An operator helped me to put the receivers to my head. There was nothing for me to touch, just a wooden apparatus box with electric wires out the back, and on the table in front a tube to speak in, standing like a curious metal flower raising its bloom for me to sniff. I stared at the box and there was a noise in my ears: 'Frank, Frank Geyer, are you there?' Into my head came this tinny voice, scarcely, but just recognisable as that of Ed Cass, like there was a miniscule Cass in the wooden box and if I opened the door at the back he would just dance out on the table. It was an urgent voice, as if calling with some portentous matter from a long, long way away, as indeed he was.

'It's me' I said, 'it's me, Ed.' I didn't know what to say, 'How are you,' I said stupidly, and felt foolish in front of the telephone operator who was standing by to help.

'The castle,' he said, 'police are exploring the castle.'

He said it twice before I go it. 'That's great, Ed,' I shouted.

'What?'

'Great. WHAT IS THERE?'

'Come and look,' he said, then some other words that were swept away in the boom and dwindle of the machine where the telephone message would come in strong and fade out.

'I'll get up there,' I said

'Come soon. Come now,' the voice said, as if it hadn't heard me.

'I'll come. I'll come,' I said, marvelling at the miracle of speech at a thousand miles distance.

Soon we were well aware of what was happening. Chief O'Brien got a cable from Detective Sergeant Norton in Englewood, the same man who had held me overnight in the cells. He wanted confirmation of Holmes' whereabouts, charges were pending for murders. O'Brien flashed back a request for clarification. 'MURDER or MURDERS?' The response was quick: 'MURDERS OK.'

Norton officially requested help with their investigation. As soon as O'Brien said I could go I was out the door, running down Broad Street looking for a cab in the main artery of the city which was clogged with horse flesh, carriages and cursing drivers. Now I was really moving, on a Pullman plunging on through night and day across America with the leaded glass, marble washbasins, pure white dinner services and the obliging porters, clean linen and clean boots, 'Yessir, nothing left to chance sir,' and the few coins placed in the pale palm of the black hand ensuring a service in excess of regulations. I lay back watching the country unfold as we rolled across the wide, flat prairie and into Chicago. When I walked into the great hall of Union Station it felt to me like a triumphal entrance. At last the powers of dedicated work in the service of justice were overpowering those of evil.

I went straight to Englewood, and to the police station, looking like the sheriff's office in a ghost town, where an old policeman emerged from the deeper reaches of the establishment to shift the wad of tobacco in his mouth and say 'everybody gone to the castle' so I took the same route. On Wallace and 63rd there was a small crowd of onlookers round the hotel entrance of the castle where the planks keeping the place boarded up had been torn off and an entrance recreated. I walked towards the couple of cops creating a police cordon in front of it and a choleric man detached himself from the crowd to ask if I was a cop. I said yes, 'You got to help me get my money back' he said, his sallow face and yellow eyes jerking as he almost squared up to me in fighting stance in his anger, 'that Holmes owes me near enough two hundred and fifty dollars for furniture I delivered right and proper and he never paid me a red cent for it.'

'I'm sorry fellow, I can't help you.' I said, 'tell the Englewood police that.'

'But he's a fraudster pure and simple,' he insisted, 'he has defrauded me! He has defrauded me!'

'Join the line,' I said and walked on.

I showed my badge and asked for Sergeant Norton. As I was explaining myself out came Ed Cass, as free and light as if he was welcoming me to a picnic. 'It's here, all the evidence is here,' he said, 'you were right, always right, Holmes is a monster. Remains... the remains here, you wouldn't believe.' His words were jumbled, he had so much to tell.

'That's great Ed,' I said, 'but tell me slowly, why don't you?'

'You got to see it,' he said, 'come in.'

He welcomed me into the hotel lobby, through the ripped open boards. Inside, the air was filled with distant banging as floorboards were prised up and cupboards taken out in a methodical search. We moved cautiously through the dim and dusty corridors, like men in diving suits, breathing in a fetid odour. In some places the castle's own power cables had been reconnected so there was electric light, at others the searchers gently carried in light bulbs on the end of cables, holding them carefully as eggs as they strung them up.

The police had been working methodically, examining room by room. There was the first floor, and two above. On the top one Cass said they'd found nothing. But this first storey was a maze of horror. He took me on a tour of the area already searched where narrow, winding passages led up to hidden stairways, cleverly concealed doors and rooms, blind hallways and trapdoors. It was even hard to tell how many rooms there were because of the half-stairs, inclining floors, the jumble of large rooms and the occasional room with a low ceiling with another room through a trap door underneath. Some rooms were fire-proof, furnished with asbestos and steel sheeting. There were secret passages where they found windowless cell-like rooms with peep-holes, some of them padded; there was a room almost filled with a huge safe into which a gas pipe had been introduced, presumably to gas some poor unfortunate who had been lured into it. I started to take notes, but the weight of information became overwhelming, Chicago police were drawing plans, making an inventory of everything in each room. It wouldn't be my case anyway, I just stopped writing and stared in awe: how could one person do so much that was so perverted?

'Look here' said Cass and he brought me into a windowless room with a steel door and pointed at a place where plaster had been worn away to the brick, all stained with brown streaks, as if someone had been clawing and clawing away till their fingers were torn to shreds, clawing in increasing desperation to get out before some nameless horror befell them. 'Jesus Christ' I said, more as a prayer than an oath. In the next room wedged into the plastering where a door sill had been torn away were a woollen shirt, a little girl's dress and a pair of shoes. It was bizarre to see them there, shoved into the structure deliberately, as if the notion was to fabricate the entire building out of fragments of people and their effects.

Cass took me up to show me Holmes's apartments with a master control for the gas in all the guest rooms. It was believed Holmes would lock a victim in the room and turn on the gas, a refinement was to lock them in an asbestos room and burn them. There was a trap door in his bedroom that opened to disclose a chute straight down to the cellar.

I stood staring at Holmes' large, comfortable bed, imagining him lying there, plotting. 'Oh, with all this I forgot,' Cass said, 'Don't let me forget to tell you – it's in the mail. It was in the mail before this came up.' He responded to my bewilderment with impatience, 'I found a dentist that can identify Pitezel from that cast. He'd never forget that arrangement of teeth, he said, damnedest thing, never seen any mouth like it.'

'Great,' I said, with no particular pleasure, 'so I think we've got him for that.'

'We've got him for more than that,' Cass shook his head, 'you haven't seen half of it. You won't believe what's here. This place is... his eyes were wide, 'like some torture chamber from story books. Do you know there's even a rack here.'

'A rack?' I said, hoping it wasn't what I thought it was.

'A rack for stretching people... for torturing them. Look you

176

won't believe it, you just have to see. Come downstairs...'

Cass was chirpy as a chipmunk, jumping from one place to another, chattering like mad, every minute a new idea coming into his head that he just had to share, like a man possessed by demons. It was as if this was all he had ever wanted: a crime scene where the evidence was everywhere, just looking around found the riches of blood, discarded clothing, instruments of torture.

On the ground floor we walked past the backs of the shops that lead on to the sidewalk, through the peeling splendour of the public areas of the hotel and down the long corridor with red carpet which I had entered surreptitiously before I was apprehended by these same Chicago police. At the mouth of the cellar there was the smell of decay as if whatever had been alive there now festered and rotted

Down the narrow wooden staircase the cellar smelled of putrefaction, but also oil, gasoline and other chemicals I couldn't identify. A string of electric bulbs shone in the gloom and a handful of officers busied themselves prising open secret places or examining finds at tables where specimens were placed for later identification. There were fragments of jewellery which must have been broken down for the precious stones to be sold; a hair ribbon, still sky blue despite the dust; a charred half of a woman's shoe. The evidence was just a collection of fragments; they had been at the work with a search team only for a day. Cass had called me almost immediately the castle had been breached and he had a message from the bloodhound-faced Sergeant Norton.

'Here,' said Cass, 'you described this to me.' He showed me the dissecting table I had encountered in such shock earlier: a stained white marble top with runnels on either side. A case of gleaming surgical knives showing evidence of frequent use stood on a table nearby. A shiver went through me at the thought of Henry Holmes pondering over the cadavers that had lain there and rendering them to bone with deft slices. There were two tanks of quicklime for reducing what was left to sludge, and a pile of loose quicklime in a corner displaying the imprint of a bare human foot that investigators had indicated with a little flag.

'Any children?' I said, my tongue thick in a dry mouth.

'Only one so far,' Cass said, and took me to a specimen table where bones were displayed which had been found in loose dirt in a hole in the middle of the floor. 'This was a child,' he said, 'preliminary results say it was a child between six and eight years of age. There are ribs, part of a spinal column, a collar bone and a hip bone.'

'Any idea of the date of death?' my breath condensed in the cold, damp air.

'They guessed at two years.' said Cass, 'and we know a Julia Conner and her daughter Pearl lived with Holmes and then disappeared. So the guess is it was Pearl, but how can you identify that?' and he waved his hand at the pathetic collection of fragments that had so recently been a living, feeling human being. We stood as if in reverence for death, with the smell of disturbed human remains in our nostrils, inhaling the dank air of decay.

Cass showed me the sights: a furnace with steel rollers like in a crematorium, with tanks of fuel – maybe gasoline, kerosene, coal oil, naphtha, benzene – things I couldn't identify. The rack was a low, flat structure with leather straps at the corners to hold the wrists and ankles of some poor wretch. A lever at one end operated a ratchet to lengthen the platform. I noted with disgust and pity a stain at waist height where someone had voided their bladder.

Finally Cass stood wordlessly over a trench, a low, narrow grave with the perfect form of a skeleton, the bones mainly brown, some with pieces of flesh adhering to them. At one end, the head seemed to be a rubber ball, with what appeared to be antennae emanating from it. I knelt down and saw in fact it was one long strip of rubber which had been wound round the head many times, completely encasing it, but from the centre, where the nose would be were two tubes, so the poor wretch could breathe while some nameless horror was practised on them.

'Can you tell if it was male or female?' I asked, trying to preserve a proper reverence for the dead while at the same time keeping my distance from a human sympathy which would expose me to a share in its suffering.

'It was probably a young woman,' said Cass. 'But it's not complete.' I looked at him, 'many bones are missing, particularly from the feet and hands - fingers, toes, wrist bones. The kneecaps are gone.'

'So Henry was dissecting,' I said, hoping we could move on.

Cass nodded, as if unwilling to go further, then felt obliged to say quietly, 'It looks like she was dissected while she was still alive.'

My stomach lurched and I turned away as if to vomit. 'Oh my God,' I said, *will it never end?*

Detective Sergeant Norton spied me and came over. 'Geyer,' he said, extending a hand, 'glad to see you.' The distraction was a welcome change from the horror. I shook his hand and stood facing him, saying nothing, waiting to hear what he had to say. He gave a look of pained resentment, 'I suppose you think I'm going to apologise and say you were right all along,' he said, 'and I should have listened better to your story, brought in Holmes and charged him with something fake and searched the castle then.'

'I'm sure I'd have done the same in your position.' I said, pausing while his countenance changed to something resembling a smile, 'and I'd have been wrong too.'

'Well, you should have come to us, not just broke in here,' he said, then relented a little and added, as if ingratiating himself, 'You being here did make a difference. People who hadn't been paid for goods were always coming to us, and people looking for lost relatives people who had disappeared. There was nothing solid to go on, but over time there was a lot of complaints about Henry Holmes and about this place. So in the end we got a court order to break in, on a warrant to look for some garbage or other, it doesn't matter. Of course, when we got some light into this cesspool we saw what you see.'

I nodded and guided him away from the subject, that apology was the best I was going to get and I'd better settle for it and move on. There was a lot of work to do here. 'Isn't there another storey here?' I asked, 'I mean, there's a tilt to the second floor that seems like subsidence, but it goes all the way around the building. Isn't there another floor under that, a very low one, that corresponds to it?' I moved my hands above and below each other to show how where one room was big, the one below would be small and tilting away from it.

'I just haven't been able to work out the structure of this place,' said Norton, 'I guess that was the idea when it was built. Holmes supervised every foot of it himself.'

'It's just a hunch,' I said, 'but an extra floor gives Holmes access to all the rooms above and below.'

'Let's go outside and look at the windows,' he said. I was pleased to go and get some air, and I wanted to extend the hand of police comradeship. Cass had gone off to talk to someone else in the cellar while I was with Norton, so I didn't tell him I was leaving, I'd be back within a minute.

We stood outside regarding the whole front of the castle, a little away from the crowd which had gathered round the entrance cordon, grateful for the light and relief from the breath of death. In the bright light the castle looked shabby and thin, the windows dusty with broken frames, the store windows with their tawdry scrollwork, the turrets shoddy. It was hard to imagine how much pain had been suffered there, by so many unknown innocents.

'There are no plans of course,' said Norton, 'and no architect, for this, he made it up as he went along. He used different builders and told them what to do day by day, so not even any of the people who built it know what's in there. Of course, he never paid them, you know...'

He stopped as he spoke, as if aware that something was happening before it took place. There was a sound like a pop, a feeling like a light punch in the face and the castle was transformed before our eyes. Glass, dust and debris came bursting out of the windows and doors like a stage trick in a wild west show. It flowed out like lava from a volcano then seemed to stop, suspended in mid-air. A great shower of debris seemed to float out on a plume of smoke. A strangled 'Uhh' sound came out of my mouth as I felt the wind rushing from the explosion. Then slowly, as if every wall was taking a long time to fall, Holmes's Castle collapsed in on itself like a card house. The lintels crashed down, the window frames crumpled in; the walls buckled and bobbed as great roof beams crashed through the rooms and tons of brick smashed to right and left, slithering about for a place to rest.

On my head, my shoulders, all around me pattered small fragments of brick, shards of wood and glass. Only now was the crash and roar of the explosion around us, a huge noise like we were witnessing the end of the world. We stood open mouthed, as if this was an act in the theatre, an illusionist's trick, and when the dust that now obscured the building had settled, the castle would still be standing whole. A silk curtain would be pulled away and there it would be.

Norton regained his self-control first. 'You,' he shouted to a delivery boy in a canvas apron who was frozen in amazement, 'get to the fire station on 62nd and Lake, ring the bell, tell the foreman it's an all stations alert. Then the police station, tell them we've got men buried here.' His voice sounded muffled in my ears partially deafened by the bang.

'Sir, yessir' said the white-faced kid and he scampered off, running in a turn so he could still look at the building as if he couldn't believe his eyes. Norton looked at me as if he was sick to the stomach at what we were going to do and we both walked forward into the billowing dust. The roar of falling and crumbling masonry had all but stopped by the time we reached the door which still stood, a solid arch, in front of the ruin of bricks, mortar and beams sticking up at crazy angles. A few guys stumbled out, dazed but helping each other through the rubble, their blue uniforms made piebald by the patches of dust. They were all police from the ground and upper floor. Cass wasn't among them, nor was anyone who had been in the cellar.

I stood at the unreal door, swirling brick dust still blocking a view of more than an arm's length, and I called, my voice sounding dead in ears numbed by the blast, 'Anyone trapped? Shout if you can hear me. Can anyone hear? Ed. Ed Cass. CAN YOU HEAR ME?'

We listened intently to the sounds of the wreck, the weighty

181

sliding of heavy objects deep within it as they settled to a new level, but no sounds made by a living thing. My ears strained to catch the smallest sound, the scratch of a mouse scurrying or a hand clawing, but there was nothing. Then there was a little crackle of sound, I listened intently as it doubled and trebled in volume, it was a voracious sound that devoured and developed into a roar. 'It's on fire,' I said through dry lips powdered with brick dust, not really speaking very loudly, 'it's on fire under there'.

We made desperate, ineffectual attempts to move some of the rubble and locate the buried men but the task was beyond us. We were quickly surrounded by men from the locality, all shouting and tearing away at pieces of timber and masonry with no order or routine, like an assault on the gates of hell by the occupants of a lunatic asylum.

Soon the air was filled with the ringing bells of the steamers and the heavy clatter of drays pulling them. When Norton appraised the fire foreman that there were trapped people, more messages went out and all the surrounding fire departments sent their full-time men, volunteers and equipment until 63rd street and Wallace resembled a battlefield with men all in helmets, some in uniform, some half-uniform, all scurrying between huge pieces of fire apparatus. The drays champed as their loads, red engine cylinders with gleaming copper and brass tubes, were steamed up until the pressure became unbearable and they began pumping with the relief of a hiss and rush of water. Coils of water pipes rolled out towards the castle in one direction and down towards the lake in the other, in a cluttered, hap-hazard collection of machines and limbs, as if a bunch of octopus had clambered out of the deep and were resting on the road in the hot night.

A great crowd of spectators had gathered that Sergeant Norton was trying to organise into teams to take out the rubble where the fire had not taken hold and it was cool enough to work. I helped as best I could, tearing at the wood and brick and lifting beams. Now the dust had cleared it looked even more like the whole building had fallen in on itself into its own foundations. The front of the building had fallen backwards like a man punched in the gut who said ugh and sat down. The frontage of the building with the flashy tiles and the decaying gilt entranceway was sitting in the cellar. The cellar, I thought despairingly, the cellar where I had last seen Cass.

It was many hours of labour in the infernal din, working all night under electric lights that were fitted up with power from surrounding buildings. So much needed to be done that I was cold and unthinking – I just had to do the job in hand. Anyway, I didn't believe with part of my mind that Ed Cass was there at all, soon I'd be telling him about the tremendous adventure I had with Holmes's castle and he would be saying 'gosh'.

We'd worked through the night and seen the sun rise over the lake the next day before the bodies came out, four of them, pulled unresisting from the dust into the dawn like dead drunk men we were trying to rouse for work. Cass was easy to identify, he was the only one not in police uniform, though his business suit was white with plaster, stained in some places with undried blood. I recognised him by his watch that was still in his vest pocket with the chain still across the stomach of the shattered body.

'Ed,' I said stupidly over the limp form, he was so obviously dead. I stood breathing hard, my hands covered in dust and my own blood where I had torn them on the rubble. I had been numb with shock until this, now the enormity of it came upon me and I choked back tears, pressing the back of my torn hands to my eyes. Ed Cass was dead, my true friend in adversity was no more, I sobbed like a baby.

They led me to the mission hall which women from the local church had taken over to give us searchers coffee and food and what medical attention we might need. The minister came and said a few words over each body as they were carted off to the dead house. Englewood put on its bravest face.

I cleaned up in the police station, they let me stay in the section house. I wanted to be among other policemen, as if they would understand better. I remember going through the motions of washing my hands, and looking at the mirror, not recognising my face covered in dirt and dust. Who am I? I wondered. I was numb with fatigue and grief. I got some sleep on a bunk or I just collapsed into unconsciousness.

In a few days I'd done what I could, and that wasn't much. I saw Cass's boss in his opulent office at Fidelity Mutual and met Hillary Cass there, a picture of sorrow in widow's weeds. She walked with a certain clumsiness, as if she had been physically hurt and had trouble moving her own weight. When she saw me she rose, crossed the room clung to my arm. I put my hand on her shoulder as she choked out his name, insensible with grief. My pity was mixed with shame, as if Henry Holmes' actions were my responsibility, as if it was my fault he had come into their home to call down ruination on all love. The devastation of lives boomed and reverberated in my mind like an echo of the explosion. She was beyond consolation, understandably: you just don't expect to marry an insurance man only to have him dug out of the rubble of an exploded torture chamber at the age of twenty-six. It was young. I didn't know he was that young, though I suppose I could have guessed.

Someone helped Mrs Cass away and I realised as I watched, with a kind of disbelieving misery, that her gaucheness was not born of grief alone: she was pregnant. I hadn't known, I guess they wanted to keep it as their secret until it became obvious. Maybe Ed was going to tell me later, when the job was over. Now it was over, for him. I had no words for all of this, the lives rent asunder, the cosmic waste of it all. I searched in my mind like a naked hand searching in a bare cupboard and found it empty of descriptive terms: I was shocked speechless.

I went back to take my leave of Sergeant Norton. We'd been through a lot together and I wanted him to know there were no hard feelings. He looked up as I walked in, his drooping jowls nearly touching his desk. 'How's it going?' I said gently.

'About as bad as could be,' he said. The evidence is destroyed. With the explosion, the fire, water damage from the fire, the way rescuers threw things around, there's not the evidence there that could hang a cat.' He held up an official paper. 'Look, I have a buildings commissioner report on it, came just this morning. It was with the typewriter when the place went up. "The structural parts of inside are all weak and dangerous. Built of the poorest and cheapest kind of material..." I suppose we know all that.' He stopped reading as if he had just got bored with it, as if he was bored with everything and was just making a special effort to talk to me to humour me, as if he'd never be interested in anything ever again. 'The walls were one brick thick in places, the gas pipes were all over the place,' he said mournfully. 'The only things I've got now are this Department of Buildings inspection and a pile of missing persons reports.

'Who were they?' I asked

'People who went to the World's Fair, mainly, I guess. Holmes ran his hotel through that period, people arrived in Chicago, looked for a hotel, saw Holmes's ad and booked in there, didn't tell their folks where they were staying. They'd only be gone a few days.' He rubbed his hand hard from his forehead down his face, as if he was going to rub his face clean off. 'That's the missing persons from the World's Fair period. Then there's people who worked for Holmes, women mainly, they're missing too.'

'How many?' I asked gently.

'Fifty,' he said softly. 'Fifty unaccounted for. Some of them nothing to do with Holmes. Most of them, I guess, were his.'

'Jesus,' I said despairingly, 'How'd he get away with it?'

'He has the luck of the devil,' said Norton, 'because it looks like he's got away with it again. We've even lost the bones, clothing, things like that. With no complete bodies, or even a crime scene, we won't be able to prosecute. Besides your Ed Cass, I lost three men. I've got no evidence. no witnesses. What can I do?..Luck of the devil.'

'I think the devil recognises one of his own,' I said. 'Anyway I suspect it wasn't your bad luck, or Holmes' good luck, my guess is it was a trap.'

'What?' he said, showing a flicker of interest.

'It was no accident. When your investigators looked into some place, maybe opened a door, they unwittingly tripped a wire or turned on a tap. It controlled gas or maybe a thin spray of gasoline or some inflammable oil. If you didn't turn it off in time, it would detonate and bring the whole building down. It was Holmes' last trick when he knew he was going to be caught.'

Norton stared at me as if he was listening but his eyes didn't register it. 'Well what d'you know?' he said when I'd finished.

'Look,' I said, 'Norton, listen. We've got Henry Holmes in Philadelphia. I'll make sure he hangs for his crimes. I won't let him go. OK?' Norton gave a false smile, as if thanking me for some minor service he hadn't required anyway. I left him disconsolately going through his missing person reports, the bold man I had encountered just a few days ago now smashed and broken like Holmes' castle.

I went to see the castle one more time before I left Chicago, now a few half-demolished walls and pyramids of rubble, some twice as tall as a man, where we flung the debris as we sifted through the building after the fire was out. The first floor was virtually cleared, as was the dreadful cellar, the reeking pit where Cass and three other men had died, now exposed to light as no more than a noisome hole in the ground in an empty plot due for development.

As I walked away I saw, standing white like a sentinel of despair in the gloom of the hopeless day, Mrs Van Tassell, both hands gripped on the handle of her purse, as if she was afraid someone was going to take that away from her too. I tried to think of a word, or even an acknowledgement, but I was too weary and walked on. I couldn't bear the weight of any more people's suffering, I had no words of reassurance to give. No, her daughter would never leave there, no one was saved, and no retribution could ever fit the crime.

Chapter 13

I went back to Philadelphia to see a man imprisoned for a crime he didn't commit. Henry Holmes was the Prince of Lies, the only crime he confessed to was one he didn't do. Henry hadn't perpetrated an insurance fraud: Ben Pitezel was insured for his life and Ben Pitezel's life was taken away from him. The insurance was paid. Where was the fraud?

Henry had been transferred to the county jail, Moyamensing prison. Or, as he put it, he had been 'placed in a crowded conveyance filled with a filthy lot of humanity' and taken there. Henry was always very particular about the company he kept, he was a murderer of refinement. A metal grille plus a wooden door screened out the commotion of the prison outside, so when I encountered Holmes in his clean, whitewashed cell it was in conditions of scholastic solitude. There was a bed, a washbasin and a small table at which Holmes sat, looking up from a legal book he was studying as I came in. 'Frank, they told me you were going to visit,' he said cordially, I almost expected him to say how great it was to see me. The jailer brought a chair for me, and one for a stenographer.

'I've been in Chicago,' I said, 'in Englewood.'

'Yes,' he said sadly, 'I heard my hotel collapsed, I read it in the newspapers.' I looked at him for the first time with contempt. For the first time he'd killed someone I knew. It did make a difference.

'Oh, don't look at me,' he said, exculpating himself with a wave of his hand, 'the insurance ran out on it long ago.'

'A lot of people died there,' I said

'Yes,' he said, looking round, as if I was accusing him or someone sitting behind him of guilt, 'but I didn't ask them to go there. I didn't ask the police to break in, or your insurance investigator friend to go snooping about. Who knows, maybe they caused the building to fall down with something they did, maybe I should claim against the Chicago police.'

I got the feeling in these interviews that Henry was trying to goad me to hit him so he could say any evidence against him was tainted by the use of police brutality. That defence sometimes worked with a jury, not least because it was sometimes true. So I never allowed Henry Holmes to anger me, and I never met him without a witness.

'There were other bodies there, Henry,' I said flatly, 'many more bodies.'

'I was an honest dealer in human remains,' Holmes said, 'I received bodies from morgues, rendered them to skeletons and sold them on to anatomy schools where they continue to assist in the onward progress of medical science. Why, I even advertised in the newspapers for an assistant to help me in my work, that's how dishonest it was. Does a crook advertise for an accomplice? There are receipts in my desk–or there would be if my building had not been damaged by the police.'

'There were more bodies than you can account for and you know it,' I said, 'there was even a rack there for torturing people

'A rack for torturing people?' he said incredulously. He looked bemused, then sprang into life 'Oh no, that was the elasticity determinator!' he said. 'I have this theory, you see, that the human body could be stretched to twice its normal length, ultimately creating a race of giants,' he beamed at me. 'The contrivance you saw was one of my inventions aimed at testing this theory.'

It was at this point that I thought Holmes might actually be mad, be stark, staring, raving mad. But I suppressed the thought, because if he was mad, then he might just get off all charges on the basis that he didn't know what he was doing. And on later reflection, I considered perhaps that was just what he wanted us to think, and it was another one of his carefully prepared bolt-holes to run down to escape justice. It was just like he could explain away the evidence or confuse it so no jury would believe it anymore, like the advertisement in the paper for the skeleton articulator, and the animal bones mixed with the human in the castle dungeon. Just put in so much innocent extra evidence that the guilty slips through – easy when you know how to do it.

'Alright Henry, I'm not here to do the job of the Chicago police.'

I said, 'You have denied that you were in Philadelphia before Benjamin Pitezel's death, and even that he is dead. The state is now able to demonstrate that the body found in Callowhill Street is that of Benjamin Pitezel, and that you were there before he died. Henry wrote it down in a blank book in a perfect, sloping script as I briefly gave him the facts about the carpenter being able to identify him and the dentist identifying Pitezel's teeth.

Henry continued to write notes on this, his brow furrowed, after I had stopped speaking and then looked up. 'Well, as you have correctly surmised Frank,' he said, 'I have lied to you in my first statement. I am truly sorry to have to admit that, but I am convinced that when you know the reason for this you will understand that my motives were pure even though I know you must do your duty by your employer.'

This had better be good, I thought to myself, knowing that it would be. Henry spoke at some length, with a wealth of detail. The point of it was that he had visited the Callowhill house three or four times, 'I had found my friend despondent and drinking heavily, then one Sunday morning I let myself into the house and couldn't find Ben on the first or second floor, that's where the office and laboratory were, so I went right up to Ben's bedroom. I found him there, dead on the floor, the stench of chloroform filling the room. He had just gone crazy and let too much worry over the care of his family send his poor brain astray and he did away with himself. His money worries had finally overbalanced his mind, he had committed suicide.

'So what was I going to do?' Henry mimed looking round as if the inanimate objects in the room with the dead man were giving him clues as to his actions. 'Yes, I decided, suicide would simply not do, for it would deny his family money from the insurance company and leave poor Ben's abandoned wife and children destitute. I had to make his clear and apparent suicide look like an accident. So I took the body upstairs – not an easy task, for Ben was bigger than me – and placed him on his back in the laboratory. I smashed a bottle containing benzene, chloroform, and ammonia and splashed some of it on his body. I took his pipe from his bedroom and laid it near his body, as if he was lighting it when an explosion had happened. Then I left the scene, confident that he would be found, and of course looking out for a notice of death so I could help poor Mrs Pitezel to claim on the insurance.'

And defraud her of it, I thought, but said nothing. Of course it was another wily and unconscionable trick to get away with murder, but juries had believed stupider things. I looked at him blankly. 'So what you're telling me Henry,' I said, 'is that you set up to commit an insurance fraud with Ben Pitezel; he killed himself in the perpetration of this crime, so you went ahead with the fraud anyway, so as not to waste good planning.'

'To provide for Ben's poor family,' he corrected. I ignored this. Henry's new line was about as clever as could be. It hinged on the slight difference between suicide and murder; it explained the fact that Pitezel really was the dead man and no substitute; and it explained why Holmes was at the house in Philadelphia. It admitted a small crime, committed in the name of charity, while concealing a bigger one.

'I have to hand it to you Henry, I said, 'you are smart. Except for one thing. Where are the kids?'

'Well I've been wondering that myself,' he said. 'Mrs Pitezel's three girls. No, no it was two girls and a boy, wasn't it? They were with Minnie Williams, my typewriter. They were going to be reunited with Ben when he was resurrected, so to speak, after the insurance scheme came off. Their mother handed them over to me to take to their father.'

'But you took the children after Ben was already dead, when you met Mrs Pitezel at Chicago Union station. You already had Alice, and you took Nellie and Howard with you.'

'Oh I don't think so,' said Holmes, his bright blue eyes sparkling with the thrill of combat at last, 'I think you'll find poor Mrs Pitezel's mind was confused by all the moving from city to city and the different plans. She's just got the dates wrong. Ben was hale and hearty when I took the children from Mrs Pitezel.'

Again, Henry had stopped a course of action for me. There were five people who might have verified the events: Holmes himself;

Alice, Nellie and Howard; and Mrs Pitezel. The children were missing and Carrie Pitezel would be taken to pieces in court by a clever defence lawyer. She wouldn't know what day of the week it was, let alone on precisely which day she met someone in a station in Chicago months previously. Holmes was the only credible witness to these events, so his version would be believed. Henry was slipping like quicksilver from my grasp as we spoke. 'Let's move on to Minnie Williams,' I said, 'you say she had the children?'

'Yes that's it' he beamed, 'that's it exactly.'

'Henry,' I said, 'that is explaining the disappearance of three missing persons by reference to another missing person.'

'Oh is that so?'

'Yes,' I said, 'it is so.'

'The last time I saw Howard,' he said carefully, 'was in Detroit, Michigan. There I gave him to Miss Williams, who took him to Buffalo, New York, from which point she proceeded to Niagara Falls. After the departure of Howard, in Miss Williams' care, I took Alice and Nellie to Cleveland, where they remained for several days. At Cleveland I purchased railroad tickets for them for Niagara Falls, put them on the train, and rode out of Cleveland with them a few miles, so that they would be assured that they were on the right train. Before their departure, I prepared a telegram which they should send me from the Falls, if they failed to meet Miss Williams and Howard, and I also carefully pinned in the dress of Alice, four hundred dollars in large bills, so Miss Williams would be in funds to defray their expenses.' He said it all neatly and slowly, so the stenographer could take it down. He had had a lot of time to practice it, sitting here in this white room with a register for heating and a sixteen candle-power electric burner and three wholesome meals a day. A lot of people in the USA didn't get that, maybe most of them. 'They joined Miss Williams and Howard at Niagara Falls,' Henry continued, 'from which point they went to New York City. At the latter place, Miss Williams dressed Nellie as a boy, and took a steamer for Liverpool, whence they went to London. If you search among the steamship offices in New York, you must search for a woman and a girl and two boys, and not a woman and two girls and a boy. This was all done to throw all you detectives off the track, who were after me for the insurance fraud. Miss Williams opened a massage establishment at No. 80 Veder or Vadar Street, London. I have no doubt the children are with her now, and very likely at that place.'

'You killed them, didn't you Henry?' I said, for the record as I hardly expected him to confess outright.

He became almost tearful, 'Why should I kill innocent children?' he sobbed, as if appalled that I could think such a thing.

'Please give me the name of one respectable person to whom I can go,' I said patiently, 'either in Detroit, Buffalo, Cleveland, Niagara Falls, or New York, who will say that they saw Miss Williams and the three children together.'

This question got under his guard for a moment, but he quickly recovered and said in his injured tone, 'That question implies a disbelief in my statement.'

'It certainly does, Henry, but you know we'll check it out.'

What was amazing about Henry Holmes, alone of the thousands of criminals I have interviewed, was that he never ran out of ideas. His world was like a gymnasium where there was always another piece of equipment to jump over, to lift, to climb up, that Henry had created to exercise my skills. At some urging about how he made contact with this Minnie Williams, he volunteered that he had made arrangements to communicate by means of a cipher code placed in the personal column of the New York Herald. It was nothing but a substitution code, but I took it down and Henry encoded the message IMPORTANT TO HEAR BEFORE 10TH. CABLE. RETURN CHILDREN AT ONCE. I was resentful that had to go off to waste time putting encoded messages in newspapers to attract the attention of people who were already dead. But I couldn't afford to pass up any opportunity to find out what had happened to the children.

I gave Henry one last chance before I left him, 'Now is the time,' I said, 'when you could produce the children with a flourish and prove me wrong. If the children are alive, you know it would be best for you to confound your critics and show them alive for all the world. Just let them return to their mother.'

'I have said all I can to help you on the matter,' Henry said, like he was a bank manager refusing me a loan.

'Then I'll bid you good-day,' and I left Henry at his table, nodding and smiling faintly that this distraction in his busy schedule had been removed.

I was arranging to get transcripts with the stenographer in the turnkey's office when I was kicked in the gut by the sight of Georgiana. I saw her through the window of the waiting room, and she didn't see me yet, so I had a chance to gaze. She stood silently in a modest blue dress looking with no great interest out of the window at the prison exercise yard. She carried on her arm a straw basket carrying eatables, I guessed, pies and fruit for the prisoner.

I normally know what I'm going to say to people, I have prepared a first line and a rejoinder, because I'm the detective and I'm the one who must control the conversation, I don't walk into situations I don't know. But here, with Georgiana, my Georgiana through a glass panel next door, a vision of peace in a turbulent world, I lost reserve, perhaps I was frightened she would go away again before I could see her.

I went straight in, 'Georgiana,' I said, perhaps too sharply, as if I was warning a child not to go near the window. As I passed the lintel I realised the inappropriateness of any remark I might make in a room bounded by the grey stone of the prison. No it wasn't so nice to see her there; no it wasn't even such a surprise; no I couldn't say 'How are you' to a woman visiting her imprisoned husband—how did I think she was?

She turned her slender shoulders towards me and gave the slightest flicker of a smile which may have been merely politeness. In the cold morning light of the prison I saw how her face was crossed with tiny lines, not there when I had gazed on her so intently as a boy.

'Frank,' she said, 'I wondered if I should see you…' Still my soul was flayed by her blonde hair; still I drowned in her huge blue eyes such that I was already tongue-tied.

'Sorry,' I said, apologising for my tone, 'I just didn't expect to see you here.'

'As you have put Henry here, it is my place,' she said, her voice softer than the incriminating words.

I was going to say I was just an agent of the law, as if excusing myself for my part in Henry's imprisonment, but that would be cowardly. 'I won't apologise for doing that, Georgiana,' I said, 'Henry deserves to be here.'

'As I understand it,' she said, in the voice of a school mistress, 'Henry is here more or less willingly. He pleaded guilty to an offence regarding an insurance policy and he has yet to be sentenced.'

'I can't talk about the details of the case,' I said with resignation, 'you are right that Henry is held on just one offence, but if he stepped outside the prison, he would be arrested for another.' She acknowledged this with a slight toss of her head as if she couldn't bear to be troubled with such pettiness.

'Where are you staying?' I said. Could I see her for dinner? I wondered, absurdly.

'I'm not staying in Philadelphia,' he said, 'I will have to go back to Burlington today so I don't spend so long away from Lucy. She's back home with a friend's mother.' I wondered if the girl knew her father was a criminal, and what would happen when she found out, how her pretty face would crumple in shock and disbelief, how it would never get better, how the rest of her life would be defined by that moment.

Georgiana was arranging her bonnet and shawl. I watched silently as she picked up her things with her delicate fingers. Soon she would be gone, leaving nothing but her fragrance, and I would be alone amid the big stone blocks of the walls, overlooking the exercise yard, as if this would always be my fate.

But Ed Cass's death had taught me something that I had pondered in the long, sleepless train journey buffeted by time and rhythmic motion: Don't wait to say what you mean for a better time, don't wait because time can stop for me just as it did for Ed. I thought of all the unfinished business he must have left, the things unsaid. Ed's lesson to me was that I must do what I want to do when I want to do it. Spontaneity.

'Don't go. Georgiana,' I said softly

She turned back and tilted her head to one side. 'I need to know,' I said painfully, 'and no time is ever right, but tell me now: Why did you leave me, that day, that night in Gilmanton, back in seventy-seven?'

I must have looked a picture of misery. I have to give Georgiana her due, that she never said that was all a long time ago, and laughed about it, or pretended it didn't matter.

She looked down, as if the secret was in her straw basket, 'Perhaps I wanted to prove something,' she said.

'To who?' I said, following her gaze round to the barred window, 'To me, perhaps?'...

'No? Who then?'

'To myself...' she said in a small, dreamy voice, 'you wouldn't understand.'

'Try me,' I said.

'Oh I don't know,' she said, as if not fully part of this conversation at all, 'False assumptions, saintly selfishness, and good intentions...'

'Can lead a road to hell?' I said. She nodded, as if careless of what she had said or whether she had said it at all. 'For me Hell is a reality,' I said, calmly but in inner exasperation, 'it's where Henry is going.'

Instead of looking angry or upset she smiled, as if enjoying a private joke, and at once I was transported back to the pine needles and the clear air of New Hampshire, with that bafflingly beautiful look of hers.

The turnkey came in for her and she nodded to me, 'Goodbye Frank,' she said, with the hint of a smile still changing her face. I mouthed 'goodbye' and smiled encouragingly. Once again Frank P.Geyer had said the wrong thing, or not said the right thing, or just been at the wrong place at the wrong time not knowing enough. I looked around at the benches fixed to the walls in a room undecorated except for the notices warning not to give contraband to prisoners. I quietly walked to the door to watch her swaying hips follow the rhythm of her demure walk down the prison corridor to the murderer's cell.

Suddenly my clenched fist came up to my breast and I was engulfed with anger. I wanted her to suffer at seeing him there, I wanted her to be in pain as I had been in pain for so many years, in a confused misery of not knowing what she had done wrong to deserve such suffering, so uniquely centred on her but so beyond her control.

I blamed Henry for that too, for making me wish suffering on sweet Georgiana, for I know I am not vindictive by nature, but he had turned love into a desire for vengeance, it was how he had made me something I was not. But I did it anyway, I watched the turnkey open the door for Georgiana and let her in past the grille then the wooden door. When she was fully inside, and both doors had clanged shut, I moved noiselessly towards the turnkey. He would stay outside for the duration of the visit but nothing more than that: Henry was allowed to be alone in his cell, he was considered a low-grade risk for violence and he had the privileges of a man who has not yet been sentenced.

I said in a low voice to the turnkey, 'I'll keep an eye on them, you come along back when their time is up.'

He agreed and went off, only too happy to get back to his newspaper and mug of the sludge that passed for coffee in this place. As he went off down the corridor I delicately raised the flap of the Judas hole and pressed my face through the bars of the grille onto the wooden door. Georgiana was standing, having just put her basket down, he was still sitting at the bare table.

I could not hear their voices as they spoke, and Georgiana's tall, slender form in her blue dress obscured most of Henry from my sight. She must be telling him how sorrowful, how outraged she was, I thought, how he had betrayed the love of her and their child, how could he do such things? I gloated in the satisfaction of at last seeing her realisation of his wickedness.

As I watched he rose, gracefully and slowly, and extended a hand to her, slowly she placed her outstretched hand in his, and the music of his melodious, voice vibrated thinly through the wooden door of the cell.

'For the fittest will always survive
While the weakest go to the wall
The handsomest men will thrive
While the ugliest head for a fall'

It was the song I had first heard in Holmes's cellar, it was one of his songs. Outrageously, obscenely, she was in his arms, her head on his shoulder as they danced a pas de deux, I saw the blue satin trimmings of her dress, the black of his coat, her dreamy face, eyes closed, saw his hand around her dear waist. I pressed my face against the cold steel, as if eager to absorb even more of the torment, until the grille dug into my flesh.

'Over the darkened down we wend
My shadow on a moonlit night
Comes up at me as my friend
Secret shadows and mystic lights
Make out of life what you may
For death there is no cure'

The song, the embrace, her blissful happiness pierced my being until there was nothing left to hurt and the tears rolled down my face like a stream.

'Time won't make a silver girl gold
Lost are the loves of long ago
Venus kissed red roses white for me but
My choice of darkness set me free.'

They parted and both laughed, she throwing her head back to expose the glorious white neck. How happy they were. He who had denied me and Ed Cass and countless others of their happiness, he was happy. He was incarcerated, convicted, stood accused of multiple murders, but still he was winning against me.

Finally I could bear no more. I walked back down the corridor wiping my eyes with the back of my hand and pulling myself together to see the turnkey. I wanted to be out of there before

Georgiana was. For years I had yearned to see her, believed I saw her through glass in every shop, in fleeting shapes in the distance. Now I knew exactly where she was and I was making sure I would be far away.

As I walked out of the yard through the great iron gates into the grey day I knew very clearly what I was going to do, as clearly as I had ever known it in my life. I was going to find those children, I was going to bring back the evidence, and I was going to see Henry Holmes hanged by the neck until dead.

Chapter 14

I cabled Scotland Yard and sent them a detailed letter that I had written by a typewriter to make it formal. I imagined Henry's glee in setting me to this dubious errand, for I had always, even as a boy, wanted to go to Scotland Yard and meet the famous detectives. He couldn't have placed the children in Mexico or Panama or somewhere, they had to be in England. He was offering me what I wanted in the hope I would grab the opportunity and high-tail it off to London. Whatever the situation, Henry's mental resources never seemed to flag.

The men at Scotland Yard were so kind as to check for Minnie Williams, by various means including looking for aliens entering the country from steamships coming in on the relevant dates. There was no record of them anywhere, nor was there a Veder or Vadar Street. I guess my trip to London would have to wait.

The children had been taken in September or October 1894, and it was now spring 1895. By now traces were cold, memories rusty, the chance of the children being alive increasingly remote. There were still some clues which pulsed with a little life, however. When Holmes was arrested, we found the tin box in Dr Oemisch's surgery that contained letters from Alice and Nellie to their mother and grandparents, and a number of letters written by Mrs. Pitezel to the children. Holmes had been entrusted with the letters but he had not passed them on, for fear of giving away his location, and the fact that the children's father was not with them as Holmes claimed. So why did he keep them at all? Maybe he wanted to use them to make out to Mrs Pitezel that the children were still alive, if she threatened to go to the police. Or maybe he just wanted to gloat over them. Who could tell what mysterious valleys and byways made up the landscape of Henry Holmes' soul, what dark cisterns and what abandoned well-holes?

Holmes must have told the children not to put locations in their letters. The kids could even have concurred willingly with the subterfuge, enjoying this life of conspiracy and hiding. From

Mrs Pitezel the letters were about domestic details and concerns about the children's comfort. Alice was the main correspondent among the children, with occasional notes from Nellie. They were written on school-book paper in a scrawled hand that tailed off in neatness and coherence as the letter went on. Most of them dealt with the normal details of childhood, 'Mama have you ever seen or tasted a red banana? I have had three... I have another picture for your album... Why have buffaloes got big rings in their noses?... We have awful good dinners pie fruit and sometimes cake at supper...' As time wore on and the life of travel and concealment took its toll, the letters became increasingly desperate, 'I want you all to write why don't you write mama... All that Nell and I can do is to draw and I get so tired sitting that I could get up and fly almost...' One of the letters, written sometime in late October, said Howard 'would not stay in at all.' This became a theme, Henry Holmes telling Alice to keep the nine-year-old Howard in, and the resourceful Howard escaping. I held the pencil-written paper in one hand and my head in the other, as if my own desperation could talk across time and distance to beg Howard to escape. If only he had got out for longer, got to tell someone what was happening, gone to the police maybe... but in his family the police were probably treated by his father as the enemy, to be avoided at all costs, and with good reason given Ben Pitezel's record. So Howard slipped his sister's clutches and made his forays on his own until one letter, also in late October or early November, when Cass and I were trudging round making our laborious enquiries, perhaps even in the city where the children were homesick in some hotel room, Alice wrote, 'Howard is not with us now.' That was the last letter.

So the children had split up, and now I was searching not for the very conspicuous Henry Holmes and three children but Holmes and one, or two children. Or had he sent them with an accomplice? My thoughts went out like scouts before an army, testing the terrain, nudging at the boundaries of the possible. The only other new clue was a real estate agents' bill, unpaid, of course. It was for a house in Cliveden that I had checked out by the local police. Yes, Holmes had stayed there a week, there were three children but the real estate agent didn't see them, and couldn't even tell if they were boys or girls. What if Henry had changed his modus operandi to stop using hotels and start renting houses? In a slow and cumbersome way, I mentally retraced the search for him. Where Cass and I had lost the trail was Indianapolis, so I decided that was where I had to go.

This time Chief O'Brien didn't even put up a show of resistance to losing me for as long as it took but he couldn't afford to spare another man, I would have to go alone. Fidelity Mutual gladly provided funds to defray my expenses, though they were pessimistic about any results. Mr Graham the District Attorney gave me letters to the authorities to help me on my way. He wasn't an optimist by nature, and feared my spending city money out of state to no good end, but he could be convinced: Mrs Pitezel would testify to the body-swapping insurance fraud if I found her children, and that would make it worthwhile to the City of Philadelphia. The Director of Public Safety Mr Honeycutt saw me for an informal talk in front of his giant desk, where he pressed his hands together and leaned forward like a Methodist minister, looking at me intently with his pleading eyes as if I was the last hope of a dying world.

While I was back I spent some time with rounded, ever-giving Molly, her little house a haven amid the decay and disaster around me. She was always asking me to stay with her, so these days I did, foresaking my fusty lodgings for the domestic life. I tried to contain my anxiety but it burst through the seams of my being in insomnia and a daytime restlessness that made it hard for me to settle to anything. One night, by lamplight, she challenged me gently, asking 'Why are you like this, what do you want?'

'I want to apprehend this man,' I said.

She pushed her black hair from her face, 'OK,' she said, 'it's your job, but I've seen you doing other jobs, you can always turn away and be, like, normal with me, why has this one got under your skin?'

'I just want to find these children, to convict this man,' I said, 'everything will be better, I promise, once I've brought in the evidence to see him convicted.'

Molly, who could see further into my turbid heart than anyone, was not deflected, 'Why did you want it so badly?' she asked, 'You've tracked bad men before, put them in jail, why should this one matter so much to you?'

'I used to know him,' I said, partly worried that this information would come out at the trial and she would want to know why I hadn't told her earlier, 'in Gilmanton, we were kids together.'

She took this information tentatively, as if I had offered her something new to eat that she wasn't sure she would like. 'Why are you so sad about Gilmanton?' she said finally.

'I guess because I grew up there,' I said lightly.

'Most people don't think that's a reason to be sad,' Molly said, emphasising each word exactly, as if she knew, as she surely did, that there was more to it.

'Yeah,' I said, with the expression that said I wanted to leave the subject, 'Yeah, maybe I just feel differently about it, nostalgia for the old times, for the country, for my folks. Maybe I should grow up.'

She hugged me, and I looked through the window into the night-time over her shoulder.

When it was time to go she waved me off from her door, I had the comforting feeling that when I got back, she would still be there. Then I was on my own in the pursuit of sadness. I was much more alone than before. It took me a long time to get used to Cass not being there, I'd be thinking a thought and want to share it and there just wouldn't be anyone. We seemed to have been together so long, though it was only a few weeks. I often saw him, or people who looked like him – vigorous, well-built young men, their hair just beginning to thin, dressed in dark business suits, striding boldly away from me through the crowds.

I was back stepping through station floors filled with bags and parcels tied up with string and the throng of travellers: immigrant women in headscarves, workmen with dinner-pails, uniformed porters, young women looking for their beaux, men looking for work, peanut sellers, newspaper vendors and pickpockets. I was back with the thundering machines eating their way through the countryside, sleeplessly staring into the blackness out of the window. It became my quest from morning to night, quest weary, quest bright, searching hotel ledgers, quizzing real estate agents, my body lying down at night on hotel mattresses rank with the smell of someone else's pleasure.

My world was recorded in the ledgers that I carried around in a growing bundle which was becoming increasingly heavy and cumbersome as time wore on. I had my notebooks, now running to three or four, and Cass' notebooks, where we each had recorded all the clues we had followed up, what witnesses had said, their addresses and leads to pursue. In addition we had begun to keep a joint book very early on, when we realised how complex it would be to track Holmes and how we were going to have to check every hotel and lodging house. In this butcher's ledger with marbled end papers, lined with red columns every known fact was written: 'H meets Mrs Pitezel in Chicago... H and three children arrive at Circle House Hotel morning September 22 1894... Alice writes from Indianapolis September 24... H and the children register as Etta and Nellie Canning, Detroit. Alice says she's staying with a couple, "They are dutch but they can cook awful nice."' Everything had to be entered in – 'Holmes arrived this station, ate at that hotel, bought paper and pencils for children' - even if it had no apparent meaning.

In time we had built up a near complete record of Holmes' travels, and it was my belief that with the slow incremental addition of information, the facts would lead inexorably to the truth, to the children. But the accretion of information was so slow, so damnably slow. I could only cover so much ground, talk to only so many real estate agents, so many hoteliers, porters, cab drivers... I knew I would get there in time, I would find the children. But I feared with a cold horror the possibility that before I found them Holmes would be due for release from the insurance fraud case. I would have to try him on the Pitezel murder, and that might fail. On a good day Holmes could charm the birds off the trees; he would twist the good men of a Philadelphia jury round his fingers and make them proud of themselves that they had been so manipulated. This was the fear gnawing at my heart, that I could not trace the clues fast enough, and Holmes would walk out of the prison and disappear under the cloak of another name, another career and another set of crimes, his dutiful wife being the only constant feature.

I was often cold and tired, going from one place to another, eating standing up at a coffee stall. I thought often of Henry Holmes in his warm, well-lit comfortable cell reading his law books and plotting to evade justice, and I thought of Ed Cass, and longed for the simple company of that honest man.

My plan was to go to the real estate agents in Indianapolis on the theory that Cass and me couldn't find which hotel Holmes had gone to from there because he hadn't gone to a hotel. So I visited all the real estate agents, always singing the same song, presenting my papers and opening up my package of photographs, Holmes' mug-shot and pictures of the children sitting round their mother in a family group, then individual pictures of two of them, standing in a photographer's studio next to the same potted plant on a stand.

Howard was a crop-haired scamp in a white sailor suit, holding a toy boat, scowling a little as if he resented standing still for the photographer in his starchy Sunday best. I looked a lot at the picture. I knew he was a disobedient, willful boy. Maybe he was a strong boy, like the country boys, not one of the sniveling alley rats they breed in the towns, maybe that's why Holmes left him somewhere, somewhere he was still alive. I buoyed myself up with these thoughts and faced every day with ham and eggs in a 'First Class European Hotel', but somewhere among the grease and fragments of food even on bright hopeful mornings was a voice which droned: despair.

It was the tenth or twentieth office on the list that I walked into where a friendly old gentleman with white hair and a face freckled dark from the sun listened to what I had to say, looked at my pictures and said without urgency, 'Yes, I remember that man renting a house in October 1894. I didn't have the renting of the house but I had the keys and one day last fall this man came into my office and in a very abrupt way said "I want the keys for that house." I remember the man very well, because I did not like his manner, and I felt he should have had more respect for my grey hairs.' I almost fell on his shoulders and kissed his old head. It wasn't just a sighting of Holmes at the right time, it was that Henry was acting out of character. Henry would be polite to his own hangman, it was his way. If he was getting impatient it was because we had rattled him, we were pursuing close behind him and he had caught the wind of it, I hoped to God that now he would be making mistakes.

I got a buggy to 305 Poplar Street, a plain two-storey building in its own ground with houses close by on either side. As I pulled up and approached the house there was movement from the house next door. It was a little buxom woman who came into her garden to look over the fence. God bless nosy neighbours. I introduced myself to Miss Hill, a spinster with straggly thin hair hardly pulled back from a face full of the audacity of old age, the point at which there was nothing left to lose by speaking your mind. She spoke out of a mouth boasting three visible teeth at most. Her conversation had a sort of petulant air, as if she was constantly tugging on your sleeve, as if every word of her prattle was urgent. I imagined with a small gleam of pleasure how Henry would have hated her attentions.

'No,' she said when I showed her the pictures, 'just one man and a boy, no girls.' She remembered Holmes very well. 'Gentleman, real gentleman he was, wonder he'd want to dirty his hands putting together a stove.'

'What was that?' I said, for like perhaps everyone else she ever spoke to, I was not really listening to her jabbering.

'Stove,' she said, 'big black round stove, for heating, not for cooking. He brung it up in pieces in a wagon; this Holmes man and the boy were sitting up front.' I looked at her somewhat incredulously, 'chimney going up, right, a furnace underneath with a door for the wood or what you put in it. I saw him put it together right there in that yard. The little boy, he watched him too, he put it together in a couple of hours.' I looked at the spot of scrubbed earth with a few mean weeds struggling through at the edges, and imagined Henry, stripped down to his shirt-sleeves, putting in the bolts and tightening the nuts of a wood-burning stove, while Howard sat on the low shed swinging his legs.

'So you spoke to him?' I asked. She needed no other prompting but repeated the conversation verbatim like it was a part in a play she had been rehearsing.

'"What you doing with that mister?" I says,

"I'm going to assemble it ma'am" he says,

"Why you gonna do that?" I says,

"I'll be burning things in it." he says,

"Why not use gas," I says, "cleaner, healthier, I never knew anyone putting in one of them things when they could just connect up to the gas company."'

She imitated Henry's supercilious tone. '"Oh," he says, like he's the smartest guy in the world, "Oh," he says, "I consider gas to be unsafe for children."'

My throat tightened. Unsafe for children. Yes, I was in the presence of a genuine, 64 carat Henry Holmes joke. Howard had watched him assemble the stove, then Howard had gone into the stove. That was the way it was. That was the meaning of the stove.

'So what happened next?' I said

'Well it was the darndest thing.' she said, fully appreciative of my attentions, 'cuz that night, the night he put the stove together, he came knocking on my door and he said, "You took such an interest in the stove you'd better keep it." And he left in a buggy early the next day.

When I had extricated myself from her clutches I pondered the story. Henry's in a buggy, not a wagon, so he's not going far, maybe to another real estate agent. So I can keep calling on them. I contemplated with grim resignation the thought of trudging round the rest of the real estate agents in Indianapolis, in towns around Indianapolis, with my ledgers and my pictures of the dead. Suddenly I realised what I was doing wrong, his modus operandi was rent a house, buy a stove. I was only looking at one half of it. The harridan was right, not many people did buy stoves now, they were from the times back in Gilmanton where we grew up. Indiana has enough cheap natural gas to last forever, tomorrow belongs to gas and electricity. So there wouldn't be so many people selling heating stoves, and there wouldn't be many people buying them. I went to the big hardware stores in East Washington Street Indianapolis. In the second, Joseph Voegtle, 'retail dealers in stoves, tin and Japanned ware,' they remembered Holmes, they didn't sell a lot of large wood-burning stoves and they had sold him two in as many days. I was right, he was getting sloppy. That part of the trail was easy, the store still had the delivery note and on it the address where they had taken the stove.

I went straight there, soon leaving the city for the highway, then tracks between the cornfields, the hooves of the horse tapping out a dusty clatter. After about six miles the driver laid down the reins as we faced a sizeable wood-fronted cottage standing in a secluded area. I went to talk to a boy mending fences in the neighbouring field. Called Elvet Moorman, he had been there in October, and he was able to identify Holmes from the picture I showed him.

He came over to the house with me, walking a long path through the rattling scream of the crickets. I stared at the wooden slats and the closed shutters in the windless evening, the wood breathing a dry smell with the accumulated heat of the day.

'You can go in, mister,' said Moorman, who was related to the owner of the place. I went up the creaking stairs to the porch and inside, imagining Holmes entering it with Howard. Though light was fading fast I was eager to see what I could, I didn't want to get this far and turn around and come back tomorrow, as if by tomorrow's daylight I somehow wouldn't be able to find the house, as if it would vanish like a mirage and I would be left clutching at air.

The house was frequently let and was furnished only with the basic necessities: beds, kitchen table and chairs, cooking pots. On a quick inspection in the fading light there was nothing suspicious, or any trace of Holmes. I got Moorman to light a lamp and we looked in the cellar but there was nothing untoward, the floor showed no sign of disturbance. Outside the house, in the space underneath it, I found a piece of a ripped-up trunk, the sort of cheap trunk that the children and Holmes had with them. I retained it for identification, it was hardly conclusive evidence but it was something. In the twilight with the sound of the crickets in my ears I tramped through the dry grass looking at the outhouses and the barn. It was in the barn that I saw it, standing pot-bellied at the end, a circular stove about three and a half feet high and just under two feet wide. I approached it as tentatively as I would an altar and raised the lamp so I could see it more clearly. On the top were stains - bloodstains? Maybe. I opened the door, held the lamp up in one hand and put the other into the dark hole. Further into the hole. Put my hand down to the floor of the stove. I recoiled with a cry as quickly as if I had touched a snake. In the bottom of the stove mixed with cinders there was something sticky, something congealed and greasy.

The boy behind me called out 'What is it? What is it mister?'

I stepped back, reaching for a rag to wipe my hand. 'I think it's what I'm looking for,' I said through a tight throat, 'I need to lock this place up, can you find me a chain or something?' I gave him the lamp and stood in the fast-descending darkness facing the black stove in whose furnace a child had been sacrificed like the children in the Bible hurled in the fire in honour of Moloch. 'God help us,' I said softly into the night.

Moorman came back with a chain and a lock he found in an outhouse. We secured the place, standing close together in the darkness and speaking in low voices as if we were conspirators. I climbed into the waiting buggy and the driver clucked and teased the tired horse all the way back into Indianapolis. I looked out at the moon rising above the cornfields and the sky filled with stars, trying not to look at my hand where I had touched what had once been a human being. When I got back to my lodgings I washed and washed that hand.

The next day I cleared everything with the Irvington police and the owner of the house. Word had got out about my work and when I arrived back at the cottage several hundred people had gathered to exchange theories among themselves, to smoke pipes and nod knowingly, to chatter excitedly or just to stare at the building, yesterday just another farmhouse, now transformed into an object of wonder, as if it was a shrine.

The local police helped with controlling the crowd and collecting evidence. We scraped samples from the stove – the congealed blood from the top and the human grease mixed with ashes in the bottom of the cinder pan. It seemed Holmes had not had time to finish the job of disposing of Howard – perhaps because his timetable was disrupted by Miss Hill showing such interest in the stove in the previous house. So he couldn't do the deed there. I imagined his nervous energy as he changed plans to obtain a new house in a more secluded spot, and a new stove. But where were the rest of the remains?

I searched the house from top to bottom, had all the soft patches of earth dug up in the barn and around it but all the searches yielded was behind a cupboard where I found a little spinning top and a tin man, the paint worn off in places through constant handling. I had a list supplied by Mrs Pitezel of the clothes and other things that the children had with them, and these were on it. Ben Pitezel had bought them for his son at the World's Fair. I knew what a smart lawyer would say about these playthings: you could buy them in any dime store, that they proved nothing. But my mind was with the lonely kid who had cherished them; these were a child's prized possessions, they would not be left behind willingly. They proved beyond doubt for me that Howard was here, had never left this place

After the first search the owner agreed that we could take apart some of the structure of the house but where to start? 'That stove probably wasn't used in the barn,' I said, 'let's check the chimneys in the house.' Soon I had strong arms and jemmies ripping out the covering over the chimney in one room after the other, then opening up the grate with a hammer and chisel.

'There's something here, boss,' someone said. There were suspicious lumps in a pile of rubble and soot that had come down when the chimney was opened. I poked around in the black pile, then ripped an old flyscreen off a window, choking in the rising dust, and used it as a makeshift sieve to pass the ashes and the soot through it. Piece by piece as the dust was brushed off them human remains emerged: first an almost complete set of teeth and a piece of jaw that I picked out of the sieve like weevils out of flour, to the gasps of amazement from the police and helpers, as if I was performing a conjuring trick. *Prestidigitation,* I said to myself... *legerdemain.*

At the bottom of the chimney we found a large, charred mass, which upon being cut, disclosed a portion of what I guessed were internal organs: the stomach, liver and spleen, baked quite hard. A piece of charred bone was also revealed, I judged it a pelvis.

In the high heat of the afternoon we labelled and packed our finds and I arranged for a builder to repair the house; a photographer to take pictures of the stove; said a few well-chosen words to reporters from the Indianapolis Evening News and the like. I dined with men from the Indianapolis police department and went home happy. I had the best night's sleep I had had in years. The business of searching for the truth is not the meanest occupation of man.

I travelled back to Philadelphia with a box that I carried with me even when I went to the bathroom, it was so precious. It contained in separate boxes or specimen jars the bones, teeth, internal organs and human grease of a child. Every now and then I would pat it, maybe to reassure myself it was still there, maybe to reassure Howard that his journey was near its end.

I displayed my trophies in the dead house to District Attorney Graham. Dr Scott declared as conclusively as he could from the teeth that this was a child, but there wasn't enough material even to determine the sex. He cut the baked bunch of internal organs open to expose the spongy pink of undercooked meat. 'Even a mother could not recognise that,' Graham said in a tone of generalised contempt.

'There's a ton of circumstantial evidence,' I said, trying not to sound pleading, 'Holmes and the boy can both be identified in the previous house where Holmes assembled a stove; Holmes can be identified in the house where I found these remains; things like the toys and the fragment of ripped-up trunk show it was Howard and not someone else. Holmes can't account for Howard's disappearance...'

Graham waved his hand, 'I know how to construct a case, Mr Geyer, and if this is what I've got to work on,' and he scanned the miserable remains of Howard Pitezel like a rejected meal, 'then this is what I'll try to convict him on. But we haven't got a clearly identifiable body here, or a motive, I've seen cases like this go down. I'm sorry.' He said it as if it was me who should be sorry for bringing him such paltry evidence.

'How long we got?' I asked with a dry mouth.

'Before I've got to re-charge Holmes or consider him for parole? About a month.'

'So I've got to find the other children, the two girls?' I said. He nodded. 'Well I'd better start doing that gentlemen,' I said, and I took my leave of them.

I gathered up my ledgers, packed a few fresh clothes and went on up to Detroit. The lead to Detroit was less slender than some of the others I'd followed, but that didn't make it strong, exactly. It was one of the few cities in the north-east we hadn't investigated fully though we knew Henry Holmes was familiar with it, so I charged the Pinkerton's man who Ed Cass and I had previously engaged in Detroit to make some enquiries of hotels and boarding houses. He came up with two girls, under the names Etta and Nellie Canning, which was Mrs Pitezel's maiden name. They were in Detroit all the time Cass and I were looking for them in Cincinnati, at 91 Congress Street at a boarding house run by one Lucinda Burns who had her staff look after them while Holmes was supposedly travelling on business. The business was killing their brother in Indiana.

Lucinda Burns was a busy landlady in a pinafore and a mob cap who left her tenants much to their own devices if they paid the rent. I talked to the people who had taken meals to the girls but like in other places where we had made enquiries, they were tongue-tied immigrants who couldn't say much except that the children were there, they were there alone, they seemed unhappy, and they ate up all their dinners.

Lucinda was a little more alert and had asked about the girls' schooling; she would direct Holmes to a local school, she offered. But Henry said he was a teacher who gave the girls private tuition. She could say nothing else except that one of the girls had said she was going north. I had talked to this lady for an hour, exhausting her patience, until I just had to leave, I had run out of questions and she of answers.

I stood outside in the quiet, unmade road, where carriage wheels had ploughed up the ground, watching the rain melt ridges of mud into black puddles. I had nowhere to go. This was the end. North? Where in hell was that? The rain trickled down my face and wet the shoulders of my coat until they were dark epaulettes. At length I trudged along to a bar where a smothering odour of pipe smoke rose in ribbons to the yellow ceiling. I put my notebook on the table and thought, as if I had Ed Cass with me and we were exchanging ideas together. I looked again at my map of the north-east, a sheet of paper with linen strengthening, opened and refolded so often it was losing the print on the folds. North. Where was that? Of course, north could be a blind, Holmes might have said they were going north in the hope one of the kids would give it away.

I tried the principle I had learned: what to believe in a man who always lied? The answer was what he didn't say. He knew there might be traces of him in Buffalo, Niagara Falls, Cleveland, so he had given us those, knowing we would find enough to think maybe that's where the real evidence was. So where hadn't he led us? Toledo, Hamilton, Rochester, Toronto. But Toronto was where he had been headed when we apprehended him at the port. He implied it was his last ditch attempt at escape, sailing off into the unknown. Maybe it was a very well known location for him. What more, really, did I have to go on?

I wired for City Hall to send on an introduction for me to the Toronto police. It took a full day, twenty-four hours to sail across, passing other stately steamers and watching the herring gulls swoop. At length, in the early morning, we reached Port Colborne and glided through the Welland Canal. I remembered sharply how Henry and me had talked about how we wanted to see that local miracle of engineering when we were boys, and I imagined how he had stood here on this deck feeling the wind on his face and thinking the same thoughts. It was another reason that I couldn't put in the report why I believed I should use my limited time searching in Toronto: it was where *I* would have gone.

The steamer pulled into the harbour with a deep whistle as the factories and warehouses of Front Street came into view. I checked in at the police station where the officer in charge had a picture of the Queen of England on the wall, and crowns on his uniform lapels. They were very English, very formal, as if someone had strapped a poker to their back to keep them upright, and had pinned their jaws so they could only talk very slowly and exactly with very rounded vowels. But they were good guys and gave me every assistance in their power.

I had to assume Henry had stayed in a hotel then rented a house, like he normally did, but the usual process of asking at hotels and boarding houses did not establish Holmes had been there at all, and I began to get a sickening feeling that I had come to the wrong place, he had never been here, he was sitting in his warm cell laughing at me. Next I tried the real estate agents. There weren't so many, but they were pretty disordered; a few were big and easy to handle but most were small, maybe there'd be one guy with five houses to let. I went to everyone I could find, but I had tied and untied my package of papers and photographs until it had become soiled and ragged from wear. My ledger was dog-eared and fraying at the corners. I was approaching the end.

Finally I went to the Toronto police and asked them if they would call in the press for me. 'Are you sure of that Mr Geyer?' said Her Majesty's Chief Superintendent, in front of the picture of her little fat majesty, looking serenely down on the ink bottle, blotter and pens on his desk. Yeah, I was sure. I knew the press was a beast which, once unleashed, could not be put back in its cage, but what had I got to lose now? I had ten days, I ticked them off.

There were a lot of Canadian newspapers, I hadn't thought there would be so many: there was Toronto World, Irish Canadian, The Empire, The Canadian Nation, Rural Canadian... about sixty of them altogether without the special interest publications like Pigeons and Pets and the Shoe and Leather Journal with a limited interest in crime.

There was a daily press call so it was easy to put out the word to call all the reporters in. Such an odd array of humanity they were, some dandies in frock coats, looking down their noses at the proceedings and not deeming it proper to sit down for fear they would have to associate with those of the cheap press; others were gnarled men, not so old but pickled in alcohol at middle age; others were whey-faced boys, all eagerness and uncertainty. All the guys were in suits but what suits some of them had; the shape gone, the elbows shiny or worn right through so that shirt showed through the frayed ends, the vest buttons not uniform, the fronts stained with food, beer and whatever else. They were coughing, smoking, chewing tobacco and making liberal use of the spittoons. Every one had a pencil and a notebook, and they wrote with extreme rapidity.

I said that I had been searching for evidence of Henry Holmes in all the cities around the north east and there was evidence he had been right here in Toronto. They knew a lot more than I thought they would, about the castle in Chicago and the people who had disappeared. I told them about finding the remains of a boy in Indiana and how we hoped to find any trace of the girls in Toronto. I gave them the dates, the Toronto city police had copies made of the photographs and these went out to eager hands.

Only one question disconcerted me, when someone from one of the fancy papers said, 'Are you expecting to find these children alive Mr Geyer?'

I looked down at my notes which were unhelpful on this point. 'I fear not,' I said, 'but I proceed in hope.'

In the evening newspaper and the following day's morning papers began the glare of publicity in decks of black headlines which now would always follow this case: 'CITY SEARCH FOR LOST CHILDREN... DID U.S. KILLER MURDER HERE?... U.S. COPS SCOUR TORONTO FOR MISSING KIDS.'

As I had feared, it wasn't that there were no clues now, there were too many: everyone had seen Holmes or someone like him, several were related to someone just similar. Everyone had seen or heard the girls; one pathetic specimen of degeneracy confessed to their murder. That was the danger of newspaper advertising, everyone wanted to be part of the show. In the following eight days I sifted the vain, the curious, the over-eager to please and the clearly demented. They knew everything until they were questioned, then it was clear they knew nothing.

The break came when I was approaching the end of my ingenuity, and I was down to looking through the newspapers for the period, in the Houses to Let column. Maybe Henry had let a house not through an agent but from the small ads. A message came in for me on a scrap of paper from a Thomas William Ryves of Vincent Street who simply said he had something of interest to tell me. It was not promising, I would rather he had come to me, but I had followed over 900 leads in the whole of my hunt for Henry Holmes and the children, and it would just not be right to ignore one at this stage.

Wearily I took a buggy to Vincent Street, the rattling on the road making me realise how tired my bones felt, deep within their padding of skin and muscle. I found the house, a practical kind of cottage in a row of similar houses, all with their own gardens. The door was opened by a turkey-necked man who clearly had been drinking. My heart sank: another vain mission, called over by a drunk who wanted to slur out his miseries, more of my precious time trickling away.

He wasn't so far gone he was insensible so I humoured him by walking in behind him to a comfortable sitting room. On the wall was a framed scroll with fancy red and gold lettering commemorating Mr Thomas William Ryves' membership of

Mystic Number One of the Knights of Pythias. Despite his current condition, Ryves was clearly a man who knew his position in society.

He sat at a table where he was drinking whiskey from a small tumbler, I declined to join him. He spoke in an accent that had a lot of Scottish in it, he was a first generation immigrant. There was a newspaper open on the table, crumpled as if it had been much used. He pointed at a picture of Alice with her low forehead and close-set eyes, 'I saw this girl,' he said, he pronounced it gir-rl, 'I didn't get a look at the other but she said there were two. Then he came and told her she'd got to go in. It was in my house.'

'What, here?' I said, looking round as if they were there now and I had just missed them.

He gulped a shot of whiskey, 'No,' he said, 'next door. Didn't have much furniture, he just brought a mattress and a bed and a big trunk. The time it said in the paper, October, name of Canning.' I almost leapt over the desk and grabbed him by his scrawny neck: 'Canning' was a clue I hadn't given out. This was it. He knew.

'So why didn't you tell me before?' I yelled.

He looked at me as if from the pit of misery, 'I wanted you to find them,' he said. Then in response to my stupefied expression he blurted out, 'I was hoping you'd find them somewhere else.'

'But if they were in your house,' I said softly, trying to conceal my baffled fury, 'I couldn't find them somewhere else.'

'I didn't want them to be in my house!' he was almost weeping.

'So what happened to them?' I asked, more gently this time.

He shook his head sadly. Ignorance? No, regret. 'I helped him,' he cried, putting his glass down so hard it hit the table with a bang, 'I helped him dig the hole.'

'You what?'

'He borrowed a shovel. I gave him my shovel.'

A moment of icy calm crept over me. I had no doubt that, but for excavation and identification, I had come to the end of my quest. 'Alright, Mr Ryves,' I said, 'let us proceed methodically. When did you first see him?'

It was next door, number sixteen, he had just the two houses and he lived in one and let the other. He had let the house to Henry Holmes who said he was looking after the children of his widowed sister. He had then taken the children in from a waiting buggy. This was when Ryves had a chance to see and talk to Alice briefly. He didn't see the children again.

The next day Holmes called to ask him if he could borrow a shovel as he wanted to arrange a place in the cellar for storing potatoes. Ryves gave him it but Holmes returned it the following day with two weeks' rent in advance. He had decided, he said, that the climate was not suitable for the girls and they would leave the next day. Ryves heard a carriage early in the morning, but never saw the children again.

'Still got the shovel?' I said. He groaned out a yes, 'then let's take it.'

I carried the regular, thick handled implement in the wake of Ryves who plodded in front of me. The house was a quaint two storey cottage of a simple style of architecture in a narrow plot of lawn with a wire net fence and a veranda tastefully decorated with a clinging clematis.

I said nothing as Ryves led me over the creaking floorboards to cellar door that was reached by lifting a large piece of oilcloth from the floor to expose a trap door, two feet square. I knelt and peered into the darkness while Ryves lit some lamps. Down below was the square shape of maybe a ten-foot cellar with an earth floor. I climbed down into the cool dampness and prodded the floor, swiftly discovering a soft spot in the south-west corner. Forcing the spade into the earth, I found it easy digging.

I went upstairs and patted Ryves on the shoulder, he looked like he could do with the rest of his bottle of whiskey. 'Is there a boy who'll run an errand for me?' I asked, and I sent the baker's boy off to the Toronto police with a note requesting urgent assistance. Then I sat on the steps, shovel in front of me, as if guarding passage to the nether regions, waiting for official help. There was no way I was going to mess up this operation, in this cellar I was going through the correct procedures. It was something Henry had taught me.

The Chief Inspector came with some men to cordon off the site, and the city pathologist soon stepped out of his own gig with his black bag as if he was a doctor come to visit a sick patient. The Chief Inspector was detailing some men to 'get down there and dig' but I stepped in and said I'd like to do it, but I'd sure appreciate some help in holding the lamp. I wanted to expose the packed earth below, I wanted to use that same shovel, my hands on the same shaft he had used.

Soon maybe five of us were down there, shapes flickering in the lamplight, while others peered over the edge into the tomb. The small cube of a room soon became murky and humid with our strenuous activities as I dug down and the other men moved the earth. After going down about a foot, a horrible stench arose. 'Ptomaine,' I said, too softly to be heard. I started to proceed with more caution, I dug while another man brushed the earth away until I got resistance, the shovel was under something that didn't want to let it go. I pulled, and shook the implement out, and from my rough-hewn hole flopped a human forearm. A couple of the men cried out with wavering, fearful voices, then checked themselves. It was a little arm, a child's arm. Though covered with soil it was clearly white. The smell grew stronger.

'This is what we are seeking gentlemen,' I said, with as much equanimity as I could muster, 'I require a trowel and a smaller brush.' They were brought for me, and some rubber gloves that the pathologist had, and a mask for the smell. The effect of the gloves and mask was to make the digging feel unreal, as if I was not doing it myself, but commanding these mechanical hands, this sweating head encased in linen to kneel and dig trowel-full by trowel-full in the damp, dark earth to expose the curled, white bodies.

A sketch-maker mapped the position in which the bodies were found as they were revealed. Alice was lying on her side with her hand to the west. Nellie was found lying on her face, with her head to the south, her plaited hair hanging neatly down her back. As Nellie's limbs were found resting on Alice's I first began with her. I lifted her as gently as possible, but owing to the decomposed state of the body, the weight of her plaited hair hanging down her back pulled the scalp from off her head, to a collective groan from my companions. I put her in the arms of the helpers, amazed at how slight a load she was.

I could see the whole of Alice's body now, lying lightly with her head to one side as if in a ghastly sleep. There were no worms: the bodies must have gone straight into the earth, the insects had no opportunity of laying eggs on them. She wore a cotton dress and shoes, one of them half off. Her flesh had the marbled, greenish-brown colour of early putrefaction. The body was in good condition, but the stench was dizzying. Her mouth and nose had a touch of foamy blood. I reached down and put one gloved hand under her shoulders, the other under her rump, closing my eyes as I drew her to me so I did not look too close into the face of death. Her head lay back, her mouth open as if moaning. I did not want her scalp to fall off as her sister's had, so I held her small head in my hand, the rest of the body in my arms. It seemed inappropriate to be so close and say nothing. I wanted to say a prayer but none would come, and instead I murmured, 'It's alright now, it's alright'. There was a sniffing sound behind me in the darkness: Mr Ryves and the policemen were muffling sobs.

White canvas was placed on the floor upstairs to take the remains, as Nellie and then Alice were lifted up and they were carted off to the dead house. Soon 16 Vincent Street was besieged with newspaper men, sketch artists and others. Everyone seemed to be pleased with our success and it was difficult to express both joy at the discovery and horror at the crime. I wired Philadelphia, and made a brief statement to the press, that it was thus proved that little children cannot be murdered in this day and generation, beyond the possibility of discovery.

A thorough search of the house also revealed part of a dress, pair of girl's button boots and other female clothing. Clothing had been stuck in chimney with straw which had been lit but had not caught as it was packed in too tightly. I put it all in boxes or specimen jars. I sent a full report back to Philadelphia and spent some time – longer than I felt it should have taken – obtaining permission to move the bodies to the US. Her Majesty the Queen had to say that was OK, in the person of her coroner.

Alice and Nellie were placed in small pine coffins that were lined with oilcloth and then packed with ice, to preserve them for the journey. For a lot of the distance I stood near to them at the back of the train, smoking cigars, watching the clean Canadian countryside flash past me. I had foolishly expected to see red maple trees when in summer the trees were green. I tried not to think too much about the experience Howard and the girls had gone through. I was exalted at my success, relieved the hardest part of the job was over, but also sad in the deepest part of my being: it was for this, this worse than monster, that my little chick Georgiana left me crying in the rain.

There were compensations. The attentions of newsmen meant I was being recognised for my skill. I had not sought personal publicity, but it did not feel bad by any means. I thought with pleasure of Molly and the crowd at the Suicide Hall reading about me. The whole story was now out, connecting the murder of Ben Pitezel to that of his children, and to the ghastly castle. The Canadian reporters had told the American reporters, they had compiled reports which were obtained from Chicago and Indianapolis. It was getting to be quite a story. Of course it was news in Toronto, but I'd seen some of the American newspapers on the train, and they had gone to town on it too.

We pulled into the new Broad Street station, dwarfed by its sky-scratching head office, and I was met by Joe Stitch with the morgue wagon who collected the coffins from the guard's van. I watched him drive off, gently clucking to his horses as he eased them into the traffic. As I lowered my eyes from the mesh of wheels, advertising hoardings and horseflesh, they met those of a boy standing in front of me. He was a freckle-faced kid of about twelve, with a bag of newspapers around his neck that he sold for a few cents apiece.

I looked at him quizzically. 'Hey mister?' he said, 'you're that detective aintcha, that caught Holmes. The one that killed all those kids and the people in the castle and all?' He looked with awe at the face he had previously seen in newspaper pictures.

'I am,' I said, swelling with pride, 'yeah, I did that.'

'Will you tell me something?'

'OK kid, what d'you want to know?'

'Just tell me,' he said, all enthusiasm, 'What's he like?'

Chapter 15

I bought a newspaper and stood at a coffee stall and read it standing. There were loud columns about 'the arch-fiend' Henry Holmes, newspapers didn't trouble themselves too much about due process, for them Holmes was guilty. But he was guilty for them in a ripsnorting, jaw-dropping, awe-inspiring way that made my flesh creep. 'His career stamps him as one of the boldest and shrewdest swindlers in the country,' I read, '... he swindled with a dash and vim that must have won the admiration almost of those who lost all.' A passable sketch of Henry showed him looking calm and confident.

Well, the confidence trickster is a colourful rogue, something of an American character, but the fascination even seemed to extend to Henry's murders, 'Did these visitors to the Fair, strangers to Chicago, find their way to Holmes' castle in answer to delusive advertisements sent out by him, never to return again? Did he erect his castle close to the Fair grounds so as to gather in these victims by the wholesale and, after robbing them, did he dispose of their bodies in his quicklime vats, in his mysterious oil tank with its death-dealing liquids, or did he burn them in the elaborate retort with which the basement was provided?...' It was pretty clear the answers these interrogatives were calculated to produce.

I thought it was enough to read these over-coloured accounts, but I was kicked in the stomach to see 'Holmes's House of Horrors' advertised on the back of a trolley-bus. It led me to a dime museum on Arch Street, standing out on even one of the busiest streets in Philadelphia, a regular P.T.Barnum show with notices outside in garish colours and pictures of Holmes outside as 'Ann Arbor Student... Doctor... Businessman... Murderer!' as if it was an evolutionary degeneration from the fresh-faced student to ogrous beast, his shoulders hunched and clasping his hands together in a personal embrace of congratulation for some fresh deed of horror.

I paid my dime and walked in. No one recognised me, even

when I stood in front of an illustration of myself, revolver in hand clutching at a fleeing Henry Holmes in the docks at Detroit. A big store had been quickly converted with pasteboard partitions painted black to provide a dark maze of corridors with cubicles for displays or tableaux. At the paying booth was touted the Castle of Torture; tableaux of the murder of the innocents; and with a jolt I saw advertised, 'the monster's two lovely wives'. My life was being retold to me in the form of a nightmare.

After a few minutes I regained a sense of balance and looked at the place squarely. There wasn't much order in the display, it had been thrown together quickly by some showman out for a quick buck when it was realised that the bodies in Canada and Indianapolis and the Castle in Chicago were connected with a man now languishing in a Philadelphia jail. Many of the pictures and sketches were not particular to Henry Holmes, they had just been put in to add bulk, like pictures of the World's Fair in Chicago and Ann Arbor University. There was a model of the castle, made rather more elaborate and gothic than the original; pictures of Ben Pitezel and the children and a faked arrest warrant – they had taken a standard warrant and put Henry's name on it.

I walked around miserably with a few other patrons of the establishment who were cracking peanuts and making vulgar remarks. There was a whole room devoted to the castle with such things as a pile of bones which were found in cellar - they had just bought a bunch of bones from a bone-yard and put them on display. They did have the Chicago police's ground-plan of castle and a fair knowledge of what had happened there. The high point was a wax tableau of Henry Holmes strangling a woman, her head thrown back and hair in disarray, he was pushing her back on a table so he seemed to be lying across the length of her as if they were engaging in the act of congress, to put it politely, but both were fully clothed. 'The monster's two lovely wives' followed this, though it was just two pictures on the wall with the supposed dates of marriage. They were both head-and-shoulders newspaper sketches, and I imagined the sketch artists waiting outside Georgiana's house in the shrubbery to catch a glimpse of her. The picture of Myrta was better, and her dark hair was better suited to the medium of black ink than was Georgiana's fair hair. Georgiana was looking awkwardly to one side as if the artist found a profile easier to draw than full face, wearing a dress with a high ruffled collar which only just revealed a pearl necklace. I wondered miserably who'd given it to her, but I suppose I could guess.

I stepped out sadly into the smell of pastries and coffee mixing with that of steaming horse dung being emitted from an animal directly in front of me. I don't know what my feelings were, maybe I didn't have any feelings that connected directly with Holmes's House of Horrors. The world was what it was, railing against its vulgarity and cruelty would not help. I had an appointment to keep at the dead house.

When I arrived the bodies of Alice and Nellie were laid out naked, the flesh still white, looking small as drowned kittens on the marble slabs made for adult cadavers. Doctor Scott was preparing his sharp silver instruments which lay on a table covered with oilcloth. He made a physical examination of each mottled body murmuring, 'no apparent contusions,' holding his face close to the surface of each body and casting his eyes over every inch. Nellie still had the bony body of a child but Alice had buds of breasts and the beginning of a woman's hips.

Scott paused at her thighs and gently opened the lips of her immature vagina, shining a light from a mirror reflector into the aperture, 'not virgo intacta', he said, then straightened up, seeing my reaction, 'but that's not proof positive of anything, Mr Geyer, no matter what the layman might say, the absence of a hymen is not evidence of the absence of virtue in so young a woman. Sometimes the hymen can be easily broken in the ordinary activities of childhood, it does not always indicate violation by a male.'

'Is it possible to tell even how long ago it was broken?' I asked with a dry mouth.

'No,' he said, not really irritated but given to routine expressions of impatience which he used with students, 'as I remarked earlier–

no apparent contusions. So there is no evidence she was forced. It may have been that she was willing; or if she was forced it could have been long enough before death for the injuries to recover; or it just didn't happen. I cannot tell.' He gave a small smile as if he was revealing a great truth quietly.

He judged suffocation as the most likely cause of death, there being no visible signs of injury. I tried a theory I had been thinking of, based on an examination of a trunk we had picked up in the trawl of Henry's things after we had arrested him. It was a big sized trunk, easily able to take two small bodies, and in the side at the bottom was bored a small hole, just large enough for a gas pipe.

'What if they were drugged with chloroform, put in a confined space and then gassed?' I said.

Scott sniffed, 'There's nothing here inconsistent with that theory, detective, but nothing to validate it either.' He fingered the eyes of one of the children to expose a black hole of decay, 'there is inflammation and swelling of the conjunctiva in cases of gas paralysis, but here the putrefaction has progressed too far to tell. As far as chloroform is concerned: it is relatively easy to chloroform a sleeping person, like a child, leaving no traces except a smell. There is no smell here but it may have been dissipated by time and the movement of the body. Is there any reason why you suspect this rather elaborate method of murdering two children?'

'Yeah: he liked trunks,' I said. In response to his raised eyebrow I continued, 'my perpetrator liked putting bodies in trunks, and he liked killing people in elaborate ways with a minimum of mess. He was a doctor,' I added.

'I had heard,' said Scott, and he gave instructions for the bodies to be made ready for identification.

I watched Joe Stitch sponge the face and mouth of Alice, now back in the dead house, where I had first seen her identifying the remains of her murdered father, the little girl who had worried about how much washing her mother was going to have to do when she returned home; a stupid, bewildered, gullible girl who was excited about going to another city. It was an adventure that cost her her life and probably her virtue before that.

In the waiting room the attendant, Muriel, was trying to keep Mrs Pitezel calm as months ago she had comforted her daughter. Mrs Pitezel saw me and ran to me, clutching at my vest, crying out, 'Oh Mr Geyer is it true you have found my Alice and Nellie buried in a cellar?' I did all I could to calm her, told her to prepare for the worst. She was supplied with brandy and smelling salts but nothing could ready her for the worst experience any mother could face, or for the terrible odour.

The children had been taken to a viewing room where they had been cleaned and laid under separate canvas sheets. The head of Alice was covered with paper, and a hole sufficiently large cut in it, so that Mrs Pitezel could see the teeth. The hair of both the children, detached from the scalps, had been neatly washed and laid on the canvas sheet covering Alice. Mrs Pitezel looked around, as if unsure about what to do, as if the lumps under the green canvas had nothing to do with her and just happened to be furniture in the room where she was standing. I gestured to the head and in an instant she recognised the teeth and hair. Then turning around to me saying, 'Where is Nellie?' she noticed the long black plait of hair belonging to Nellie lying on the canvas. Her mouth opened to produce a shriek such as I have never heard from man or beast. I would pay a lot never to have heard the noise from that poor forlorn creature.

Muriel helped her out of the room, and out of the building which had quickly become surrounded by onlookers who had detected from the presence of the press that there was some celebrated case taking place. Mrs Pitezel, suffering beyond description, was led through the crowd oblivious of their gaze.

As the shrieking of Mrs Pitezel was being reduced by distance to a whimper there was no sound in the room, you could hear yourself swallow. The turning of the papers in the ledger tore like an avalanche through the silence. Finally I said, 'Let's get this to the coroner,' and we began to collect the paperwork. With Dr Scott's autopsy report; my account of finding the bodies and Mrs Pitezel's identification we had enough to have an inquest that afternoon. I was moving towards the completion of my task.

The coroner judged that Alice, Nellie and Howard Pitezel had been murdered, and their bodies concealed. DA Graham had already drawn up the papers, so I went back to Moyamensing Prison to charge my old friend Henry with the murders for which he would hang.

Twilight was descending on the foreboding face of the jail when I arrived with a stenographer who by convention remained silent throughout this interview. Henry was looking relaxed, sitting in his cell in a collarless shirt. A deal of correspondence was piled on his table, I could see a couple of them upside down. They were on lightly coloured paper in exotic colours of ink, the usual letters from female admirers attracted by major criminals. Henry was looking bright and cheerful, as if it was him who would be walking out of the prison at the end of our encounter, not me. I went through the charade of introducing myself formally, for the record and said, 'We have found the bodies of Ben Pitezel's children.'

'Yes, I read about that,' he said

I waited for a further remark but none came, another man might have been uncomfortable, but Henry was a master of silence when it suited him. 'Do you have anything to say about these children who were in your charge until they were killed?' I asked.

'That is to be demonstrated,' said Henry, 'but no, I don't have any comment to make.'

'Then I must formally charge you, I said, that you did willfully and feloniously take the lives of Benjamin Pitezel, Alice Pitezel, Nellie Pitezel and Howard Pitezel...'

I let the leaden words of the official charge fall against the stone floor of the cell. Henry listened, as if he was appreciating a piece of verse or a particularly testing sermon. 'So it has come to this Frank,' he said finally, as if I had somehow let him down.

In my mind I could still smell the bodies of the girls, 'You have destroyed an entire family, man,' I said, my calm finally dissipated by his insouciance.

'Family values,' he said chirpily, 'the best kind, dont'ya think?'

'Do you have anything constructive to say?' I asked.

He pondered for a moment and then said in his lilting, melodic tones, 'the finest musician in fairyland, and perhaps ever, in all time, was Orpheus. It was said that when he played his lyre and sang his songs even the wild beasts of the woods were tamed by him. Some said he could even charm the rocks themselves, but in my view that was a little far-fetched,' what the stenographer made of it all I cannot think, but he took it all down faithfully, and there was no way I would impede due process by stopping the recording of an accused man's response to a murder charge, however bizarre. Anyway, I always liked Henry's stories, they took me back to an earlier, happier time.

He continued, 'Now Orpheus married a beautiful nymph, Eurydice who was his whole life, but their happiness was not to last. While walking one day in a lonely place by a river-bank she met a bee-keeper, Aristeus, who was so taken with her he had to have her. As she was running away from him she trod on a serpent which sunk its poisonous fangs into her flesh. Orpheus came looking for her but found her only in time to see her die. The divine singer was inconsolable at her death, and his lyre was silent for months until one day, sleeping fitfully on the bank where Eurydice died, he hit upon a scheme to relieve his torment. He went to the mouth of hell – everyone in fairyland knew where that was – and he played his lyre and sang his songs until the very trees wept and the god of hell, Hades, called him in to ask why he sang such mournful music. He explained in song the loss of Eurydice and his pitiful plight, in tones so beautiful, that all the guardians of hell wept for him – the ferryman, the many-headed dog, the judges of the dead. He played so plaintively that his music suspended the tortures of the damned. Hades and his wife were so moved they gave permission for Orpeus to lead his beloved Eurydice out of hell. There was one condition: that she should go and not look back during her journey out, until she had reached the light of the sun. The couple went a slow and stony way, taking much longer than the journey in, for the descent to hell is easy, but the road back is hard. They had almost reached the gates of hell when Eurydice could not resist one glance back and in that moment there was a rush of wind and at once she disappeared and the road too disappeared and the mouth of hell closed. Orpheus found himself alone on the grass outside where it had been, now doubly inconsolable, for not only had he lost Eurydice, but when he went even to hell to reclaim her she was so faithless as to need to look back to her former master.'

Henry sat silent again in front of his pile of delicately coloured love letters. 'What do you mean by that, Henry?' I asked gently, though knowing the answer only too well, 'I mean, why tell that story now?'

'It was for you, Frank. You got me... but you'd rather have got the girl.'

The anger and pain of years flashed before my eyes in a blinding torrent as my body tensed to strike him such that the stenographer flinched in expectation of violence. I regained control in less than a second. Not for the first time Henry was taunting me in the hope I would hit him and he could claim police brutality and appeal to the jury. He knew how to get me, in that way that it is so much easier to be angered to blows by people that you love.

'One last time, Henry,' I said, controlling my quavering voice, 'Will you just confess to save Mrs Pitezel at least the pain of testifying in court?'

'I'll take my chance with the twelve men of the jury and the solid principles of American justice,' he said

'Then I'll see you in court Henry,' I said. I needed a drink after that. I took my leave of Henry, the stenographer, the prison, and went to McQueen's Suicide Hall. There in the smoky fug where a mandolin orchestra played coon songs and tired girls in ostrich feathers and ribbons danced for tips, I probed at the pain which Henry had alerted, like touching an aching tooth with my tongue, waiting for Molly to come in.

How could Georgiana possibly believe Holmes' lies, how could she love a moral degenerate who could murder even little children in the most calculating fashion? Could there be a meaning to this, some way through it? I remembered something Cass had said to me when I had mused months before on Holmes' duplicity and her willingness to believe the most outlandish lies rather than question his integrity.

'A bit like being a parson's daughter, really,' he said, which sharpened my senses, for Georgiana of course was a parson's daughter, and though Cass's insights came ponderously slow, they came. 'I mean, if you're a parson's daughter,' he said, 'you don't go discussing evolution or the age of the world with the smart kids, do you? Not if you want to be known as a good girl. I mean you just take it as written: the world was made in six days, all the animals came out of the ark two by two. If my pa said Jonah was inside a whale, then he was, and anyone who says otherwise is just trying to make trouble and I shouldn't listen to them.' He was right, of course, Georgiana had taken Henry as a matter of blind faith not swapped one set of beliefs for another, but just added Henry's infallibility to the truths of a good, country, Christian upbringing. I now often remembered as nuggets of wisdom things Cass had said which I paid little attention to at the time. How I missed him.

But now Henry had opened up a huge frontier of vulnerability by introducing my relationship with Georgiana, even in an oblique way, it was a warning to me. Now I was open to attack from all sides: Henry, the lawyers, the police department. My pursuit of Henry became not a single-minded crusade for justice but the vindictive action of a jilted lover. Of course there was a defence: I pursued him because it was my case, and it was my case before I even knew he was involved. I come like him from Gilmanton, which is a coincidence but no more. Of course once I'd seen him I recognised him, but a policeman knows hundreds, maybe thousands of people, and a lot of them he has met in the course of his duty. It's no wonder a detective might know a criminal. It is usually considered to be in the interests of the justice system that he does know a criminal. *'And share the same girlfriend?'* I could hear Chief O'Brien's voice saying. It was a good question, and I lacked an equally good answer.

'My hero,' said Molly, coming up behind me and putting her hands on my shoulders. I shrugged this off with a smile, but she said she'd been reading about me in the papers, keeping cuttings about the Holmes case. She had just come in and was still wearing her coat, her face fresh and flushed from the cold air outside. I took her soft hand across the table and looked into her eyes, realising with a quick jolt that one thing I did not want was for this caring woman to find out about Georgiana from anyone but me.

'There was a girl in Gilmanton,' I said without introduction, 'she was my girl, but Henry Holmes ran off with her, that's why this case has been so personal,' I said, and looked down in shame.

'Yes,' she said, her head to one side, her blue eyes sparkling. 'I guessed that.'

I looked up in surprise, 'You...'

'Well...' she prevaricated, 'I guessed it was about a girl. It doesn't matter, you know,' she said, '...it was a long time ago.'

I took her in my arms. It didn't matter to her that I had loved someone else. So had she, after all. That was the simple and unaffected way she looked at it. We were both damaged goods.

'Have you got a word for it?' she said,

I shrugged, 'Reciprocity' I replied.

She had to start work. I didn't want to stay long in the drinking hall, I didn't want to be drunk, I had a full day's work tomorrow. I walked along beside the winding black river towards Molly's house to let myself in with the spare key she had given me. She would be pleased I was staying with her when she came back late tonight, her hair smelling of smoke from the bar. If I had done anything wrong, she would absolve me. My own actions had led me naked into the jungle, but I could not have with integrity done any different from what I did. If I had given the case to someone else, Henry might not be in jail right now. I had followed the irresistible momentum of my own life, the success in capturing Henry and my danger now I had done it were part of the same thing. For good or ill, chance and personal inclination propelled me down that path. Whether it was heroic or sick it was me, and

I was going to get on and do my job.

The next day and for many weeks after I was in a nervous ecstasy of organisation, of people, plans and paper. I had to be able to open the ledgers we had painstakingly kept and track Henry and the children from location to location until we could prove one day he was there with a child, the next he was there alone, and the remains of a child were there to be revealed. Every step had to be linked by a logical progression and a signed witness statement, every individual had to agree to give evidence and as the trial date drew closer I was busy pulling them all together: the diminutive hotel manager in Cincinnati; the loquacious spinster in Indianapolis; the old real estate agent in Irvington who felt Holmes should have respected his grey hairs; busy Lucinda the Detroit landlady; all had to be boarded and paid for, even the Mystic Knight of Toronto with a fondness for whiskey whose expenses almost certainly included a visit to a house of Spanish dancers at the docks. They were the army of the unknown whose collective testimony damned Holmes to hell.

I needed rail passes, hotel bookings, special pleading to a reluctant witnesses who had been planning a vacation out west to see her sister; another who didn't want to leave his business. I had to take special care of poor Mrs Pitezel, with whom I spent many tearful hours at the Rossin Hotel where she was boarded, tended by the ladies of the Christian Endeavour Society who had volunteered to look after her.

In the end with the detectives' office and the DA's department working together, nominally under Chief O'Brien but in fact directed by me, I had assembled a cast of thirty-five witnesses in hotels all around Philadelphia at the city's expense. It was the biggest trial the city had ever conducted, a show-case to demonstrate how to do it to the rest of America. I strode around City Hall from dawn till the electric burners blazed long into the night, making arrangements and giving orders, a tyrant of justice.

I was nervous about everything: every arrangement that could go wrong, every detail of evidence that had to be supported by a network of other details like an iron bridge dependent on all its struts – if one went the rest would become unstable and shake apart. Henry was conducting his own defence, which made me edgy. He could say anything, I could still be mentioned, but there was nothing I could do but move on towards the appointed date with all the efficiency under my command.

In the evenings I now usually went to stay with Molly, or went straight to the bar after a long day and work into the night, and took her home from there, weary but full of satisfaction that I was achieving something that mattered. I considered leaving my lodgings altogether and moving in with her, and she suggested it half-jokingly.

'Let me get this case finished,' I said, 'let me win this case and put it behind me, and things will be better between us, I promise.' It might not have been the most romantic of proposals, but it was all I could manage at the time. These weeks were the happiest of any I had spent in Philadelphia, I was looking towards a kind of redemption: Henry Holmes would hang for his crimes, and I could be free from the chains of the past.

At last 29 October 1895 arrived, the trial of 'the greatest criminal of modern times' in the Court of Oyer and Terminer. It was a fabulous, breathing, wooden-panelled courtroom with the judge in his black robes sitting in a raised area with two banks of four wooden pillars on each side, topped with elaborate Corinthian foliage, the whole thing looking more like an altar than a seat.

The well of the court was packed with curious lawyers and spectators from the world of the courts well as with newspapermen. About five hundred people crowded into the public gallery, many of them standing in line since early in the morning. This trial truly was being held in the eyes of the world. I edged around to get a glimpse of Georgiana, still glorious in a white and yellow outfit, sitting quietly in a bonnet, holding her gloves in her hands in her lap, as if she was patiently waiting for a church service to start. It was a relief to see her: if she was present in the well of the court Henry can't have been intending to use her as a witness, which soothed my nagging doubts that Henry might involve my relationship with Georgiana in his defence.

All necks were craned and people literally did stand on their toes to catch the first glimpse of Henry Holmes, who walked into the court in his black, double-breasted suit, with a vest with a gold watch chain, still jaunty and confident. He thanked the wardens guarding him in a perfunctory manner as they opened the wooden gate to let him into the dock, as if they were his personal servants, not his guards. The dock had been moved closer to the bar of the court and a small table furnished with pens, ink and paper had been placed here so he might have the privileges ordinarily accorded to attorneys. He had even been given a special cell in the court where he could receive messages from his admirers.

I nodded to DA Graham, sitting with his papers before him and his team on either side, no expense had been spared on this one. Graham did not acknowledge my greeting, except by looking at me longer than he would if he was just peering round the room, he was saving his energy for the fight. The clerk charged Henry under his own name of Mudgett. Henry did now seem nervous, and he looked away when the names of his four victims were intoned, that he did feloniously and against the common good murder Benjamin F.Pitezel, Howard Pitezel, Alice Pitezel and Nellie Pitezel. 'How say you?' he was asked, 'Guilty or not guilty?'

'I'm not guilty sir,' he said.

'How will you be tried?' the ritual words were intoned.

'Before God and my countrymen' replied Holmes in a thick voice.

'May God send you a safe deliverance,' responded the clerk and Henry sat down for the long procedure of empanelling the jury. Holmes went about the questioning of prospective jurors with enthusiasm, challenging jurors over and again, asking them if they had seen the 'sensational display' of the Dime Museum in Broad Street; or if they had formed opinions about the case from reading newspapers.

'It is no longer a reason for challenge,' the Judge interrupted him, 'It was at one time. It was found impossible in these days to enforce it as a reason for excluding jurors. Newspapers are so numerous that everybody now reads them.'

It wasn't until after the lunch recess that the trial proper could get moving, though nerves deprived me of appetite. DA Graham ran through the basic events for the first time: the renting of the building in Callowhill Street; Ben Pitezel's death; Holmes identifying the body with Alice; the insurance payout; Holmes meeting Mrs Pitezel and taking the other two children; travelling from state to state with them; the discovery of the bodies.

Henry was passionless throughout most of the opening statement, only coming to life when Graham speculated that he had ruined Alice, perhaps rendering her insensible with chloroform or alcohol. Suddenly he sprang up, 'Your honour excuse me but it is quite outrageous to suggest that I, who never allowed liquor to pass my lips, would administer the same to one of tender years.' The judge shut him up. Henry was hoping such protestations of petty virtue had an effect on the jury who were property-owning, respectable folk.

What convincing defence could there be? Though he was not tall, Henry's stature was enhanced by the attentiveness of the eyes fixed upon him so he seemed to grow and dominate the courtroom. Even I who knew him well felt myself holding my breath as he stood calmly to make his opening speech.

'Well this court is presented with a catalogue of heinous crimes,' he said, like a country lawyer moving to deflate a big-city windbag, 'and I think we can all agree that these cases should be tried, but...' He cleared his throat and looked at his notes, 'nowhere has Mr Graham been able to demonstrate why they should be heard in Philadelphia. I submit that all but one of these cases is beyond the jurisdiction of the Philadelphia courts and they should not be heard by this court...'

DA Graham was up immediately, his blue, razored cheek flushing a little pink, 'I must object. Your honour this is outrageous. The public prosecutors in Indianapolis and Canada have given us permission, explicitly and in writing, to proceed here in this city in this court with these cases. Their representatives sit here today to observe their wishes being carried out,' and he motioned to some of the black, beetle-like lawyer figures crouched over their papers in ranks behind him.

'The question is not,' the judge said benignly, 'whether another court has given us permission to deal with this matter, but whether this court is proceeding in its own competence in doing so. Your objection is over-ruled. Continue Mr Holmes.'

Henry addressed the court with a readiness that would have done credit to the most experienced lawyer at the bar. He was cool and collected, not once did he display the least signs of nervousness. He passed through the tomes of legal books, the names and dates of past cases, with smoothness and efficiency, building up precedent by precedent before our eyes and ears an escape-raft from justice. 'I want to be quite explicit here,' he concluded, 'I am arguing that there is no case to answer. I did not kill these people as I am accused of doing. However, if there was a case to answer I submit it should be heard in the place where the crimes were alleged to have been committed, not in Philadelphia.'

There was a pause after he had spoken, as if the court was going to erupt into applause; then a small rustling as people turned to each other to comment appreciatively on Henry's presentation. The judge called them to order and indicated DA Graham who went to the fray with a bullish vigour. 'There is no separation here,' he cried, 'these other murders of the little children have been compounded because the abduction and murder of the children was part and parcel of the murder in Philadelphia. These killings were all part of one design: the extermination of the Pitezel family. The evidence of this design is admissible in proving the motive and purpose of the prisoner. The accused killed the children to wipe out the story from human knowledge or the possibility of human detection. It is a monstrous thing, but its very monstrosity must not deter us from believing it, because what we have here is not the proof of some shadowy thing but the actual proof of the commission of these crimes.'

My heart was with him, but even as he then proceeded through the cases, attempting to put counter-points to Henry's, it was slow going. He blundered forward like a man wading in molasses. I peered around the wooden foliage to observe Georgiana, holding the baton of her fan on her cheek or her hands folded in her lap, one clasping her pair of gloves, as if for all the world she was listening to birdsong, not her husband's trial for murder.

The judge who had been listening attentively and taking notes did not retire to consider his decision. 'It seems pretty obvious from the precedents brought before me that I must decide for the defendant. The prisoner is now on trial for the murder of Benjamin F.Pitezel in the City of Philadelphia, and that is the only case to be tried here. Evidence of his subsequent killing of these children elsewhere will not be admitted. If he is found not guilty of this offence, he may be sent to Canada or Indiana for trial for the other offences, but he cannot be tried for the other offences here.' The judge's voice fell into a silent court, broken by the sound of DA Graham's chair scraping the floor as he got to his feet. There was a pause and I realised, as others must have, that unusually for a lawyer he actually did not have anything to say. There was a second's silence then, 'Will your honour admit the letters of the children identified by Mrs Pitezel?' he said somewhat desperately.

'They had better be kept out,' said the judge and Graham made no more efforts, he was a freshly whipped dog.

The judge had ruled against us. The simple-minded son of a bitch had chosen the multi-murderer. I had a vision of the fluted pillars of truth and justice crashing about me; the chandeliers wrenched from their moorings, the wooden foliage and the elegant plaster mouldings falling from the roof and walls, the whole building tumbling down like the palace of the Philistines. *'You might catch him, Mr Geyer, but you won't keep him.'* I saw Georgiana get up in a flurry, cross the courtroom and embrace Henry as warmly as decorum in a public place would allow. I did not want to see this, I wanted to be alone.

I pushed through the double doors and walked out open-mouthed and into the room where the witnesses waited playing cards, knitting, drinking coffee. Of course, they knew nothing of the case, as witnesses they weren't allowed in the courtroom until they had to give evidence, but they had heard the commotion of the exiting crowd and looked to me for an explanation.

The newsmen were crowding into the door in a roar, asking questions. I pushed them back and closed the door behind me. I explained, dry mouthed, to the faces that I had coaxed and cajoled into coming hundreds of miles to see righteousness triumph that most of them would not now be required. I explained as well as I could, and shook hands with some who commiserated with me. In the end there was Mrs Pitezel, a skeletal indictor dressed in black, staring at me wordlessly across the polished table with her sunken eyes, looking at me with horrified betrayal, accusing me in her despair, I who had reassured her of the certainty of justice for the killer of her children; I who had failed.

Chapter 16

An hour later the prosecution team were sitting in the DA's conference room, too shocked yet to be dispirited. On a table to the side were still strewn newspapers calling today's debacle 'one of the great legal contests of the century.' Most of us were silent in front of bundles of court papers but Director of Public Safety Honeycutt held open a law book. 'The law,' he said, looking this way and that like an animal in a trap, 'let me tell you how our legal procedure is fantastically employed to aid the criminal... fantastically. Look at this,' he looked himself, saving us the trouble, 'in Alabama, a verdict of murder is set aside because the word "aforethought" is omitted after the word "malice" in the indictment. In Missouri an indictment for rape is held defective because it concluded "against the peace and dignity of state" instead of "against the peace and dignity of *the* state."

'Look here's one you're going to like, here's one you are really going to like,' he was shouting towards me, red-faced, as if I was personally responsible for these miscarriages of justice, 'a murderer is discharged because the prosecution neglected to prove that the real name of the victim and his alias represented one and the same person.' He finished and looked round at the bemused faces. He hissed, 'The double murderess Lizzie Borden walks the streets in Massachusetts as free as the wind while the very children playing in the street chant songs about her guilt. Little children know but the law does not.'

He seemed to realise now what a spectacle he was presenting, got a grip on himself and sank down in his seat. 'It's utterly unknown in Europe,' he whispered, 'that such tissues can be spun to defeat the ends of justice.' He had finally lost control, poor bastard, he was a good man borne down by absurdity. I was sorry for him, but DA Graham eyed him with a sort of pitying contempt which made me realise Graham would be running against Honeycutt for his job at the next election.

'So it's round one to Dr Holmes, gentlemen,' said Graham

with more control than I guess he felt. 'The judge has refused a continuance to reassess our case, and we are going on tomorrow. Any questions?'

'What is our chance of conviction?' Chief O'Brien asked, chewing on a half-smoked cigar.

'The evidence for the murder of Pitezel is only as good as the evidence for suicide, or even accident.' Graham said coldly.

'So what we looking at after all this?' growled O'Brien, 'If we get the murder conviction, will he hang?'

Graham looked down at his meaty hands and half shook his head as if himself declining to tie the noose. 'With a sympathetic judge... a murder of an accomplice while involved in a criminal activity... it could be only five years... with time off for good behaviour...' Holmes's behaviour was always good, I reflected miserably, 'it could be no more than three years six months.'

'Then at least he's some other bastard's problem,' said O'Brien, 'we give him board and lodging in our jail, then he's extradited to another state: to Chicago, to be tried for the murders there. To Indianapolis...'

'Maybe,' said Graham, 'maybe not. Remember the evidence in Chicago is burned. On the other cases: witnesses move away, or die, or lose interest; a new administration at City Hall in Indianapolis could have different priorities: not want to spend money expediting criminals from one state to another. Detectives get onto other cases, they leave the police service, they forget... they don't all have the commitment our Mr Geyer has...' he looked at me as if acknowledging the abilities of a moderately gifted child, 'everything just drifts into ashes and is blown away. If we don't get him now, maybe we'll get him later... but maybe we won't.'

Everyone was in bad shape here, and Graham was not improving things. I had to make this work or we were going to go in demoralised tomorrow morning, we'd walk in feeling defeated and our defeat would be confirmed. I had to turn this around, 'Tell me, DA,' I said, 'why do you rate the chances of conviction on the Ben Pitezel murder so low? We only need one murder to hang

Henry Holmes.' It no longer felt somehow disloyal to be talking about hanging Henry with strangers, out loud, as if I had joined a conspiracy against my friend, for once I was unequivocal. 'We always had a great case with Pitezel,' I said, 'we just have to make it stick. There was a body and a crooked scheme. Holmes had means, motive and opportunity, we have Mrs Pitezel's testimony about the money as evidence.'

'With Mrs Pitezel about as steady as a leaf in fall,' said Graham, 'without the carpenter putting Holmes in Philadelphia prior to Pitezel's death, the case is not strong, Mr Geyer.'

'What do you mean without the carpenter?' I burst out.

O'Brien said, 'When we sent a man to confirm that your Eugene Smith was standing by to give evidence he withdrew his statement...'

My stomach tightened into a ball of ice. 'What?' I said.

'He didn't want to proceed,' said O'Brien, 'didn't want to testify. We could force him, put him up as a hostile witness, but that normally doesn't create too good an impression with the jury.'

'Nah,' I said, cursing myself for not spending more time on the Philadelphia angle. I was so busy with the other stuff I wasn't worried about it. The evidence of the children was so fresh, so good, juries are so eager to convict in cases of child-murder, they'd hang the court janitor if we let them. I didn't think we needed more than the children. No wonder Henry was always so confident, even once caught, even when the bodies of countless innocents had been uncovered from his castle, children from the chimneys and cellars of suburban homes, still he was going to walk free. I had seen justice go as far as it would, and what it would then do was to release Henry Holmes to kill again. My case was dissipating into the night, my thirty witnesses standing separately in crowded stations waiting to go home. Now Henry had somehow leaned on the little carpenter to withdraw his evidence. It was injustice made manifest, it was the rule of evil.

I suddenly had the vision of walking into the Suicide Hall and saying I had lost the case, that Henry Holmes was free or receiving a nugatory sentence, of telling Molly, who so believed in me, that I had failed. I stood up, 'Mr Graham,' I said, 'I will see you tomorrow before court for a conference. I must go now and prepare the case. The carpenter will give evidence in accordance with his original statement. This will be a successful prosecution for the city, gentlemen. Good evening.' I left with more confidence in my stride than my voice, the guts hadn't been kicked out of me yet, but I'd taken a pretty hard hit.

I half-ran along the echoing corridor and downstairs to the detectives' room that was plunged in gloom. Only a few of the team had stayed, the rest had gone to a bar to drown their sorrows. I located the file on Eugene Smith but there was little in it to help, 'Declined to give full statement,' was the last note written in it. I stood chewing the side of my cheek thinking what I must do.

I just had time to get to Smith before it became so late it would be an intrusion, you can't go banging on someone's door at midnight and expect them to help you. This had to be calm. A breathless messenger came running up as I stood thinking. 'I've been looking for you Mr Geyer,' he gasped, 'visitor waiting for you in the interview room.'

'No, I've got no time,' I waved him away, and he cowered as if expecting a blow and started to run away so I felt mean. 'Who is it anyway?' I shouted after him.

'Mrs Holmes,' he said, 'Mrs Henry Holmes.' Not for the first time that night a sickening lurch tilted my world like an earthquake had hit it.

'OK,' I said quickly, 'I'll see her.'

I tried to move fast but my limbs slowed me, as if I did not really want to tread that hard polished floor, go down that blank corridor, into that airless room. I looked in through the grille and caught my breath as I saw her sitting, the same curve of the chin, the same beautiful neck with the soft gold curls around her ears. I was ashamed to find myself still vibrating with love for her like a plucked string. I breathed deeply and opened the door. 'Frank,' she said, standing, her big blue eyes as gorgeous as they had always been.

'Geor...' I said but my mouth was dry and her name was lost in a swallow.

'I hope you will forgive my coming here,' she said with exact diction, as if she had been practising this address, as I guess she had.

'Of course, you are welcome.' I said, as if inviting her into my parlour, and lamely added, 'all this must be very difficult for you.'

She acknowledged that with a nod, as if it was agreed between us and that wasn't what she wanted to talk about. Her face was drawn and her skin was powdery white, as if it had been lightly dusted with flour, emphasising her vulnerability, which only made her more attractive.

'So why did you want to see me?' I prompted gently. Maybe, I thought, it was to say sorry. I caught the scent of her perfume, or perhaps it was her own, musky odour. I was letting my desire for her cloud my mind. She remained silent, lips pursed. 'Did it never occur to you,' I said, 'in the long years after you left, that I would have been loyal and true and always put you first?'

'Mmm,' she said sharply, a small noise as if of longing, one she might have made in passion, that made me want to take her in my arms and love her there and then, and damn the consequences, damn the trial.

She looked at me from a lowered face, a lock of her hair which she had been fiddling with now hanging down straggly like a schoolgirl's. 'This isn't easy for me,' she said, 'but Henry has two wives, I do accept that. So if Henry is acquitted he must divorce one of us, or have the marriage annulled. It could be me, and then I would be free.'

'Free.' I said stupidly, 'To... to marry me, you mean?'

'Yes, Frank. If you would ask,' she said a little coyly.

'Why would you do that?'

'To make amends,' she looked up at me through long lashes, with face downcast so I was tempted to just touch her gently on the chin to raise her face. Her dress rustled softly as she moved closer. This was a dream, it was what I had always hoped for, yearned for, but even here, intoxicated by her beauty and my long longing, I knew every boon desires payment.

'What would you want me to do, Georgiana?' I asked quietly.

'Just for you to drop the charges against Henry,'

'I breathed out, as if I had been holding my breath all the time since I saw her, 'Oh, that just can't be done Georgiana.'

'Well,' she said, 'a reduction of charges. You have it in your power, I know, to make this unjust case against him fail...' even now she had to convince herself it was not a fair trial, or she couldn't go through with this devil's bargain.

I regarded her sweet, imploring face and my heart ached for her, as if I could go back to the time before she left Gilmanton, the long humid summers and the crisp winters amid the granite and pine trees. It would be easy not to get the carpenter. If I didn't go to the carpenter, or didn't ensure he would testify, then I could be free of the memory of the years of anguish, I could escape the past. The case was almost lost already, it just needed a push and Henry would escape the murder charge, could serve his time for the insurance conspiracy then take his chances with other states. I would have fulfilled my part of the agreement and Henry would still be out of the way.

It was what I had always imagined would happen, it was Georgiana coming to me, begging for my love, it was Henry's life in my hands. So this was why Henry had never used my earlier relationship with Georgiana to undermine my credibility. As always, Henry was playing for larger stakes: he held back on accusing me then in order to bribe me with Georgiana later. He not only read me like a book, but he guessed the next few chapters.

I took her by the shoulders, looked into her cornflower-blue eyes, the closest I had touched her in more than ten years. I said quietly, 'And I am to believe that when you love Henry Holmes so much that you would even go off with another man to save him, that you would then stay away from Henry if he was free? You'd go to him as soon as my back was turned.'

'Do you doubt my word, Frank Geyer?' she said, bristling, the parson's daughter again.

'I doubt everything,' I said, 'but I am sure you are still in love

244

with Henry and will not stop being...' My words fell heavily in the tiny room. 'He must have made you very happy,' I added, with a soul full of regret.

She looked down, reddening, 'They weren't all good times' she said quietly

'How can you talk about good times with a multi-murderer?' I asked, as always unable to conceal my irritation with her.

'I guess your answer's no then, Frank,' she said, 'Goodbye'.

I might have hoped for more. Even a rejection could take longer, I could spend a little more time with her. For the second time in my life she had walked out on me. Appalled, I watched her leave down that corridor, seeing her heels click on the polished wooden floor, while at any time I could have called her back. I sat down in the interview room with my head in my hands, my heart thumping. I'd gotten the biggest murderer in American history, but I'd rather have gotten the girl. Well, we'd see about that.

I took the elevator and left through the main lobby, in time to see Georgiana get into a cab and go off in the direction of Moyamensing Prison, presumably to tell Henry his plan had failed. What was his next one, I wondered. Well, he had only another twelve hours before the trial started again, as I had, most of them hours of darkness. We would see.

I took another carriage from the hack stand. It had been raining heavily and still was, covering the cabman and his nag in a coat of water that glistened in the electric burners of City Hall. The man grumbled about being asked to go so far, into the tenements where he'd never get a fare back.

We rattled down Thirteenth, through the trampled garbage, the waste and the shit of the city, past the shops with their blinds raised and the shut-up stalls. I thought angrily of how Henry had put her up to it, with a promise of reunion later, as soon as my back was turned. She might even have been involved in everything, even down to the disappearance of the children, and even her display of surprise when I met her at her house was just another way of tricking me, but how could I know? I didn't really know her. Her sweetness and beauty was a snare, a pit of deception.

Soon the broad avenues and tall buildings gave way to small, mean streets where came immigrants looking for liberty enlightening the world, to find narrow passages in overcrowded tenements, windowless rooms, the sky perpetually dark with smoke, the lungs always coughing phlegm, streets constricted and verminous, bodies weak and diseased.

We turned into one of the small streets then up another, in some kind of fancy short-cut the driver had, but then found ourselves behind a bread-wagon with its wheel broke, the driver cursing and kicking it in the rain. I pulled out my watch. Time was passing in sickening thuds. The nag might be able to back up, more likely the driver would have to unharness her and lead her around then pull the cab backward by hand through the narrow street. It was all too much. I leapt out and handed some dollars to the driver who was waving his arms and shouting 'Awwww' in the rain. 'I'll walk,' I said.

'Thanks a bunch mister,' he shouted at me, 'thanks a bunch.'

The garbage was turning to mush underfoot. I realised I didn't really know where I was. Rain had washed the slouching ruffians from the corners, there was no one to ask the way, it was just the street, and the rain, and me; me in the gathering darkness as lamps were extinguished for the night's rest. I started moving faster, quickly looking down streets with tall buildings so old and weak they leaned toward each other in their decrepitude over the cinder paths and black mud. I slipped on some kind of shit and crashed down into the puddles gashing my hand and bruising my leg. I got up cursing wildly and limped onward, the hard raindrops hitting my cheek like cold steel needles. Through thin walls and from saloon doorways came the chatter of immigrant voices – Swedish or Dutch. I dived into a saloon to be hit by a wall of warmth full of the smell of smoke, beer and sweat. I took directions from a man with an ear like a muffin and two missing front teeth who was sitting by the door, he may have been a bouncer but he was so deep in liquor himself he was more likely to be bounced than to bounce. Even he looked at me in my desperate, mud-besmeared state, as if he was as like to refuse me entry.

I limped on in the rain, now confident of my direction, not bothering to look at my watch as I couldn't move any faster whatever the time was. I walked down one alley and another and found Eugene Smith's tenement. I had been there before, but hadn't recognised how mean it was, maybe it needed that combination of rain, cold, darkness and desperation to bring it up. I raised myself up the stair and knocked on his door. Through a grimy pane I could see a lamp was still lit, its wobbling light came towards the door. I realised that I didn't have anything to say, the misery and the rain had driven away my pre-emptive powers. I, who was always prepared, I just stood there by the dripping sills, gasping.

'Who is it?' came Eugene Smith's thin voice through the door.

'Hi, Mr Smith, Frank Geyer, you remember... I'm sorry to call so late,' by now he had drawn back the bolt and was opening the door, 'can I have a moment?'

Smith was holding a lamp, a sandy, wiry body in a collarless shirt like a streak of white in the darkness. 'Why hello,' he said, peering at me as if he was trying to see someone through my head.

Indeed it was pretty late for a social call. Normally I would have implied I was just passing, had called in to see how he was getting on. 'Look, I know it's late, and I'm so sorry...' I stumbled.

'Nah,' he said, 'we were up, don't worry, my wife has just gone to the laundry.' I thought that curious until I realised he meant she had gone to work there, on the late shift, toiling through the night so the folk on Rittenhouse Square need not be without a single shirt, petticoat or handkerchief for a day, everything neatly cleaned and ironed and returned to them before they had breakfast.

'I guess you know the trial's been going on Mr Smith,' I said, 'can I come in and talk to you about it?'

He hesitated, then shrugged, 'Yeah,' he said, 'we got to be quiet because of the kids, but Pearl's not asleep yet. Through a tiny hallway he guided me into a small room which functioned as the living room and the children's bedroom. There was a crib with a baby's round, pinkish features peeking out, and a sofa

247

which served as a bed on which sat a thin-nosed girl with freckles wearing a patched slip of dingy material. She looked at me with interest in the shadowy glow of the lamp.

'Hush, you sleep little one,' Smith said, softly pushing her into a reclining position on the sofa and covering her with a quilt.

'How many children do you have?' I said, touched by the gentle scene amid the squalor. We spoke in whispers which gave this late night conversation a desperate urgency, as if we were plotting a crime.

'Two,' he said 'fifteen months and five years. There was a middle one but,' he looked down, 'he died. This is Pearl. She knows her letters and can read some,' he said with evident pride.

'That's great,' I said, and pondered whether to apologise again for disturbing him but thought better of it. I was in now. 'I understand you don't want to testify in the trial,' I said, 'did someone come here to ask you not to give evidence, offer you anything?'

'Hell, no, it weren't like that...'

'So why did you decide not to testify?' I whispered in the darkness.

'Well it was a long time ago,' he said, 'I can't rightly remember what I did or didn't see.' We made a pretty pair. I must have been a sight, smeared in mud and dripping wet, facing this feeble specimen, his bony body visible through the threadbare clothes, but the conviction of a man who had killed and killed again rested on the testimony of this faltering tradesman.

'But when I came to you a while ago you said you could remember Henry Holmes, you described him to me. What moved you to withdraw your testimony?'

'Weeel,' he said, scratching his head, 'well I saw all this stuff in the newspapers about him. He's the arch-fiend and such like, devilish cunning and all...' I stood, mystified, 'well I'm just a working man trying to make a living. I thought... maybe I should just let you guys get on with it, I don't want no dealings with no arch-fiend.'

'But if you don't, it helps him to get away,' I said. I saw a ray of the lamp glow on the alert face of the little girl on the sofa, 'He has killed *children* before,' I hissed, 'I know. I dug up their bodies. He will do it again.'

His shudder was visible even in the dim glow. This was the wrong thing to say. 'Hush, man, you will give them nightmares' he whispered.

'I'm sorry, Mr Smith, I'm just trying to get across to you how serious it is.' I was losing him here. 'I'm sorry, Holmes' crimes were terrible, he has to be punished.'

'Yeah, a murderer,' Smith mused, 'and he was so pleasant spoken too'

'Don't you want to bring him to justice?' I said.

'But isn't he already on trial, why do you need me? I don't know nothing about no child murders.' He said the last words so softly, his face glowing with the tension of sweat in the dark, he was almost inaudible. I explained why the trial had failed, and it would have to be done in another state. It was all too complicated for him.

'Hell, I don't know,' he said, 'what do I know about murder? Maybe I'll just sit this one out. I'm sorry and all.'

I was the end of the interview and I had failed. The implications went swimming inside my head. Holmes would escape the gallows and, I felt with a guilty eagerness, I could lay claim to Georgiana. I had failed in my mission, and now I could have what I wanted more than anything else in the world. I choked and glanced around. Something unexpected in the gloomy poverty of the place caught my eye: standing on the single table was a square device of wood and metal with clamps and wheels.

'Is this the saw setter?' I said, 'that sets any dull saw in seconds with no excessive labour?'

His freckled, pale face smiled with genuine satisfaction, 'You remembered,' he said.

I looked at the device with admiration, 'It's a fine thing, did you get anywhere with getting a patent on it?' I asked.

'No, I think after the last time, I had tried and it all went so wrong, I just felt I ...'

'I could help you with that,' I said calmly, though it was my last chance and my heart was pumping hard.

He stared at me intently, 'You could?' he said..

'I've got friends in the newspapers, reporters,' I said, 'I could get someone to do a story about your saw setter...'

'Is that so? Could you really?'

'Yep, an honest man's brilliant invention was a victim of Henry Holmes cruel schemes. If he hadn't killed Ben Pitezel, who knows what the future would have been for your fully patented saw-setter.'

'Yeah,' he said, 'that was like it was,' his face beamed in the shadowy room. 'But... hey... I suppose this depends on me going and giving my testimony?' He pronounced each syllable separately, 'tes-ti-mon-y' like he was worried he would get it wrong.

'Well, yeah,' I said, 'it's got to be part of the trial, otherwise they can't report it. But I'll make sure you get the publicity, and who knows, maybe some rich sponsor will come and make you an offer for your saw setter.'

'Well, I suppose you've got me,' he said, the tension in his face relaxed. He was a man who did not like to displease, he did not want to send me away unhappy, he wanted an excuse to do the right thing. I arranged travel for him, I would send a carriage, and I left the cramped tenement, almost weeping with relief.

I stumbled out into the stinking alley where rats fought one another for fetid garbage and I breathed the pure air of the night now the rain had relented. Yes, I would get the man, it would be one for Ed Cass, one for Alice and Nellie and for Howard, for the nameless number rendered down as meat in the dungeon of Holmes' castle. But most of all it was one for me. Redemption.

Chapter 17

I was too exhausted to sleep, my mind was racing through the possibilities of Holmes's release, of my disgrace. I was punch-drunk with the exertions of the night after weeks of ceaseless labour. I was early at the court, pushing through the crowds who seemed to begin waiting for public gallery seats before dawn. Some, like the society women in silk dresses and costly bonnets, had servants keeping their place for them so they wouldn't have to sully themselves waiting in line for the pleasure of seeing Holmes on trial. I caught up with DA Graham who came out of a meeting with the prisoner looking like a shaved bulldog. 'Your friend Holmes,' he said, and my heart jumped as it did when I though anyone suspected what my real relationship with Holmes was.

'Yep?' I said.

'He's rolling the dice again,' Graham said. I nodded, holding my breath for him to continue. What new misery was this? 'He's not gonna take the stand. He's gonna rely on the fifth amendment.'

'So what does he get out of that?' I struggled to understand.

'We don't get to cross examine him, but he doesn't get to examine our witnesses either.'

'So does he say anything?'

'He gets to make a statement,' said Graham, his patience nearly exhausted.

'So what is he doing?' I asked, genuinely incredulous.

'He's taking a chance,' said Graham wearily, 'taking a chance that the jury won't appreciate the inconsistencies in his account. He doesn't want to be challenged in a place where he can't get away with a quick lie and a bolt through the door.'

'Yeah,' I said, 'I think you've got the measure of him.'

I watched the people crowd in, waiting for my glimpse of Georgiana, who passed wordlessly as I stepped back into the shadows thrown by the tall pillars. I still peered around the wooden foliage to see her, but now with more regret than anguish. I didn't want her to hate me, but I wouldn't save Henry.

The prisoner was less buoyant now, no longer the carefree individual of yesterday. He seemed to have shrunk in his clothes, his collar looking too large for him, his face pale and thin. He gave the appearance as if you might want to pat him on the shoulder and tell him it was all going to be alright. I felt a pang for Georgiana, to be sitting there alone with her gloves and her purse, acting like she wasn't seeing the man she loved on trial for his life.

As soon the crier declared the court sitting Henry announced his choice to remain silent. There was a flurry of excitement through the crowd and the reporters looked quizzically at each other. What did it mean? It meant Henry didn't want to question witnesses, didn't want to tear poor Carrie Pitezel to pieces, didn't want to confuse the carpenter or question me about my dubious motives. Once again, Henry was playing another game which left us standing, wondering what was happening.

He made a brief statement without the flourishes which had distinguished his earlier performance. He stood guilty, he said flatly, of the conspiracy to commit insurance fraud but he did not kill his friend Benjamin Pitezel, he arrived to find Ben dead and arranged the body to look like a suicide. He said he may have done some wrong things and who has not? But he has always cared for his wife and little ones, had been a good provider, and wished only for the freedom to continue to do so. He made no further attempt to answer the prosecution case, he just relied on his plausible manner and the luck of the devil.

This time it gave out. His luck failed him. The little carpenter gave as good a testimony as if I had carved him out of wood and set him working myself as a witness automaton. He was transparently honest, entirely convincing, and put Henry on the spot in Philadelphia before, not after the death of his bosom buddy Benjamin Pitezel. Mrs Pitezel, a picture of misery, came accompanied by a nurse who administered smelling salts and a spoonful of medicine during the testimony. She spoke so feebly a court crier was appointed to repeat her words after her. She testified to the insurance money being paid to her which she then paid over to Henry. Dr Scott told us a good deal about Ben Pitezel's internal organs, and how the pattern of burning in the oesophagus showed that chloroform had been administered to a body rendered insensible, perhaps with whiskey. There were no convulsions: Ben didn't drink that chloroform of his own free will.

Throughout this Henry was sitting upright and seemed to be paying attention, but he was taking no notes. He seemed to have moved on, passed the trial stage, as if he had just lost interest in it. Eventually Graham made his closing speech to the jury and demanded a conviction in a hectoring tone which I think was misjudged. Henry made a slight bow to the jury and went off with the dignity of a small man under duress, trying to appear taller.

It was always a long, dull wait when the jury was out, people went out to smoke and the reporters chattered. I could see the back of Georgiana's head, her lovely neck, as she sat still facing the altar with fluted columns with carved leaves and fruits.

I took myself down to the cells to see how Henry was doing. I didn't want to speak to him, he might think I was gloating. The time of waiting for the jury is a special form of torment I would not wish on the vilest miscreant. I approached through the close, subterranean atmosphere to find that the guards down there were around Henry's cell, which had open bars so the prisoner was clearly visible, for fear some wretch might rob the gallows by committing suicide. I peered through the heads and saw Henry, sitting at a small wooden table in the cell, now cheerful and lively, his old self again, spinning a silver dollar.

'Come on gentlemen, place your bets' he was calling like a fairground barker, 'heads acquittal, tails conviction. Don't be shy, now, try your luck on the outcome of this important trial. Heads not guilty, tails guilty. The uniformed wardens crowded in with fistfuls of notes and stood back to let the play begin. As they did so, Henry spotted me and winked conspiratorially. He said nothing, but gestured to the table and the pile of soiled banknotes, asking if I would like to join in. I shook my head and smiled sadly at this bravado in extreme circumstances.

He span the coin and I turned on my heel as the silver disc whirled on the wooden table, I was half way down the corridor before I heard the cry go up from the crowd, 'Oh, tails.'

Very soon after, when perhaps only twenty minutes had elapsed, the court reconvened for the verdict, too quick for a real deliberation of the evidence. I knew what had happened: they had reached their decision immediately but for the sake of decorum thought it better to wait for a while or it would seem they were sending a man to his death at a second's notice.

The jury shuffled in with eyes on anything but the man they had condemned to death. A jury never did meet the eyes of a man they had convicted. The court room was so quiet you could hear a chair creak. The clerk addressed the foreman who looked like a store-keeper or wholesaler or something, out of place in this awesome business, 'Jurors, look upon the prisoner; prisoner, look upon the jurors. How say you gentlemen of the jury, do you find the prisoner at the bar guilty of the murder of Benjamin F. Pitezel or not guilty?'

'Guilty of murder in the first degree, sir,' he said, in a voice husky with tension

'Is that the verdict of you all?'

'It is sir.'

Henry stared with a haughty demeanour at the foreman, as if he had just sold him a short measure of cloth and Henry was contemptuously waiting for him to correct the error.

The rest of the proceedings passed in a daze for me. The judge said that the facts spoke for themselves as the jury had realised, Henry Holmes was sentenced to be hanged by the neck in the prison yard according to the custom and practice of the Commonwealth of Pennsylvania. That was it, the case was over. The judge stepped down from his high altar, it was finished, we could all go home, except Henry who went down without saying another word, or even glancing towards Georgiana, his face a mask of indifference. I could only see the back of Georgiana's bonnet from where I now was. Her head stayed stock still. In the well of the court there was one long collective exhalation. Some were looking at each other with pleasure, others in glum resignation - they had realised that sending a man to hang is not a joke. Others were paying out bets.

I stood and looked through the melee, not satisfied nor elated, just tired. A few bodies away Georgiana passed me on the way to the cells, biting her lip fiercely, her eyes red in her white face. She didn't notice me, and I didn't try to attract her attention. I followed her with my eyes but everyone started to mill around and I lost her in the crush of jabbering people.

I suppose I had succeeded, I suppose I ought to feel proud. I suppose this was what success felt like, this empty feeling like a hunger that had gone past pangs and was now a gaping emptiness at the centre. I looked around for someone I knew who would make me feel less alone and sidled up to Chief O'Brien and DA Graham who was shooing away a greasy fat man who was pleading for a hearing. It was the proprietor of the dime museum Holmes's House of Horrors who was putting in a bid for the trial exhibits.

O'Brien had a glazed, distant look, as if he was half dreaming about the farm he'd retire to, not really in the courthouse at all. He saw me and looked cheerful in a determined kind of way. 'I still don't get it, Geyer,' he said, 'a torture chamber, people killing children. In my day there was plenty of murders, there was tough men, but college educated men going around killing for nothing… it's all too much for me.'

I knew what he meant. He was telling me he wasn't going to do the job for long, it was mine if I wanted it. He was a man for a hot chase and a brisk clubbing, a policeman of the old school. He had judged correctly: this was too much for him.

'I know what you mean,' I said, 'I've felt like that a lot in this case. Dungeons and castles, hell, it's more like the middle ages in England or something. The way I look at it, Holmes was atavistic,' in my exhilaration I had used a word he wouldn't understand, I explained: 'a throwback to an earlier time, a throwback to a dark and savage past, we won't see the like of him again.'

O'Brien was a well-built man but now he looked old, his solid chin was jowelly, what had been muscle had turned to fat. 'Yeah,' he said and punched me affectionately on the shoulder. But he didn't look convinced.

Over the following days there were loose ends to tie up: Jeptha Howe, the attorney who had handled the money, pleaded guilty to insurance fraud claiming he knew nothing of the murder. We couldn't prove otherwise, and I was inclined to believe him anyway. He got his career destroyed and six months in prison, drank himself to death within a year of his release. I talked to a reporter on the Philadelphia Post to make sure Eugene G.Smith and his saw-setter got some coverage: an honest citizen who was a victim of Henry Holmes' cruel ruses.

The judicial process in the United States has difficulty with finality – there were a series of appeals mounted for Henry: for a new trial...for the judgement to be set aside because of some irregularity in procedure...each attempt less hopeful than the one before. Henry was like a salmon trying to leap the rapids as it swam upstream: in the end too tired by the journey to leap any further, but still making the effort out of courage or blind instinct.

An approach that even I had some sympathy with came from doctors, craniometrists and other men of science who had been granted permission to examine Henry. It was established that criminals are such from birth and recognisable by certain physical features – throwbacks to a more primitive stage of human development, or even animal nature. The doctors argued from the most modern premises that Henry should be kept alive for medical science as an example of moral degeneracy. They described him as 'a moral idiot', yet he cannot always have been so or he would not have been able to get a college degree and work plausibly in respectable society. Moreover his moral disease seemed to be progressing, he had the established signs of degeneracy as marked by the Bertillon system: a prominence on one side of the head with a diminution on the other side; a marked deficiency of the nose and ear on one side, resulting in an almost malevolent distortion of the face.

The signs of degeneracy were not obvious to me, but a deep line of crime was said to have marked the side of his face such that a United States Government criminologist who knew nothing of the case declared Henry Holmes guilty within thirty seconds. The doctors were fascinated too at seeing one of their own in this condition, remarking that, 'As a medical man himself Holmes has a unique insight into the physical and moral changes which he has been undergoing.' *I'll bet he does*, I thought. The appeal court decided there was no reason to stay the execution but ordered that the medical men should have every access so at least, I thought, Henry would have some company.

At some time after the trial the wasted, spectral figure of Carrie Pitezel came my way again. Sorrow had drawn ravines in her cheeks under the sunken eyes. With her were an older girl, almost a woman, cradling a youngster in her arms, these were Dessie and Wharton, the eldest and youngest children. She had brought them for no obvious reason, it was just as if she was afraid to let her two remaining offspring out of her sight for fear they might never return.

'Mr Holmes,' she said in her wavering voice, still referring to him with the dignity afforded his status as a professional man, 'Mr Holmes sent me a letter. I wanted to see you about it.'

She handed me two sheets of fine writing paper in Henry's angular script. It commiserated with her for her loss, said he was distraught at the anguish he had caused her, and that he knew nothing could compensate her but he could hand over to her the ownership of a house and lot which he owned under a false name. This might go some way to making recompense, particularly as he now knew how poor she was with no husband to provide for her. For this, however, he would need some time. Would she approach the governor of the state of Pennsylvania and ask for a delay of execution? He helpfully added the name and address of the governor in case she was in any doubt about it.

'And you've come all the way from Galva, Illinois to show me this?' I said gently to the body shrouded in black bombazine. She nodded meekly. 'When will you learn to stop believing in him?' I asked, partly in genuine wonderment that Henry, trapped and at bay though he was, even condemned to death, could still weave a web of intrigue to ensnare the one person in all the world who should know better.

'I've got to believe in something,' she said, defiantly.

I agreed without enthusiasm to look into it, though I really didn't mind having an excuse to see Henry again. My interest was quickened when, on the same day as Carrie Pitezel trudged in to see me, news came that William Randolph Hearst had seen fit to buy Holmes's story. The sum mentioned in rival newspapers denouncing the deal was $10,000, more than most people earned in many years of work. Hearst's paper trumpeted his coup: 'The multi-murderer confesses: twenty-seven lives sacrificed to his monstrous appetite.' I read it with gloomy disgust, but also a kind of excitement that the case to which I had devoted so much was still headline news. It continued, 'The nerve, the calculation and the audacity of the man were unparalleled. Murder was his natural bent. Sometimes he killed from sheer greed of gain; oftener, as he has himself confessed, to gratify an inhuman thirst for blood... All were deliberate, planned and concluded with consummate skill. To him murder was indeed a fine art; and he revelled in the lurid glamour cast upon him by his abnormal genius.' It said that the story was presented before the public as a warning and a moral example and such like, before a final flourish describing Henry, 'One could almost see the fiendish grin on his thin and bloodless lips as, in the gloom of his cell, he set down the terrible tale.' Serialisation would begin on Sunday. I knew it was an outrage that Henry should make money from his crimes and that Hearst Newspapers should help him, but I wanted to see it just as much as any other sucker, just from morbid curiosity, maybe more because it might fill in the spaces, the gaps in my knowledge that still gnawed at me in the morning hours of wakefulness before the sun rose.

Henry seemed to bear me no ill will. Indeed, he was pleased to see me. As a man condemned to death he had been moved to a slightly better cell, in accordance with the idea that a man on death row should have all reasonable comforts as his punishment was not being imprisoned, he was just in prison awaiting his punishment. Still, I was glad no relatives of Henry's victims were there to see his last home. It was larger than before with shelves of books and a few small touches that I guessed had been provided by Georgiana: a bowl of fruit, a vase of flowers sitting on a lace napkin. There were piles of newspapers, letters and pages of manuscript, some of them on the floor so they curved off the hard edges of the cell and made it look more like a regular room.

Henry was sitting in his shirtsleeves writing on a piece of paper just like the one he had sent to Mrs Pitezel. More schemes for Henry, I thought wistfully. He rose as normal, 'Frank, they said you would be coming,' still referring to the prison staff as if they were his personal servants.

I explained Carrie Pitezel had come to me after getting the letter. 'Really?' he said, 'from Galva, long way to travel. I thought she'd just write to the governor.'

'Can you give me any details, Henry, which would demonstrate that you had any property to dispose of ?' I asked.

'I'm unwilling to do that, Frank,' he said.

'I'm going to take it that you can't,' he gestured to indicate it was immaterial to him. 'Hasn't the poor woman suffered enough?' I asked, more in desperation than anger.

Henry looked at me quizzically, as if the concept of there ever being enough suffering was alien to him. 'You know I can't give you that information,' he said

I could see there was nothing in this for me so I changed track, 'I see you're in the papers this Sunday.'

'Yeah,' he said cheerfully, 'they're giving me a good show.' Seeing my expression he added, 'If you wonder why I'm doing it, look at this.' He handed me a thin book like you might get from a dime store. In big garish letters it said on the front, 'Holmes The Arch Fiend or A Carnival of Crime, The Life and Trial of H.H.Holmes. Innocent Lives Sacrificed to this Monstrous Ogre's Insatiable Appetite.'

'Yeah,' I said, handing it back, 'I've seen stuff like this.'

'It's mainly invention, of course,' he said, 'but I couldn't let it go without putting my side.' I assented, I well understood Henry's reluctance to see someone else cheat the public with lurid lies when he was so well positioned to do so.

He handed me another book, far better produced, on good quality paper, with a picture of himself on the front with a luxuriant beard and moustache, in a smart collar and tie, looking out at the reader with a sort of insolent contempt. It was titled 'Holmes' Own Story' and the selling line said, 'The only true account of the greatest criminal the police have ever handled. Accused of more crimes than any other man living. Price 25c.'

'It's the book the papers are running in serial,' said Henry. 'This copy is for you.'

'Why thank you Henry,' I said, attempting to summon the appropriate etiquette to thank a murderer for a copy of his memoirs. I looked for inspiration, flicking through the pages of type. I couldn't prevent myself from reading where the book fell open, because it was about the children, the murder of Nellie and Alice. Even with Henry standing before me, I read with a fascinated horror, 'I compelled them to both get within the large trunk, through the cover of which I had made a small opening... I ended their lives by connecting the gas with the trunk. Then came the opening of the trunk and the viewing of their little blackened and distorted faces, then the digging of their shallow graves in the basement of the house, the ruthless stripping off of their clothing, and the burial without a particle of covering save the cold earth which I heaped upon them with fiendish delight.'

I wordlessly showed him what I had read, 'That's not what happened Henry,' I said, 'I dug up those poor girls myself, they weren't naked.'

'Well, how should I know?' said Henry

'Because you did it,' I snapped, mildly exasperated that he was playing games when we were talking about the bodies of these wretched children.

'I didn't, as a matter of fact,' he said, 'I had a confederate and directed him to do the job. I gave him instructions to carry out the murders in a certain way, I did not know whether he had followed my instructions...'

'You are saying you had an accomplice?'

'Oh, I always had a man, whether it was Ben or someone else, I couldn't do it all on my own, and it was always safer to have a front man.'

Maybe, I thought, that would explain why he was so difficult to find – not one trail but two, and he was right: it was safer to have another man like Ben around. And he had worked with other people besides Ben Pitezel. 'So where do I find this accomplice?' I asked.

'I'll happily lead you to him,' Henry said, 'if you will be so good as to ask the governor for clemency. Then I can stay in prison, or in your custody, while I assist you in your investigations.'

I sighed with something like relief, there was no accomplice, it was another of Henry's schemes, 'You haven't lost your touch, Henry,' I said, 'you had me for a moment.'

'Not long enough, it seems,' he said, as if apologising for some minor failing in courtesy.

'I suppose it's always worth a try,' I said, almost sympathising with him for not fooling me.

'Force of habit,' he said lightly, as if wishing to brush off his failure, though we both knew this was one of the last gasps of a dying man.

'So why did you do it?' I asked, flicking lightly through the book. He looked quizzically as if I was asking why write it, or why sell it. 'Why did you kill all those people? Will I find the answer here?'

'Oh,' he said, as if it was an old question he was tired of answering, 'It's a big country, Frank, big railroads, steamboats, sky scratching buildings. America deserves big crime, don't you think?'

'Couldn't you have been respectable,' I said, 'with your brains and your charm, you could have done anything, lived a long and happy life as a respected member of the community?'

He shrugged and held out his hands expansively like a peddler showing off his wares, 'How many businesses have I founded, how many women have I loved? What would I do with more life?' He looked down to the floor of cold stone, 'I suppose I had the choice, like Achilles,' he said wistfully, 'a life which was long and distinguished and dull; or glorious and eventful, but short. Guess I chose the latter path. "Choosing darkness set me free"' he sang lightly.

'You can't say you chose to be bad?' I asked, incredulous that anyone should say such a thing, 'have no conscience?'

'Conscience, what's that?' said Henry, 'Can you eat it? Can you spend it?' Now he was playing.

'I'd better take my leave, Henry,' I said, 'thank you for the book.'

'Hey,' he said as I called for the warden to let me out, 'come and say goodbye.'

'What?'

'On the morning, you know,' he nodded as if to the scaffold in the prison yard, through the layers of stone walls, 'come and say goodbye.' He turned, feigning preoccupation with his papers, and for the first time mentioned his fate. 'Barbaric method of execution, hanging,' he said disdainfully, 'the electrification chair, now that's the humane method of the future, that's the way of civilisation.' I tended to agree with him and so said nothing. It was the only time he had spoken of what was to happen to him with something approaching human emotion but it was general, as if addressed to all hangings, not merely his own personal appointment. I promised I would come, a friend at the scaffold. I didn't resent the request, I did want to see it through.

In Molly's house I sat at the table by the window reading until the wick on her lamp burned down. I was eager to see any references to Georgiana but there wasn't anything except "the shame I have brought upon my family" and the like, and nothing about me but a generous note about my skills as a detective. I showed it to Molly when she came in, she was impressed that this educated murderer should regard me with such professional admiration. There was little about Gilmanton but a few sentimental words about his Ma who was still alive, poor woman.

I set down here as much as I care to recount. The prose style was lurid and decorated with frequent exclamations. Some of it was detailed with gruesome accounts of killings, some so sketchy

262

that though there were said to be twenty-seven murders, it looked more like twenty-two were being described. Henry said cynically that as he had been accused of the murder of every disappeared person in the last ten years, he would profit from it. In some cases, like that of the Pitezel girls, Henry had just lied about the circumstances, for whatever warped reason. I wish I had Ed Cass with me to talk it through and sift the fact from the fiction.

First Henry killed Dr Robert Leacock of New Baltimore, Michigan, a fellow student, whom he dispatched with a large dose of laudanum for $5,000 insurance money. Then he developed the bodies-for-money scheme where he stole a cadaver and claimed it was the body of an insured friend. He claimed this raised him $40,000, an improbably large amount. In this series of crimes Henry recounted his own death, the story I had already heard from his old comrade in crime Dr Grant in Battle Creek: how he dressed a cadaver in his clothes and took it by rail into the forest, setting up an accident with a fallen tree with the body underneath it, and having the insurance claimed on his behalf.

He obscured his marriage to Myrta Belknap, and his move to Chicago, and the disappearance of Mrs Holton who hired him to work in her drug store, but he described the store with enthusiasm. He wrote with pride that no matter what sort of pills were ordered in his drug store, or what the cost, the customer received powdered chalk, occasionally coloured and perfumed, as if it was a matter of honour with him to cheat everyone even if the counterfeit cost more than the genuine article would have.

Julia Conner died as the result of an abortion. Pearl, her daughter, was poisoned next, because she was old enough to know what was happening. Henry was paid from $25 to $45 by a dealer in bodies when he sold them on as dissecting material. Later he found he could make more for skeletons and he dissected them himself. The sums involved were not great, I guessed it more likely he just enjoyed the work.

It was as he wrote, 'I roamed about the world seeking whom I could destroy.' Some murders had clear objectives, others just seemed to happen: a man called Rogers was killed on a fishing trip with a blow on the head with an oar; a Southern speculator by the name of Charles Cole killed by a blow with a gas pipe; a Dr Russell died by being struck with a heavy chair. Did Henry alone have the strength to lift a heavy chair unknown to the victim, I wondered.

There was a maid called Lizzie who grew too inquisitive, so he suffocated her in the basement death chamber after forcing her to write letters to relatives saying she had left Chicago for a point further West. Mrs Sarah Cook and her unborn child were next dispatched, then Miss Mary Haracamp of Hamilton, Canada. She kept house for him and came upon him while he was preparing his last body for shipment. He led her into the safe which filled one room in the castle and killed her after compelling her to write a letter saying she was tired of living with him, had left the city and would not return.

The statuesque Emmeline Cigrand of Dwight, Illinois, known as Amelia, a stenographer employed by Henry, went the way of all those who got close to him in the castle. She was his mistress though she was engaged to be married to a young man whose life he had vainly tried to take. Henry lured her into the huge safe, then closed the door, 'and she met death in a slow and lingering form,' after writing a letter to her fiancé under duress, breaking off the engagement. Poor Mrs Van Tassell's daughter Emily was doped with a poisoned ice-cream, and invited into a back room to lie down and recover, whence she never returned. Both these became fine specimens of skeletons, dissected by Henry and Charles Chapman, the dancing hop-head he employed in the permanent night of the cellar.

Henry recounted how he tried to kill three women who worked in his restaurant by trying to chloroform all of them without success. They escaped and ran into the street whereupon he was arrested but not prosecuted. Not for the first time I questioned the veracity of the tale: would he really have attempted to kill three adult women, who were used to physical work, in the same room?

Rosine Van Jassand was poisoned with ferro-cyanide of

potassium and buried in the basement. Robert Latimer, who was employed by Henry, knew too much and attempted blackmail. He was subjected to the secret room and slow starvation and his body went to a medical college. Latimer was the one who attempted to claw through the solid walls of his prison with his bare hands, Ed had shown me the bloody marks on the wall before the castle blew up.

Anna Betts was killed with the substitution of a poisonous ingredient in a prescription he had filled at his drug store. Gertrude Conner was killed in the same way though she got to Iowa before she died.

Holmes and a partner – a young Englishman – forced a banker from North Wisconsin to sign drafts of $70,000 by depriving him of food and nauseating him with gas. He was then killed with chloroform and his body sold. Nannie Williams was brought to the castle to sign away her real estate–perhaps lured there by Minnie Williams. She was murdered by gas poisoning, along with Minnie who had now served her purpose.

The killing of Ben Pitezel, Howard, Alice and Nellie was described in a detail made more repulsive by the fact that much of it was invented in order to render a ghastly story still more horrible. He said of Ben Pitezel, 'I proceeded to burn him alive by saturating his clothing and his face with benzene and igniting it with a match,' and that Ben begged for mercy pitifully while this torture was taking place. It was complete invention – I knew Ben Pitezel had been rendered unconscious and killed in that state and had not been burned. Henry was embellishing details merely for sake of lying, or to bolster his claim that he had a confederate, so I would convince myself as I read through that we ought to keep Henry alive to help track down another dangerous man.

The book was like an emetic: the tales of murders came gouting out like a flow of vomit. As something of an afterthought, a final spit, and presumably added for the sake of completeness, Henry noted he had shot Baldwin Williams in self-defence in Leadville Colorado.

I looked into the shadows thrown in the dark by my lamp,

turning over fragments of information in my mind, trying to conceive the enormity of it all. Crimes amerciable, crimes beyond retribution. I never had to see Henry Holmes again, except to see him hang, and that was the way it should be. I need never again see Georgiana, she had betrayed me for that monster of depravity and had even tipped him off when I was looking for him. She could burn in hell too. I lay in bed beside Molly that night, listening to her gentle breathing and thinking about a world without Holmes.

Chapter 18

As time passed the horrific details of the crimes receded and what remained was my memory of Henry as a companion, his laughing voice, his sparkling eyes. Over that bright, cold winter which was filled with accolades for me for catching Holmes, Georgiana became an astral figure of light and gossamer, hardly even living now, more an idealised woman than ever. I didn't ask for that, it was just what my mind served up to me.

Finally, after the appeals and counter-appeals had been made and the schemes and cunning ruses had run out, the bright day of 7 May 1896 dawned and I dressed next to Molly's sleeping form, with the dawn splintering through the shutters, to see Henry off.

Hang days were always the tense festivals of the prison service. There were crowds at the west gate waiting for I don't know what, some evidence of drama. All they would see was a notice posted up on the studded wooden door just after eight to say the execution had been carried out.

I signed in at the turnkey's office and went up and around the long row of cell doors. There were none of the usual raucous shouts echoing through the corridors, prisoners were usually pretty subdued on hang days, it was the condemned man's ceremony and they didn't want to intrude. Henry had a guard permanently outside his door who when I approached was letting out a man in black... it was a cassock: a priest.

I was surprised to see him, 'How do you do Father,' I said awkwardly, and introduced myself.

The priest's face was face shining fervently with a light gleam of perspiration, 'P.J.Dailey from the Church of the Annunciation,' he said, 'I have brought him to God.'

'How is he, father?' I asked, genuinely curious about this – could Henry truly have turned to religion?

'He is in a state of contrition, I have blessed him and we will face this ordeal together,' Dailey said, pressing his hands together.

'I thought I knew Henry Holmes well, and I didn't know he

267

was a Catholic,' I said.

'Now he is, he has been received into the church,' said Dailey. I wished the priest good day and smiled. He swished off in a sanctified glow. A Catholic convert... Henry never ceased to amaze me.

The door opened and Henry rose to greet me. 'I met your priest, Henry,' I said.

'Yeah,' he said, with a dismissive wave.

'Father Dailey was under the impression he had converted you,' I said, with probably more levity than the situation demanded, but Henry's vitality was infectious.

'So he went away happy,' Henry said, 'is there a problem?'

'You mean you haven't converted?'

'Oh yes,' Henry said defensively, 'I've given a first general confession and everything, learned the responses, taken communion and all.'

'But do you believe in their faith?'

Henry shrugged, 'Well, you never know, they may be right... and redemption is guaranteed with them.'

'You are not saying you are trying to cheat the Almighty?' I asked, my exasperation with him now exhausted, it could serve no further purpose.

'Well, somebody has to,' he said, my blank expression prompting him to add, 'If I didn't, then someone else would.'

I almost wished him luck for such an act of celestial audacity. The twisting vipers' nest of emotions in my chest had quietened down, now all I wanted was to understand. 'Well, Henry,' I said, with a smile probably entirely inappropriate to the circumstances. I didn't want to talk about crime, now that had ended, I wanted to ask him something which would give me a token to remember him by, the essential Henry. 'So what happened to the musician Orpheus, when he got back from the underworld, what was the end of the story?' I asked.

He smiled at me with a wan pleasure, he had always so enjoyed telling stories. 'Orpheus was inconsolable,' he said, in a melodic voice which took me back to the scent of pine in the morning air of Gilmanton and the school room where the ink froze in the desks in winter and in summer the airless heat hung still despite the open windows. It could have been so different, as a boy I could have imagined us meeting again under any circumstances but this, I could have embraced him, for the pity of it. 'And some say Orpheus killed himself,' Henry continued without a shudder as if he had no care in the world, 'others that he was torn to pieces by the women of Thrace who were infuriated at his single-minded love of his wife. They tore him limb from limb and scattered his dismembered body, throwing his head in the river. But even after he was dead his head went floating down the stream, still singing as it went, down through the green countryside to the sea.' He looked down at his hands which lay in his lap.

'That doesn't mean anything to me,' I said.

'Nor me neither,' smiled Henry, 'kinda peculiar creatures, women.' He was straightening papers that were already straight, patting neat piles of clothes.

In the silence of the cold stone room I couldn't help asking gently, 'what were you trying to achieve, Henry?'

He looked at me with an almost gay expression, 'Oh, my whole life has been dedicated to a scientific experiment on the people around me to establish whether suffering ennobles.'

'And does it?' I said blankly.

'No, no it doesn't,' he said. 'But it was fun finding out.'

'It wasn't about the murders was it?' I said, making a last attempt at understanding, 'It was about... about the life. The murders were just part of the life. We fixed on the murders, we were obsessed with them, but murder wasn't it, murder was just part of the life, you just did them and moved on.'

Henry pondered, contemplating this, 'Then you know,' he shrugged, 'so why do you keep asking?' He smiled warmly, 'I wanted to say goodbye old friend,' he said. 'Remember, when you think of how I did you wrong, think too of all the times I could have killed you and didn't. Remember as well that if your name is ever known a hundred years from now, it will be because it is linked with mine.'

'Maybe,' I said, knowing it to be true.

'Congratulations,' he said 'you've caught the biggest mass murderer in American history.' He made a long pause, for he knew I was filling in the rest of the line myself, *but you'd rather have got the girl*. 'Goodbye Frank,' he said, extending his hand. I took it and found it cold. The dark-clad wardens were at the door. Henry made no show of cowardice nor wish to keep them waiting. It was the old Henry, the old bravado on show for the last time. I could hate him for what he had done, despise him for taking pleasure in it, but had to admire his style.

He was led off to the prison doctor who, in a burlesque of civilised barbarity, would certify him as medically fit to hang. The cell door was left open: there was no prisoner to escape, after all. I stood at the door, as if fearing I was intruding, and looked at the piles of paper neatly placed on the table, the crucifix above the bed, the folded bedclothes, the slippers on the floor not to be worn again, the picture of Georgiana on a shelf by the bed. That was Henry, that was what Henry had been reduced to, the brilliant wit and fiendish schemes, all the diabolical power over people, now this little pile of human detritus.

I went on past the silent rows of cells to the gallows where the state officials waited. The rest of the apparatus was prepared, only the man was lacking in the courtyard where stood the scaffold, permanently erect, a high, sturdy wood platform with a cross-bar for the gallows. On one side, behind a wooden screen, was the hangman with his mechanism, a lever he pulled towards him to open a trap door and send a bag of sand with a rope attached hurtling ten feet to the ground. On the other side of the scaffold, on the other end of the rope, would be placed the wretch who was to hang.

A small number of subdued witnesses and court officials stood before the structure as if waiting for a theatrical performance. Dr Scott was one of the few I knew so I stood next to him and we watched as the hangman adjusted the bag and checked the mechanism. 'Fine art that,' mumbled Scott through his whiskers, 'bag's too heavy and it rips the condemned man's head clean off.

Shade too light and it just lifts him, balances him like scales with the bag on one side and him on the other, and he strangles slowly. But I bet that bag's just right.'

'That's very reassuring, doctor,' I said, my mouth dry. I was feeling a chill in the air.

There was a flurry of excitement as the little crowd turned to see the main attraction. Henry walked with his hands behind him, as if he was going to a podium to deliver a particularly distasteful speech to an assembly of schoolboys, about their very bad conduct in the preceding term. As he passed me he turned and his blue eyes looked into mine, 'Darkness falls in fairyland,' he said, and winked. Against all my will, my training and inclination, a smile flashed onto my face. He had tricked me for the last time.

Henry ascended the platform with his priest, who stood to one side. He then walked to the edge of the scaffold with the gallows behind him, looking down at us in the courtyard, resting his hands on a low rail. Prison food and the prison air had taken its toll: he was pallid and his hair unhealthy-looking, though it had been trimmed for the occasion. When he spoke his tones were steady, as if he was going to make his speech then go off to do a day's work. 'Gentlemen,' he said, 'I have very few words to say. In fact, I would make no remarks at this time were it not for the feeling that if I did not speak it would imply that I acquiesced in my execution. I only wish to say that the extent of the wrongdoing I am guilty of in taking human life is the killing of two women. They died by my hand as a result of criminal operations. I am not guilty of taking the lives of any of the Pitezel family, either the three children or the father, Benjamin F.Pitezel, for whose death I am now to be hanged. I have never committed murder. That is all I have to say.'

There was an intake of breath from some of the witnesses, from shock at this supposed revelation or outrage at his audacity, I couldn't tell. It would not have been Henry if he did not die with a lie on his lips. What was the point? It was one last drip from the shrunken pool of his powers, to fool just one more person, sow doubt in the mind of maybe five others, so he never had to relax control, even when all was utterly lost.

Henry knelt and Father Dailey prayed with him for two minutes and he kissed a crucifix which the priest held. He rose and the priest stepped back, his place being taken by the hangman who moved with a swift, mechanical efficiency, handcuffing Henry's hands behind his back and drawing a black hood down over his face. Now he stood like a grotesque mannequin or a performer in an illusionist's act. The hangman pulled the rope from about the beam above them, drew out the noose and placed it over Henry's head, tucking it under the black hood, drawing it tight at the same time in one fluid movement.

The hangman acted so fast it was difficult to register. He pulled the vital lever and the mechanism said *scholck* as the bolt holding the bag in place was levered out, *click* as it sat smartly in its new position. Of course, it was the bag which moved first, not the man. The sandbag descended into the void. It must have been a split second but it seemed a long time, a long wait before the jerk came and Henry, his head knocked to one side, was way up in the air, his legs kicking this way and that like a dancer in an Irish jig suddenly deprived of the floor. My first thought was: *man in trouble, got to help him* but I did not lunge forward. I stood and stared as the legs swung out then my friend turned round and round on the rope with the legs swaying backward and forwards as if he was struggling to break the rope. As his back swung round we could see his fingers, handcuffed behind him, opening and closing in spasms. 'Jesus, make it stop,' I breathed. There was a gasp and a soft crash as one of the witnesses fainted, another slid onto the wooden benches around the courtyard.

When I looked back from this distraction the jerking had ceased and the body hung limp. Henry was cut down like a sack of grain and the mask removed so Dr Scott could certify death over a face with eyes stained red, bulging from the head, the blackened tongue lolling out as if in a permanent gesture of impudence. The noose had sunk deep into Henry's neck such that it would not be removed without cutting, so finally one of the prison guards did so with a pocket-knife, digging into the flesh with the sharp point to find the strands of hempen rope. Cut away, it left a deep, pale furrow with a mark under the ear where the knot had caught. Dr Scott, wheezing as he knelt, pressed a stethoscope to Henry's chest in a mockery of a caring gesture and after two minutes' silence, stood and said, 'Yep, he's dead.'

The witnesses filed past, most taking a brief glance at the grotesque, broken figure, some gazing in horrified fascination, some looking away. He was placed in a simple pine coffin and the body was surrendered to me, for I was to oversee his last request. Henry had left instructions with an undertaker to have his body encased in cement. I had balked at this but he had said, 'Think of it as a deterrent to crime.'

'What are you talking about?' I had asked.

'Well, if there aren't any bodies available, there won't be the temptation to steal them and defraud some good upstanding insurance company,' he said.

I had advanced that this was not a temptation felt keenly by very many citizens, but I agreed to oversee the performance of the task. I went along in a wagon accompanied by the lugubrious undertakers from J.J.O'Rourke, with the coffin bumping in the back, on to their office at the corner of Tenth and Tasker. There in the back of the depot I watched Henry's wish being carried out. The undertakers opened the coffin and exposed Henry, his face now a little more like the real man as the contorted facial muscles had somewhat relaxed in the aftermath of death. The undertaker's boys mixed up five barrels of cement and began to pour it over the body. Bucket after bucket of mortar was poured, steaming in the cold air, until the face of Henry Holmes became an island in the pool of sludge then that was gone too and nothing remained but a still lake of cement in the pine box with a little stirring of scum on top.

The undertakers nailed the box down and went for lunch while the cement set. In the afternoon, with a deal of effort, the weighty box was hauled onto one of the wagons used for hauling stone for tombs. The wagon groaned off, heavy on the axis, horses straining under the weight, towards Holy Cross Cemetery. I did not go to the funeral, I didn't think it was my place, I guessed there would be family there, guessed there would be Georgiana.

I did see her, however, near dusk on that day. I had gone back to the prison and was now leaving when I saw two figures across the yard, two women dressed in black. I was going to do nothing but tip my hat to them but as they approached I was irresistibly drawn to their graceful and sedate walk. It was Georgiana, Georgiana accompanied by Myrta Belknap, Henry's other wife. One was carrying a psalter, one a posy, I forget which, they were looking so alike now, especially in mourning and with their bonnets on, they were like bookends.

They were not exactly gay, but they were not so gloomy as I might have supposed. Henry's death had been anticipated for so long that when it came it must have been a relief.

'Hello Frank,' said Georgiana. Myrta barely acknowledged me. 'We came to collect Henry's things from here,' Georgiana indicated the black gate of the prison, 'I couldn't stay still, I had to come out.'

'Yes,' I said, and I did understand, that to do it today meant that all the worst jobs had been done with the gritty taste of bereavement still fresh in the mouth, and tomorrow could dawn a new day. 'So you two got to be friends.'

'Yes,' said Georgiana, clearly more comfortable with my presence than was Myrta.

'I'll leave you two to talk,' Myrta said, 'I'll see you inside Georgie,' and she went off with barely a nod towards me.

I took a long look at Georgiana, seeing her in daylight for the first time since I visited her in Burlington. There were lines appearing around her mouth and her forehead showed signs of being creased with tension. The trial and the publicity had taken a lot out of her. She made a delightful, small smile, 'Myrta and I corresponded after Henry's arrest,' she said, 'She looked after Lucy, with her two children, while I attended the trial.'

'What are you going to do now?' I asked, 'have you plans for the future?' Georgiana looked over towards Myra, now at the prison gate, 'we're going to set up house together,' she said, 'and bring up the children as best we can. We are two widows, after all.'

'Yes,' I said. So it would be a house, I reflected, with the presence of Henry always presiding over it. As always, the urgency of time tormented me: there was little I did not know, but I had taken this route like a fairground hell-ride through the suffering and murder of Henry's story. If I did not say it now, would there ever be another occasion?

'Georgiana,' I asked, commanding the full attention of her pretty face and her enormous blue eyes, 'so why did you go? Why did you leave Gilmanton?' I asked.

She smiled reproachfully, 'When you saw me in Burlington, you said you wouldn't ask why,' she said.

'I think it's time now,' I replied, 'why did you go with him, and not me?'

'You wouldn't understand.'

'Try me.'

'I suppose...' she said, as if herself trying to puzzle it out, as if this was the first time she had addressed her mind to the question which had tormented me morning and night for all my adult life, 'you were so good and steadfast and true and all... you knew so well where you were going, what you were going to do with your life...' she gestured hopelessly.

I felt as if a trap door had opened in my stomach and my whole being was falling through it. 'I would have thought these were virtues,' I said, almost dumbfounded.

She just smiled. 'I said you wouldn't understand,' she said gently with the same perfect curve of chin and neck, the same turn of the head that I knew from time immemorial. I must have gulped like a fish, and no more words came out. She took pity on me, 'Do you know Henry's story, about the two islands, the nymphs and the satyrs?'

I nodded, 'Is that how he seduced you, with that story?' I asked flatly.

She blushed scarlet and looked down, a picture of vulnerability, 'It's not really the place for that talk,' she said. I wasn't going to argue, though I didn't see any impropriety in talking thus in the public square in front of a prison where her husband had just been hanged.

'Nor the time I suppose,' I said weakly, 'though it never is the right place or the right time.'

She made a gesture as if to leave, Myrta was waiting,

'Do you think things will get better, Frank?' she said.

She was thinking about her own feelings while I was thinking of the century that was to come. 'Yes,' I said, 'things will get better.'

'And will there be an end to it, the finger pointing and whispers?'

'People forget,' I said, understanding the drift of her question, 'or if they don't forget, they get interested in other things. What will you do?'

'I'll look after the children, I'll keep on teaching, if any school will have me,' she looked at me frankly, as if inviting compliments on her choice.

I wanted to say it would be hard without a man around, and I'd call in, but it was all in the past. Whatever might have been had already happened. The puppet dancing on the end of the rope that morning had already determined our fate.

'So what are you going to do, Frank?' She asked.

'I'm going to do my job,' I said, 'year in and year out, I'm going to do what little good I can.' It was a pusillanimous answer. It was true as far as it went, but the truth was I would go back to the untainted love of Molly, take her out of the Suicide Hall, make an honest woman of her, go back to the life which was long and distinguished but dull. Maybe I would write a book, to put all these words together that I have in my head. I would learn to sing again.

'Maybe it never ends,' I said. She extended her begloved hand for me to touch, mouthed goodbye soundlessly, and off she walked into a world of evil with the fearlessness of the perennially beautiful.

ACKNOWLEDGEMENTS

Much of this story is literally true. The responsibility for excessive irony in some of the locations lies with providence, not me: Henry Holmes really was born in the New Hampshire of Thornton Wilder and Robert Frost; and was hanged in Moyamensing Prison after a crime committed in the city of brotherly love.

I have used the name Henry Holmes throughout, in fact his family name was Mudgett and Holmes was one of at least eleven aliases. Holmes was the name by which he came to be generally known, however. I have often made adjustments to accommodate the enormity of the events of Holmes' life, to reduce the scale of matters which, though true, are too preposterous to fit in a work of fiction or, like Holmes' marriages, just too numerous to encompass in a novel's structure. He was married at least three times in his thirty-three years. Anyone interested in the bare facts of Holmes' life may read my account in *Double Indemnity: Murder for Insurance* (1994) or David Franke's *The Torture Doctor* (1975) which additionally contains many details about Holmes which I have found valuable in writing *Choice of Darkness*.

Frank Geyer's tracking down of Holmes was a complicated and painstaking exercise which would sorely try a reader's patience if set down in full. It was the more remarkable because it was achieved with leg work and persistence, employing few of the devices which aid a detective today. Geyer deserves a place as one of the forerunners of modern policing, using the dogged tracking down of clues and patient deduction, an approach even more notable because it was done at a time when muscle and bribery were more common tools. Geyer's own book, *The Holmes-Pitezel Case*, was published in 1896.

While there is a deal of poetic licence in my story, most of the sheer fact about public affairs is true, and can be verified from such sources as *Violent Death in the City: Suicide, Accident and Murder in Nineteenth Century Philadelphia* by Roger Lane (1979) and *American Police Systems* by Raymond B.Fosdick (1920). In early chapters I have borrowed freely from two personal memoirs: Cornelius Willemse's *Behind the Green Light* (1931) and Jacob Riis' *The Making of an American* (1901).

Hillary Wootton kindly checked my manuscript for Anglicisms. Diana Tyler and Meg Davis gave helpful and encouraging advice on the first draft of the manuscript. Bevis Hillier's punctilious attention to the manuscript saved me from many grammatical and other errors. Any which remain are my responsibility.

Most of all I must thank Julie Peakman who read the manuscript in its early stages and made comments, and who took me to live in Thessalonika where I started this work. Thanks also to the other girls at Aristotle University: Stella, Eva, Anna and Jennifer, who kept me entertained when I was not preoccupied with beginning this book.